CW00692653

Amie

and

The Child of Africa

Lucinda E Clarke

Amie and The Child of Africa

First published 2015
ISBN 9781517119867
Republished 2020
ISBN 9788409201419
This edition Copyright © 2020 Lucinda E Clarke

Cover art and design by Dazz Smith
darryl@nethed.com
http://www.nethed.com/book-covers/

Editors:
Zoe Marr   zlm@gmail.com
Gabi Plumm   gabiplumm@bigpond.com
www.facebook.com/plummproof

Compiled by: Rod Craig

This is the second book in the Amie series set in Africa and follows on from *Amie an African Adventure*. I would suggest these are read in order, as to explain too much in this sequel might spoil the first book.

The Child of Africa may rekindle memories for those who have left this bewitching land, or introduce some of its wonders to the reader who has never travelled there. It has given me the opportunity to go back to the Dark Continent from the comfort of my home in Spain, and remember the people, the wildlife, the breathtaking sunsets and the vast open spaces.

While Amie's story is a figment of my imagination, many of the scenes are true to life, and recall some of the fascinating and amazing people I met. This book is dedicated to them and to friends and readers who have supported and encouraged me to write more about Amie's adventures. In particular I would like to thank: Rod Craig, Zoe Marr, Patricia Steele, Kathryn Hearst, Nancy Utterson Lynch and Gabi Plumm - PlummProof Proofreading for manuscripts gabiplumm@bigpond.com

I hope you continue to enjoy my books.

I cannot thank my longsuffering husband enough for all his love, help and encouragement as he has once again endured the lonely hours when I have been glued to my laptop.
As I have said before: While you may leave Africa, a part of Africa will never leave you.
Spain 2020 ©

Also by Lucinda E Clarke

FICTION
The Amie series:-
Amie – an African Adventure
Amie Stolen Future
Amie Cut for Life
Amie Savage Safari
Samantha (Amie backstories)
Ben (Amie backstories)

Psychological Thriller series:
A Year in the Life of Leah Brand
A Year in the Life of Andrea Coe

MEMOIRS
Walking over Eggshells
Truth, Lies and Propaganda
More Truth, Lies and Propaganda
The very Worst riding School in the World

HUMOUR
Unhappily Ever After

Contents

1 THE CAMP IN THE BUSH

The silence of the night was shattered by the sound of approaching vehicles. Bright lights split the night, illuminating flying insects in their beams as the trucks drew nearer. There were excited shouts and one driver blasted his horn which immediately woke everyone in the camp. Whoever had been on guard duty barely had time to shout a warning as the new arrivals thundered towards them.

Jonathon wriggled out of his sleeping bag and seized the rucksack that was always next to him before pulling Amie to her feet.

"Run. Run," he whispered loudly. "Run as you've never run before." Stopping only to grab their shoes, they left the tent and raced off into the darkness.

Amie didn't need to be told twice. They'd been discovered and the only thought she had was to get as far away as fast as she could. There was no time to jump in the two trucks parked next to the tents, their only chance was to make for the other side of the valley on foot and hide in the trees on the lower slopes of the mountain range.

She ran blindly, trying to keep up with Jonathon. His legs were so much longer, he was just over six foot tall and she was a good seven inches shorter, so he was forced to slow down to keep pace with her. She didn't stop to think she

1

termite mounds she couldn't see in the dark. Nor did she stop to think of all the dangers beyond the safety of the camp. There were lions out here, hyenas, buffalo, jackals, wild dogs and elephants. Anything they might bump into could easily turn round and attack.

As soon as they were on the other side of the wide, dry river bed, they stopped to put on their shoes, Amie's feet were already bruised and bleeding and it was more painful with her shoes on.

They set off again, running over the veldt, not caring what was in front or to the side of them, not even stopping to see who else was also running. They only knew certain death lay behind them. Low hanging branches slapped their faces and legs, and twice Amy stumbled over shrubs as she tried to zigzag round the odd acacia tree that loomed in front of them. The only piece of luck was the moon. It was bright enough to cast deep shadows near the larger objects which lay in their path, but not bright enough to make Jonathon and his wife too easy a target.

Amie's breath became ragged, her chest felt as if it was going to burst open and she gulped for air.

"I, I, can't..." she gasped. Even the fear of the unknown people, who had approached the camp in the dead of night, wasn't enough to make her to run any further. She had no idea how far they'd come, but she knew she couldn't run any more.

Jonathon pulled her on for a few more steps and then yanked her down on the ground behind a large rock. They crouched and listened, every sense alert to the slightest possible sound, but all they could hear was silence. Not even the usual sounds they'd come to expect once the hot African sun had disappeared below the skyline.

Amie tried breathing deeply, in and out, in and out, until her heart slowed, then she started to shake. Jonathon put his arms round her and held her tight as she leaned against him. At least this time she wasn't alone, but what were they going to do now?

Amie woke with a start, bathed in sweat. She reached out an arm and felt for Jonathon who was sleeping peacefully beside her. She was safe, her terrifying adventures were over, so why did she have these nightmares? She'd never run away from any camp in the bush, with or without Jonathon. When she'd been in trouble before, she was on her own, her personal long and lonely fight for survival. Were these new dreams a psychic look into the future?

It was only a few years ago that Amie had been living at home in a suburb near London, newly married with her future all planned out. She recalled the day Jonathon had announced out of the blue he'd been offered work in Africa.

Moving to Togodo had been a shock, but not long after settling in, civil war had broken out and Amie was caught right in the middle of it. Eventually, she'd met up with her husband again and they'd stayed with Dirk and Helen in their temporary bush camp since then. No one knew how long they would have to survive out here before government differences were settled and life could go back to normal.

Amie felt safe in Dirk's camp. He'd grown up on this continent and knew more about its plants and animals than most. She'd fallen in love with Africa and was keen to learn all she could about her newly adopted home, but survival was paramount and to eat they needed to kill.

Amie sat motionless as she watched the kudu grazing peacefully on a short tuft of grass. Even after weeks of practice she found this the hardest part of all, remaining quite still. It never seemed to bother the African people; they appeared quite relaxed, squatting down and remaining immobile for hours on end. Amie had seen the women in town sitting on the pavements, legs stretched straight out in front of them, unmoving, as they gazed into space. She found it almost impossible to sit like that even for a short time, and if she got comfortable to begin with, after a while some part of her would begin to ache and hurt. Unlike Jefri, born and bred in Africa, she couldn't squat. It wasn't a position she'd ever used, so she had chosen to kneel. Now her left knee was sore, the pressure from a large stone pressing into her kneecap. She was quite sure she'd brushed the ground before kneeling down, but the pain was getting worse.

To take her mind off things she focused on a dung beetle as it struggled past, rolling a dung ball much larger than itself. It fascinated her that these little creatures always travelled in reverse, hind legs gripping their ball of dung, head down they pushed back with their legs. They can't have any idea what obstacles they were going to meet mused Amie and shook her head and smiled.

Suddenly, alerted by her slight movement, the kudu sensed danger. Its head snapped up, its ears swivelling swiftly to catch the slightest sound. It stood quite still for several seconds, before deciding it was safe.

Amie breathed a sigh of relief. Jefri would be thoroughly disgusted with her if she spooked the antelope and sent it running off out of range. He'd think it was yet another example of how much these newcomers had to learn about living in the bush. She was surprised she no longer felt any pressure on her knee, thinking about other things had helped, but glancing at Jefri she saw he had not lost concentration, for a moment.

The kudu lowered its head again and Jefri let loose the arrow which pierced its neck. Time stood still. The animal bounded away and ran for about half a kilometre before stumbling, rising, running a few more steps, and finally sinking to its knees.

They followed the thin trail of blood and the disturbed dust tracks to where the animal lay on its side, and Jefri quickly put the animal out of its misery by cutting its throat with the knife he took from his pocket. As she helped him gather some large stones to cover the carcass, Amie wondered if she would ever get used to watching such a beautiful animal die.

She knew tomorrow night, and for a few nights after that, they would all have meat to eat and yes, she would enjoy the taste and it would give her strength, but each time she accompanied Jefri or Kahlib on the hunt, a small part of her hoped they would not find any game and there would be no need to kill anything.

It was an unrealistic hope. In fact, it was stupid. There was not much vegetation left close to their encampment to feed them all, and if they dug up everything near the tents there would be nothing left to re-grow. As it was, they now had to travel farther and farther each day to gather the berries, leaves and roots they needed to survive. There had even been some talk of moving on if the rains didn't come soon, and they would be forced to take refuge in the bush to the south.

There also were dangers in this, as most of the land was claimed by one tribal group or another, and if they encroached onto owned territory, their cover would be blown and it would lead to conflict. They were not in a position to defend themselves, despite the few guns they had in the camp.

Amie took one last look at the fallen kudu. Already the sheen was disappearing from its coat, and its eyes were glazing over. The flies had arrived and were feasting around the wound and crawling into the nose and mouth of the dead animal. She whispered a silent prayer, thanking the kudu for providing life for her and her new tribe and commending its soul, if it had one, to heaven. She had learned the Bushman, or San, the original inhabitants of Africa, had always prayed over their kills and she much admired them for it.

Jefri would return with one of the other men to drag the carcass back before they strung it up, skinned it and prepared the meat.

What had life been like for the animal? Amie wondered as they walked back to camp. Was it constantly on the alert for danger? Did it worry about unfamiliar noises and movement in the bushes? Did it ever relax, even when sleeping? We've become like that she realized in surprise. They were ever watchful themselves, aware that unknown eyes might be observing them, even now at this very moment. But the only sounds came from a noisy troupe of vervet monkeys in a large acacia tree on the other side of the ravine.

Back at the camp Amie flopped down onto her sleeping bag and closed her eyes. Who would've thought remaining still for so long, waiting and watching, could be so exhausting? The sun didn't help either, beating down on the dry, dusty earth. It sapped her energy, caused her to sweat uncomfortably and urged her to curl up and sleep.

But Amie couldn't sleep, there was something nagging at the back of her mind, and not too far back either. She had tried to talk to Jonathon several times, to ask him the question she was itching to have answered. Each time, he had brushed her off, deflected her words, changed the subject or given her such a ridiculous answer she knew he was avoiding telling her the truth. She remembered his exact words when they had found each other again after the civil war had torn their lives apart.

"But how can I stay in Togodo? They accused me of being a spy!"

"A spy! Then they caught the wrong fish didn't they?" and Jonathon Fish had laughed.

What had he meant? Was her husband a spy? Had he really been working for some secret service outfit besides trying to build a desalination plant in Apatu, the capital? Was that only a cover? And if it was, was she a part of that cover? Or was it some silly joke? Was Jonathon only teasing her? If he denied there was any truth in his statement, how could she be sure? Spies were probably taught to lie

7

convincingly in their first week of training.

One moment Amie believed she was being totally irrational, making something out of nothing. The next, her gut reaction told her there was at least some truth in what he said. She sensed something wasn't right, and she needed to know didn't she? Here they were living off the land in the middle of nowhere, in a country that had recently been embroiled in a civil war. She had only survived by the skin of her teeth, and she wasn't sure if they were still looking for her. She had appeared to be co-operating with the losing side.

Jonathon and Dirk had been working on the Land Rover for days, trying to fix some problem, so she would have to wait even longer to get him on his own and ply him with questions.

"Amie, are you there?" Helen appeared in the doorway of her tent.

"Oh yes," Amie sat up and rubbed her eyes.

"Are you OK? Not feeling ill or anything?" Helen sounded worried, it could be a disaster if any of them needed medical help.

"No, no I'm fine, a little tired that's all. Did Jefri tell you, we, or rather he, killed a kudu?"

"Yes, good news travels fast. He took Kahlib to go and collect it. We won't go hungry for a few days." Helen paused. "Are you sure you're all right?" she asked again.

"No, I mean yes. I'm fine, really." Amie had a horrible feeling she was being disloyal to Jonathon, but did Helen know something she might let slip? Anything was worth a try otherwise she would worry until she really was ill.

"Helen, can I ask you a question?" Amie indicated for Helen to sit on the log that served as a makeshift dressing table, chair, desk and stool in the small tent.

"Yes of course you can dear. I noticed something's been bothering you, but I didn't like to ask."

That was so typical of Helen, she would never intrude, never pry. Yet she was also the most - what word would best describe her – serene? Yes, that was it. Helen was the most serene person Amie had ever met. She too had grown up in England but after meeting and marrying Dirk, had moved out to help run his small game lodge several kilometres south of Apatu, the capital of Togodo. She had told Amie she would never live anywhere else and didn't even enjoy the regular trips into the capital to stock up on essential supplies. Rural Africa had captured her heart and, in over ten years, she'd never had any regrets. Nothing seemed to faze her; nothing was ever a problem and her glass was always more than half full. Was it the result of living the simple life deep in the African bush among the wildlife, far away from the big city, its materialism and all its problems? Whatever it was, Helen was someone you could talk to and trust. She ran her fingers through her short brown hair and her green eyes focused on Amie, waiting patiently to hear what she had to say.

Yet Amie was reluctant to voice her fears, she was going to sound stupid. Helen would think her paranoid, even if she didn't give an opinion.

There was a long pause, broken by Helen. "Are you unhappy here?" she asked gently.

"No, no it's not that," replied Amie staring at the

ground. "I like being here, it's been the best three months of my life. If you'd asked me a few years ago if I'd be content living off the land, somewhere out in the middle of nowhere, I would've had hysterics. I'm amazed at how much I've changed, it's unbelievable. I had such a conventional upbringing on the outskirts of London, followed the expected path, had my life planned out and then – it all turned out so differently."

"You've been through a lot," Helen said softly, reaching out to squeeze Amie's hand. "These experiences take you to a new place, both physically and mentally. You can never go back to what you were, you know that don't you?"

"Yes, I do. I've changed beyond recognition. Even a trip home to England showed me how I no longer fit in with the people I've known all my life. And that was before the civil war here had even begun."

"You've been so incredibly brave," Helen smiled. "I'm not sure I would have coped as well as you did."

"Nonsense," Amie said firmly, "you would have coped much better, and not done stupid things like eating poisonous plants."

Helen laughed, "You can hardly be blamed for that. Do you still have nightmares about the war?"

"No, not anymore." Amie considered this wasn't really a lie, since her nightmares now had nothing of the war in them.

"But something is making you unhappy," Helen persisted.

Amie sat silently for several minutes. How was she

going to ask the burning question?

"You don't have to …" Helen began to say but Amie interrupted her.

"I don't know how to say it and you're going to think I'm not quite sane but …"

"I never judge, my dear. If it bothers you and if I can help …"

"I think Jonathon is a spy!" Amie blurted out. She stopped and held her breath.

Helen sat quite still and said nothing.

"There, now I know you think me quite mad. I didn't mean to blurt it out like that," Amie spoke so fast she stumbled over the words; she was afraid of Helen's reaction. There was such a long pause that eventually when she did glance up; the older woman was staring out through the tent opening. She finally turned to Amie and looked into her big grey eyes.

"I won't lie to you," she said, "but sometimes information is not yours to give. I think if you want to know the answer you must ask Jonathon. He's the only one who can tell you."

To Amie, that told her nothing. Helen had not jeered at her, suggested she was stupid, nor that she was imagining things. So perhaps she did have reason to worry. Even if Helen knew something she wasn't going to share what she knew. Amie decided to change tack.

"We can't stay here forever can we?" she asked.

"No, no I don't suppose we can, although I have no idea where we would go. We've managed very well for the last three months, but it can't last. Now that's something I worry about," said Helen. "Sooner or later someone will stumble upon our small camp and ask why we're all living out here in the bush. Dirk sent one of the boys back last week to see if there's anything left of Nkhandla Lodge, and then to go on to Apatu and check out the lie of the land."

"Jumbo?"

"Yes. Kahlib says he'll be back later today."

"How can he possibly know?" asked Amie in surprise.

"I have no idea. After years in Africa, its people never fail to amaze me. Sometimes they 'know' but don't ask me how. Come, let's go and top up the water supplies and make ourselves useful. It's cooler now the sun's going down."

Amie got to her feet and when they emerged from the tent it was to see Kahlib and Jefri approaching the camp, dragging the kudu back on a makeshift stretcher.

It was later that evening, while they were all sitting around the camp fire, when Jumbo appeared out of the shadows. Without making a sound, he squatted down beside Dirk as if he'd only been to the corner store for a loaf of bread. There were murmured greetings but he would eat and drink before he could tell them his news.

The lodge, he told them, was still uninhabited, but some parts of it had been dismantled and the thatch had been stolen from the rondavels. The water pump was broken beyond repair and several birds had moved in. It sounded much the same as Amie remembered it from her last visit.

In Apatu, life continued as before, but although the new government was firmly in charge, many people were not happy about the changes. Those who'd worked for the last government had lost their jobs, and only a few had been lucky enough to hold on to their homes and even their lives. There were many rumours of discontent, but no one seemed prepared to do anything about it. It would probably continue that way for quite some time, until the old government supporters felt strong enough, and collected sufficient armaments, to rise up in retaliation. Then the whole cycle would start all over again.

"Were there any foreigners in the streets?" asked Dirk.

"Yes Boss, one or two, all dressed in smart suits with important-looking cases. They may come to do business with the new government," Jumbo replied.

"We should go and have a look," Jonathon remarked to Charles who nodded in agreement.

"Any white women?" asked Helen.

"No Miss Helen, none that I saw."

"It sounds as if things have moved forwards a little in the last few months," said Dirk, "getting back to normal, well normal for Africa!" Everyone chuckled.

Amie ran her fingers through her short, fair hair and looked around the group. On her left was Jonathon, her husband. Like her he was now deeply tanned and his fair hair was almost white, bleached by the sun, a stark contrast to his blue eyes.

Next to him sat Charles, one of their friends from the days they lived a carefree life in Apatu. He was another expatriate from England and Amie had been shopping with Kate, his wife, when the first bombs dropped. Charles and Jonathon had been on the last plane out after the civil war had erupted, but he'd accompanied Jonathon when he flew back to look for Amie. She'd never been quite sure why he returned, but when she asked him, he'd only grinned, and told her Jonathon needed someone to hold his hand on the plane. More than that he wouldn't say, even when she pressed him for more information. Did he still hope Kate had somehow survived? No, she was positive he believed her when she described how she'd watched one of her best friends being crushed to death, although she'd been reluctant to go into any graphic detail.

Charles was a comfortable sort of person to have around. He wouldn't have been out of place in a heavyweight boxing ring; tall, solid and all muscle. He had more strength than two men put together, yet he was always gentle. Amie had once watched him carefully pick up a chameleon and place it out of harm's way when it wandered too close to the cooking area. He was easy going and always ready to calm things down if there were words between any of the others. Yet Amie sensed the sadness deep inside. Even though Jonathon was over six foot tall, his slender frame made him look tiny beside Charles.

There was Dirk and his wife Helen. They'd been forced to leave Nkhandla Lodge and live in the bush with their workers, all of whom came from the far north and belonged to the Luebos tribe. They were one of the two smaller tribes, less warlike than the M'untus, the tribe now in power, after overthrowing the Kawa tribe who were the largest and most intelligent tribe of all.

Dirk's family had been in Africa for over three hundred years, one of the first white settlers to leave Europe and carve out a living from farming the virgin land. As a child he'd run free across the plains, learning all he could about the native animals and plants. Apart from the years he was away at boarding school, he'd been here all his life.

The last six members of the camp were all former workers from the lodge: Kahlib, Jefri, Jumbo, Reibos, Kaluhah and Sampson. Eleven of us altogether, Amie thought, living near the furthest guest lodge on Dirk's land. She'd thought they would use the building to live in, but Dirk was adamant they slept in the tents he'd rescued when they fled. They'd managed to salvage cooking utensils, boxes of matches, sleeping bags and anything else useful for survival in the wild. With only one Land Rover to use, they'd been forced to leave the rest behind, as everything had to fit in, or on, the vehicle. While Helen drove, all the men walked, it left more space for the supplies and equipment. Now, even if they went back, there was nothing left, and several of their vital supplies were dangerously low. The biggest piece of luck had been the second Land Rover and the extra provisions the camera crew had left them when Amie had been re-united with Jonathon. But even those additional essentials were almost exhausted.

"All the traditional Africans in the rural areas use some goods from the city," Helen had remarked to Amie one day. "Dirk may have lived here all his life, but we still mixed the old and the new. No matter where you go, you take your culture, food preferences and religion with you."

Amie's thoughts flashed back to England, and the groups of immigrants she'd seen. Even though some had been in their adopted country for more than a couple of generations, they still held fast to many of the customs from their original home countries. The locals may grumble about newcomers not integrating, but how much have we integrated, she wondered. This group more than most she decided, but she remembered Helen's words, 'we can't stay here forever'.

Amie was close enough to hear Charles as he whispered to Jonathon.

I think it's time to go back over the border to Ruanga. We should visit the Robbins in Umeru."

Helen had overheard too. "I'll give you a shopping list," she exclaimed. "We need more shampoo and soap and a couple of new buckets and …"

"Whoa!" laughed Jonathon, "We weren't exactly planning a shopping trip were we Charles?" Seeing Helen's downcast face he added, "But we'll see what we can do. And yes there's lots of stuff we need, only teasing."

"Can I come too?" asked Amie. The thought of seeing Alice Robbins again, and having a hot shower or a proper bath and a bit of civilization was very appealing.

Jonathon thought for a moment then shook his head. "I'd rather you didn't, we'll have to run the border at night, and it might be dangerous. I'd be happier if you stayed here safely at camp."

Amie was bitterly disappointed. She chewed her lip and said no more. She wondered if it would be possible to persuade Jonathon later when they were alone. She would do her best to get him to change his mind. But even if he refused to take her with him, she was determined to get the truth out of him before he left.

2 RETURN OF AN OLD FRIEND

Her chance came the next day as they walked from the camp to gather firewood. Each foray meant walking farther and farther away, as they'd already exhausted the area close to the camp.

Seeing a low, flat rock and after looking around for signs of danger, Amie took Jonathon's hand and practically pulled him over to sit beside her on the warm stone.

"I can't live with this anymore, Jonathon," she told him. "I promised myself I wouldn't talk about it, but it's got too much so I have to know."

"Have to know what?" he asked. There was some hesitation in his voice as if he could guess what was coming.

"That remark you made, about being a spy. I need to know if it's true. And no, don't brush me off," she added as she saw the smile on his face. "I'll know if you're lying to me." Amie wasn't at all sure about that. She knew Jonathon could lie through his teeth and she wouldn't be any the wiser.

Jonathon was silent for what seemed like an age.

"I don't want you to *know* anything," he said. "The more you know, the more danger you might be in."

"So you *are* a spy."

Jonathon sighed and turned to look at her. "You're one

17

of the bravest people I've ever met. You're honest and true and a seriously good person."

"That's not answering my question."

"Put it this way, when they questioned you at the police station, you had nothing to tell them. However much they beat you, you had nothing to hide. That kept you safe."

"Nonsense," snapped Amie. "I could have cooked up any old story to satisfy them. They weren't to know if it was the truth or not. They were ready to believe what they wanted to believe. I've thought since, if they'd kept me there much longer I would've made up some nonsense to shut them up. So don't palm me off with the 'I want to keep you safe by keeping you in the dark' routine because it won't wash."

Jonathon sighed. "I guess you do have a right to know," he said, "but it's not the James Bond stuff you see on the movies. It's really quite mundane. Listening, talking, asking subtle questions, and reporting back the answers to those who have an interest. That's all there is to it, really."

"I suspect there is a lot more to it than that. Was that what you were doing when you were away for those months after you finished at university?"

"Yes."

"Up in Scotland?"

"Yes."

"And what did they do with you up there?"

"They weren't dishing out Jaguars with ejector seats or exploding pens if that's what you're thinking." Jonathon smiled.

"Obviously. But they did teach you something?"

"Survival techniques, how to defend ourselves, a bit about codes and communications, enough to help us keep our cover, not a lot more."

"And was I part of your cover? Were you really building a desalination plant?"

"Oh yes, that part was all above board. It was being built with British government aid. My job was to report back to the embassy on anything I might hear."

"But why didn't they use the embassy staff? There were plenty of them." Amie knew she sounded querulous, but she couldn't help herself.

"Far too obvious, Amie. People are more likely to let things slip if they think you're totally apolitical. And while we're on the subject I have a question for you, madam."

"What?"

"Why didn't you come to me and tell me about the scenes you had filmed when the rebels were murdered? Why did you go and have a private chat with Vivien at the embassy?"

"I didn't go to the embassy."

"Don't split hairs, I know you met her at the club, but you didn't tell me. Why not?"

"Isn't it obvious? You'd have sent me home wouldn't you? Put me on the next plane back. I didn't want to go, I wasn't going to leave you here on your own and I wasn't going to ruin your career either as I thought. Of course, I didn't realize then you had two careers did I?"

Jonathon nodded. "Fair point. So, are you satisfied now?"

"No."

"Well, I don't know what else I can tell you."

"Charles, too?"

"Charles?"

"Don't be obtuse Jonathon, is Charles another spy?"

"Not exactly, more a reliable eyewitness."

Amie thought it was beginning to sound like one big boys' club where they played games behind closed doors and whispered secrets about what they heard.

"Did you know that war was going to break out in Togodo?"

"We suspected it in the long term, but it took us by surprise. If we'd known about the massacres in the bush earlier, we might have been able to take action sooner."

Amie gasped. It had never occurred to her she could have played a part and even saved lives. She had procrastinated for days before approaching anyone in authority and the consequence of her actions didn't bear thinking about.

"There's one more thing."

"What?"

"I want you to teach me to take care of myself."

"What?"

"I mean to fight, use a gun, unarmed combat, that sort of thing. I want to be more prepared if anything happens again."

If Jonathon was surprised he didn't show it. "I can teach you a bit, but after everything you've been through, I think you can take very good care of yourself."

"There's always room for improvement," said Amie. "When are you going to Umeru?"

"Charles and I plan to leave tomorrow. We thought we might also go on down to Atari and touch base."

Amie counted on her fingers. Three days to get as far as Umeru, say two days staying with the Robbins, another day to the capital, two days there and …

"We'll try to make it back in a couple of weeks," Jonathon replied to her unspoken question.

"And you won't take me with you?" Amie asked again.

"No," replied Jonathon firmly. "It would be much too dangerous and you've been in enough tight situations to last a lifetime." He scrambled to his feet. "I think we'd better start looking for some wood."

It was amazing how much there was to do around the camp. Amie had never fully appreciated the amount of time most species spent simply gathering or finding food. For people there was also the preparation; none of them had got to the point of eating raw meat, if you didn't count the biltong. Amie had often bought the dried meat at her local butcher as she and Jonathon enjoyed it, but she was surprised to see it was made from raw meat, and Dirk had been making it all his life. He had a supply of spices and she watched in fascination as he rolled the strips of raw meat in them and hung them to dry on hooks.

"We need to make as much as possible," he explained as he worked. "When the rains come, if they come, we won't be able to keep a fire going as easily. We'll need protein to stay healthy."

They got their water from a deep hole the men had dug in the river bed, not too close to the camp, for the smell of easily accessible water could attract predators. Collecting water and firewood took many hours each day and at least two members of the party were out hunting for most of the time.

Amie had always believed the African savannah was teeming with wildlife, and there was possibly more in this area, since they were still on the edge of Dirk's land. Whether anyone would respect Dirk's right to own the land now was a moot point, but at least they had the semblance of living legally. No one had mentioned what might happen, should people from the city decide to investigate. It was a subject they hadn't wanted to raise.

It was three days since Jonathon and Charles had left. The sun was sinking in the sky and Amie and Helen were sitting on the ground sorting berries when Jumbo and Kaluhah appeared, dragging between them what looked like a small antelope. Amie only gave them a quick glance then she gasped. It wasn't an animal; it was a man, or at least the body of a man.

Dirk jumped to his feet and ran to take a closer look.

"Boss, look what we found," said Jumbo. "A filthy Kawa," and he spat in the dust to emphasize his disgust. "He was spying on us, he would tell the city people we are here."

"Good God!" exclaimed Dirk. "He's barely alive!"

"I wanted to …" and Kaluhah drew his finger across his throat. "But Jumbo said to bring him here so you could deal with him." He dropped his half of the burden, which fell and remained quite still.

Dirk rolled the man over and felt for a pulse as the

women hurried over to look.

"There's a faint sign of life," said Dirk, "but he's not in good shape."

Helen recovered her wits first and went to fetch a bowl of water and a flannel. She sat beside the man and began to wipe away some of the dirt on his face. Amie gave a small cry.

"What's the matter?" asked Dirk. "Don't worry, we won't kill him, even if that's what some of us want to do." He glanced briefly at his men.

"But Boss," argued Jumbo, "it is dangerous to let him live. We only brought him here so you could get the truth from him," and he kicked the man in disgust.

"I certainly want to know who he is and why he's out here miles from anywhere." Dirk continued before Amie could interrupt him.

"I, I can tell you who he is," she said under her breath.

"You know him?" Dirk looked at her in surprise.

"Yes, I do. At least I think so," replied Amie as she bent down to take a better look. The man was barely breathing, although he stirred as Helen cleaned his face and gently prodded him to see if any bones were broken.

Amie peered more closely and nodded. "It looks like Ben Mtumba. I worked with him on the video shoots. I'm almost sure it's him although it's difficult to say with his face in such a mess."

"It certainly is," agreed Dirk. He looked at Jumbo and Kaluhah. "You guys certainly gave him a good work over."

Both men looked defiant. "But he is the enemy Boss," complained Jumbo pulling himself up to his full height. "He must not live."

"We thought you might like the honour," added Kaluhah.

Dirk shook his head and thought for a moment. "That's not how we do things. Come on guys you should know better than that by now."

Amie thought both men looked quite sulky as they shuffled their feet in the dust.

"He's possibly suffering from shock. I can't find anything broken," said Helen. "Lots of bruises, but I don't think it's as bad as it looks." She looked up at Amie. "You say you know him?"

"Yes, I'm sure it's Ben, though what he's doing here is a mystery. He lived somewhere in Apatu. I never went to his home, but he was with me on all the shoots and he's a good man I'll swear to it."

Jumbo growled and spat in the dust again. He was obviously not convinced. As far as the Luebos were concerned, all those from the Kawa tribe were enemies and dangerous even though they'd been overthrown.

"Make up a bed for him Helen, we'll put him on the spare groundsheet. Let's see what he can tell us when he comes round."

Reluctantly Jumbo and Kaluhah picked Ben up and half carried, half dragged him over to the plastic sheeting Amie and Helen were stretching over the ground. They knew better than to complain to each other. Dirk was fluent in many of the dialects and he would understand every word they said.

"At least we must tie him up, Boss," protested Jumbo.

"That might be wise," agreed Dirk and went to fetch some strong, nylon rope.

Amie looked down at the unconscious man. What was Ben doing here? Was he looking for them, or did he simply come across them by accident? Was he a spy sent to search out any dissidents? Surely not, she had spies on the brain. She couldn't wait for him to come round so she could talk to him.

"I'm not sure Jumbo and Kaluhah are right," she said to Helen as they finished preparing the meal that night. "When I worked with Ben and Themba, I always felt Themba was all for the rebels, but I'm not sure about Ben, I don't think he really favoured either side. If he did, he certainly didn't let on."

"That's not very easy in Africa," responded Helen. "If you're not with me, you're against me. My friend will always be my friend and my enemy will be my enemy until the day he dies."

"Do you think Ben ran away from Apatu after the fighting?"

"Why now? The fighting has been over for months, and while they might root out those they thought were ringleaders, I doubt if all the Kawa were slaughtered. They're the biggest tribe. I would be surprised if the M'untus can hold on to power for very long."

"Oh," said Amie. "But surely if it's all gone quiet, and a few visitors are coming in to Togodo now it must be stable, I mean …"

"There will always be a few brave souls who will take a chance if they think they can land a contract for their companies," Helen continued, grinding up a pile of baobab seeds. "Remember, the latest uprising started because they'd found oil and other minerals in the north, in M'untu territory. They were convinced the Kawas would take all the money. And I'm sure they were right to believe that."

"I'm so glad I'm not in any tribe," said Amie. "But I guess if I went far enough back in history, my family would have been in one tribe or another."

"For sure. Dirk has said time and again tribalism is holding back progress on this continent. Until they all live together as one, and learn to co-operate I'm afraid entering the 21st century will take many generations. There's so much distrust and jealousy. It breaks my heart."

And mine too, thought Amie. She still couldn't believe, after all that had happened to her, she loved this land so much. Why? It wasn't only the wide open spaces, was it? Or was it the people? Though she had seen how savage and cruel they could be. Was it the presence of the wild animals? Sadly she'd seen far fewer than she'd expected. Even living out here in the bush, they'd only observed one herd of elephants as they meandered along the bottom of the valley. Had Amie chosen the campsite, she would have pitched their small tents lower down, closer to the dry river bed, but Dirk knew the old pathways followed each year by the huge beasts as they traversed the same trails used by their ancestors. Not for the first time Amie thanked whoever was looking after them that Dirk, understood the animals and knew the plants so well. Twice now he'd stopped Amie chopping up certain roots and leaves for their evening meal because they were poisonous. To her, they looked exactly the same as the ones she'd prepared only the night before, until he pointed out the minute differences.

26

Amie voiced the worry that was nagging her. "Helen, what do you think will happen to Ben? Will the boys kill him, do you think?"

"If Dirk wasn't around, without a doubt, yes," she answered. "As it is now? I'm not sure. A lot will depend on what he has to say when he decides to tell us."

Amie glanced over to where Ben lay quite still on the plastic sheet under a shade awning, securely tied to the bumper on the front of the Land Rover. "He's been lying there for hours," she said. "He's not said a single word."

"I suspect they gave him quite a beating. I'm surprised they didn't break any bones, well not as far as I could see," said Helen. "Still we'll make sure there's enough food for him when he does come round. There's not a lot for any of us, supplies are getting to be a problem, even with two people not here. At least Jonathon and Charles will be able to bring back plenty of stuff from Ruanga. I suggest you keep well away from this Ben; the other men won't like it if you appear to be friendly with him. They might easily have doubts about you as well, and that won't help things. I'll get Reibos to take his food over and see to his needs."

Amie wasn't happy to hear Helen's warning; she'd been waiting impatiently for the first opportunity to talk to Ben as soon as he regained consciousness. Her brain was teeming with questions, but she could see the sense in what Helen said. It was so easy to forget how jealous and distrustful the Africans were. Did they live in a cloud of perpetual fear she wondered. Often the Africans in the rural areas seemed so happy and content, wanting only food and shelter for the day and believing tomorrow would take care of itself.

I wish Jonathon would hurry back, thought Amie. She found her mood improved one moment, and she was able to enjoy the simple life, take satisfaction from finding and preparing food, fetching water and taking the time to chill out.

Other times she experienced waves of despair as she fretted about their future. Her thoughts flew across the miles to her family back in England. Last time she'd spoken to them she'd told them she was off on a video shoot in Alaska and would not be able to keep in touch. But she'd been here for three months now and surely they were worried about her? When he returned to England, Dave from the camera crew would've updated them, but even though they knew she was back with Jonathon, they would still fret.

Before he left to go south to Ruanga, she'd asked Jonathon if there was some way he could contact them and tell them she was safe. He'd promised to do that and she trusted he would find a way of explaining where she was and what she was doing. Not that it would stop them worrying though.

She could picture her sister Samantha collecting Dean and Jade from school and playgroup, before going to pick up a few essentials from the local supermarket, a whole world away. She imagined the high street shops, pavements glistening in the rain, with the traffic racing by and people coming out of the train station on their way home from work. It was surreal, it was not only a world away it was life on a distant galaxy.

For the next few nights Amie couldn't sleep. She tossed and turned, conscious that Jonathon was not lying next to her in his sleeping bag. She wondered where he was and what he was doing. Was he asleep in a proper bed in the Robbins' house where she had stayed when she'd been in Umeru? Had he enjoyed a hot shower and dinner served on warm plates sitting at a table? Had he even got across the border safely?

However many times she closed her eyes, tried to relax and drift off to sleep, her brain cells sprang into action and she was off on another flight of fancy. In the end she wriggled out of her sleeping bag, put on her boots and stepped outside the tent. It felt cold out in the African night, so she reached back in and put on her coat as well. Dirk insisted they sleep at night fully dressed; if they were discovered and attacked they would not have time to put clothes on, especially if they had to make a run for it. He had lightened his warning with a funny story about a party of campers who had to vacate in the middle of the night and were seen hopping around totally naked, causing much mirth and derision from the poaching party.

"It's amazing how vulnerable you can feel without clothes, even though common sense tells you a couple of layers of material won't stop a bullet or a knife," Dirk said at the end of the tale.

She stood quite still checking for danger. There was little wind and she couldn't detect any smells that might warn her that a lion, a hyena or a jackal was nearby. She saw no unfamiliar shapes, so she wandered over to the cool boxes looking for any leftover raisin bush berries. It was then she noticed that Jumbo, who was supposed to be on watch, was sitting in a very odd position.

29

She tiptoed over and gently shook his shoulder, thinking he might be asleep. If Dirk discovered he'd dropped off there would be all hell to pay in the morning. But as she touched him, he keeled over and collapsed. For a brief moment Amie wondered how deeply asleep he was, and she bent over to give him a really good shake. Horrified, she realized he wasn't asleep. He was dead!

She couldn't move. What should she do? Should she scream to wake everyone up, or creep over to rouse Dirk as gently as she could?

She had just decided to do the former, but before she could cry out, a hand wrapped itself around her mouth and another hand clamped her arms by her side. She was dragged backwards away from the camp area. She fought as hard as she could, but she was no match for her captor who was holding her so tightly she felt as if her ribs were going to cave in. She was gasping for air, and she blacked out for a few seconds. She tried to raise her legs to kick her assailant, but it was impossible as her feet bumped along the ground jarring her whole body. Her teeth felt as if they'd come loose and her head was swimming, and it seemed to go on for a long, long time. Every now and again Amie made a feeble bid to pull herself loose, but then, there was an uncomfortable pain in the side of her neck and she remembered no more.

3 I SAW ANGELINA

When Amie came round, she saw they weren't moving anymore. She wasn't sure how far they'd come, she didn't know how long she'd been unconscious, and she'd lost all sense of direction. Her abductor kept her head held tightly against him, still covering her mouth so she couldn't cry out.

"Amie, Amie," he hissed. "Don't scream. If you do, I'll have to break your neck. Do you understand?"

Amie tried to nod, but it was impossible to move her head.

"Please, please you must listen to me. I need to talk to you."

Amie didn't know whether to feel relieved or terrified, she recognized the voice. Everything would be all right, but then she remembered Jumbo's body and shuddered. She wanted to ask him not to hurt her, but it was impossible to speak, she couldn't even make eye contact with him, he was still holding her tight from behind.

"Amie, if I take my hand away will you promise not to scream? I need you to listen to me, please!"

Again Amie tried to nod but she still couldn't move. It would be foolish to scream, to break someone's neck only took one quick yank and no one was around to come to her rescue. She had no choice but to do as she was told. If he was capable of killing one person, he was quite capable of killing her as well.

She wriggled frantically trying to indicate she would remain quiet. Much to her relief he took his hand away from her mouth and she gasped, filling her starved lungs with fresh air.

She turned round. She had guessed correctly. It was Ben.

"What, what, are you doing?" she croaked. Her throat felt like sandpaper and her head was still swimming. Was this only a terrible dream? Had she really left her tent in the middle of the night? Surely any moment she'd wake up.

"Amie I am so sorry to hurt you, I don't mean to, but I am desperate," whispered Ben. "I need your help."

"My help! How could you possibly need my help?" Amie was amazed.

"We are friends, right?"

"Ben, I thought we were friends but now I don't …" Amie stopped herself. Watch what you say you idiot, she thought, or your big mouth will get you into trouble. You really should have learned your lesson by now. She began again. "I really don't see how I can help you. I don't think for a moment Dirk was going to kill you, it's not our way, and as white people we're not at war with the Kawas or the M'untus. This is your country and you'll find a way to sort out your own problems," she added paraphrasing what Dirk had said so many times before.

"Amie, you are the only one who can help."

Amie recovered a little and twisted round to look at Ben. She had never seen him look so dejected, so unkempt, so unlike the Ben she'd once known, the chatty one who always made her laugh when they were out filming together. He'd told her a little about his family, how proud they were of him, how hard he'd worked to get a college education. How he was so close to his two sisters and three younger brothers. As the eldest he had plans to help pay their college fees when their turn came. He'd asked endless questions about life overseas and adored looking at the few photographs Amie had shown him of her house and family in England. But this Ben was different. This was a scared and frightened man who looked as if he was suffering.

"What's happened, Ben? Why are you here?" asked Amie.

"I was looking for you."

"For me! Seriously? Why?"

"I told you, I need your help. You are the only one who can help me."

"That's nonsense Ben. You have no idea what I've been through, where I've been, the prison, the shooting, the riots, the war ..."

"Many people died or disappeared in the war," Ben said softly, "but it has not stopped. It is still going on, only much, much worse."

"Wait a minute Ben, how long is it since you've been in Apatu?" Amie wriggled a little further away and settled herself more comfortably on the ground. Was she mad to trust him? If she was sensible, she should get up and race off back to the camp screaming her lungs out. But something stopped her, she wasn't sure what, but it seemed only fair to hear what he had to say. "How long is it since you've been in Apatu?" she repeated.

"Several weeks," he admitted.

"There you are. Jumbo only came back from the capital a few days ago and he said it was all calm, no fighting. There were even some white foreign visitors on the streets. Unless he was lying," she added. The thought she was sitting next to Jumbo's killer sent a shiver down her spine and she inched a little further away. Should she try and make a run for it after all?

"No, I believe him," said Ben. "In the capital it is quiet, it's what is happening out in the bush that is frightening. This is where the bad stuff is going on. Not in town, out here," and Ben waved his arms to indicate somewhere inland.

"What sort of bad stuff? What are you talking about?"

"Bad men, not Kawas, not M'untus, not Luebos, not even the Tsaan. I think they come from a country to the north. They have set up a large camp far away from anywhere, there are many of them with guns."

"But why would they set up camp if they wanted to attack? Surely they would come across the border and take over one town at a time and march towards the cities? What reason would they have to hide out? It doesn't make sense if they'd come to invade Togodo. And why haven't we heard about it? If the camp is as large as you say, someone would have noticed surely?" She added. "We thought no one knew where we were, but you found us."

"I followed Jumbo," Ben admitted.

"But, how did you know Jumbo would lead you to me?" Amie was puzzled.

"One of my neighbour's cousins knows Jumbo and he often went into town with Mr Dirk. You told me you had visited their game lodge so I came to try and find you because you know me and you can persuade Mr Dirk, and the people he knows, to help me."

Yet another of those long shots most people in their right minds wouldn't even consider, Amie thought. Yet another example of a bizarre coincidence, or was it the workings of fate? She gave herself a firm talking to; this was not exactly the time for philosophical musings. She was still in a tight spot and she still didn't know what Ben wanted or how dangerous he could be. He'd threatened to kill her; she mustn't forget that.

"I was surprised to see you were hiding out here with him in the bush. I felt you were alive, but many people died in the fighting."

"Yes," Amie replied sadly. "I've been back to look, but I couldn't find any of them. Not Pretty, or Angelina or Mrs Motswezi from the school. Ben, those bastards burnt the school and orphanage to the ground. I don't care which side you are on, but that was barbaric, those poor little children had done no one any harm." She shook her head to prevent herself from bursting into tears.

Ben grabbed Amie's shoulders and gave her a hard shake. "They would grow up one day and become dangerous men." Then, seeing her expression, he added, "that is the reasoning behind it. I need help from Dirk and his men and you can persuade him. Now I have some hope. I knew he was hiding out here somewhere."

"But how? I don't understand …" Amie was puzzled,

"we're not hiding out as such, simply keeping a low profile until things settle down between the warring factions. We're still on Dirk's land and while the troops were running high on blood lust it was best to keep out of the way. It's as simple as that, lying low." As pictures of the still-burning orphanage and all the fighting and killing she'd seen flashed into her consciousness, she took a deep breath. She wasn't going to break down now and blubber like a baby in front of Ben.

Ben dropped his hands and sighed. "You are the only ones who can help. Would you believe me if I told you the Kawa did not burn down the orphanage? We were only fighting the M'untu. We were going to share the new wealth with all the tribes when they brought out the oil deep below their tribal lands. When their chiefs would not even talk to our government, there was nothing we could do. And then they made war on us and now everyone is suffering. They do not know how to run a country. Many governments will not even recognize them and the oil, and other minerals which would bring wealth to many is still there under the ground."

"Always the African way," Amie said bitterly. "If you can't get what you want, you fight, and who cares who's caught in the middle?"

"And I suppose it is so different where you come from?" Ben asked sarcastically.

"Yes, of course, we discuss things, work arrangements, come to an agreement in a civilized manner," replied Amie.

"So, the big wars in Europe I learned about in my

history lessons at school did not happen? With millions killed?"

Amie felt ashamed. Who was she to judge? Ben was right, was it so very different in any part of the world?

"If the Kawas didn't burn down the orphanage, who did?" she asked. "I can hardly see the government troops attacking it. They would have no reason to. What would they hope to gain?"

For a moment Ben said nothing and then it dawned on Amie. "You mean a third group was involved?"

Ben nodded.

"Not from the Tsaan, surely?"

"Goodness no, they are the most peaceful of all our peoples. It was chaotic, there were people running everywhere with guns. No one was safe; no one knew what was going on."

Amie shuddered. "Don't remind me. I still have nightmares about it."

"Think," continued Ben. "It is the perfect time for others to move in, no one would be aware."

"And who is this third group?" asked Amie. "Though Ben, I don't want to get involved, I really don't. All I want now is a quiet, peaceful life. I've had enough excitement for a dozen lifetimes. Dirk might be able to help you, but I don't need to be part of it."

"Would it make a difference if I told you Angelina was in the group?" asked Ben.

"Angelina? Don't be ridiculous Ben. I can't possibly believe that! She's only a child. She can hardly be ten years old! Well, no one knew her real age for certain. Are you telling me she's running around waving an AK-47? That's so ridiculous. I've heard enough," and Amie went to stand up.

"Wait," Ben grabbed her arm pulling her back down. "Let me tell you the whole story."

Reluctantly Amie sank back onto the ground and pulled her coat around her to keep out the cool wind.

"The orphanage was attacked, yes, and many of the children were killed and some of the teachers too. They say the rest were all taken and driven away. Angelina was with the ones they spared, and the headmistress too I think."

"Mrs Motswezi?"

Ben nodded his head. "They were driven inland and no one knew where they had gone, or why they had taken the children. No one heard anything for many, many months, until bit by bit the rumours filtered through. They had set up a huge camp and were training their troops to fight."

"But what would they want with young girls?" Amie asked the question before she had time to think, and the answer left her cold. "You mean?"

"Yes, to have a woman keeps the men happy. And many men like very young girls."

"Don't!" Amie retorted. "No, not Angelina, not ..." She started to sob. Appalling images crowded her brain and she squeezed her eyes tight, trying to block them out. Dear, sweet, shy little Angelina, thumb stuck in her mouth, clutching Amie's skirt, waiting by the gates to the school, never leaving her side, Angelina hiding behind the sofa, sitting on the kitchen floor playing with the saucepans, her big, brown eyes gazing adoringly at Amie, the one person she had put her complete trust and faith in. And what had happened? Amie had been out shopping when the fighting started.

"I don't believe you," Amie said. "Angelina couldn't possibly be in this camp. When I left the house, she was with Pretty. She would have been nowhere near the orphanage. This is all a pack of lies. And anyway you probably only caught the odd glimpse of the child, how can you possibly say she's now in a camp with a group of child abductors?"

"When I went to your house to see if you were safe, Pretty told me she took her to the orphanage," replied Ben. "It was the safest place she could think of in case the riots spread as far out as Spring Glen."

"So, Pretty survived as well?"

"I don't know. When I last saw her she was still in your old house. I did not see her in the camp."

"But you say you saw Angelina though," Amie tried hard to keep the sarcasm out of her voice.

"I'm sure of it. She was sucking her thumb, I remembered that."

"Lots of children suck their thumbs," snapped Amie.

Ben sighed. "I know, but she was also cuddling a blue teddy bear."

Amie gasped as she recalled that day at the mall. She'd ignored all the warnings about choosing any one child as a favourite, and had unofficially fostered the little AIDS orphan after meeting her at the orphanage. For many weeks Amie had fought her impulse to whisk the child off, and even had wild ideas about taking her back to England. It wasn't until Angelina had run away from the school hostel and turned up on the doorstep one day, that she finally allowed herself to become emotionally attached.

She'd sent her to the best school that catered to the children of the ministers and expatriates, and treated her to a complete wardrobe of new clothes, to replace the one threadbare cotton dress she'd always worn.

But it was the blue teddy bear that rang bells for Amie. Angelina had never asked for it. She never asked for anything. But seeing her little hand stroke it in the shop, it too had gone into the basket along with the dresses, jackets and underwear. Angelina had taken that bear everywhere, to bed, to school, when they went out in the car, when they went shopping. Amie would laugh and suggest Angelina should call it 'Glue Bear'.

It was the only blue bear Amie had ever seen in any of the shops, but Ben might have noticed it too. He was astute enough to know it was one sure way of getting Amie's cooperation, simply by suggesting Angelina might be in danger. Could she trust him? Was he telling the truth? And what could he possibly want from her?

As if in answer to her unspoken question Ben blurted out. "Do you still have your camera?"

"Don't be so ridiculous," snapped Amie, "after all I've been through!" She stopped. Ben didn't know about her capture, her imprisonment and her escape. Of course, the bush telegraph was way ahead of Vodacom and any of the other cell phone companies; way ahead of the news broadcasts on television, but no one heard everything.

She paused. She did have a camera. Before the video

crew left, Dave had given her the small hand-held camera, saying it might come in useful one day.

"Think of it as my present to you," he'd said with a smile. "To thank you for all you have done and, who knows, you might be able to capture some amazing footage. When you come back to England you'll be instantly famous!"

Was this how fate worked? They say there's a reason for everything, but what use was a camera if the idea was to rescue Angelina? What difference would that make? "So, what good would a camera be? How could that help?"

"We need to tell the outside world what is going on," he replied. "How will people believe us if we tell them about all the suffering, the inhumanity, the cruel things they are doing? We must get them to help us stop it, and kill these evil people."

Amie sighed. "It's a nice idea Ben," she said, "but I'm not sure the world will take too much notice. I know we don't get up to date news here, but the last I heard, no one had officially supported one side or the other. Their attitude was, 'it's just another African conflict, and we are not getting involved. Once there's a clear winner, we might be prepared to do business with them'. And I think that's what has probably happened. I hear there are a few foreigners visiting Togodo again. Everyone will want to get in and grab a piece of the action knowing there's lots of oil."

"But you still don't understand, Amie," Ben knew he was not getting through to her. "What I'm talking about is not some Togodians wanting to make war in Apatu against the new government. These men are not from here, they are foreigners."

"So where do you think they've come from? One of the African countries near here?" asked Amie. "Are they after the oil as well?"

"I don't know what they want. It could be more land for their people and our minerals as well. But I do know they are killing my people and they have caused much suffering."

Amie drew in a sharp breath. "Look Ben, I think we need to go back and talk to everyone else about this. I can't help you on my own, perhaps we shouldn't get involved at all." Even as she said it, Amie knew she would do everything in her power to rescue Angelina and take her to Ruanga or some safe place. No way could she leave her to her fate, even though common sense was telling her to leave well alone.

She stood up. "The sun will be up soon, I should get back to camp." For a brief moment she wondered if Ben would try and stop her leaving, but he made no move to detain her. She walked a few paces and looked back. "Let me return on my own and talk to everyone, and when I've reassured them, I'll come and fetch you." She paused. "But, wait, you killed Jumbo, they'll not forgive you for that." Amie sat down again.

"He's not dead. I only made him look like that. If you press the side of the neck, people go to sleep, but they wake up again."

"Where did you learn to do such a thing?"

"One of my cousins had a boxing club in Apatu. He taught me."

"Oh," said Amie. There were a lot of things she didn't know about Ben now she came to think of it. If only she was sure she could trust him. "Which way is the camp?" She had lost all sense of direction the night before and she wasn't sure how far Ben had dragged her.

It took Amie some time to find her way back. Her legs were still shaking and she was shivering from her ordeal. Once or twice she looked back over her shoulder to see if Ben was following her and really letting her go. Or, would he change his mind, pounce on her and drag her away again?

As she approached the tents she was expecting to find everyone getting up, for most Africans rise with the dawn. The early beams of the sun were peeping over the mountains to the east, long golden fingers of light that gently warmed the air. Later in the day those same beams would blast the ground with a fierce intensity, making the sun more an enemy than a friend. For now, Amie welcomed the warmth as she hugged her coat around her, but she arrived to find the camp in an uproar.

Kaluhah and Jumbo were in a heated discussion and Amie was relieved to see Ben had told the truth; he'd not killed Jumbo after all. But she also realized having a guard on duty each night was no guarantee of safety. Not if Ben had managed to escape, then creep up and disable Jumbo so easily. Like many Africans whose names foreigners found hard to pronounce, he'd looked for an adopted name, and since Jumbo described his size and strength, Jumbo he became.

Everyone was very nervous when they found Ben had disappeared. Dirk's men were convinced he'd come to spy on them and was now going to tell the authorities where they were. Jefri and Sampson were arguing fiercely with Reibos, blaming him for not making sure Ben had been tied up securely. He'd been in charge of the prisoner so it was his fault.

Amie walked over to Dirk who was trying to calm everyone down.

"I need to talk to you."

"What, now?"

"Yes, right now. It's about all this uproar, it might help." He hadn't noticed Amie had arrived back into the camp, or even that she'd been missing in the first place.

"Let me calm the boys down first, I'll get Helen to serve breakfast right away. We'll talk later," and Dirk went to try and make peace between his workers. They looked as if they were about to kill each other. Looking back and seeing Amie's face he added, "After breakfast we'll find a quiet spot and listen to what's bothering you. I'm sure it's something we can easily sort out," he said with a smile.

Amie wasn't so sure.

When she recounted the events of the night before it was difficult for Amie to guess what Dirk was thinking. His face remained impassive and when she'd finished, he sat quite still for what seemed an age. She didn't tell the full story; she made out she'd willingly walked a little way into the bush to talk to Ben. She said nothing about the fact he'd overpowered her and dragged her away by force.

"I can't make a decision on any of this, except to say Ben is welcome to stay here with us, as long as he pulls his weight, and Jumbo is prepared to tolerate him. When

Jonathon comes back, we'll discuss it further." Then Dirk added, "I can see you want us to rush around and go and find this group of foreign men and see what they're up to, but then what? Storm the camp? Mount a daring rescue and free all the captives? This is not a Hollywood movie, Amie, and we need to be realistic."

"Yes, I know," she said with a sigh, scuffing the soil with the toe of her shoe, disturbing a line of ants busily marching past.

"We'll have to be patient. That's one good lesson we can all learn from this, patience."

While Amie watched Dirk walk away she felt sad. Patience had never been her forte. He would talk to Jumbo first and try to persuade him of the importance of allowing Ben to join them without any repercussions.

Amie tried to put aside all thoughts of Angelina, and what she might be suffering. She performed her daily tasks and did her best to shut out the images that kept jumping into her head, of Angelina being physically or sexually abused. She mentally kicked herself for not asking how recently Ben had spied on the camp. It might already be too late. Angelina might not even be alive. She hadn't even asked how far away the site was, how many days had it taken Ben to walk there? Had he even come straight here? For all she knew it might have been months ago, the men might have moved away by now.

Helen could see something was bothering her, but she neither questioned nor pried, so they went to fetch water in silence. Nothing was said as they cleaned and tidied the tents and swept the area with branches.

Amie had learned the importance of keeping the space around their sleeping quarters free from vegetation and rubbish: it was easier to see the odd scorpion or snake that might venture too close.

She worked with Kahlib repairing the wooden stands for the sleeping bags, holding the logs close together while he tied them tightly with twine. Dirk was always reminding them how important it was to avoid lying directly on the ground.

It was later in the day when Dirk told her he'd spoken to Jumbo, and since no one had even noticed Amie had been absent from the camp, it might be best not to mention it to anyone. Jumbo was angry he'd been tricked and put out for the count, but he'd reluctantly promised not to harm Ben. Dirk wasn't sure he would keep his promise, but Ben must decide the risks for himself.

Having got permission to invite Ben, Amie had no idea where to find him. She walked in wide circles around the camp but could see no sign of him at all. It was possible he'd changed his mind, but as it grew dark, he appeared on the other side of the Land Rover. Amie walked over.

"Come and meet everyone more formally this time," she said, as she gripped his arm and pulled him closer to the small, enclosed oven where Helen was removing the tubers and chunks of kudu she'd left to roast earlier.

"Goodness, I didn't expect to see you again!" she said as she kneeled back and looked quizzically at Amie.

"I should introduce you properly. This is Ben. He worked with me on the shoots when the Colonel blackmailed me into filming for him. Ben became a friend and I still think of him as one," replied Amie. Ben shot her a quick look of gratitude.

"Nice to meet you 'properly', Ben," Helen smiled and held out her hand. "I hope you'll forgive us for ..." she pointed to indicate where Ben had been tied up.

"No, no," he cut in, "I understand. The whole world has gone a little crazy. No one knows who to trust these days."

There was a loud snort from Jumbo who was watching Ben like a hawk. Amie was convinced that at the first opportunity, Jumbo would harm or even kill Ben. He hadn't forgiven him, and wouldn't forgive him any time in the future.

Despite their reservations, generally Dirk's other men were reasonably friendly and shook hands half-heartedly. They weren't used to working with someone from another tribe. At the lodge, it had been a tightly-knit community, all Luebos from the same family. But if Mr Dirk wanted them to welcome this stranger into their midst, they did not have a say. The only exception was Jumbo, who glared at the newcomer and brushed off his proffered handshake.

Whatever they might think about Ben everyone was keen to hear news of the outside world. He had little to tell them. It was his tribe that had been overturned and he was not about to share the news he was related to the President who'd been deposed in the bloody fighting. He'd been keeping a very low profile since the war had broken out and he'd never even told Amie how well connected he was.

Listening to Ben, Amie wasn't sure if they could trust him. She wondered if he had an alternative agenda. She was sure the Kawas were itching to get back into power again.

Jumbo made some disparaging remarks under his breath at this point but no one except Amie, Dirk and Ben himself knew why he was being so rude. Amie couldn't have expected Ben's welcome to be particularly warm. Was she wise in vouching for him? Introducing him into the camp as a friend? She reminded herself that her brief abduction was a secret she must keep, and never tell anyone else, especially Jonathon. If she changed her mind about Ben, and if he ever became a threat, it was ammunition she could use against him.

4   LEFT BEHIND

A few days later Amie and Helen were digging down into the sand in the river bed when they heard a distant drone which got louder and louder. They saw a dust cloud on the other side of the valley coming closer and closer. For a moment they didn't move a muscle, and then they looked around for somewhere to hide.

"Relax," said Helen after a couple of minutes. "I think it's Jonathon and Charles. I'd recognize that engine anywhere."

A few weeks before, Amie would have run off to meet them, but now she was more cautious. What if Helen was wrong? Better to wait and see if it really was Jonathon. They watched as the vehicle approached the camp and with a whoop, she raced over and flung open the door. Jonathon jumped out and gave her a massive hug.

"You're back! You're back and you're safe!"

"Of course I am, and we've had a good trip. We saw hardly anyone on the road. It was all quiet and peaceful."

Dirk slapped Jonathon hard on the shoulder, "Good to see you back, man," he said

"What have you brought? Did you get the shampoo and the soap and the blankets and the ...?" Amie was bouncing up and down as if it was Christmas and her birthday all rolled into one.

Charles laughed. "We got everything on the list and a lot more besides."

"And how are the Robbins?" asked Amie peering into the back of the vehicle, poking and prodding the packages and plastic bags.

"They're fine and send you their good wishes. It's all so peaceful the other side of the border. It was quite a culture shock seeing everything so normal."

The next couple of hours were spent unloading all the new supplies. Spices for Dirk to make more biltong, a comb and mirror for Helen, who'd been sharing with Amie since hers had broken; even some new clothes to replace those that had been washed so often they were falling apart. Everyone admired the plastic bowls and buckets as if they were treasures from some Aladdin's cave, and grinned when they saw all the tins of corned meat, vegetables and other foodstuffs.

"I'm amazed the old truck held up under the weight of all this," Dirk remarked when they'd finished unloading.

"Well, we got stuck in a lot more sand on the way back than we did on the way in," said Jonathon. Looking up he saw Ben. "A new person in camp?" he frowned.

"This is Ben," Amie explained. "I don't think you ever met him, Jonathon. He was one of the guys with me on those shoots."

"Thought I recognized the name," said Jonathon, holding out his hand, "and thank you for taking care of her."

"My pleasure," murmured Ben.

It crossed Amie's mind that Ben might worry she would tell her husband how they'd met again and how he'd practically kidnapped her and threatened her. He might be feeling a little uncomfortable about what he'd done.

Jonathon paused. "So does this mean that things are now back to normal? Is it all quiet? OK to go back to the capital? We didn't pick up a lot of news about what was going on here in Togodo, but lots about events in the outside world."

"Nothing much has changed, sir," said Ben. "There are a few foreigners in Apatu now. Not many, but I would think it is safe to return."

"It might be right for some of us, but not for me," Amie muttered to herself. She was not convinced there wasn't a price on her head even now. She'd been working for the Kawa government when all the fighting broke out, and she could only guess that her captors had been M'untus. It would be a lot easier if we, as outsiders, could recognize which tribe people belonged to, she reasoned. She also wondered why Ben had said nothing about the mysterious camp in the bush. She guessed he would choose his moment - since men never liked to rush these things - and many Africans could rarely see the need for making a fuss and demanding instant action. She noticed Ben didn't join in the general chatter that evening, but melted away into the shadows.

There was no more serious talk until after everyone had eaten, and they were sitting beside the heat coming from the underground oven. It was the safest way to cook, allowing no smoke to drift into the air and alert any curious passer-by. As an added bonus, Helen was able to brew up coffee on the small camping stove now she had a new supply of gas canisters.

"I've really missed my coffee," said Amie, savouring each mouthful from her tin mug.

"I brought as much back as I could," said Jonathon, "as a special treat."

"So, what news?" asked Dirk.

"Seems the whole world has gone mad," replied Charles. "We were appalled at what we saw on the television, and from what Tim Robbins told us."

"It's a gruesome repeat of the Crusades from the Middle Ages," added Jonathon. "There are Muslim fundamentalist extremist groups operating all over the place."

"They've launched attacks in twenty-one countries," Charles continued.

"Twenty-one?" repeated Helen in amazement.

"At first most people thought these were only random killings of Christians as the groups don't co-operate with each other. But it looks as if the problem is spreading," said Jonathon.

"There are horrific pictures and videos posted on the Internet showing them beheading hostages, boasting about rapes and training children to fight with guns. They have reintroduced slavery and buy and sell women and children. Fathers have abducted their children and taken them away to fight. Mothers have left their families and converted to fundamental Islam."

"We've not been aware of any of this," murmured Helen.

Jonathon continued. "They go by a variety of names, al-Qaeda, Boko Haram, the Muslim Brotherhood and so on."

"When did this all start?" asked Amie. "Why haven't we heard more about it? Surely all this hasn't happened in the last three months?"

"No, it seems to have begun in the late eighties when a fanatic called Zarqawi founded a group called 'Oneness and Jihad'. Five years later he pledged his fighters to support Osama Bin Laden and changed the name to al-Qaeda."

"That we've heard of, even in rural Africa," Dirk remarked. "But as far as we knew, the Americans killed Bin Laden. But you're saying that wasn't the end of it?"

"I suspect it was only the beginning," replied Jonathon. "The Americans built a huge detention centre in Iraq and threw in hundreds of militants. It kept the so-called terrorists out of circulation, but fermented discontent."

"It didn't help that some of the military were accused of brutality, so the place actually became a ground for training fighters. It's started a new Jihad or Holy War against the infidels, and the attacks have been getting more frequent, more ferocious and more brutal," Charles added.

"They renamed themselves as the Islamic State or IS," Jonathon continued, "and there could be twenty to thirty thousand strong in one group alone."

"At first the western powers weren't too bothered," said Charles. "The fighting was in Iraq and Syria, but it seems to be spreading."

Jonathon poured himself some more coffee. "But the West is now worried the fundamentalists are recruiting fighters from Europe to join the cause. No one knows how many, but maybe as many as 2,000 westerners have gone to Syria alone."

"How bad is it?" asked Helen.

"Don't ask me how they worked this out, but with US$2 million a day in revenue, they've been able to launch thirty to forty attacks a month."

"Where do they find all these new recruits?" asked Amie.

"Over the Internet and through religious study groups. In the United Kingdom alone, there are two hundred Muslim schools, and some are accused of teaching fundamentalist principles."

"Most Muslims aren't going on the rampage!" exclaimed Helen. "Surely it's a religion of peace?"

"Yes, it is, and the Koran states it's a sin to kill. But in any religion you'll always get a few who will interpret holy words for their own purposes," Jonathon reminded her.

"A few! You were talking about thousands just now," said Dirk.

"From Turkey alone, there are thousands being abducted or lured into Syria to IS controlled areas, but it still breeds distrust against a huge number of peace-loving Muslims," Charles opened a can of beer as he spoke.

"Don't those who want to live in peace have any authority over the rest?" Amie couldn't imagine sitting by and saying nothing if she saw her own people beheading and raping innocent victims.

"In some parts of Turkey people are now flying the IS flag in their windows and on their cars, despite the fact that IS have dozens of Turkish prisoners and even beheaded two American journalists," her husband replied. "There have been incidents in Kenya, including an attack on a shopping mall killing innocent people, and the fundamentalist movement has been active in West Africa too."

"I seem to remember a group called Boko Haram killing people in Nigeria," said Amie thoughtfully. "It was on the news in England. They kidnapped over two hundred schoolgirls."

"At least one and a half million have fled the area since," Charles added. "The refugee problem is another aspect of this whole disaster. Men, women and children are flooding out of the towns trying to escape the fighting. Yes, people are horrified but nothing much is being done about it."

"It looks as if people are too scared to stand up to them," Jonathon said. "Possibly worried it might escalate and get out of control."

Amie wondered if it would be wise to talk about what Ben had seen here in Togodo, not so very far away. Was the camp he'd seen one of these fundamentalist groups? She wondered how safe they were.

"I had some really good Muslim friends before coming to live in Africa," Helen said sadly. "I can't believe they would want to harm anyone because they're Christian. As a woman I think the most worrying thing is the introduction of Sharia Law. I guess many Muslims might be in favour of that."

"I don't know anything about Sharia Law," said Amie. "Does anyone?"

"Basically it's the law as interpreted in the Koran," replied Charles. "Cases are brought before a council of men who listen to both sides of a dispute, and make a binding decision."

"I know from my friends, that women are highly regarded and protected," Helen said, "and if you've been brought up in that faith you can accept their rules. But it wouldn't be for me. I couldn't adapt to keeping separate company from men, and covering up whenever I left the house, or only being allowed out at all if I was accompanied by a male relative. To me, that's taking away my freedom, especially my freedom to drive."

"From what little I know," Dirk broke in, "it's relatively easy for a man to divorce a woman but not so simple the other way round. And if I remember correctly the Sunni and Shia Muslims have some differences that go way back in history. That complicates things."

Amie remembered her one excursion back to her old home in Apatu when she'd been swathed in a suffocating, black burqa. Goodness, it was still packed away at the back of the tent somewhere. She'd been meaning to cut it up and fashion a mini skirt out of it, but the material was thick and heavy and not really suitable. She had a brief premonition, almost a déjà vu in reverse, that she might need it again one day.

It was late by the time they went to bed and Amie had not had a chance to tell Jonathon how Ben had suddenly turned up out of nowhere and the story he'd brought with him. She was still trying to decide if she should mention it to him while they were alone, or if she should invite Ben to tell it in his own words. While her maternal instincts towards Angelina made her want to rush off and rescue her, she was aware Jonathon might flatly refuse to help, insisting it was none of their business. Angelina was a child of Africa and her life and fate were inextricably bound to this continent. Thoughts of daring rescues which would amount to kidnap, or whatever they called taking someone illegally across an international border, would not sit well with Jonathon. Amie wasn't sure she would have the courage to sneak off without him, even if she had Ben beside her. The moment they entered their tent, Jonathon had flung himself down on the camp cot and went out like a light. Amie had no chance to discuss anything with him.

The following morning, while she did her daily chores around the camp, Amie could feel Ben's eyes on her, and she tried to avoid him as much as possible. It had been impossible to get Jonathon's attention, as he'd been crawling under the Land Rover, helping Dirk fix some problem that had developed on the journey back. Although she'd deliberately found reasons to walk as close to the vehicle as she could, at no time did she hear them talking about any camp, or about possible militants not too far away. Had Dirk said anything to the others about what Ben had seen? Surely this was a threat to them all? Did they think he was making it all up? She wondered why she herself had not mentioned it last night around the camp fire. She was desperate to tell Jonathon.

In the end it was her husband who took her by the arm and pulled her over.

"We need to talk," he said.

Amie breathed a sigh of relief. "Yes," she agreed, "and I think Ben ..."

"I've already asked him to meet us over by the baobab tree."

The baobab tree was about seventy metres from the camp. Fully twenty metres in circumference it thrust its branches to the sky, looking as if it had been planted upside down. Amie had remembered sheltering in one on her first night alone. Helen had told her it was known as the 'tree of life', providing shelter, clothing, food, and water for animals and humans. The bark could be used for making cloth and rope, the leaves for condiments and medicines and the 'monkey bread' fruit, full of vitamin C, tasted like a cross between grapefruit, pear and vanilla. Best of all, the tree was fire resistant, and so escaped the fierce fires which raced across the savannah every few years, devouring all the dry vegetation in their path. Huge swathes of veldt could be engulfed in a matter of moments.

A few feet from the tree Amie paused. "Oh! Look Jonathon, zebra. They're so beautiful!"

"From a distance yes," smiled Jonathon. "But they can be vicious little buggers if you get too close. They're very handy with their hooves."

"And the stripes on each one of them is different, I still find that hard to believe," added Amie. "I wonder if they recognize each other by their stripes or by their smell."

Jonathon chuckled, "We'll never know for sure."

She stopped to admire the small herd, as they gracefully nibbled and tore at the sparse clumps of stubbly grass. She remembered a long forgotten word. A 'zeal' of zebras, not a herd. Now whoever had taught her that at school? Not a particularly useful thing to know, she mused. Their tails flicked from side to side, whisking away the troublesome flies, moving steadily across the landscape, yet every now and again they turned their heads, swivelling their ears for sounds of predators and any signs of danger.

"I can only see zebra, there are no other animals with them. Isn't that unusual?" Jonathon asked. "Don't they often graze with other species?"

"Yes," replied Amie. She remembered sitting in the kitchen in Spring Glen showing Pretty, her new maid, how to cook a particular dish she liked, and Pretty telling her the zebra had got its stripes after fighting with a baboon over a water hole. The zebra kicked so hard it fell over backwards and into the nearby fire and the sticks left scorch marks on its white skin. She still wasn't quite sure if Pretty really believed such a tale, but at the time she seemed quite serious, assuring her madam it was true.

Thoughts of Pretty brought her back to the present and the story Jonathon was about to hear. For a brief moment Amie couldn't see Ben, but as they walked around the tree he was there on the other side, watching the zebra. He stood up as Jonathon came into view.

Jonathon nodded briefly and sat on the ground next to the massive tree and rested his arms on his knees. Amie slithered down beside him, still watching the animals in the dip between the hills.

"Amie says you have information," said Jonathon.

"Yes. I saw a camp, by a river. It is a very large camp and there are many soldiers and several women and children too."

Amie was trying hard to gauge Jonathon's reactions, but he was not even looking at Ben. He was busy using a couple of stones to crack open a wild marula nut before scooping out the kernels inside. He chewed the pulp slowly and thoughtfully before asking, "How long do you think the camp has been there?"

"I have no idea, many weeks?"

"But wait!" exclaimed Amie. "That can't be right, it must be about two years since you said Pretty took Angelina back to the orphanage, and that was torched right at the beginning of the uprising, so where have they been all this time?"

Ben said nothing. He just sat there and didn't respond.

"There could be a lot of different answers to that one," Jonathon said.

"You do believe Ben, don't you Jonathon?" It suddenly occurred to Amie he would simply ignore the whole thing and insist they not get involved. Then what was she going to do? She glanced sideways at her husband who was nodding, deep in thought.

"How far away is this camp?"

"It could be seven days' walking," answered Ben.

"Hmmm, that's probably about 200 kilometres give or take a bit," Jonathon muttered. "And in what direction?"

Ben indicated inland, towards the north-west. "I don't think it is too far from the border with Relawi. Perhaps they think if they run there they will be safe."

"That can work two ways," Jonathon observed. "They can launch an attack in either country from such a good vantage point. I suspect relations are not good between the new government here and Relawi?"

"I have not heard, but they say many countries will not recognize the new regime."

"That's true. Most are sitting on the sidelines waiting to see how things go."

"But for two years!" Amie was still worried about the length of time. Angelina couldn't have been in captivity that long surely?

"International affairs don't move that quickly," her husband reminded her. Jonathon sat in silence for a long time, then said, "Well I think a look-see would be the best. See what's going on."

Amie's heart jumped. She hoped and prayed Angelina would be there, she could rescue her and save her from all the abuse she must be suffering. Her imagination flashed into the future. She would need to be very patient with the child; it would be like the traumatic stress disorder Amie had suffered herself. But time and patience would help the healing process. She was so lost in her thoughts she missed what Jonathon said next. He was planning to go and check out the camp with Ben and Charles.

"When are we leaving?" she asked.

"*You're* not leaving at all," replied Jonathon. "*You'll* be staying here safely in camp."

Amie wasn't quite sure whether it was the arrogant tone in Jonathon's voice, or the words he used, but she was incensed.

"Oh yes, I am coming."

"It would be foolish of you, and downright irresponsible of me, to drag you on a two week trek through the bush." Jonathon snapped. "It'll be difficult enough as it is without you slowing us down. So, no more arguing Amie, no pleading, the answer is 'no' and that's final."

Amie seethed. It took all her self-control not to get up and walk away before she said or did something stupid. How dare he, she raged. How dare he tell her what she could or couldn't do. He was the one who'd forced her to come to Africa in the first place and she'd coped, way beyond what most people were asked to cope with, and she'd survived. Now he was acting as if she was a foot soldier in his army. She was damned if she was going to 'do as she was told'.

To work off her anger, she attacked a nearby fig tree, but most of the fruit was not yet ripe and her efforts wore her out after she managed to knock only a few mottled, yellow specimens to the ground. She picked one up and bit into the thick skin, nibbling on the soft seeds. She was determined to go and look at the insurgents' camp one way or another.

Once Jonathon had made a decision about anything, he organized what needed to be done with total efficiency. He and Charles made up lists of equipment and planned the route as far as Ben could advise them. They discussed if it was a good idea to take the Land Rover and drive part of the way there, but decided against it. Leaving it abandoned in the bush was asking for trouble and they would be lucky if it wasn't stolen or vandalized. Although they had the two vehicles at camp it would be stupid to take the risk of losing one of them.

Over the next couple of days Amie tried every possible way to get Jonathon to change his mind. She tried pleading with him, getting angry and sulking. She called him all the names under the sun, argued she would be a valuable asset, boasted about how capable she was and burst into tears a couple of times, but all to no avail. He stuck firm to his refusal to allow her to go with them.

Ben was going, of course, and Charles and Dirk asked Jefri if he would like to go as well. That made four, all men of course Amie fumed. There had to be a way to be invited along, if only she could find it.

While Amie was desperate to go, she was also very afraid. She might have experienced a heroic journey before, but at the time she'd had no choice. If she ventured out this time, it would be from choice, her own conscious decision. Was she being wise in begging to be included in the party? Would it not be easier to stay here with Dirk and Helen and sit patiently waiting for Jonathon's return?

But then, she asked herself, why was Jonathon so keen to go and check out the camp? Not out of pure curiosity. No, she guessed it would have something to do with his work for the British government; he was going on a spying mission. So, he wouldn't be too bothered about Angelina, and as far as Amie was concerned, that was the only reason for going, to rescue her child.

For the next two nights she tossed and turned in her sleeping bag, weighing up her determination against her common sense, and against her anger at being treated like a child. There was only one answer; she would wait for them to leave, and an hour later, she would follow them and once she caught up with them, they wouldn't be able to send her back. Yes, she decided in a fit of desperation, she would go, in such a way they would be stuck with her.

She felt quite smug about her decision. She had taken control of her life, and if Jonathon noticed she'd stopped nagging him, he didn't say a word.

Helen gave her a few thoughtful looks, almost as if she could hear Amie's thoughts, but as always she kept her opinions to herself.

Amie watched as the men packed up the essentials they would need. The small primus with a couple of mini gas canisters, warm clothing, a hat, groundsheet, mug and plate each, tins of corned meat, a compass and GPS, lighters, water bottles, several energy bars from the camp supply, first aid kit, lightweight raincoats, a torch each with spare batteries, safe water tablets, extra socks, a couple of tea lights, serrated knives, sewing kit, small axe, dry tinder for a fire, a spade, duct tape and plastic bags and of course they each carried a gun.

"Why are they packing so many plastic bags?" Amie asked Helen, she was damned if she was going to ask Jonathon or any of the soon-to-depart-party, who all seemed in the highest of spirits.

"To keep things dry," Helen stated the obvious. "Most plastic bags don't seal that well, so you secure them with the duct tape, which can be useful if it rains or if you have to cross a river. Wet equipment is one of your worst nightmares."

"Of course," murmured Amie. Now why didn't I realize that, she thought as she made a note of everything the guys were stuffing into their rucksacks. She would have to duplicate some of this stuff when she packed, as she wanted to be independent and no one would be forced to share with her. This time, she reasoned, I'm going to be really well prepared.

There were some extra things wrapped in black plastic that Jonathon stuffed to the bottom of the bag, but he didn't explain what they were, and Amie was not going to ask him.

Jonathon announced they would be departing the following day and that night, as they sat round the cooling oven, chatting quietly, he was extra attentive to Amie. She had no illusion he would change his mind, but he seemed to be saying sorry to her, except she was not yet ready to forgive him. I thought marriage was supposed to be a partnership, she reasoned to herself, not only the one half having all the adventures and the little wife sitting at home. No way, not for Amie.

During the afternoon she had gathered together a copycat list of things she planned to take. She wouldn't have the primus of course, nor the GPS, but she was sure once she caught up with the men she could share the spade and the axe. She was also happy for them to be in full charge of the guns as well. She paused when she considered packing the burqa. It would be a great disguise, but would she really need it? It was thick and heavy and wouldn't fit into her backpack. Reluctantly she decided to leave it behind. All she was going to do was catch up with her husband, and once they were all together again she would be safe.

As they settled down into their sleeping bags that night, Amie had mixed feelings. She was terrified about what she was going to do, but reassured herself she would only be on her own for a couple of hours. That wouldn't be too difficult. She was not relishing Jonathon's wrath when she joined them, but she'd cope with that when it happened. She was prepared

5   AMIE SETS OUT

She didn't sleep well, drifting in and out of unconsciousness, waking at the slightest sound. However, it wasn't until the pre-dawn light shone over the eastern hills that she sat up and realized, to her horror that Jonathon had already left.

Frantically she pulled on her clothes: long trousers which tied around the ankle, several layers of light tops, and a warm parka for the nights. She jammed a jersey and some spare underwear into her backpack and began to stuff in the supplies that she'd hidden in the corners of the tent, checking each item off her mental list. Damn, she only had one can of meat; she'd been meaning to grab another couple after the men had left. Now she'd have to creep round to the kitchen area where Helen put all the clean dishes, and grab her mug and plate as well. She'd need to be quick and very quiet.

She had no idea who was keeping watch at the moment; another danger to avoid, she reminded herself as she grabbed her hat. She felt like a thief as she sneaked into the food storage area and grabbed another couple of cans of meat, several energy bars, together with chunks of biltong, and stuffed them with her plate and mug into her backpack. Ah, let's take a knife, fork and spoon as well, she decided, might as well be civilized. Leaving the note she had written the day before for Helen and Dirk to find, she slipped out of the camp.

It wasn't difficult to see Kaluhah. He was standing under an acacia tree. If he stops me, I'll simply explain I'm going for a walk, she decided. He's hardly likely to try and prevent me from taking a very early morning stroll, even if he thinks it is a little suspicious, because I'm dressed for travelling and carrying a backpack. But the moment she ducked out from behind the cover of one of the Land Rovers, he turned and walked towards the other side of the camp, and Amie was able to slip away unnoticed.

She knew the general direction the men had taken, so her plan was to head out for a few hundred yards and scout around for their tracks. Her tracking skills were nowhere as good as Dirk's guys, but she had paid close attention when they'd shown her the evidence left behind by a wide number of species. She wasn't able to tell the difference between all the big cats, but she could guess the size of the animal, and the dung left behind was also a good indicator of which animals had been around recently.

She walked briskly with the sun rising behind her, confident she was heading in the right direction. This early in the morning there was less guesswork, and the previous day she'd practiced with the compass and noted the exact bearings in relation to the layout of the tents and the vehicles.

A couple of times she thought she saw signs of their progress, very shallow indentations on the hard ground, a few twigs broken by a boot, and blades of flattened grass.

When she came to a dry river bed, she was delighted to see evidence of footprints in the sand. She recognized the distinctive pattern from one of Charles' boots and wondered how far ahead they might be. She was confident she would catch up with them very soon. She would stalk them for a while, possibly half a day and, by then, they would've gone too far to turn back to escort her to camp. She felt pleased with her plan. It was going to work.

On the far side of the river, the grasslands gave way to more bushy shrubs and there was more ground cover, which helped to conceal any evidence of travellers. Amie was beginning to get a little worried and feel a little panicky. She couldn't lose their tracks now, not now! She took a couple of minutes' break. The sun was getting hotter and, up to this point, she had been walking briskly. She realized the men would be able to make better time than she could, so she only allowed herself a short break to catch her breath before setting off again.

There was a path of sorts through the areas that were more overgrown, and she guessed it would make sense to follow it. She also wondered what animal had fashioned this pathway; it was unlikely to be one used by man. She frequently glanced behind her, in case the owner of this rural freeway was using it at the same time.

She was making better progress now, and she didn't stop while she rubbed insect repellent over her face and neck, it might keep some of the small, biting flies at bay. The trees grew closer together and she was aware she was less likely to spot any dangerous animals. She reminded herself not only to look at the ground in case she stepped on a slumbering snake, but also up into the trees, excellent hiding places for leopards, and the occasional lion or cheetah could also be found in the lower branches.

Amie plodded on despite the rising heat; the distant landscape shimmering gently in undulating waves. Surely she must be keeping pace with the men, but she would have to walk even faster to close the distance between them. She got into her stride, the sweat running down her face, trickling past her collar and welding her shirt to her back. The occasional breeze helped to cool her a little as she walked.

She paused when she came to a log and looked over it to see what was on the other side. A large puff adder lay in the path and Amie paused, there was no way she was going to step over it. She looked to see which way it was facing. Left, I'll go left, she decided, noticing its head was on her right, but to make sure, I'll give it a very wide berth. She was relieved to see part way down the snake's body it was hugely distended, indicating it had eaten recently, but even if one of Africa's laziest snakes had recently dined, she wasn't going to take the risk of being bitten. While most snakes disappeared fast when they sensed waves from approaching footfalls, the puff adder rarely moved to get out of the way.

Amie was not too comfortable stepping off the pathway, but she didn't have a choice. Cautiously and carefully, looking closely where she put her feet, she walked in a wide circle around the reptile and breathed a sigh of relief when she got back onto the path. The trees offered a little shade, but soon they thinned out again and the open savannah lay before her with no signs of other humans.

Amie glanced at the sun, she was sure she was still going north-west, but she started to have her doubts. This was insane. What did she think she could possibly accomplish by following Jonathon? She must've been totally stupid to leave the safety of the camp. This time she only had herself to blame for her brainless actions.

She saw a lone baobab tree in the distance and decided when she reached it, if she saw no further evidence she was going in the right direction, she would turn back. She was fairly confident she could retrace her steps, as she'd taken note of several landmarks along the way.

Then, on a wide sandy patch she saw another clear imprint made by Charles' boot. Yes, I'm right! Now all I have to do is speed up, she told herself and took longer strides making good progress across the low-lying grass. Here the vegetation was low, so unlikely to hide even a party of sleeping lions, so feeling more confident and full of energy she pressed on.

There was a shriek to her left and she watched in awe as a young impala, its coat a glossy red-brown, bounded past her closely followed by a cheetah that raced out from the shade of the trees. They were moving so fast they were a blur as they passed Amie. The big cat kept its eyes focused on its victim as it twisted to the side to outflank the antelope. The sheer strength and beauty of the animal and the rawness of the hunt kept Amie rooted to the spot. All thoughts of danger to herself flew out of her head as she watched the action.

The impala was running for its life, or rather racing in

leaps and bounds, using its back legs to push upwards and onwards. But while it might have stamina, the animal was no match for the cheetah, whose speed allowed it to overtake. With one last bound the cat leapt on its victim and almost fell on top of it, curling its two front legs around the struggling impala before dispatching it with its teeth. The unfortunate antelope kicked wildly, making several attempts to escape, and for one brief moment Amie thought the small antelope was going to make it, as it bounded forwards a few steps before collapsing on the ground.

Amie realized she'd been holding her breath during the action and it dawned on her she might be in considerable danger. She reached into her backpack and got out the large knife she'd taken from the kitchen. It was all she had to defend herself with, but on this occasion, it seemed the cheetah, after one slow look around, was content to start feeding ferociously, allowing Amie to walk swiftly past while keeping a close eye on it. The fast chase had taken them some distance away, and Amie prayed the big cat wouldn't need to kill again. She thought it unlikely, as Dirk had explained many times, most animals would only expend their energy to hunt to eat. Unlike humans who murder for gain or revenge, animals kept to a higher, more ethical, code of behaviour.

The terrain now was sandier and Amie was able to follow the spoor left by the men. Although she was both hungry and tired, she kept on walking, pausing only to grab an energy bar from her backpack. In one hand she carried her water bottle, and after seeing the cheetah in action, she kept hold of the knife in her other.

The straps from the backpack were beginning to cut into her shoulders making them ache, but she put up with the pain, as the majority of the weight she was carrying was from the water bottles. That was a lesson she would never forget; water was essential. Neither was she going to discard any of the empty water bottles, when she found water she would refill them.

She remembered cheetahs rarely strayed too far from a water supply, but she was not going to hunt around now, she still had to make up ground. She must also look for a place where she could spend the night.

Back at the camp, Dirk and Helen were horrified when they realized Amie had gone.

"How can she be so stupid?" exclaimed Dirk. "Has she no idea how dangerous it is? She doesn't even have a weapon."

"She's taken a knife," said Helen reading the note she'd just found. "We should go after her, Dirk."

"We'd need to track her, so the Land Rover won't be much use," Dirk observed glumly. "And I'm loathe to leave even fewer people here in camp." He scratched his head. "She's a tough one," he added, "and she's a lot better prepared than last time."

"I don't care about any of that," said Helen. "You have to go and find her. If you don't, I'm getting in the truck and going myself. She could be in terrible danger and I could never live with myself if anything happened to her."

"I guess the least we can do is to drive west for a few kilometres and see if we can catch sight of her, but I don't hold out much hope, when we're not even certain which direction she took," grumbled Dirk. "And if we find her, do you think you can persuade her to come back to camp?"

"I'll have a damned good try," said Helen. "You've always said I have good persuasive skills, and I'll use every one of them if I have to. I've grown very fond of the girl and I'd be heartbroken if she got herself into trouble."

"Well if she has, we might never know," Dirk replied reasonably.

Helen shook her head. She knew what Dirk meant. If Amie had fallen prey to a hungry animal they might never find her remains. She could only pray for her safety.

Amie spent her first night in a shallow cave cut into the rock on the side of a slight incline. She knew such territory was a favourite place for leopards, but she had to trust to luck. She disturbed a pair of elephant shrews that were thoroughly put out at having to share their sleeping quarters, but Amie ignored them as she squeezed into the narrow space. There were a couple of bats near the entrance but, by now, she'd become so tough they didn't bother her at all. Those silly movies showing bats getting tangled in hair and flying into people's faces were as fake as the vampires they showed sucking blood.

She spent quite a comfortable night, enjoying some of the delicacies Jonathon had brought back from Umeru, which she'd helped herself to from the food stores. She hoped Helen would forgive her.

Although Charles was convinced he was fit, he was beginning to realize he was more out of shape than he thought. Jonathan seemed oblivious to the heat, and as for Jefri, he appeared to have an unending source of energy as he loped onwards mile after mile after mile. He took short sharp steps, seeming to skim over the ground at an amazing rate, often stopping to wait for the Europeans to catch up with him.

Charles was worried about slowing them down, but when his heart began thumping faster in his chest and his breathing became more ragged, it was time to own up and beg them to take a rest.

Jonathon looked at his friend as Charles wrenched the backpack off and collapsed onto the ground. Jonathon grabbed his wrist and took his pulse. "We'll need to slow down," he said to no one in particular. "The camp is not going anywhere in a hurry, and I'd rather we didn't half kill ourselves to get there a few hours earlier."

Ben nodded. He hadn't wanted to admit it, but the pace set by Jefri, which Jonathon had matched with ease, had been telling on him as well. He was much fitter than Charles, but he was more used to city life and riding in cars and taxis than traipsing over the open African veldt in his native land.

Jonathon offered Charles a drink - water laced with sugar - and suggested they rested for a couple of hours before looking for a suitable place to camp for the night. So far their trip had been uneventful. Only a few peaceful animals grazing on the grasslands peered at them before moving a few steps away. There'd been no sign of other people either which he thought strange.

"Why haven't we come across any villages, or people? I

can't understand it," he turned to Jefri and Ben.

Jefri shrugged, but Ben answered. "This is an area the government chose as a nature reserve. All the people were moved out and they were not happy, but the government told them they would make money from the tourists coming to look at the animals. And some hunters would pay lots to shoot the big animals."

"And it never happened?" asked Jonathon, although he already knew the answer.

"No. No tourists came and no lodges were built and the people were afraid to move back into the area. They were scared of what the government might do to them," Ben added. "It is such a shame, my country could be a paradise for people to come and visit."

"Why am I not surprised to hear that?" said Charles, whose breathing had returned to normal. He mopped the sweat off his face with a handkerchief.

"Very few people understand that Ben. You're one of the few," observed Jonathon.

"How far have we come?" asked Charles.

Jonathon looked at the GPS. "We've made good progress, exactly on target for a six day hike." He looked at Charles. "How are you feeling?"

"It'll get better," Charles said with more optimism than truth. "Give it a couple of days for the joints to loosen up and I'll be fine."

"Another ten minutes and we can push on," said Jonathon, deliberately not looking at Charles to gauge his reaction. He saw that Jefri looked as fresh as a daisy and hadn't even sat down when they stopped. He was rummaging in a nearby bush looking for edible berries and leaves.

Amie was not giving herself the luxury of a rest either. She was worried that if she stopped, she would find it difficult to get going again. She kept up a steady pace, neither too fast nor too slow and when she looked behind her, she was surprised at the distance she'd covered. She hoped the others weren't too far ahead, but just as she was congratulating herself on how well she was doing, she heard several loud crashes to her left. It sounded as if a fleet of trucks was trundling straight through the bush. For a brief moment she didn't move, and then she looked around wildly to find a tree. If she got off the ground, she'd be less visible. She spied a good-sized acacia but the thought of the thorns tearing at her clothes and her hands gave her second thoughts. Although the thundering noises were coming closer, they didn't seem to be moving very fast.

Not far away was a manketti tree that looked easy enough to climb. Amie rushed over, dropped her water bottle and knife on the ground and began scrabbling up the trunk. She would need both hands to climb and she didn't have time to pack them away.

She scraped her hands as she pulled herself up, but she was in such a panic she hardly noticed the pain. Breathing heavily, she rested for a moment, squatting on the first major fork and looked down. She was only a few feet off the ground, possibly twice the height of a man. She decided to climb higher but the vegetation was thicker and the branches closer together. As she reached out along the largest lower branch, she was unable to move, her backpack was now wedged between the branches. Bit by bit she released the straps and eased it off. Slinging it over one arm she stretched out along the branch. Grabbing hold of it she pulled herself higher, and reached for the branch above that, but her hand slipped and jerked downwards, allowing the strap of the backpack to slide down. Gravity completed the bag's journey and it landed with a thud on the ground at the base of the tree.

For a brief moment she considered climbing down and trying to retrieve it, but the noises that had panicked her in the first place, were much, much nearer. She wriggled up onto the next high branch and clung on for dear life. From her perch she saw a large grey shape below, then another, and a small herd of elephants moved into view beneath her. It was impossible to tell how many there were, but she thought she saw at least two small calves, still none too steady on their little legs.

Her heart missed a beat as a trunk appeared below her, waving backwards and forwards, before it moved away to attack the nearby acacia tree. Which way round is it? Amie tried hard to remember. Was it poor eyesight, good sense of smell or, poor smell? No it must be a better sense of smell. As long as I stay absolutely still they might not see me at all.

The first elephant below the tree moved on, followed by a second one that rubbed its back against the trunk. Amie held on to the tree, like a drowning sailor clinging to the mast of a ship at sea. Common sense told her that, in general, elephants were not a danger to humans. It was unlikely she would be trampled to death, but they were also curious creatures and she had no desire to be used as a football should they find her and feel playful.

The moment that thought crossed her mind, she saw to her horror, one of the smaller elephants had noticed her backpack at the base of the tree. He poked it with his trunk and managed to roll it a little way, but was interrupted by one of the fully grown females who came to investigate. She smelled it and gave a low rumble, which to the rest of the group, seemed to be a signal to move on. Another elephant came to poke the unknown foreign object, picked it up and tossed it high in the air. It came to rest several yards away. She ambled over and curled her trunk around it again, but one of the straps flew up and flapped onto her nose so she tossed it to one side in contempt.

Amie had no idea how long the elephants grazed below her, while they tore the leaves off the trees and investigated the ground. To her it seemed like hours, but eventually, much to her relief, they moved off. Despite her fear, she could only admire the great beasts as they meandered along a pathway their herd would have used for thousands of years. The gentle giants were awesome and the thought of them being slaughtered simply for their ivory was heartbreaking.

She waited until they were almost out of sight before she plucked up the courage to come down from the tree. When she first lowered herself onto the next branch below, she found her fingers refused to let go of the branch she was clutching so tightly. It felt as if they were wrapped permanently around the wood, and she'd have to prise them loose one at a time. Eventually she slithered and fell, rather than climbed down and landed with a thump at the base of the manketti tree, jarring her whole body.

Gingerly she got to her feet and poked and prodded herself all over, but although she was bruised, she didn't appear to have any broken bones or suffered any real damage. She staggered over to her backpack. Luckily it hadn't contained anything breakable, but she wondered if the elephants had been able to smell the water bottles inside it. The knife was still lying in the grass, but her almost-empty water bottle had been squashed flat, so much for keeping it for a refill she thought wryly.

She checked out the position of the sun and realized with relief the elephants were heading east not west; she guessed they were heading towards Dirk's camp. She set out to walk north-west as best she could judge it, the dying rays blinding her on her left, as the sun sank lower in the sky. It was more difficult now to get into an easy stride, each step hurt and she guessed she might have pulled a leg muscle in her frantic attempt to get out of the elephants' way. It could be a lot worse she consoled herself.

Back at the camp a rather dejected party had returned after searching for Amie for most of the day. At first it had been easy to track her, but then the heavens opened and the rain had come down in torrents, washing away all traces of her journey. It was a sudden cloud burst, localized, but enough to persuade Dirk and Kahlib to give up.

"It's in the lap of the gods now," he told Helen sadly. "She survived once and I wouldn't be surprised if she makes it a second time."

"I hope you're right," replied Helen. "I hate to think of her out there all alone. I don't know what possessed her to try and follow the men. She must really love that child, even after not seeing her for all this time. I'm not sure what the outcome will be if they do meet up again."

As the sun sank below the horizon it cast a bright orange glow across the sky. Amie stopped for a moment to gaze - Africa in splendour. But there was no time to linger; she needed to find as safe a place as possible for her second night. An acacia might be a better bet if she could climb it carefully and avoid most of the thorns. They were more plentiful and gave a lot more shade. Of course, it didn't matter which type of tree she chose, the mosquitoes would inevitably find her. She only hoped the repellent in her bag hadn't been ruptured after playing elephant football.

Nestled in the middle of the forked trunk, a good distance off the ground, she devoured two snack bars and drank about a third of a bottle of water. She had gathered a few juicy berries and leaves as she walked, confident this time she'd chosen ones that were quite safe to eat. She wriggled around and managed to get herself quite comfortable and was settling down when she thought she heard voices. She stayed stock-still, thinking hysterically that all this excitement was getting too much for her.

Her ears pricked up, alert for the slightest sound, and even though they'd stopped talking, she heard footsteps approach and pause at the base of the tree. Looking down in the rapidly-fading light, she couldn't make out at first how many of them there were, at least four, possibly more. She didn't move a muscle, and breathed as quietly as she could.

"This would be as good a place as any for the night."

"Is it not too open?"

"No, we can see anything coming from a mile off, and if we make for the more wooded areas, we'll be going back on ourselves."

The men started to unpack, lit the primus and put water on to boil.

"We'll cross a river tomorrow," said one of them, "and we can top up the water supplies."

"That's good news."

"I think we've come further today than I thought, another three or four days?"

"It won't be too soon for me, even though the ground is quite level, it takes a lot of energy to walk in this heat."

"Ah, but we need to go over those low hills, the camp is on the other side."

"Coffee anyone?"

Soon the smell of coffee was joined by the sound of cans being opened, and little was said while the men ate.

Amie leant back in the tree and smiled. What were the chances of both her and Jonathon settling down for the night under the same tree, it must be millions to one. This would only happen in some silly book, never in real life. There were several acacia trees dotted all over the veldt, although this one was much larger than all the others, so it was the best choice. Now, how was she going to plan their reunion?

Looking down through the leaves, she saw Jefri nudge Jonathon and whisper to him. Jonathon looked as if he was about to leap to his feet, but Jefri grabbed his arm and spoke softly again in his ear. Jonathon nodded and swiftly reached behind him, picked up his rifle and aimed it up into the branches.

6   WAITING FOR JONATHON

"Jonathon! No!" shrieked Amie, as she tried to scramble out of the tree. "It's me, it's Amie!"

Jonathon dropped the gun as if it was red hot and stood up.

"What the hell are you doing here?" he roared.

If Amie had stopped to think, she would've realized her behaviour was likely to make him very angry, and she wouldn't have been mistaken. Walking off alone into the bush had been a very stupid thing to do, putting not only herself at risk, but causing worry and inconvenience to other people as well. For the first time she wondered if Dirk and Helen had gone out to look for her.

She clambered down to the base of the tree and was a little reassured to see the wide grin on Ben's face, he obviously approved. Jefri looked nonplussed, Charles looked as if he'd seen a ghost, but Jonathon was furious.

"I can explain …" began Amie.

"I don't care what you have to say," said her husband. "You had no right to go wandering off by yourself. Anything might have happened to you."

"Well it didn't," Amie responded. "I'm fine, I'm in one piece and it looks as if I made better progress than you did!" she added in a fit of bravado.

Jonathon ran his fingers through his hair and sighed. "I can't believe you would do such a thing."

"Well I have, and now I'm here and it's too far to turn back, so you're stuck with me," Amie decided the best form of defence was attack.

Ben held out the can of meat, but Amie shook her head. Despite the fact she was hungry, she wasn't going to admit it. "No thanks," she said, "I've already had supper."

Jonathon gave her a dirty look and sat back down.

Charles spoke for the first time. "I'm sure an extra pair of hands will be useful and Amie might even be a help."

"I have no idea how," grumbled Jonathon, "she's more likely to be nothing but a bloody nuisance."

"Thanks," replied Amie. His words hurt. He was being totally unfair; she'd already proved how capable she was in getting this far.

There was an awkward silence and the atmosphere was strained. No one knew quite what to say. Eventually Jonathon said, "Well you're here now and there's nothing we can do about it. Just be sure you don't hold us up."

While everyone else got out their sleeping bags and prepared to settle down, Amie climbed back into the tree. She felt safer above the ground and this particular tree was quite comfortable. As on previous nights, she knew she wouldn't sleep deeply, as her sense of survival was wired and she would wake frequently to check for danger. However, apart from a lion roaring in the far distance, the rest of the night passed peacefully.

They set off not long after the sun rose, eating on the move as they pressed on westwards. Ben reckoned the camp was possibly a couple of days march ahead, but he warned they had guards around the camp and he was not sure how far out they patrolled. He told them it was next to a river, wide and fast flowing, and he had counted fourteen tents in all.

They walked for two more days and, on the last night after the evening meal Ben attempted to draw a diagram for them. Using a stick, he marked the outline in the sand. "They have three tents close together at this end; I think these are for those in charge, as they have guards outside. This tent here is where they keep the women. The rest, along the other side of the central area, are used for the soldiers, but these two at the far end, I think that is where the stores are. That is all I know."

"And they cook here in the middle?" asked Jonathon pointing to the area between the tents.

"Yes. I saw some of the women cooking, closely supervised by several soldiers and twice a day they are escorted down to the river to wash or collect water."

"So they're being used for labour," said Charles.

"Yes, and uh, for other purposes. I saw a couple of girls taken at night to these three tents at the end here. That is why I think the main men are in these ones."

"Do you think they are Kawa, or Tsaan?" asked Charles.

"I do not recognize them as being from Togodo. We do not make our women wrap themselves in the black cloaks from head to foot."

"Wait a minute," said Jonathon sharply. "You didn't mention that before! You mean like Muslim women are dressed when they go out of doors? But we were talking about the fanatics at supper with ..." Then he remembered Ben had not been sitting with them.

"Yes, like that," admitted Ben. "Is it important?"

"It makes a huge difference," replied Jonathon, while Charles nodded in agreement.

"But why?" Ben did not understand.

"Because, there's been a huge insurgence of fundamentalists in several different countries, who are fighting to spread their religion. Some towns have been razed to the ground and Christians have been butchered and killed. This is a new Holy War."

"I did not know," muttered Ben.

"What is even more terrifying, these soldiers are fighting for a cause they totally believe in, and they're quite prepared to commit suicide and die for the cause. Many have strapped explosives to their own bodies and then set them off in crowds of people. We're not talking about fighters who'll listen to reason as we know it."

Both Jefri and Ben looked very uncomfortable and Amie suspected they might make a run for it, slipping away into the night.

"We didn't ask you how many soldiers there are altogether," Charles said.

"I think twenty-five, thirty," replied Ben. "There is also a white woman ..."

He got no further before Jonathon broke in. "A white woman?"

"Yes, but she is in the tent with the other women. I do not know if she is with the soldiers or a captive as well. I saw her with the child with the blue teddy bear."

"Angelina," Amie murmured softly.

"How do you know she's white if the women are all wearing burqas?" Charles cut in.

"When they were down at the river, they take them off while they wash, not completely, but I saw one had white skin."

"It could be one of our friends, someone from Apatu, even from the club," Amie suggested.

"Unlikely, not after all this time," replied Jonathon. "We were amazed to learn from Tim Robbins in Umeru, dozens of people from different European countries have left home and come to fight in this Holy War. No one can quite work out why. Apart from having the same religious beliefs, they must be aware of the savagery of many of these groups."

"Innocent journalists have been beheaded," Charles said.

"And many innocent villagers, simply because they were Christian," Jonathon repeated. "So we must make a plan."

"Are we going to rescue all the women?" asked Amie hopefully.

Jonathon gave her a scornful look. "Is that what you thought we were going to do? No, not at all, we're simply going to have a look-see and go back to camp."

"But I thought ..." Amie wailed.

"No Amie," Jonathon interrupted. "We're only here to report back ...."

"... to the authorities in Umeru," Charles finished for him.

"Oh," Amie was devastated. "But I thought, I mean ... not rescue Angelina? Just leave her there?" Amie's eyes filled with tears.

Jonathon put his arm round her, showing compassion for the first time since she'd appeared. "Be sensible Amie. You don't even know for sure if it is Angelina."

"But the blue teddy she ..."

"Might have dropped it anywhere, another child may have picked it up or stolen it from her. Maybe it wasn't the only blue teddy in Apatu. You want it to be Angelina I know that, but it is best she's not anywhere near here. It would be heartbreaking to see her and not be able to do anything about it."

"You mean, even if we see her, you would just walk away?" Amie couldn't believe what he was saying.

"Be sensible, there are four of us and up to thirty of them and they'll be armed to the teeth, not only with guns but possibly explosives as well. And they are fanatics; they'll kill first before asking questions. I don't know whether it's safer to leave you here, or have you with us. Either way this is dangerous." He gave her a shake. "Now do you realize how stupid it would be to rush in there?"

Amie nodded her head. She really hadn't thought things through in a logical sense. In her imagination she'd visualized clutching Angelina and comforting her as she helped her away from the horrors and the fear. She'd pictured herself returning to the camp, loving the child and planning a wonderful new life for her. Now it seemed all they were going to do is look and walk away. She decided to keep her eyes open for any opportunity, surely she'd be able to do something. She couldn't walk away. She couldn't.

When Ben got the opportunity, he drew Amie to one side and asked her if she had remembered to bring the camera, so they could get footage of the camp. Amie shook her head, in her hurry to leave Dirk's camp she'd completely forgotten to pick it up. She felt very ashamed as she admitted this to Ben, but convinced herself it would have been damaged beyond repair after the elephants had played football with her backpack.

The following day Jonathon, Ben and Charles planned out their strategy. They would hide their supplies and leave Jefri and Amie to guard them. Hearing this, Jefri looked more than a little relieved. The men would approach the camp staying on this south side of the river, hide out below the summit of the high ridge closest to the camp and observe as many details as they could. Jonathon marked out the places for the three of them. It would be safer not to descend the ridge on the camp side, he suggested, but keep each other in sight in case they needed to warn of any danger.

The fanatics had set up right next to the river with their tents occupying the widest part of the flat land before the ridge that rose steeply behind them. Charles remarked that the camp was probably in the flood plain, which made him think they were not the brightest soldiers in anyone's army.

After much debate, it was agreed the patrols would be more frequent east and west of the camp, so they would be safer on the high ridge behind looking down.

It was difficult to recognize either Jonathon or Charles as they covered their faces with wet mud mixed with a dark dye Jonathon produced from his backpack. They covered their hands and wrists and, much to Amie's astonishment produced two pairs of night vision goggles. Then they assembled weaponry that was stored in small pieces in the rucksacks. She had no idea what kind of guns they were, and she didn't want to know, but then Jonathon really surprised her when he pushed a small pistol into her hand along with some ammunition.

"This is a Walther PPK, I can't even show you how to fire it because the noise might carry too far, but I'll show you how to load it and what to do if you feel you need to kill someone before they kill you."

Amie gulped. This was all getting very real. This was what she'd got herself into. A moment of guilt went through her as she realized Jonathon would be more vulnerable without the extra gun, because he'd now given it to her. She concentrated hard on what he was demonstrating, quite certain she would never have the courage to pull the trigger. Yes, she remembered asking him to teach her some self-defence, but now it was all too real.

Jonathon showed her several times how to load the bullets into the magazine, push it into the grip, release the safety catch and - in theory - how to fire the gun. He made her load and unload it herself at least a dozen times until he was satisfied she knew what she was doing.

Grabbing her arm he guided her away from the group. He walked with her towards the shade and suggested she sit down. "It's probably too late for this," he said, "but once more, do you trust Ben?"

"Yes, yes I do trust him. Why do you ask?"

"It's not impossible he's leading us into an ambush.

This could be a trap. Not everyone is as they seem you know." Jonathon gave a wry smile.

"You don't have to remind me," Amie replied, "you had me fooled for years. But yes, I do trust him, as much as I trust anyone."

The time dragged once the three men had left, and after chatting to Jefri for a while, Amie wandered around, poking sticks into a termite mound trying to entice the little insects out, but they were having none of it. She gathered small pieces of thin branches and wove them into plaits to make long ropes, but this wasn't very successful either. The night passed uneventfully, but the next day as the sun rose higher in the sky, and beat down on the earth; Amie and Jefri took shelter under the shade of the wide acacia branches.

They drank sparingly, since there was no obvious place to replenish the water, nibbled on pieces of dried meat and dozed in the heat of the day.

Amie lay gazing at the sky, imagining all kinds of scenarios where she raced into the camp, firing her pistol, scaring everyone, who took one look at her and ran away. She rescued all the prisoners single-handedly and guided them back to Dirk and Helen who welcomed them with open arms. In her dream, Jonathon was standing on the sidelines admiring her courage and congratulating her. He was apologizing profusely for doubting her, when she woke with a start, to see a stag beetle running down her arm. She gently shook it off.

In the distance a few zebra and wildebeest moved leisurely across the landscape grazing as they went, and a small herd of buck joined them, keeping a sharp look out for danger. Amie thought she would never tire of watching these beautiful creatures living wild in their own habitat. This is where they belonged, not in zoos, though those were necessary as breeding venues to make sure species didn't die out.

The men had been gone for over twenty-four hours. They'd left before dusk and now the light was fading on the following day and there was still no sign of them.

On the second day, Amie and Jefri gathered a few leaves to eat, and walked around a little and Amie climbed a tree to while away the time. Jefri showed her the tracks made by a dung beetle, and how giraffe had been past here in the last few days. He pointed to the hoofmarks made by what Amie understood was some kind of antelope, but Jefri only knew the local name for it so she wasn't sure which variety he was describing.

When the sun sank on the third day, Amie began to feel unsettled, but reasoned the men would wait until it got dark again before leaving their hiding places. The next night passed and they still hadn't returned and now Amie was worried. They hadn't heard any shots, but she wasn't sure exactly how far away the camp was and how far the sound would travel. Jonathon hadn't wanted to take a chance when he was teaching her how to use the gun. Ever since he'd given it to her, she'd kept it in her pocket. It was such a small gun, she guessed he'd worn it on his ankle, but looking at it, she was amazed it might be capable of really killing someone. She held it in her hand, even something so tiny looked dangerous and lethal. It might give her some courage, but it was unlikely to be used, certainly not by me, she thought.

The patience shown by the Africans was something that always amazed Amie. When Jefri saw her pacing backwards and forwards the following morning he tried to calm her down.

"They will come in time," he said. "Many things can stop them from coming."

"That's what I keep telling myself," Amie moaned.

"We must sit and wait," remarked Jefri lying back and closing his eyes, "and they will come."

Patience is not high on my list of talents, thought Amie, and wandered off to torment the termites again. Anyway, she reasoned, we can't sit here forever, we'll need to go and find water soon. She walked back to rummage in the bags to count the number of full bottles they'd left. If they took care, there was enough for two more days.

The sun sank in the sky and disappeared below the low hills on the horizon, and still there was no sign of the returning party.

Amie scrambled into her familiar tree, convinced she would not be able to sleep a wink, but at some point she must have dozed off. Her dreams were full of images of war films she'd watched on the television back in England. They were never her favourite genre, but Jonathon liked them and she would often curl up on the sofa and read, pausing only to look at the screen occasionally. Now her dreams were full of the battles and skirmishes where soldiers from both sides fired hundreds and hundreds of bullets at each other. None of the movies had seemed very realistic to Amie, despite the high tech visual effects. She knew the moment the director called 'cut', everyone would wander off to the catering van, both warring sides laughing and back-slapping on the way.

But none of that bore any resemblance to the position she was in now. How had she got into a situation like this? She dozed off again and this time she returned to the town she grew up in. Her dream was peppered with images of her family, her mother, father, Sam, her sister and her brood. She could see herself floating over them as they went about their day-to-day lives, all so normal, all so conventional. They knew which roads to take, which shops to enter, which television programmes would blare into their living rooms tonight. It was all safe and secure and yes, predictable. That was the only word to describe lives lived in first world countries by millions, who in past generations had ironed out all the wrinkles caused by tribal in-fighting, wealth management and land ownership.

When Amie finally opened her eyes, she felt as if she'd not slept a wink. As she stretched her arms and twisted her neck, she had a feeling something was different, something had changed.

Cautiously, she got down from her tree and noticed the bags containing their supplies were no longer there. She looked around. Jefri was not there either. She was alone.

She fought down a feeling of panic and took deep breaths as she realized she was shaking from head to toe. He must be here somewhere she thought. She wondered if he went off to find water, so she scouted round looking for signs of his footsteps in the sandy soil, but there'd been so much activity in this small area over several days, it was impossible to be sure which particular prints belonged to Jefri.

She looked a little farther away from the home tree, as she thought of it, but after two hours of frustrated searching she gave up in despair. He can't have gone and left me, he can't, he can't. How could he do that? She crouched down and started to cry. She was on her own and she had never been so terrified in all her life. This wasn't running blindly away from danger, this was her own fault; she had no one to blame but Amie. She felt very sorry for herself.

A screeching hadeda flew low overhead, followed by its mate and several more which snapped Amie momentarily out of her self-pity. She couldn't sit here and wait to dehydrate or starve to death, she needed to take action, but what? What were her options?

The sun bouncing on a sparkle of light from low down in a nearby bush caught Amie's attention. She dashed over to investigate and to her joy she found all their bags and, most importantly, their water bottles nestling in a hollow under the leaves. At least Jefri hadn't condemned her to starve to death she thought, as she wrestled a snack bar out of its wrapper and took several swigs of water.

She returned to the shade to plan what she was going to do next. It's pointless staying here, she reasoned. What if the guys never came back? How long should she wait until she too made her way back to Dirk and Helen's camp? She could only believe that was where Jefri was heading right now. Why hadn't he told her he was going? I suppose there were dozens of reasons she thought, but he had gone, so did it really matter why?

There was another option of course. She could make for the fanatics or terrorist camp or whatever name applied to it, and see if she could find out what had happened to Jonathon, Charles and Ben. That would take a lot of courage Amie, she told herself, are you brave enough to do that? To get closer to the enemy?

For the next couple of hours Amie mentally listed the pros and cons of going back to Dirk's camp, or sitting and waiting. She made an inventory of the remaining supplies and weighed up her chances of survival.

The day dragged on and on until at last Amie could no longer sit and do nothing. She had to take action. She rummaged in Jonathon's large backpack, past caring if she violated his privacy. There were several things she'd never seen before and didn't recognize, certainly stuff Jonathon had never shown her. Firstly there were three box-shaped squares with a flat piece of plastic on the side, and each one was about the size of an extra-large Rubik's cube. She had no idea what they were for or how to use them, and she dared not fiddle with them, but put them into her pack anyway, they might come in useful. Next she pulled out four long, cigar-shaped tubes with a ring at one end. Amie twirled them around in her fingers turning them this way and that. She wondered if they were grenades of some kind, but the ones they showed on the movies always resembled small brown pineapples. She thought it would do no harm taking those so she put those in her backpack as well.

She found the tin full of gunk the men used to darken their skin, mixed it with a bit of mud, and plastered it all over her face and hands. She pulled her hat low over her blonde hair to hide it as best she could, glad she had persuaded Helen to cut it short. She tied the bottom of her long trousers tightly and tucked them into her boots. She put on her darkest t-shirt, with her long-sleeved brown jacket over it and pushed the gun into her pocket. She filled her backpack with water bottles, a couple of cans of meat, several packets of biltong and the remaining snack bars. She looked at the knife which was now a little blunt from use, and found a suitable stone and sharpened it.

She was ready, or as ready as she would ever be. She wasn't feeling any braver, but if she ran away now, she'd feel such a coward. She had to find out what had happened to the men. She sat as patiently as she could and waited for dusk to fall before she set off towards the fundamentalists' camp.

7   A CRUEL DEATH

If Jonathon had planned to observe the encampment from the low-lying hills close to the tents, Amie decided to observe it from across the river. She would wade over further downstream to the far side, rather than make directly for the camp, so she needed to circle round. First though, she had to find the river. Usually this wasn't too difficult, for where there was water, the trees grew more abundantly alongside the banks. She hugged the more densely wooded areas, keeping her pace slow and steady. She deliberately put her feet only on the bare ground, and she kept an eye on the trees overhead. She doubted there would be too many large carnivores in the area with so many people around, but there was still plenty of danger, snakes, scorpions and spiders and, of course, the dreaded mosquitoes. She had no idea if they would take a liking to the gunk she had spread all over her face, and she was reluctant to smear on the anti-mosquito cream in case the colour came off.

As she approached the top of a low rise, she took off her backpack, got down on all fours and crawled to the summit. There, way over to her left, she could see the camp, exactly as Ben had described it with the river beyond it, the water sparkling in the moonlight. She wriggled like a snake over the brow of the hill and slithered down, looking out for any patrols. She had just reached the cover of a line of small bushes when she heard muted voices. She lay still, hugging the ground.

There were two of them and if they were supposed to be guarding the camp they were making a very bad job of it. They were standing not far from Amie, laughing and joking as they lit their cigarettes. It was unlikely they would have seen her crouched low under the bush, and it didn't appear they were on the alert for any signs of danger.

After a couple of minutes they wandered off towards the tented area, and Amie waited for several more, before she crawled away at a tangent. She was hoping she could find enough cover to hole up in, ready to get a good view when the sun came up in the morning.

Amie made her way towards the river. She would need to cross it and as she approached, she saw with relief the water was not very deep and she would easily be able to wade across to the other side. She squatted down next to an overhanging willow tree that reminded her of the one in her father-in-law's garden. Next decision, should she attempt to walk across and present a more visible target, or keep low and try to swim over? She mentally listed the contents of her backpack, was there anything that would spoil if it got wet?

She kicked herself, one thing at a time, Amie. The first priority was to replenish her water supply, and while she was doing that, she could take an extra few minutes to make a decision.

She slithered down the muddy bank, pulled out the empty bottles and waded a little way into the water. She filled all of them and screwed the tops back on. The backpack would be considerably heavier now, but that was a small price to pay when tomorrow the African sun beat down on her.

Everything appeared quiet and peaceful, but Amie did not let her guard down for a moment. She kept trying to remember little bits from the films she'd watched, in what now felt like a previous life, on how to act like a commando. If only Jonathon had given her some lessons in self-protection.

She remembered the gun, surely if that got wet it wouldn't work? So swimming was out, she would need to wade across, but she would wait a little longer until there was no sign of life from the camp. She also remembered all those plastic packages she'd taken from Jonathon's bag, it might not be a good idea to let those get wet either, for all she knew they might explode if they came into contact with water. It was no contest; she would have to walk across.

The half moon had risen high in the night sky before she decided to make a move. Clutching her backpack securely in her arms and bending forwards slightly, she waded into the warm water. It was approximately twelve metres from bank to bank but it felt the length of a marathon course to Amie as she tried to create as few ripples as possible. At this depth, the water only came half way up her thighs, so she didn't think it would be teeming with crocodiles or hippos. She shook at the thought, while her back crawled as she imagined someone taking aim and shooting her from behind. Time seemed to stand still as she crossed and at the last minute she fell forwards into the water as her foot hit the bottom of the slope on the far side.

As quickly as she could, she scurried up the bank and crawled beneath the vegetation. She was some way upriver from the camp, so she decided to rest for a while and dry out a little, before she eased her way along parallel to the water, to get as close to the tented area as she could. It looked as if the bag hadn't got wet on the inside, and she wiped it as dry as she could with her sleeve.

Amie still had no idea what she was going to do once she'd taken a look at the camp. She could hardly walk in and demand they return her husband and his friends, assuming that's where they were. They might as easily shoot her on sight, but it would be worse if they questioned, tortured or raped her. She went cold at the very thought but she couldn't second-guess what was going to happen. She would have to make decisions as she went along.

After about an hour, she shuffled her way further along the bank, crouching low, and moving a couple of steps before she paused to look and listen. She thought if someone saw her, they would expect her to keep moving. Well, that was the plan. She allowed herself a brief moment to feel smug. Was all this infiltration business simply common sense?

At last, when she felt close enough to the furthest tent, she used her hands to dig down and make a hollow under a particularly dense bush, and curled up to wait for morning. She was doubtful if she'd be able to doze off for more than a few moments at a time, and so far she had been running on pure adrenaline. One moment she felt brave, the next, terrified out of her mind. What choices did she have? Could she have left without finding out what had happened to

Jonathon? Was she fooling herself if she thought she could do anything to help? What of her desperate longing to rescue Angelina? In fact what was she doing here at all, huddled in a hole by a river, in the African bush, next to a fundamentalist camp run by people who were not known for their kind and welcoming hospitality? It was all so bizarre! Would she wake up in her own bed tomorrow morning as her mother brought her an early morning cup of tea?

No, the reality was here and now and she must make the best of it.

The long night dragged on and on, but eventually the pre-dawn light showed Amie a clearer picture of her surroundings. She was very relieved to see the vegetation that hung over the hole she'd dug for herself was thicker than she'd thought, it had been difficult to judge in the dark. She had a good view of the camp a little way along on the far side of the river, though she would have to rely on her own vision. Charles had taken the binoculars, and Jonathon had that nifty little gadget that showed things at night.

What now? She could only wait and see what happened. At some point someone was bound to come down to the river to wash or collect water.

Shortly after the sun rose there was a call, its eerie tones splitting the air and Amie saw people rushing out of their tents, slipping down briefly to the river to wash before bowing down in prayer. So these people were fanatical Muslims after all.

All the time she had lived in Apatu, there had only been one mosque and only a few women were seen in the streets wearing the all-encompassing burqas. So, this was definitely not a camp of Togodian rebels.

The next flurry of activity was the raising of the flag, which had a black background with a white circle and some Arabic writing Amie couldn't read. Although she didn't have a clear view of the middle of the camp, it looked like most of the soldiers had gathered round to stand to attention while one of the soldiers pulled on the halyard that took the flag to the top of the pole.

This told Amie something else. Either they were not bothered if they were seen, or they were quite happy to engage with anyone who got too close. If they were as fanatical as they were described, it was likely they were happy to die for their cause. She recalled one of the great African leaders who'd sent his warriors into battle with the promise that all the bullets from the British forces would turn to rain and would not cause them any harm. Of course this was far from the truth and hundreds were mown down in the first charge. Even in this modern day, belief in witchcraft and magic was alive and well among most people, including the very well educated.

Amie shrank back into her hiding place, checking to see there was nothing of hers that might reflect the sun's rays. She removed her wedding ring, recalling some Hollywood movie where the sparkle from a ring had alerted a sharp-eyed guard, and the infiltrators were seized and put to death.

Next, it was time for breakfast and the soldiers milled around holding plates as they queued up at one of the tents. To Amie's eyes they didn't appear to be very disciplined, pushing and shoving and behaving more like schoolboys than trained fighters. They were a rag-tag bunch, no two men were dressed exactly the same. While they all sported a black uniform of a sort, it was mismatched and scruffy. Most had boots, but a couple of them wore sandals. She tried to count them but it was difficult as they wandered to and fro. She estimated there were twenty to thirty in total.

Amie massaged her arms and legs to prevent them cramping up, and wriggled into a more comfortable position. So far, no one had even glanced in her direction and she was not unduly surprised to note that no one was on patrol on this side of the river. For now, she felt she was safe if she remained hidden.

A little later a few soldiers approached one of the tents that backed onto the river, opened the flaps, went inside and after some time, dragged out several women, at least Amie guessed they were women as each one was draped from head to toe in a black burqa. Several of them were wailing, shrieking and protesting, and Amie had to bite down hard on her lip to stop herself from crying out.

She counted a total of seven altogether, who were forced to sit on the ground before each one was handed a plate. One of the soldiers went back into the women's tent and dragged out two small children. They too were forced to sit and made to eat. One little girl refused, and shook her head from side to side. A soldier shouted at her and backhanded her across the face, sending the child sprawling in the dust. He heaved her back up and pointed to the bowl of food she'd rejected. Reluctantly she picked it up and dipped her finger in it. The soldier continued to glare at her and indicated she should put it in her mouth.

Watching closely, Amie thought the captives were local

Togodians. It looked as if they didn't speak the same language as their captors so Ben had told the truth. But there was also the possibility he'd led Jonathon and Charles into a trap and he was in league with the group. Two white men might be good collateral for a ransom. Someone outside must be funding all this. Amie prayed if the men had been captured, they were still alive.

Her eyes tried to pick out individual faces, but she was too far away to distinguish one from another, and to move closer would put her in danger. She tried to focus on the two children, was one of them Angelina? It was impossible to say.

As soon as the women had finished eating, they were handed piles of the soldiers' dirty plates and herded down to the river. Although they were a little way upstream from Amie, she now had a clearer view, but it was still impossible to make out who was who under all the black material. At the river they rolled up their sleeves and washed the dishes. Two of the guards were standing idly watching them, but as they huddled together sharing a match to light their cigarettes, one of the women gave a shriek. Like a wild animal she ran as fast as she could across the river away from the camp. Her heavy burqa weighed her down and for a moment, Amie thought she might be pulled under, but the water was not deep. When the woman picked up her hem she moved faster, putting more distance between herself and the camp.

For a few brief moments the soldiers stood there in shock, and then they leapt into action. Running back to the tents, one of them reappeared with a rifle and took aim at the woman. He fired wildly, missing time and time again, giving the desperate woman the chance to get further away. She paused to try and wrestle off the burqa, but it was a big mistake, as more soldiers appeared further down on the opposite bank and a whole barrage of bullets flew until one found its mark.

The woman shrieked and fell face down in the water. Oh my God, oh my God, Amie whispered to herself, and while every instinct urged her to try and save the poor soul, self-preservation and shock made her quite unable to move.

For good measure, some of the other soldiers appeared and shot at the heaped black bundle, part floating, part dragging in the water, as it moved in the slight current. Amie could only console herself that at last the woman's suffering was over and she was now free. She was worried the men would come and retrieve the body, so very close to her hiding place, but to her enormous relief no one seemed inclined to do so.

After a few moments of cheering and backslapping and self-congratulation, the men scattered around the camp, some to form a loose cordon around the rest of the women who were standing in shock like waxworks. But the soldiers harassed them, and reluctantly they went back to washing the dishes under the eagle eyes of their guards.

Amie quaked, what am I doing here? She asked herself for the hundredth time. What have I got involved in now? She glanced back at the body that was half floating in the current, at first bumping gently against the shore. Then it began to glide gently down the river.

Her attention was drawn back to the camp where she

could see one of the soldiers, who looked as if he was in charge, rounding up a group and marching them to the edge of the camp. She could only surmise it was lesson time, as the portly leader was shouting at them, waving his arms around as he screeched strings of words without appearing to draw breath. He waved a variety of different weapons at them, presumably demonstrating how they worked or what damage they caused.

The men crowded forward, eager to get their hands on the weapons, but the commander, if that's what he was, kept them at bay. He was determined to explain the theory before the practical.

Two men appeared rolling a small drum that they filled with earth and propped against a large boulder. One by one the men were lined up, and handed a weapon. If the idea was to hit the target, not many of them succeeded in getting anywhere near it. Shot after shot rang through the air, but the drum remained pristine.

The leader moved the men closer and closer still, but not one bullet found its mark. As the sun rose higher the men began to falter, and one or two tried to back off and look for shade, but their leader was ruthless and didn't let up for one moment. He screamed, shouted, threatened and once again they would form up and attempt to hit the target.

If Amie hadn't been in such a precarious position, she would've found the whole display rather funny. It was like a parody from a television show, as they continued to load and fire, load and fire without hitting anything at all. This continued for some hours, until at last even their leader gave up in disgust and dismissed them all.

It was at that point Amie realized the women were no longer in sight. She had been so absorbed watching the men's antics she hadn't thought to watch them. They were gone, possibly herded back into the same tent but she wasn't certain where they were. She noticed one small girl being pushed towards the river, the soldier behind her urging her forwards with the barrel of his rifle. She walked one slow step at a time, looking at the ground, dragging her feet and in her left hand she clutched a bedraggled, blue teddy bear. When she reached the river she walked in a little way and turned to face the guard but not before looking in Amie's direction.

It's her! It's really her!

Amie gasped under her breath. It's a miracle she's still alive and I've found her, after all that's happened, after all this time. I'm sure it's Angelina! Is it Angelina? Or am I hallucinating? She was finding it difficult to think straight and as the heat waves oscillated the scene in front of her, she began to have her doubts. Yes, the child certainly looked like Angelina but it was probably only wishful thinking. Amie exhaled and stared as hard as she could. The child wasn't allowed to stay in the cool water for very long, before the guard on the bank shouted at her and reluctantly she climbed the bank and was pushed into the tent which Amie now guessed was the one where the women were kept. She wondered if they'd be allowed out again at lunch time.

Twice during the day the women were let out, and escorted away from the camp, on each occasion closely surrounded by at least a dozen armed guards who kept them closely packed together. Amie could only guess they'd increased their surveillance after the morning's attempted escape.

The afternoon looked as if it was designated as time for siesta; the camp lay quiet. Amie took the opportunity to doze off in a deliberate attempt to stop her thoughts from racing, asking herself questions she couldn't answer. Each time she woke and there was no sign of life, Amie took the opportunity to dig further down and widen the depression in the ground where she was hiding. It was hard work, for the sandy soil was deeply packed and her nails became torn and ragged. She opened the backpack and retrieved the spoon, asking herself how she could have been so stupid not to think of using it before. It must be the heat, preventing her from thinking straight. The sweat dripped from under her cap, ran down her face, stung her eyes and made her clothes stick to her body like a second skin. What was worse a small swarm of biting flies had found her and were having a feast. She didn't dare swat them too vigorously in case she was seen, but they were making her life a misery.

She mentally mapped the camp layout as best she could, which was very similar to the way Ben had described it. She had also decided what she was going to do once it got dark, so all she had to do now was wait, and hope and pray no one noticed her.

Eventually, after what seemed like an aeon, the sun finally slipped down behind the hills. There was another ceremony in the camp as they lowered the flag, after which they sat and ate in the glow of the firelight, laughing and talking and pushing each other around. Now and again one would get up and disappear off into the bush, not always in the same direction. At first Amie thought they'd gone out on patrol, but later realized it was only the call of nature. All she could do was to sit as still as possible, only changing her position when it became unbearable.

Amie had always thought it was cruel to force women to dress in black clothing in hot countries, everyone knew black absorbed the heat and was to be avoided. Was that why the men usually dressed in white she wondered?

She waited until it was almost dark before she squirmed out of her hiding-place.

Her first task was to replenish the water she'd used, so lying flat on her stomach she pulled herself the few feet to the river's edge and submerged the bottles. She'd drunk as much as she wanted during the day, knowing she was right next to a water supply, which, although it tasted sandy, she felt sure wasn't polluted.

She dragged herself back up the shallow bank, packed away the bottles and buried the bag as deeply as possible into the hole before pulling a couple of nearby branches over the top. Checking she had the gun in her pocket and the knife in her hand, she squatted down and made her way along the river. She had no idea how far the body of the poor, unfortunate woman had drifted, but her first task was to find it.

The night was surprisingly still for Africa. There were few signs of animals on the hunt, or scurrying through the undergrowth, but the presence of the men with all their shooting on the opposite river bank was probably the cause. Amie crept along, peering through the night into the water that lapped like beer froth back and forth against the bank. She was relieved when the river swung to the left, and she was now out of sight of the camp. She took the opportunity to straighten up, but at first her body refused to co-operate. It had been crunched up for so many hours, it was agony to stand straight and walk normally.

Amie took a few steps away from the river, and slipping behind an acacia tree she swung her arms in circles until she'd loosened up. Next she practiced kicking with her legs and bending backwards and forwards until she felt more supple. Only when she felt she was in near working order, did she venture back next to the river again.

It took a good half hour walking at a sedate pace before she saw a large black heap in the water. It wasn't against the edge as she'd hoped, but stuck against a log which had blocked its free flow further downstream. Feeling around her, Amie pocketed the knife and grabbed a strong branch, and keeping as close to the bank as she could, she prodded the bundle to bring it closer. Her first few attempts were futile, but at last it wobbled to one side and floated free. Amie took a couple of tentative steps into the water and grabbed the edge of the burqa which slipped out of her hands. She leaned out again, and this time she got a better hold and managed to pull it right to the edge.

After a day in the heat the body had swelled up and bloated, which had kept it afloat but the smell was indescribable. A wave of nausea swept over her and she threw up what little contents she had in her stomach. She took several deep breaths and straightened up, pulling hard on the cloth that came away more easily than she expected.

She saw the reason why.

The log which had stopped the body from moving had itself moved, and as the body floated free from its clothing, a pair of jaws snatched it and somersaulted back beneath the water. Amie went weak at the knees and sat down hard on the bank, her fingers now welded to the burqa while she watched the scene in horror. She'd been so certain there wouldn't be crocodiles in the shallow river. That might explain why the soldiers were not patrolling on this side of the water, and why they'd not bothered to retrieve the body.

She stumbled backwards dragging the wet clothing behind her. She was aware crocodiles spent some time each day out of the water to warm up, and she had sat in her hole all day with never a thought she could be lunch just there for the taking. She hoped as the river appeared to be a good deal deeper here, they would not venture further upstream. She could only hope.

It was Amie's plan to wear the burqa, but it was going to take a good deal of courage to put it on. To her relief, the water had washed away the blood but it still smelt foul and there were several bullet holes in it.

Watching the crocodile as it grabbed the body and sank beneath the surface, Amie shuddered. It was too gruesome to watch, yet she could not tear her eyes away from the scene. The crocodile surfaced once more then disappeared from sight.

Once her legs had stopped wobbling and her shakes had subsided, she walked back the way she had come. A little further on, she immersed the burqa in the river again, hoping to wash away at least some of the smell. Even at night, it should dry out a little. So, should she hole up for another day or try and put her plan into action now? As she approached the bend in the river, she looked at her watch. Of course she was going to cross over and go into the camp, but she was still not sure where the men were patrolling, or if they were keeping a lookout. One more day? Even though it was an uncomfortable hole, it gave her a false sense of security and another few hours of daylight would help her to plan better.

The following morning was a repetition of the one before; until around lunchtime Amie heard the sound of a truck approaching on the other side of the river, and saw a large cloud of dust. It was closely followed by a second vehicle and she wondered if the new arrivals were friend or foe.

It didn't take long for her to see they were friends, as several men got out and walked into the camp. From her hideout, Amie could only see part of the action, but at last her patience was rewarded. A couple of the soldiers walked over to a tent she hadn't noticed being used, and dragged out Ben, Charles and lastly Jonathon. Amie exhaled. They were here! She had found them! She could set them free!

A horrible thought occurred to her. Had the trucks come to take them away? Had she endured all this to have the prize snatched away at the last minute?

As the people walked between the tents, Amie caught glimpses of action. It looked as if the new arrivals were questioning the men and several times she heard cries as if they were being beaten. She watched them leaning over the captives who were sitting on the ground, and screaming at them, words flying back and forth, none of which made any sense to her. When they had finished, the three men were pushed unceremoniously back into the tent and several armed guards were stationed at each corner.

Amie was distraught. She wanted to rush across and attack the men who were hurting the man she loved, but all she could do was watch, wait and hope she could rescue all of them.

It was obviously time for some celebrations as the visitors were treated to a meal, and then, much to Amie's horror, the two young girls were dragged out of the women's tent and although she couldn't see what was happening, her imagination filled in the blanks. Tears streamed silently down her cheeks as she pressed her finger nails into her palms. The animals! They're nothing more than animals she raged inside. No, animals have a higher code of conduct. How dare they? How dare they treat poor defenceless children like playthings? These were the very people who openly vowed to protect both women and children. These men were doing neither, it was obvious to Amie they were exploiting the women for their own ends. While the anger boiled inside her, she realized she'd learned more. She now knew which tent they were keeping the men in, and the location of the women's tent. Now all she had to do was crawl in under cover of darkness and set them all free.

8   AN UNEXPECTED REUNION

Right Amie, she mocked herself. It's all so simple isn't it? Is that the best plan you can come up with? The answer was yes, because it was her only plan, and she hoped the burqa would be the disguise that would see her through the ordeal.

She wriggled around in her hole, and between snoozing to try and keep up her strength, nibbling on some biscuits, chewing biltong, and taking sips of her warm water - there was no way she could keep it cool - she waited for the sun to go down on the second day. But the minutes dragged by and she felt the day would never end. She heard raucous laughter from the other side of the river and she suspected the men were getting very drunk. Earlier they had unloaded several boxes from the trucks, and some looked suspiciously like crates of beers and boxes of whiskey. They were not planning on leaving this area any time soon. As far as Amie knew, Muslims didn't drink alcohol, but that didn't appear to apply to the visitors and those officers in charge of the camp.

Towards the end of the afternoon she retrieved the tin of black gunk and spread it all over her face and hands. She thought it must have deterred the mosquitoes, because they hadn't bothered her at all, but several biting flies seemed attracted to it.

Amie tried to work out what to do first. There are six women in the small tent, she reasoned, the children aren't in there but while the women's tent was closer to the water, Amie thought it would be better to try and rescue the men first, then they could help set everyone else free. So, that was the plan, she just needed to choose the right time.

The carousing went on for hours. The sun had set, but the moon hadn't risen yet, and the few figures Amie could see stumbling around in the dark looked very drunk indeed. Was her luck in? She felt a huge wave of hope coursing through her body while she waited. She tried to remember if crocodiles hunted at night, or if they were mainly active during the day? She wished she could remember all the things Dirk had taught them about the wild, but if that was what fate had in store for her, it was better than being captured and raped by these human animals.

Eventually the noise died down. It was impossible to see in which tents the new arrivals were being housed, but she doubted they would be in with the prisoners. She hoped they'd left as few guards as possible on duty.

Cautiously she wriggled out of her hiding place and wrapped the burqa round the top half of her body, she didn't want it to get wet as she waded across the river. She tucked the knife into her waistband, slithered down the bank to the edge of the water and looked long and hard both ways. She could see no shapes, nothing that would suggest a crocodile was lurking anywhere close by. She grabbed a stout branch just in case. It might help her to escape if one of the enormous reptiles attacked.

As she waded through the water, she was careful not to

make waves, but she didn't stop after every few steps as she
had before, there was danger in the water too. With a sigh of
relief she reached the far bank, and leaving the branch
beside the water, she crawled up the shallow incline. She
melted into the shadow of a tree and let the burqa fall to her
feet. It still smelled foul from its previous occupant, but it
provided excellent camouflage. Amie paused to get her
bearings. Despite looking at the camp for over two days
from the other side of the river, it didn't look as familiar
from this angle. She would keep to the shadows and try to
skirt round the outside of the enclosure and approach the
men's tent from the far side.

Her plan had gone well so far, but when Amie peeped
round the corner of one of the tents, to her horror she saw it
was surrounded by armed guards who didn't seem
particularly drunk. But they did not appear to be particularly
alert either. The two at the front of the tent were whispering,
and the couple on the other side, were standing smoking,
drinking from a whiskey bottle and gazing up at the night
sky.

Amie could see no way of getting close to the tent
without the guards seeing her. She retreated a little way deep
into the shadows and wondered what to do. If she waited
would they eventually go to sleep? Or would they be
replaced by other guards who were more sober when they
arrived on duty? There was simply no way she could tell.
She was stuck and she could only hope they considered their
captives important, or they wouldn't be keeping such a close
watch on them. There was no one guarding the women's
tent so perhaps that was a better target, could she create

some sort of a diversion?

She dithered, as she stood next to the corner tent and looked round. She wrapped her arms tightly around herself and took a deep breath, she had to make a decision, and soon, she couldn't wait there all night.

One of the soldiers standing at the rear of the tent went to sit with the two at the front, and the low sound of their voices carried over the night air. They passed the bottle back and forth between them. The remaining guard at the rear staggered straight towards Amie. She held her breath, sure he would see her, even though she was enveloped in the black burqa. He came so close she could smell the smoke from his cigarette, the alcohol and the sharp, unpleasant tang of sweat from his unwashed body. Amie realized that in all the time she'd been watching the camp, not one of the men had been down to the river to wash properly, except for a brief trip before prayers.

Amie held her breath and half closed her eyelids. She was afraid he might see the whites of her eyes. She had no idea if that was a sensible thing to do, but he tottered straight past her and disappeared further out into the bush. She guessed he would be back as soon as he'd relieved himself. All she had to do was stand completely still and wait for him to pass her again.

But that didn't happen.

Something bumped into Amie's side and she fought to keep her balance. She felt the impact of the man before she had time to react. He swayed drunkenly to one side and pulled her into him, wrapping one sweaty arm around her head, forcing her mouth closed. His hand pressed hard against her lips. With his other arm he gripped her in a bear hug round her chest, crushing her tightly.

She kicked and struggled, but the burqa bunched up around her nose so she could hardly breathe. Another soldier got up, staggered over and the men conferred in a language Amie couldn't begin to understand. She had to get air into her lungs. She was on the point of passing out when the first soldier released the pressure on her chest and they dragged her over towards the women's tent. While one held her, the other untied the ropes holding the flaps together and threw Amie inside before re-securing the canvas.

She fell over in the dark and landed on something, or rather someone. There was a muffled cry of pain from the person underneath Amie, muttering and some squeals. Amie struggled to unwrap the burqa which had coiled itself round her like a winding sheet and she fumbled about in the dark trying to make out what was around her. She fell backwards onto another body causing more grunts and complaints from the other women.

"Sorry, sorry," mumbled Amie.

"English?" an astonished whisper came from the far corner.

"Yes, yes," Amie gasped. She still hadn't got her breath back and every time she tried to free herself from the thick black burqa, it felt as if she was pulling it tighter. By the time she was free she felt quite exhausted.

"Yer English?" the question was repeated.

"Yes! You are too?" Amie could hear that the voice didn't belong to an African, the accent was wrong. It sounded like a very broad Birmingham accent.

"I don't effing believe it," came the loud whisper. "Another girl from home? How long since they got you?"

"About five minutes," replied Amie feeling around her in the dark.

"What? But, but we're in the middle of effing nowhere. Did you come with those trucks we heard?"

"No. Look it's a long story. I was hoping to rescue you."

"Fat chance. They keep a good watch over us here."

Amie felt other hands reach out to touch her, pairs of hands that gently poked and prodded as if to make sure she was real. "How many of you are there?" she asked, as her eyes became a little more accustomed to the dark. Now she could make out shapes, but not individuals.

"Eight women, no, seven of us now," the voice broke a little. "And two kids," replied the girl.

"And you're all here?" asked Amie.

"No. The kids and Phumelo ain't in here now, they're busy with the big-wigs."

"And how long have you been here?"

"Dunno. Several weeks I think."

"Is anyone else here English?" Amie asked.

"Nope, only me. I were separated from the rest. We all went to different places."

"But from where?" Amie was puzzled.

"That's a long story, and I'll tell you later, but for now can you rescue us? Please! That'd be flippin' great. Help us get free."

"I didn't see any soldiers outside this tent tonight, why haven't you tried to escape?" Amie asked.

"Ah, you can't see. They tie our hands and feet together at night." A hand touched Amie's arm and guided it down so Amie could feel for herself. Amie gasped, no wonder they'd not been able to escape.

"They didn't tie you up?" the accent was definitely English Amie decided. She tried to work out the best thing to do.

Many of the others were now murmuring in what she thought she recognized as Togodian, certainly an African language.

"Shush," she said, "Shush, I'm thinking." She had no idea what time it was but she'd have to move fast. Even if she blended in with the women when they let them out in the morning, she was certain tomorrow she'd be discovered and she'd also be tied up. Tonight was her, and their, only chance.

She pulled out the knife from her waistband and reached out in the darkness and felt for a length of twine and started to saw through it. It only took a few seconds. The rope gave way and there was a gasp from one of the women.

As she worked, Amie's mind snapped back to one Christmas when she and her mother went to a local farm selling fresh turkeys. The carcasses had all been thrown into a large wooden box, their pale bodies stripped of feathers with their feet tied together. When they'd tried to pull one out, it got tangled with several of the others and eventually one of the farm workers had come to help them free the bird her mother had chosen.

Amie worked as fast as she could, hacking away on another length of twine. It was like trying to untangle a huge ball of wool in the dark she thought while she worked as fast as she could. Her wrists ached and she could feel the muscles in her arm as she sawed away.

"Do they tie you up like this every night?" she whispered.

"Yeah, don't you think we'd have tried to escape otherwise?" the reply was delivered with a fair amount of sarcasm.

"I'm sorry," Amie replied, "I should've guessed. I'm working in the dark here, and I've no idea if I have even freed anyone yet."

"I can move," said a new voice that gave Amie a start. She thought she recognized it. "Mrs Motswezi?" she whispered.

"You know me!"

"Yes, yes I do," Amie didn't let up for a moment, sawing backwards and forwards with the knife. Relief washed over her. Now, they might stand a chance, with an interpreter she could organize the women.

"You remember me?" she asked.

"No, but your voice ... you sound familiar."

"It's Amie, I used to visit your school and play with the children."

"Aieeeee, I remember you well!"

Mrs Motswezi's voice rose as she grasped Amie in the dark to the sounds of lots of shushing from the rest of the prisoners.

"You don't know where, if, is ..." Amie was almost too afraid to ask the question but she had to know. "Is Angelina here too?" she asked in a rush.

"Yes. The poor child is one of us, but she is not here now in this tent, she is one of the favourites so they take her …" Mrs Motswezi's voice dropped.

Tears coursed unbidden down Amie's cheeks and her whole body shook causing the person she was trying to set free to yelp in pain.

"Sorry, sorry," she murmured and tried to concentrate on the task in hand. As she worked away she mentally tried to add up how many pieces of twine she would need to cut through.

"Is anyone else free yet?" she asked.

Mrs Motswezi translated and told her that she had released two more.

Amie paused and tried to concentrate. Which side of the tent faced the river? "Tell me where the door is, take my hand and point it in the right direction."

Someone reached out and moved her arm and pulled it out behind her. Amie pushed one of the women in the opposite direction. "The river is that way," she whispered as loudly as she dared. "We can start to dig under the canvas and slip out and over the river, but we have to be very fast and very quiet."

Mrs Motswezi translated and the two women who were no longer tied up scrambled to the back of the tent. The women were crawling, pulling and pushing to reach the other side, while those who were still tied up tried to get out of the way. There were grunts and groans as feet trampled over stomachs and bodies fell onto arms and legs and heads bumped together. Amie despaired. If she had only freed three people so far, how much longer was this going to take?

She managed to free two more of the women, but the next piece of twine she was hacking at gave way suddenly and she fell over backwards. The knife flew out of her hand and landed somewhere in the darkness. Amie wanted to scream, as if it wasn't difficult enough.

There was frantic scrabbling behind her until a small grunt of satisfaction announced someone had found it. Another pair of hands started to cut through the rope while Amie rubbed her sore arm and tried to feel her way to the back of the tent where at least three of the women were scrabbling at the hard earth.

"Wait," hissed Mrs Motswezi, "there is a spoon here, I took it at supper, we must use that too."

"No!" gasped Amie, putting the heel of her hand against her forehead. "I'm not thinking straight. We have the knife, it's a bit blunt now but we might be able to cut through the canvas."

"We is all free," whispered the English voice. "Here, here, the knife is here. I got it. Run it down the wall."

It seemed to take an age to get the knife to even make a hole in the canvas, but once it poked through it was easy to slice it downwards and the pale moonlight flooded into the tent.

"Put your burqas back on," hissed Amie, "they won't see us so easily in the dark."

There were a few discontented murmurs, but one by one the women crawled out of the back of the tent and scuttled towards the river. Amie thought it best not to mention she'd seen a crocodile further downstream.

One behind the other they waded across, with Amie

bringing up the rear, constantly looking over her shoulder to see if there was any activity from the tents. She could feel the hairs tingling on her back. She imagined a bullet smashing into her at any moment, but she gritted her teeth, slid down the bank, holding her burqa above the lazily flowing water.

Once they reached the far side, some of the women raced away from the camp as quickly as they could, but Amie stepped forwards and grabbed the English girl's arm. "Wait, I have to collect my bag, it's further along here in those bushes."

For a moment Amie thought the girl would rush away, but reluctantly she followed Amie while she retrieved her belongings. They set off after the others, barely able to make them out in the dark as they stumbled towards higher ground.

One by one they ducked low as they crested the skyline and rolled or fell down the other side. Once at the bottom, they paused, out of breath, exultant and fearful all at the same time. They were free, but for how long?

On this side of the ridge the land was not as flat, but rose in gentle waves interspersed with towering rocks. On the far side of the wide valley rose another ridge with an even higher range of hills in the distance. They set off across the valley floor, making for the next incline. Amie thought she could see dark holes that might indicate caves in the hillsides. She wondered how far it was safe to go, that wouldn't take them too far away from the camp.

"I have to go back," she whispered to the English girl.

"What! Yer mad, we only just escaped goddammit,

what the hell would you go back for?"

"My husband and friends they are still there I can't abandon them," Amie replied.

"Well, you can bloody well count me out," replied her new 'friend'. "Yer won't catch me back there in a million years. Yer on your own."

A hand grabbed Amie's and a gentle voice said, "I will stay with you. I could never leave behind my children. It is God's wish for me to protect them. They are in my care. My sister was not in the tent with us. I cannot leave her behind. She is the only family I have left."

"Mrs Motswezi," tears welled up in Amie's eyes. "I hadn't forgotten Angelina. We must go back for her too."

"Nuts the pair of you," spat their companion. "I'm outta here."

"And which way are you going to go?" asked Mrs Motswezi in a calm voice. "Do you know where we are?"

"Well, no, but I do know I'm getting as far away from that hell hole as it's possible to get. You two can please yerselves." With that the girl got up and squinted into the darkness, and it was then they noticed the other three women had melted away into the night. They were on their own.

"My name is Amie," she put out her hand, though it seemed a ridiculous gesture standing there in the African night. They had practically been lying on top of one another only a few minutes ago.

"Shalima," the girl said reluctantly, and briefly grasped Amie's hand in a limp handshake.

"We need to move further away," said Mrs Motswezi,

pointing back towards the terrorist camp. "They will come to look for us in the morning, we need to hide."

"Well, I'll be off then," said Shalima. "Good luck, hope you manage to free all the prisoners, though I don't think much of yer chances," and she set off across the shallow valley, striding out as if she was walking along her local high street on a Saturday afternoon.

"She has no water, no food," muttered Mrs Motswezi.

Amie pulled a face. There was nothing either of them could do to force her to stay, and perhaps she would catch up with the other women and they would all make it to the nearest village or town. She had no idea how large the previously designated National Park was, but it couldn't go on for too many miles.

"We need to find a cave," Amie whispered, "to hide in."

"Yes, over there," Mrs Motswezi pointed further along the ridge where they could see dark, round holes in the hillside. "If we go over one more mountain there will be holes on the other side."

Amie smiled at the idea of them climbing over a mountain and then for no reason she could explain, she suddenly reached out to Mrs Motswezi and gave her a big hug. For several seconds the two women clung together. Was it for comfort, a show of solidarity, or simply because they'd escaped and were alive? Amie didn't care about the reason, it was simply an expression of her love for the brave woman who was prepared to help her set the children free and return them to a normal society.

Wrapping their burqas up round their waists, the two set

off parallel to the ridge, looking out for a suitable cave, but to their disappointment they could see nothing that was easily accessible. They crossed another valley and looked for a refuge on the far side of the next ridge. The rising moon and the almost cloudless sky made it easier to pick their way over the ground, avoiding the rocks and tree roots

Mrs Motswezi stopped and grabbed Amie's arm. "We will need to hurry, there is rain coming."

Amie looked at her in surprise, and glanced up into the sky where she could only see a couple of fluffy, white clouds floating in front of the stars. She wondered if the horrendous experience Mrs Motswezi had lived through had somehow unhinged her mind, but for some inexplicable reason, many Africans knew these things. Nothing in science or rational thinking could possibly explain this innate sense many of them had about the land or their affinity with it. So, if her old friend was still sane, and believed it was going to rain, then Amie believed it was going to rain too.

Struggling under the smelly, restricting burqa, Amie scrambled up the next slope. As soon as she reached the other side, she collapsed on the ground and lay there puffing and panting. Her chest heaved from the exertion and Mrs Motswezi didn't look in much better shape, when her roly-poly figure flopped down beside Amie. I don't know if I am out of shape for my age, or Mrs Motswezi has hidden strengths I can't even imagine, thought Amie. She looks horribly overweight, yet she has the resilience and tenacity of someone half her age. Now that she thought of it, Amie had no idea how old the headmistress was and she wasn't about to ask; it would be considered most impolite. She could only look at her companion and marvel.

"Look, up there," Mrs Motswezi was pointing to a ledge a little further along. "That looks like a safe place to shelter. Come, we must go, go now. Come, we go."

Despite the urgency of the situation, Amie had to smile, 'come, go, go, come'. Slowly she got to her feet, feeling as if every bone in her body had been battered with a hammer. At least her trousers had dried out in the cool night air, but her boots were still wet and had rubbed the tender skin on her feet. She was not looking forward to taking them off to inspect the damage. Earlier events had pushed all thoughts of discomfort away, but now she was beginning to calm down a little, she was aware of every bit of her body with all its aches and pains. Amie had recently passed her thirtieth birthday, but right now she felt twice as old as Mrs Motswezi who got to her feet with ease, picked up a long, dry branch and made for the dark shadow which suggested a cave, its entrance partially concealed by a large, leafy bush clinging to the rock face.

As they approached the entrance they paused and listened, but there was not a sound. Mrs Motswezi tapped the ground gently at the opening below the overhang and getting no response, took a few steps forward and poked the stick out in front of her, repeating this several times.

"I think it is safe," she said softly. She moved in a little further and sat on the dry floor. Her companion sank down gratefully beside her.

Amie examined her rescued backpack. It looked exactly as she had left it, no holes had appeared and the straps were still secure. She pulled out a bottle of water and offered it to her friend. The older lady took it, drank and handed it back. Amie rummaged further into the bag. "Are you hungry?"

In the gloom she saw Mrs Motswezi shake her head. "No, those animals made us prisoners, but we ate well."

"How did you? Tell me what happened." Amie was not sure where to begin, as she folded up the burqa to use as a blanket and contemplated the painful task of removing her boots.

In a voice that was quiet and unemotional, Mrs Motswezi described how she'd been sitting in her office when Pretty, Amie's maid, had rushed in dragging Angelina by the hand. She had some foolish story about men who were shooting in the streets and she was leaving and going back to her village far away from all the trouble. Her problem was that her madam, Mrs Amie, had left Angelina in her care and she could not leave the child, so she was now the responsibility of Mrs Motswezi. She assured her that her madam would come to claim the child as soon as she came home from the town. And if she never returned? Then Angelina was now where she belonged, in the hostel with the other AIDS orphans. Pretty had done what she could.

No sooner had Pretty left, when some men had driven in though the gates. They'd leapt out of the vehicles waving guns, shouting, and screaming at everyone to leave the buildings. They fired bullets into the air while they watched the dazed children and their teachers rush out into the playground. While some herded their captives into a large group in the central playground, others raced through the buildings to make sure no one was hiding. Any who were found were dragged out by their ears, beaten and roughly pushed towards the other children and teachers. Mrs Motswezi had tried to reason with them. These were only innocent children who had never done harm to anyone, but her pleas fell on deaf ears. They might be children now, but one day they would grow up and they would turn on the new government, they would remember this day and want vengeance.

The men were not very organized and there was much discussion and argument as they formed a loose cordon around their prisoners and herded them towards the boundary. When they opened fire on the children there was pandemonium. Mrs Motswezi shook her head and tears filled her eyes as she recounted her story.

9   ATTACK ON THE ORPHANAGE

Some of the children went rigid in fear, others screamed, while many tried to run. The teachers were helpless, they couldn't decide whether to stay and comfort those who were in shock, or run in a futile attempt to save their own lives. And still the firing went on and on and on. Yet more threw themselves flat on the ground and lay still, indistinguishable from those who were already dead.

The men turned their attention to the school buildings, gathering up the meagre bedding to use as kindling. Two more lorries drove in through the gates, bumping over the rough ground to where the heap of innocent bodies lay. A few of the younger, prettier teachers were spared and forced at gunpoint to stand in a group a little way off. Mrs Motswezi had wondered if it would be better to die there and then. Who knew what fate the men had in store for them?

Soon the buildings were alight. They went up like a torch, the flames reaching up into the sky, creating huge, billowing clouds of smoke. A few of the men were ordered to collect the little bodies and load them into the back of the lorries. None of them looked too happy with their appointed task, especially as the wind came up and the plumes of smoke blew in their faces making it difficult to see. Soon they were working in a thick cloud of ash and it was at that time a few of the survivors were able to escape, among them, Mrs Motswezi who was still holding Angelina's hand.

"How awful it must have been," murmured Amie. "How awful." She sat silently for a moment. "But that was months and months ago, where have you been since?"

"I went back to my village. Pretty had the best idea, she said it would be safe in the rural areas."

"And ...?" Amie waited to hear the rest of the story.

"Angelina and I lived in the village where I had come from." Mrs Motswezi sighed. "I worked so hard, so very hard, to escape the village life. I had studied my best at school, my parents sold two cows so I could go to attend the high school in the nearest big town. And they sold another four to pay for my fees so I could train to be a teacher." She paused for several moments lost in thought. "I did very well at the college," there was pride in her voice. "I came out the top student and I was offered many teaching posts, but I chose one in Apatu. Ah, yes, the big, capital city, that was what I had been working for all those years."

"And you taught in Apatu for many years?" Amie enquired.

"Yes, and I was a good teacher. But I heard about the many children who now had no parents, they had died from AIDS. These poor little souls had no one to care for them and so I told myself that I would make them a good home. Many had been turned away from their villages as the stigma of AIDS made them unwelcome. I persuaded some of the church people to spend money to put up the buildings, and we employed a teacher and a housemother. We opened the doors."

"When I first visited the orphanage, you had several teachers and lots of classes and the hostel too," Amie added.

"Ah yes. That was good. We teach the children in English and that made us to be popular, so more children came, even those who still had parents. We grew and grew and grew."

"Exactly like Topsy," Amie smiled, but Mrs Motswezi only looked puzzled.

"I'm sorry?"

"Oh, nothing, it was a book from my childhood," said Amie.

Mrs Motswezi said nothing for a moment and continued her story. "But now after all the struggle, I was back in my home village, back with my parents again. The fighting was in the capital and we thought we were safe in our kraals, living off the land. But it was not so many months when different soldiers came." She indicated the direction of the terrorist camp. "We had no idea where they come from, or why they had come. They appeared in their trucks one Sunday morning while we were at our prayers. They drove in and got out and seized the cross and assaulted our preacher. Poor man he only travelled to our village once in a while, and now he was being beaten by these strangers, and he did not know why. Everyone was told to lie on the ground and they began more shooting."

Mrs Motswezi sat silently for a moment. "They picked out a few of us, me and Angelina and my sister, two other girls from our village and they had some other women already. They killed everyone else, all of them, no one escaped. They set fire to our huts, they drove out our cattle and goats and chickens and they took the things they wanted. And all the time they were screaming strange words."

"Was it Allah Akbar?" asked Amie.

Mrs Motswezi thought for a moment. "Yes, that was it, and they often cry it in the camp. I think it is part of their prayers?"

So, Ben was right, thought Amie to herself. "And then they brought you to this camp here?" Amie asked.

"No," Mrs Motswezi replied after thinking for a while. "There was another camp first, where they forced us to cover our faces and wear these heavy cloaks. They told us we were whores, like street girls, to allow men to see our faces. They said we were to learn to be subse … subsi …"

"Subservient?" suggested Amie.

"Yes, I think that is the word. We must be that to the men, because we are special and precious. They lock us up in a tent for most of the day and stand over us when we clean their dishes, even me, Mrs Nomphsela Motswezi who was trained to be a teacher and ran a school all by myself. Now I must hide away from the world because they tell me their God wants this from me. I do not understand. What is happening? They are not Togodian, where have they come from? What do they want with us?"

Amie didn't know what to tell the older lady. How could she explain it was a twenty-first century crusade, fundamentalist Muslims against everyone else, and it was springing up in so many countries. The two sat there in silence for a long while, deep in thought when they heard sounds from outside the cave.

There was a loud crack of lightning, thunder rumbled and the heavens opened. The rain came down in torrents, while bright shafts of light illuminated the valley below them. It was during one of these that Amie noticed something coming towards them and nudged Mrs Motswezi who had begun to doze off.

Amie first thought it was some wild beast also looking for shelter, and she searched round for her knife and patted the gun that she'd stuffed in her back pocket. She wasn't sure the sound of the pouring rain would muffle a gunshot, goodness she didn't even know how loud the gun would be if she was forced to fire it, but the feel of it in her hand was reassuring – if she ever had the courage to use it.

They both sat silently, leaning back on either side of the walls of the cave almost holding their breath as they watched the creature come closer and closer. It seemed to be making for the cave and it would arrive very soon.

"I think it is a person," whispered Mrs Motswezi. "It does not walk on all four legs. But it could be a spirit. I have heard they walk out. I am so frightened. The Tokoloshe takes many forms," and Mrs Motswezi made the sign of the cross over her ample breasts and put her hands together as if in prayer.

"Yes," breathed Amie. "It is a person." She tried not to smile, watching her companion whisper prayers under her breath like any good Christian, while worrying about ancient spirits from African folklore.

Like two statues they sat quite still.

Amie glanced behind her to see if there was any way they could hide further back, but the cave, if it was large enough to be called a cave, was shallow and there was no tunnel leading deeper into the hillside. Her hand tightened on the gun and she nursed the knife in the other. Armed to the teeth without the ability or will to use the weapons, she thought. One day Amie, one day you may have to inflict harm on another creature, but please, don't let it be tonight. I'm not ready yet, please not tonight. Amie had no idea who she was actually talking to. She had long ceased to believe in God, and hadn't been to church except for weddings and christenings for years, even though she and Jonathon had been married in church. But someone, somewhere out there might hear her, and spare her the agony of killing another human being.

The waiting seemed to go on and on, as the figure walked steadily towards them. He or she must be totally drenched by now, and was bending forward to protect themselves from the driving rain. Reaching their side of the valley, the figure climbed up the slope, a shapeless mass that reminded Amie of the old Hammer horror movies she'd watched as a child.

The creature had almost reached the entrance to the cave when it pitched forwards and collapsed in a heap almost falling on top of Amie and Mrs Motswezi.

"Oh bugger," said a voice and Amie only just managed to control her giggles.

"Come on in Shalima," she said. "You're dripping wet. Take that ridiculous burqa off before it soaks everything."

Shalima looked up from her prone position on the ground. "Bloody hell!" she exclaimed. "What you two doing here? How did you get in front of me?"

Amie reached over and helped her further in under the overhanging rock. She moved over to make more space and let their new arrival sit down in the dry.

"I don't think we overtook you," she said with a smile. "I think you walked round in a circle."

"Yer kidding ain't you?"

"No, it's very easy to do that in the dark, landmarks aren't easy to follow. At least you're safe now." She offered Shalima a bottle of water, but the girl shook her head. "I've had quite enough water to last me, ta," she said.

Amie passed the bottle they'd already opened to Mrs Motswezi, who broke off a couple of leaves from the overhanging bush at the entrance to the cave, and fashioned them into a funnel. She placed the bottle outside the overhang to top it up with rainwater.

"I ain't staying more than a night," Shalima was on the defensive. "I'm on me way home and nothing and no one is gonna to stop me."

"To England?" asked Amie.

"Not if I can bloody help it. There's lots better places to go," grumbled the girl.

"What are you doing here in Africa?" Amie asked her, as a flash of lightning lit up the interior of the cave like a searchlight.

Shalima leaned forwards and peered closely at Amie who shrank back a little at having her personal space so rudely invaded.

"You that woman who was on telly!" exclaimed Shalima. "You was in the war and you got into all kinds of trouble."

So, Dave had made the programme after all and it had

been shown. Amie shrank back even further at the thought she might be recognized anywhere in England. It made going home less than desirable. For the moment she would remain non-committal.

"What are you doing here?" she asked again.

"What you bleedin' think? Getting outta the rain," replied Shalima sounding more than a little grumpy. "I guess we're sleeping here tonight?"

"Well, that is what we'd planned. We didn't know you were still around."

"Yeah, well, if I'd had my way I'd be like, miles away by now. Hell knows how I ended up here again."

Nothing more was said that night as the three of them made themselves as comfortable as possible, wrapping their heavy burqas round them before they settled down to sleep. Amie had wondered if it would be wise to take turns keeping watch, but either they were safe at this distance, probably no one had noticed yet they were missing, or it was simply best to get a good night's sleep. The one thing she did realize was that she was quite exhausted and doubted if she could stay awake much longer. Her last thought before sleep overtook her was the worry they were trespassing in some creature's home and it might return after the rain had eased off.

There was pandemonium in the camp the following morning when it was discovered all the women had escaped. The commander flew into a terrible rage and ordered everyone to line up in the square so he could get to the truth and find out how it had happened. Which soldiers were untrustworthy?

Did they have a spy among them? Had anyone sent messages with the women to alert the outside world and give away their location?

He glared at his men as they shuffled uncomfortably in two untidy rows in front of him. No one even dared suggest they raise the flag. No one dared say anything at all. They all knew the women had escaped, that piece of news had flown round faster than a cruise missile, but none except two, had any knowledge of what had happened, and they weren't about to say a word.

Mukhtar and Abubakker remembered little of the previous evening, it was all very hazy in the glare of the early morning sun. They'd been furious to be selected for guard duty the previous night, when the visitors arrived bringing with them news of the outside world and a crate of whiskey. Everyone knew alcohol was forbidden, but last night was the first time Mukhtar had ever let it touch his lips. He had no idea who had stolen the bottle, probably from the higher-ups as they got progressively more inebriated, before crashing out in the commander's tent. Word had it they were even too plastered to manage it with the girls.

Someone had sneaked the bottle out and they'd all had a few sips. For many of them it was their baptism with hard liquor and it only took a little to make them feel woozy and sleepy. Mukhtar remembered going off into the bushes and bumping into something wearing a burqa, he assumed it was a woman, and he vaguely thought he'd thrown her in with the rest. Could it have been a man and not a woman? And, yes, he hadn't tied her up, although it was most unlikely he would have been in a fit state to tie any knots. Whatever had happened, whatever he had done, he decided to keep his mouth shut. He didn't even remember Abubakker had helped him by untying the tent flaps.

The commander paced up and down, shouting and screaming at his men, going red in the face while trying to ignore the pounding in his head. Still he continued to rant and rave for over an hour until it dawned on him he was getting nowhere.

He pulled one poor unfortunate out of the back row and had him dragged forward, stripped of his uniform and bound to the rather unstable flag pole. Not having any whips to hand, he instructed one of the men to make do with a branch from a nearby acacia tree, complete with thorns.

The soldier who had been ordered to beat the chosen victim tapped him timidly on the back to start with, but under threats of receiving the same treatment, he hit him harder and harder, until his back was a mess of blood and exposed muscle. The screams from the wretched and innocent man resounded across the valley, and put the fear of God into the rest of the men. When the punishment was over, he fell to the ground in a heap, no longer conscious and very close to death.

Still the commander was not satisfied, he still had no idea who'd helped the women escape, so he ordered all but two of his men to go out and search for them. On hearing this, they set off in twos and threes to scour the surrounding areas. While some were anxious to find the women and bring them back, others were not so keen and had decided before leaving the camp they weren't going to look too hard.

Since most of them were not allowed access to the women, the females were more trouble than they were worth.

The first light of the morning woke Amie and she sat up and rubbed her eyes. Now she could investigate their refuge properly and she was surprised to see the floor of the shallow cave was reasonably clean. She'd been expecting to see bat droppings at least, but looking up she saw the surface of the overhang looked quite smooth. She could see right across the valley, the bushes and trees glistening in the sunlight, as the last of the rain was absorbed into the air. It never failed to amaze Amie how fast everything dried once the sun rose high enough in the sky. Now, the earth was a deep chestnut brown, but in only an hour or so it would revert back to its normal sandy colour. She took a deep breath of the fresh, clean, dust-free air, and turned to look at her companions.

Mrs Motswezi was snoring softly, curled up tightly in her burqa blanket, but Shalima was sprawled out, taking up far more than her fair share of the available accommodation. Amie's movements woke her with a start and she sat bolt upright.

"Where am I?" she looked around her. "What am I doing here?"

"You arrived last night in the storm."

"Huh?" Shalima took time to remember, then nodded. "Well, guess I'll be off after breakfast. Sooner I get going the better."

"Where's home?" asked Amie, she was more than a little curious as to why a white woman had been in a terrorist Islamic camp in the middle of Africa.

"Birmingham. Well, I grew up there."

"So what are you doing here?" Amie asked yet again.

Shalima eyed her suspiciously. "I could ask you the same question. Yer not African are you?"

"No, there are a lot of white Africans, their families emigrated generations ago. But no, I came out here with my husband's work."

"Oh yeah, I remember now yer that chick on telly who was ... ah yes, of course, but I thought you were home now, all back to normal."

To me, Africa is home, Amie thought to herself. Once it gets a grip it won't let you go, except she didn't think the open skies, the wild animals and the majesty of the landscape had gripped Shalima in quite the same way. The magic had bypassed her completely.

Shalima changed the subject. "Got sommat to eat? I'm starving."

Amie was trying to like Shalima but it was difficult. The girl was demanding, rude and full of herself. Considering Amie had helped her escape, she didn't seem particularly grateful and hadn't even said thank you. She pointed to some bushes outside the cave. "Some of those leaves are edible and nutritious, but you have to be careful which ones you eat. While some are OK, others are poisonous."

Shalima blinked several times. "So how d'you tell the effing difference?"

"By learning about them one at a time, and if you're not sure, you try each one, chew a very small piece and wait to see if it has a bad effect on you." Even as she was talking, Amie felt a bit mean, as there were a few biscuits in her backpack and some survival rations she was saving for an emergency. While she was happy to share with Mrs Motswezi, she wasn't so keen to share with Shalima. The girl was simply rubbing her up the wrong way with her attitude.

Their chatter had woken Mrs Motswezi who stretched, unwound her burqa and went to crouch by the entrance scanning the surrounding countryside.

"Anything moving?" asked Amie. She had great respect for the sharp eyesight of many of the Africans she had known.

"No, nothing. Ah twiga."

"What the ef's a twiga?"

"A giraffe," Amie whispered, her arms tightening around her backpack.

"Oh, they don't attack do they? They dangerous?"

"No, not unless they feel threatened. If you get too close to them they might attack."

"So you run away huh?"

"Not unless you can top forty miles an hour," Amie replied with a smile.

"So what are we going to do?" Mrs Motswezi asked after taking a drink from the water bottle Amie handed to her.

"I think we should stay here for the day, and let the camp settle." Amie thought that the best idea.

"Yes. They will be out searching, so we stay hidden," Mrs Motswezi agreed nodding vigorously.

"You gonna stay here all day! You could get miles away, we should leave now!" Shalima obviously did not agree.

"We're going back, Shalima."

"Back? Back where?"

"To the camp."

"You gotta be crazy in yer head. They'll go ape if they see you."

"I can't leave. My husband and close friends are still there, and a child I am very fond of …"

"And my sister too," added Mrs Motswezi sadly.

"You said your sister is one of the young girls?" asked Amie putting her arm around the teacher.

"Yes, we have the same father but a different mother. There are many years between us. We were both taken from my village. Everyone else they killed, I have no one else. I cannot leave her."

"Well, I think yer both nuts," Shalima was disgusted. "I ain't staying around for no one."

"You still haven't told us what you were doing there in the first place," Amie spoke more sharply than she intended.

"Came out to fight, didn't I?" Shalima seemed proud of it, but Amie was beginning to suspect it was all bravado.

"To fight? For IS or ISIS or whatever they're called?"

"Yeah, there was a whole bunch of us, seen it on the Internet. Fight for the cause, the next Jihad."

"Do your parents know where you are?"

"Course not. Heck they would've tried to stop us. But it was gonna be a great adventure. Learn how to shoot, blow things up, become a hero!"

"But I guess it didn't quite work out that way did it?" Amie asked quietly.

"Yeah well, you know." All of a sudden Shalima's eyes filled with tears and she bent forwards and started to sob.

10 SHALIMA'S STORY

Mrs Motswezi took Shalima in her arms, rocking her backwards and forwards like a small child, murmuring softly in Togodian.

"You must have been through a lot," Amie said softly.

"It was all gonna be such fun, different to the boring life at home. My dad never let me do nuffing. He was always going on about how a good Muslim girl should behave and how he would choose a good husband for me and how I could set up a good home for this great man of his choice and cook wonderful meals and bear him lots'a children and …"

"You're Muslim?" asked Amie in surprise, "and your father was going to choose a husband for you?"

"Yeah, like they do in Pakistan, that's where he comes from. Me mum's English and she didn't agree neither, but she has no say at home. She has to do as he says."

"Do you have brothers and sisters?"

"Yeah, three brothers and two sisters, but they're all as good as gold, never do nothing wrong. It's always me what's in trouble. Like the day I took me hijab off to go to the mall with friends. When me dad found out he hit the roof, and had his brother take me to and from school. They locked me up in the house for a month to teach me a lesson."

Amie was lost for words. She had read stories in the newspapers about children from cross-cultural marriages, or newly arrived immigrants whose children had grown up in England. They mixed with British children, went to the same schools, played the same games, but they weren't free, many were still bound by the old customs from their parents' home countries. She could understand how this could cause major conflict.

Shalima sniffed and continued. "Then me uncle took Shebia back to Pakistan to marry some old goat, least twenty years older than she was, 'cos he said it was a match wiv a good family. Geez you should see him, he wheezes and smokes this disgusting pipe and is a real slob. He only took a bath once a month, and never changed his clothes, he stank! Sure it was done so he could come and live in England as he was now married to a Brit. And they never have no money as he sends it all back to Pakistan to his first wife! Imagine that, he has five children with her. Shebia refused to sleep with him and the family got mad and she got beaten up and the police got called. But she was too afraid to tell them anything and she got beat up even more. She tried to run away, but like she ain't got no money and she was on the streets and someone saw her and dragged her back home."

"But surely there was someone she could turn to?" Amie was horrified by the story. "Social Services?"

"Yeah, right. She told one of the teachers and they said that until she was eighteen she'd have to stay and put up wiv it, or they'd put her in some kind of children's home. And she didn't want that."

"That must have been so awful for her!" Amie was not sure if Mrs Motswezi understood everything Shalima was saying as, apart from her broad accent, the words came tumbling out in a steady stream. It seemed that once she started talking she couldn't stop.

"Yeah, gave me folks a fright, and they was extra vigilant with me and my sisters. We had no freedom, and there were so many rows in the family. We heard about one girl who was killed by her father and brothers 'cos she had brought such shame on the family by walking out on her husband. She weren't gonna to take no more beating and she claimed refuge in a woman's shelter place. She only went out the once, but they was watching out for her and as soon as she walked across the road they grabbed her and stuffed her in the car and that was the last anyone saw of her."

"Do you think they sent her back to Pakistan?" Amie suggested.

"No, they'd never have got her on a plane, she would have screamed the whole way. No, we heard they done her in."

"Murdered her! But that's illegal," cried Amie. "The police would investigate and …"

"What, you joking ain't yer? No body, no one to spill the beans, no one to complain. No, she's a gonner I tell you. Only they weren't gonna do that to me, no way."

"So what did you? Uh, how did you …?"

"They helped me at school."

"What! To escape and come and fight for IS?" Now Amie was really shocked. "In a British school? I don't believe you!"

"You ain't got no idea what them teachers tell us in class. There's plenty of them who follow the cause, and teach us about salvation and being a martyr and gonna heaven and all that stuff. The world must be rid of infidels and the faithful must get revenge for what them Americans and them British have done to their people in the Middle East, killing them and putting the rest in prison, and beating them up and torturing them and all just 'cos the West don't like their leaders and the way they behave." Shalima rushed on without a pause.

"You do have a point there I suppose." Amie had never thought of her own country as an aggressor. Even coming to live in Africa she had spent most of her time cocooned with other British expats and kept her own customs and culture close to her heart. Yes, she had grown to love Africa and her peoples, but inside, she still felt herself British and proud of it. Now, she wasn't quite so sure how she felt. There was a lot going on that seldom came to light. There had been no Muslims at her school although she had seen plenty in the streets. How many of them, especially the women, led lives of quiet desperation? How many were happy to follow the age-old customs of their families, and how many envied the western youth with their freedom, their dress, their music and their open interaction between both sexes? And how many feared arranged marriages? She shuddered to think what it must be like to be told to go with some elderly man, especially if he wasn't even clean, possibly didn't speak the same language, and considered you a kind of possession. It was too awful to think about. In comparison she had had it so easy; loving parents, a great sister, even if they did fight sometimes, and a happy, stable home. They'd always been supportive and she knew they would be there if she ever needed them. Her home was the safe haven she could turn to at any time. She'd never had the problems Shalima had experienced.

"And it's not only on the Internet. They is on Twitter and Whatsapp and Facebook and you know what? They even boasted they hacked into the Twitter and YouTube accounts of the US Central Command. How clever is that? These guys are on a mission, I tell you"

"But the school?" Amie asked. "How could they possibly ...?"

"They made us all feel special, part of the new uprising, and they suggested we log on to these sites and there was plenty of them, where they told us they was looking for recruits."

"To come and fight?"

"Yeah, help the cause. And there are plenty of kids leavin', they even helped us with money for the plane fares too."

"So, where did you go? How did you get away?" Amie was both fascinated and appalled by the story.

"Packed up a few things, they sent a taxi for us, all the way to Heathrow and we got on a plane for Turkey. Knew where me dad had me passport, think he was getting ready to take me to Pakistan and marry me off as well. No way was I having that! And when we landed we was taken to a camp and they trained us and showed us how to handle guns and stuff and explode bombs. It was quite cool really. We was taken in a pick-up to Syria, but that weren't such fun.

Lots of fighting and bodies and kids with no one to look after them. It was all a bit gruesome."

Shalima paused. "One day some other soldiers arrived and there was a big powwow. Next thing we know we was split up and I was taken away from me mates, even away from me boyfriend, and I was flown to Africa and landed up in a camp and they don't seem so keen for us to fight. And then to be bloody maids and service the men, disgusting creatures. Hell I don't even know what country I'm in now."

"We are in Togodo," Amie told her, while thinking there was usually a boyfriend in the picture somewhere. "And I'm not sure any government knows there is an IS camp here. They seem to be spreading all over the place, there are also groups in Libya, Chad and Nigeria and now here as well. I only heard about this a few days ago. Shalima, I don't know if you still feel any allegiance to them but do you realize how brutal they've been? I'm not talking about the street fighting in Syria, I hear that's bad, but Jonathon heard when he was in Umeru these people had publicly beheaded journalists and aid workers. They posted videos on the net and they've killed people for speaking out against them. And they attacked a magazine office in Paris and twelve more people died. How could you support people like that?"

Amie's words seemed to sear into Shalima's brain. She adopted her tough girl attitude again, pushed Mrs Motswezi away and gathered herself together. "I must be off. It's givin' me the creeps bein' so close to the camp and all. So I'll say g'bye."

"Wait a moment Shalima." While Amie would be

happy to see the back of her, she couldn't let her wander off on her own, it would almost certainly lead to her death. "Think this through for a moment," she said. "What will you do for food, and drink, and do you even know which direction to go in?"

"Yeah, well, I guess, I'll start walking and see where it takes me."

"Shalima, use some common sense!" snapped Amie. "You won't last two days out there." But who am I to talk she asked herself. I walked out into the bush didn't I? And I survived. Still she felt she couldn't sit and watch the girl walk away.

"Been all right up till now, ain't I?"

"So far, but you should at least have some breakfast before you set out." Amie opened her backpack and laid out the contents on the floor of the cave. She gasped when they heard a rumbling sound outside, but Mrs Motswezi smiled. "Thunder," she said, "our tracks, they will all be gone now."

"That's a relief, I'd almost forgotten they'll probably be looking for us," Amie had got so carried away by Shalima's story that recent events had slid temporarily to the back of her mind.

She counted up the biscuits and energy bars she had left, and the three cans of meat and she was pleased to see there were also several packets of foil she had not investigated. As she emptied all the contents out Shalima gave a whoop and pounced on the black plastic bundles.

"Bloody hell!" she exclaimed. "What was you doing sneaking around the camp when you had all this lot? You mad or what?"

Amie looked puzzled. "Frankly I have no idea what they are," she said. "They were in Jonathon's bag, so I thought they might be useful."

Shalima looked at her in amazement. "You honestly don't know?"

"No. I suppose they are explosives or something like that? But I've no idea how to use them."

"Well, I bloody do," replied Shalima with satisfaction. "They might be bastards, but they trained me well. We could blow up half the camp with this lot."

"Then that's what we'll do," said Amie, "though we'll have to blow up the right bits."

Mrs Motswezi smiled again. "We can rescue my sister, and Angelina and your man too, Amie."

"You really are going back? No shit?" Shalima obviously thought they were mad.

"We don't have an option," replied Amie. "I can't walk away and leave them to their fate, even if I don't feel very brave about it." She looked at the young girl. "Shalima, can you show me how to use these?"

"Bloody wonder they ain't gone off already," she replied, "seeing you swinging that bag all over the place."

A shudder ran down Amie's spine. "I didn't think of that," she muttered.

"Sure, I'll show you, after breakfast," Shalima said slyly.

The rain was coming down heavily. Long streams of water poured off the overhang and bounced onto the floor of the cave, sending small sprays over its inhabitants as they eased back as far as they could to keep dry.

"So, what's yer plan?" asked Shalima while chewing on a stick of biltong.

Amie unscrewed a bottle of water and took a few sips, before answering. "To go back as soon as the sun goes down, or say late afternoon, before it gets dark, and hide out again and see what's happening."

"What if they see you?"

"I was watching the camp for hours before I crossed the river," Amie said with not a little pride in her voice.

"Ah, but they didn't know you was there did they?" Shalima pointed out.

"No, but do you really think they would expect us to go back?" Amie queried.

"Um, no, guess not," Shalima admitted grudgingly. "Only mad people'd go back."

"Which makes us stark, raving mad," agreed Amie.

"We should not go today," Mrs Motswezi said firmly, the tone of her voice suggested the decision was final. "We must wait to see how much rain comes."

Amie realized the river was likely to be much deeper now, perfect for a crocodile who might fancy swimming a little way up stream. She decided to keep that information to herself, she didn't want Mrs Motswezi to freak out and disappear along with the other three women who had vanished into thin air.

"Mrs Motswezi, where do you think the other women went?" she asked.

The elderly lady looked puzzled. "Who knows? It was only me and my sister from my village and there is no village there any more to go to." She paused while she wiped a few tears away. "They said they were from another village away from the sea, they go there, or possibly they go to Apatu? Where there are many people they can find help."

"Will they tell the government people about these men?"

Mrs Motswezi didn't answer her.

Forgetting the fear many local people had for government people and anyone in authority, Amie pressed on. "Surely they'll report it, and they'll send out Togodian soldiers to attack them?"

Mrs Motswezi remained silent again.

"But these men are foreigners, they're not African, they shouldn't be here, they're trespassing," Amie was trying hard to push the point home, but Mrs Motswezi simply held her hands out and continued to look nonplussed.

So, Amie thought, there was unlikely to be any help coming from the city. We're on our own.

The rest of the day was spent dozing, nibbling the food sparingly, collecting water in the water bottles as it poured off the roof, and keeping a look out for any movement in the valley. If anyone was scrambling down the cliffs towards the cave, they would not have heard them as the thunder rolled and the lightning erupted from the clouds.

Amie and Shalima played noughts and crosses in the loose sand on the cave floor and half-heartedly tried a couple of games of 'I Spy'. As soon as the rain eased off, taking a lot more care this time, Amie removed the grenades from her backpack and Shalima showed her how to arm them and explained how much damage each one could do.

They slept again that night and remained where they were for one more day. It was towards the late afternoon when the rain stopped altogether and Amie felt it was time to move. It had been such a headlong dash from the camp no one was quite sure how far they'd come. For a while they discussed if it was a good idea to go and scout around and then return to the cave, or make for the camp and try to creep in as soon as it was all quiet. Both Amie and Mrs Motswezi agreed they should, if possible, try the rescue that night. They were worried the camp might move on, or more recruits might arrive or, no one put into words the thought that their loved ones might not be alive.

Amie didn't say a word, but she noticed Shalima was discussing the venture as if she intended to be part of it. Was she coming along? Was she going to help? Amie was afraid to break the mood by asking her outright, but her advice was invaluable.

They had drawn out plans of the layout in the sand, but it seemed Ben had done a thorough visual search when he watched the camp, as Amie learned nothing new. The commander was in one of the three tents at one end, two tents on one long side of the rectangle next to the river housed the ordinary soldiers, with the women's tent sandwiched between them. The three tents on the opposite side served as the sleeping quarters for more of the fanatics, with the ammunition and stores tent in the middle. The remaining short side was where they kept the prisoners, and the women thought there was another store tent there as well, but hadn't seen people walk in or out.

"So, do you think that is where they store the weapons?" asked Amie.

Shalima looked thoughtful. "Well," she replied, "we have a choice of two tents, and they most probably have the weapons in one and the food and ordinary stuff in the other."

"And nothing to tell us which is which?" Amie.

Both of the other women shook their heads.

There was further discussion about whether to wear the hated burqas. Would they provide camouflage or mark them out as Muslim women the guards might recognize? Mrs Motswezi was most reluctant to put hers on again, although she did admit it was good as a blanket. It was all right for her, Amie thought, she could pass as a local Togodian walking from one village to another, but Amie had blond hair and white skin, although the deep tan she'd acquired helped. Shalima was halfway in between, neither one nor the other; her Asian parentage had given her a very light brown complexion.

What a motley crew we are Amie thought, as she handed out pieces of biltong, and what are we planning to do? Take on twenty-five trained soldiers? Not that well trained, but possibly even more dangerous than disciplined troops. We must be out of our minds.

As the sun sank behind the hill on the far side of the valley, the three women made their way up the slope above the cave and peered cautiously over the top. Everything looked quiet, with only a few buck grazing peacefully below them. Taking a deep breath Amie led the way down into the next valley.

"I can't see anyone searching for us," she whispered to Mrs Motswezi beside her. Shalima brought up the rear. Not a single word had been said about the girl from Birmingham returning with them to the camp, and Amie was not about to raise the subject now.

The rain held off and Amie was amazed to see how many new green shoots had appeared in such a short time. The parched earth, which looked so barren in places, had released the dormant seeds hiding below the surface, and new life was springing up everywhere. There were still plenty of clouds floating high above and Mrs Motswezi whispered there was a lot more rain coming. Amie thought this might be both a blessing and a curse. While rain would lower visibility, it would also provide more water for the crocodiles. She wished she could remember if they lived in packs in the wild. She felt very guilty she hadn't mentioned them to the other two women, but she didn't want to scare them and it was a comfort she wasn't going back on her own. If it was at all possible she would never go walk about on her own in the bush again. She'd done it twice and while the Africa of the twenty-first century was not exactly teeming with wildlife any more, she preferred not to push her luck too far.

As they got closer to the incline on the far side of the valley, she went over and over what they planned to do. It had been decided she would make for her hideout opposite the camp and watch for a while, leaving the other two on this side of the last ridge. She would signal them if she thought it safe to cross the river and creep in between the tents. Shalima would make for the tent where she thought the ammunition was kept, while Mrs Motswezi would check out the women's tent. Amie would attempt to get into the tent where the men were held and, if possible, set them free.

Should anything go wrong, or they were discovered, Shalima would set off one of the explosive devices close to the ammunition tent and in the chaos they would have to improvise.

It is such an amateurish plan, Amie fretted. This is not the stuff of movies. No one was going to call 'cut' if things didn't go to plan, but it was the best the three women could do with few resources and no experience. They could only trust to luck and hope for the best.

Peering over the last ridge and looking down on the camp, everything looked almost peaceful. As far as they could see, the two extra vehicles had gone, so hopefully there were fewer guards. They hadn't made a huge effort to recapture the escaped women after all. At any rate it meant fewer adversaries and that could only be in their favour.

Lying on her stomach and pulling herself along by her elbows, Amie leopard-crawled over the ridge, slithered down the bank and crept towards the overhanging trees that marked her previous hideout. As she slid down into her hole she was horrified to find it was half full of cold water. She should have guessed that would've happened. It seeped into her boots and half way up her trousers, and as she ducked down it swirled round her hips.

Only just in time, Amie remembered she had tucked the gun into her waistband and wrestled it free before the water reached it. She would have to hold it up to keep it dry. While it was a comfort to feel it nestled in her hand, and it gave her lots of courage, she thought she was probably fooling herself. She was convinced she would never, ever have the guts to actually fire it, not at a living, breathing human being. Inside, she was still the suburban girl from England who'd had a pampered and sheltered upbringing, wanting for nothing. The only inconveniences were things like the bus arriving late or the car refusing to start.

She scanned the camp observing it from one end to the other. She could see they'd already removed the flag, and there was only one fire burning low in the middle of the open space between the tents. Voices reached her on the gentle wind, and she saw one or two of the soldiers walk past. She would have to wait until most of them had turned in for the night.

She hoped she wouldn't have to wait for long. She'd left her backpack with the others as the idea was to go in as light as possible, and make their escape back across the river. Amie looked at the water for several seconds. It was gleaming silver in the moonlight as it flowed steadily on its way to the sea. It looked quite a bit deeper than it had before, but she thought they could still walk across. She could see no sign of anything in the water and hoped and prayed that any predators would stay away.

There was a loud roar from somewhere to her left. A lion, but how close she was not sure. For a few minutes there was silence, then another roar, and this time it alarmed the men in the camp. She saw soldiers appearing from tents, while others ran to get their guns, and they gathered in a group behind the tent where she thought Jonathon, Charles and Ben were held.

The men were arguing and Amie could only guess some of them wanted to stay right where they were, while others were eager to go hunting. The discussion became more violent with lots of shouting and screaming, until the commander approached the group. More talking followed, until at last, six of the men broke away and with their guns held high, they hurried off in the direction of the noise.

At least that left fewer soldiers to avoid, Amie thought, but the rest were now fully awake and she knew it would be unlikely they'd settle down into a deep, untroubled sleep if they thought there were lions nearby. She sat and waited patiently.

Should they go in now, while there were fewer people? For several moments she considered it, then reasoned their chances would be better if most of the camp was fast asleep.

All remained quiet, until there was another roar, dozens of shots and distant shouts of triumph. Amie groaned, yet another of Africa's magnificent creatures slaughtered for no reason. It was most unlikely any pride would attack a camp of several tents and pose any risk to the inhabitants. She settled down to wait some more.

The next disturbance was the sound of the men returning to the camp, dragging behind them what could only be the carcass of the lion. How utterly stupid, thought Amie. Don't they realize the smell of blood would attract every predator within miles? They might as well have set up neon lights announcing free food for every hunting dog, jackal and hyena in the area. It told her they knew nothing about bushcraft.

The carcass was rudely dumped outside the tents near the parked Land Rovers as the rest of the men came to poke and prod it. They were full of bravado, slapping each other on the back, laughing and punching each other playfully. It was sickening to watch. She might have the courage to use the gun after all.

Shalima had tried to explain to her small audience how to use a firearm. She'd described how to load one and how to fire different makes. But without the hardware to look at or practice with, it was not going to be much use. Amie was convinced Shalima would have no hesitation whatsoever shooting anyone who stood in her way, and that was why she'd returned with them, for revenge. She'd come to do battle for a glorious cause, for her faith, and they'd trained her and made use of her as a prostitute for oversexed soldiers. She had plenty to be angry about.

After all the excitement it was finally time for the men to sleep, and one by one they all disappeared into their tents. Amie couldn't see a single guard on duty.

It was time.

11 THE RAID ON THE CAMP

Amie gave several 'huhu-huhu' noises, trying to make them rise in scale and end with a whistling sound. Mrs Motswezi had made her practice over and over again, assuring her it was the call of the Greater Eagle Owl. It was like no owl Amie had ever heard in England, but it was a call she was more familiar with in Africa. She hoped it was loud enough to carry over the ridge.

She kept an eye on the camp while listening for the approaching women. When fingers suddenly grabbed her shoulder she nearly jumped up in alarm, but the hand held her down firmly. Mrs Motswezi squeezed her arm and Shalima materialized in the deep gloom beside her. Amie hadn't heard a thing, not a rattle of pebbles, not a footfall, but whether it was because they'd moved silently or if Amie's hearing was to blame she wasn't sure. For now, she was just happy they were all re-united.

Staying close together, they crept down the bank to the river and one by one they stepped into the water. Where before the water had come halfway up Amie's legs, this time it was waist high. Shalima was in the lead with Mrs Motswezi in the middle and Amie bringing up the rear. When they approached the opposite bank and hauled themselves out, there was no sign of life from the camp and they wrapped their wet burqas around themselves. Amie shivered in the cool night air, and when a thick band of cloud drifted across the moon they were all but invisible. Their hands reached out and clasped together for a brief moment before they disappeared in different directions.

Like a wraith, Shalima made for the stores tent. The sooner she was armed the better, even if the other two idiots didn't know how to fire a gun, she sure as hell did. It was time to feel like a real fighter again. She was looking forward to it.

Mrs Motswezi prayed she would find both Angelina and her own sister in the women's tent. If they'd been taken away tonight by one of the soldiers, it was going to be near impossible to rescue them, and all this would be for nothing. Like many Africans, Mrs Motswezi was fatalistic about life and death, but if she had a choice, she would prefer to live many more years. She'd been born a teacher and she believed that was her mission in life; to love, care for, protect and teach the little ones.

Amie crouched and ran towards the tent she thought housed Jonathon, Charles and Ben. She'd only caught one quick glimpse of them, and she had no idea what state they might be in. She tried not to think what she would do if they'd been tortured and couldn't walk, or if they'd been drugged and resisted her attempts to help them escape.

To her surprise, there were no guards near the tent and she wondered if they'd only been there on show for the visitors. She tracked a wide circle around the outside of the encampment, and approached the rear of the tent. She knelt on the ground and tugged at the thick canvas, hoping to peep under it and check if it was the right one, but it held firm. She felt along the edge to see if she could pull out one of the ground pegs to loosen the tension. The rain had softened the earth and she managed to wriggle one of the steel spikes clear, but when she went back to yank at the bottom of the canvas, it remained stubbornly in place.

The only other option she had was to cut the canvas with her knife. Since they only had one knife between the three of them, and possession being nine tenths of the law, Amie had not handed it over. She poked the point of the knife into the tent wall and jiggled and rotated it to make a hole in the canvas.

Shalima stood silently in the shadows and studied the two tents she thought housed the stores. She wasn't interested in the food tent, although after a couple of days chewing on hard biltong and a few spoonfuls of canned meat, her stomach was feeling extremely sore. Amie had collected some leaves which she'd assured Shalima were good and wholesome to eat, but they'd tasted of nothing much and hadn't given her that nice, full feeling you get after a good meal.

When she'd signed up, she thought she was going to the Middle East, at least within a shout of civilization. She'd even dreamed about visiting interesting places there. She hadn't expected to be dumped in a hellhole in the middle of the African nowhere. It was hot, the flies were pesky and there were all kinds of extra dangers, not so much from the wild animals but from the small stuff: mosquitoes, snakes and all kinds of ugly-looking creepy crawlies. Perhaps Birmingham wasn't such a bad place to live after all? No, what was she thinking? She'd escaped once and she would never, ever go back. She wouldn't tell her parents or any of her family where she was or even if she was alive. Let them worry about her; it would serve them right.

She snapped out of her trance and went to investigate the nearest tent. Now, if she'd been in charge of the camp, would she have placed the weapons store on the outskirts in case there was an accident? Or further into the middle between two sleeping tents for security? There was a fifty-fifty chance she'd get it right and she might not have time to try it twice.

Mrs Motswezi was shivering as she tiptoed to the front of the women's tent. They'd cut a long slit in the back wall facing the river when everyone escaped before, but this tent looked new, so they'd replaced it. She checked to see if the coast was clear but there was no one in sight, no soldiers on guard duty that she could see. In the centre of the compound the last embers of the fire burned low inside the circle of stones, and the smell from the carcass of the dead lion wafted past her on the wind. She edged round to the front of the tent, keeping her back close to the canvas, and felt with her right hand for the fastening. The old tent flaps had been secured with rope, but this one was closed with a zip.

Frantically she put her hand to the top of the tent and felt around for the slider to pull the zip open but there was nothing there. Then it dawned on her the zip might open from the bottom so she bent over and grasped the metal tag.

She pulled it up, just enough for her to duck down and crawl into the tent.

A whimper from inside greeted her but the occupants tried to scramble away. It was too dark to see how many people were huddled in there but Mrs Motswezi stretched her hand out and whispered, "Do not be afraid. It is me, Nomphsela. I have returned for you."

The nearest person threw herself forwards sobbing quietly.

"Is it really you Nomsa? Have you come back for us?"

"Yes, but you must be quiet. We must crawl away very, very quietly. Do you understand? How many of you are there? Who is here?"

"Sister, it is only me and Angelina. We are the only two. The other woman was taken away and I think now she is late."

"Come now. We are going to creep out and cross the river."

As quickly as she could, Mrs Motswezi untied them and wrapped them in their burqas. Then pushed them out of the tent and they wormed their way towards the river.

Amie made a hole large enough in the canvas to rotate the knife before she could begin to slice it downwards, shredding the material. It was a lot thicker than the tent which housed the women, and she had to saw backwards and forwards, inch by inch until the split was large enough to see inside.

The knife was, by now, very blunt and Amie sweated in the cool night air, she felt it run into her eyes which made them sting. Impatiently she paused to wipe her face on her burqa and continued until she had an opening wide enough to put both hands in to rip the material. But however hard she pulled, it refused to tear and she didn't have the strength to make the opening any larger. She picked up the knife again and continued to saw her way through.

She gritted her teeth and wished she had the courage to go round the other side of the tent and untie the laces, but the opening faced the commander's tent on the other side of the compound. It would be faster, but she was afraid of being seen. This was slower, but safer.

Shalima made a decision and crept to the tent she figured housed the ammunition. Since she didn't have any means of cutting her way in, she had no option but to lie flat and wriggle along the ground until she could reach the front flaps. She pulled the zip up a couple of feet and wriggled inside.

It was almost pitch black, and she was unable to see much at all. There appeared to be rudely constructed shelves on either side, but at first glance it was impossible to see if they were holding saucepans or armaments. She raised her hand to explore the nearest shelf, but to her disgust all she could feel were small round tins which probably contained food. Further along, her fingers came into contact with a canvas bag followed by paper sacks. She rubbed her fingers over the paper and licked them. They tasted of flour. Shit! She'd broken into the food tent. What bloody bad luck was that? But as her fingers explored further along, she felt a sturdy handle. Excited she pulled it down. It was a large knife. Of course, they would also store the kitchen utensils in here along with the food, now why hadn't she thought of that? Running her thumb along the side, she could feel it was razor sharp.

As cautiously as she could, she crawled backwards and turned round. She would have to start all over again on the next tent, but at least she now had a combined weapon and tool. As she swung around, her hand passed over something made of canvas with buckles on it that was lying on the ground. On impulse, Shalima opened it, reached up and grabbed several tins off the shelf and pushed them into the bag. Personally she was sick of trying to chew her way through all that hard, raw meat Amie called biltong. If they got away from here, she was going to get inside these tins and have a proper meal for a change.

By now, Mrs Motswezi, her sister Phumelo and Angelina had reached the river bank, but they had a problem. While Angelina was quite prepared to walk across and even try to swim a little way, Phumelo absolutely refused to get into the water.

"We must cross," the headmistress hissed into her ear. "It is the only way we can escape. Come, it is not far," and she attempted to half push, half pull her into the water. But Phumelo shrank back, curling up into a small ball on the bank of the river. She was terrified and had gone into a state of shock. She wrapped her arms round her legs, put her head down, rocked backwards and forwards, and refused to move.

Angelina came round the other side of her and tried to shove her into the water, but the child was not strong enough and Phumelo wouldn't budge.

Mrs Motswezi turned to her. "Angelina, you go across now, as quickly as you can. You will be safe on the other side. Look, see those bushes up there, near the big tree?"

Angelina nodded.

"Make for those. Hide and stay very still and I will come. Good girl. Go! Go now!"

Angelina hesitated for a second, turned away and waded into the river. She gave a gasp as the cold water wrapped round the bottom of her burqa, trapping her legs. Mrs Motswezi leaned forwards and tugged it as hard as she could and part of it came free. "Drag it behind you with one hand," she instructed in as loud a whisper as she dared. "Don't let go of it, don't let go. You understand?"

Angelina nodded and started to wade out towards the middle of the river, while her old headmistress turned back to her sister. Looking over her shoulder, the child could see Mrs Motswezi giving Phumelo a good shake. She hoped and prayed they would follow her soon, she did not want to be hiding in the bushes all by herself with no one to help her. What would she do, where would she go? She was very scared.

Shalima crammed as many tins into the bag as she could, and dragging it behind her, she scanned the area for somewhere to hide it. Just then, she saw something which gave her an idea; it might tip the balance in their favour. But first, she had to break into the other supply tent and see if she could relieve her previous captors of their weapons. It's a pity I don't have time to disable them, she thought, but most of the soldiers kept their guns with them at all times.

Silently, she crept around the back of the sleeping tents, counting them to make sure she got the right one. For a moment she paused. One, two, three on this side of the compound, it must be the middle one. She poked a hole through the canvas with her new knife and peered in. It was difficult to see anything, but she'd have to take a chance. She slashed downwards making the gash large enough for her to squeeze through.

By now, Amie had finally made a hole large enough for her to wriggle into the prison tent. There was only one person inside. He was staring at her, the whites of his eyes shining in the dark face. Amie's first thought was she'd broken into a tent where the soldiers slept, and any moment the soldier was going to grab her and raise the alarm. She was expecting the worst. But this figure didn't leap up and alert the whole camp, it just stared at her.

Amie didn't move a muscle, she didn't know what to do. She felt for the gun and gripped it firmly in her left hand. Taking a deep breath she hissed, "Who are you?"

"Amie?" was the astonished reply.

"Ben? Is that Ben?"

"Yes. Sssh."

"Where are the others?" Amie knew she was wasting time talking when they should be escaping, but she had to know.

"Gone. They took them away this afternoon in a vehicle. I think they went with the visitors."

Amie's heart sank, all this was for nothing. She was too

late, she'd waited too long. She was no nearer rescuing Jonathon, and now she had no idea where he was. She snapped herself out of her stupor and sprang into action. Grabbing his arm she tried to pull him to his feet. At least she could rescue Ben.

"Come, follow me," she hissed, "this way." But when she saw the way Ben was struggling to get up onto his knees, she realized he was hurt.

"What's the matter?"

"I cannot walk," he replied. "But I can crawl."

"It's the best way of getting around this camp in the dark," Amie whispered. "As soon as we get outside, we go straight into the bush and then bear left and cross the river. Do you think you can manage that?"

"I will try my hardest," and Ben followed Amie on all fours, but as she poked her head out of the tent she came face to face with Shalima.

"New part of the plan, right?" hissed her new friend. "I'm gonna try and take that Land Rover and if we drive down river, we can meet you further downstream. OK?"

"But …"

"Look, I have supplies," Shalima indicated the canvas bag. "It's too heavy to carry far, but with wheels we can get away much faster. He can help me," she pointed at Ben. "We'll use the farthest one. Where are the others?"

"They're not here. They were taken away," Amie sighed.

"OK, you cross the river with the women and go downstream. We'll meet you later," and with that Shalima disappeared into the darkness.

Amie helped Ben out through the torn gap in the tent and, pushing her shoulder under his arm, she helped him to shuffle towards the vehicles parked beside the tents. They were making good progress when Amie realized the carcass of the lion was between them and the vehicles, which wouldn't have been a problem - except for the hyena. Drawn by the smell of blood, it had been the first to arrive, and was now gorging itself on the fresh meat.

The animal had heard them and lifted its head, its muzzle smeared with blood. It glared malevolently at them. Amie had no idea if it was likely to attack, or, if they gave it a wide berth it wouldn't feel threatened and carry on eating. This new danger was blocking their path to the vehicles, so what were they going to do?

Amie froze. She knew that hyena attacks on humans were extremely rare, but Dirk had warned her they were not cowardly creatures. They'd been known to chase lions off a kill and they didn't always scavenge, but killed for themselves. Sadly the patterns and behaviour of many of Africa's wildlife had changed due to declining habitats and the intrusion of man. They'd always followed the rules, but now the rules were changing.

That doesn't help, thought Amie, but she had little choice. There was no way Ben could cross the river in his condition. They'd come this far; there was no going back now. While she was still hesitating, Shalima appeared on the other side of the carcass and aimed a rifle at the creature.

Amie wanted to scream at her to stop, but her throat closed and although she opened her mouth, no words came out.

But Shalima didn't fire the gun. She turned it around, and like an ace cricketer at a one-day match, she swung the butt against the hyena's body as if she was going for a six. The animal was flung into the air, somersaulted and fell back onto the corpse of the lion, emitting a sound somewhere between a screech and a howl.

As fast as she could, Amie urged Ben forwards. Shalima raced over and together they dragged him to the nearest vehicle and bundled him onto the back seat. He stifled his groans as best he could, while Shalima disappeared under the steering wheel. Less than a minute later the engine roared into life, she clambered into the driver's seat and engaged first gear.

The Land Rover was not the only thing to come to life. The scream from the hyena had woken several of the men and dark figures rolled out of the tents.

"Go," hissed Amie, "I'll go back to help the others. Go!"

She sprinted away from the truck, the smoke belching from its exhaust pipe. Shalima roared off across the savannah, swerving violently every time she approached a termite mound; some were taller than a man and as solid as a rock. She used the sidelights sparingly, putting them on long enough to see a few metres ahead and then turning them off for a few seconds. She had no idea if this would confuse her pursuers, but she hoped so. Bullets whistled around her when she pulled away, but very soon the vehicle was out of range.

Taking advantage of the chaos in the camp, and the men running into the clouds of dust left by Shalima, Amie managed to slip unnoticed back to the riverside. She couldn't believe she hadn't thrown herself into the front seat beside Shalima and raced to safety. What had happened to the shy young girl from London? She only knew she'd acted on pure instinct and having found Angelina, she wasn't going to leave her again.

The sound of the vehicle revving up, had galvanized Phumelo into action and she finally allowed herself to be dragged into the water. They started to wade across the river, but she lost her footing and disappeared under the surface, kicking and thrashing. Mrs Motswezi grabbed her, but one of the soldiers had seen them. He raised his rifle and took aim. The first few bullets flew over their heads, but the next volley sprayed the water all around them.

Mrs Motswezi tried to propel her sister towards the far bank, but by now she was panicking and out of control. As her head came out of the water, she dug her fingers into Nomsa's shoulders and clung on for dear life. She was threatening to pull them both under and all the while the bullets danced around them like shooting stars.

The commander screeched when he saw what was happening. He didn't want them killed but taken alive. Snatching the gun out of the soldier's hands he shoved him towards the river. The soldier hesitated, but another stream of abuse from his superior persuaded him to run down the bank. He sat down to take his boots off, but in response to violent yells from the shore, he waded into the water towards the two scared women.

There was a flurry as the river turned into a washing

machine and an enormous hungry crocodile grabbed the soldier in gaping jaws and pulled him under. The soldier screamed in terror before he disappeared. For a second no one moved, but the spectacle was enough to galvanize Phumelo into action and they both made for the opposite shore at breakneck speed.

A group gathered on the bank and peered into the darkness. One of them shone a torch on the river illuminating the bloody stain as it rose to the surface. They all watched in horror as the crocodile corkscrewed over and over tearing its prey limb from limb. No one was prepared to venture into the water now, despite the screamed commands from their leader.

The monster's tail appeared briefly, and another shape slid silently through the water to join in. A battle ensued under the rolling spray. Mud churned from the bottom of the river, mixed with blood and white froth which caused a maelstrom of images, only revealed as the clouds drifted away from the moon.

Amie had hurtled away from the camp further downstream, but was still close enough to have heard the drama. She now knew no stretch of the river would be safe. She took stock. There was no way she could go much further on the camp side of the river. There were fewer bushes along this stretch and she'd be right out in the open, a perfect target for a bullet. She slipped her burqa off and wrapped it round her left arm over the gun, and holding her breath slipped into the water. If she was attacked, maybe, just maybe she could hit the creature hard on the nose and stun it long enough for her to escape. She thought of Angelina, Mrs Motswezi and Phumelo on the far side and didn't stop, even when she heard another shot ring out. She didn't think it was aimed at her. Were they trying to kill the crocodile or the escapees?

She waded through the waist-high water, trying not to attract attention, and holding the burqa-covered gun out of the river. She was tempted to swim; she could keep a lower profile, but by doing that, there was no way she could keep the gun dry. She clamped her jaws tight and kept her eyes focused on the far bank. If she looked back now she'd lose her nerve.

More bullets were fired. There was another scream and Amie imagined the water changing colour as it mixed once more with blood. Was it from the soldier, the crocodile or one of the women? It was tempting to run, but safer to make as little turbulence as possible. She was terrified of attracting more of the prehistoric beasts. Step by step she got closer to the opposite bank, and it took all her willpower not to leap onto the shore at the last minute. Crocodiles were quite capable of galloping out of the water and dragging their victims back below the surface. It was no accident these reptiles had survived for millions of years, they were superbly adapted assassins.

Amie crawled to the nearest bushes and heaved a sigh of relief. At that moment the clouds parted again and the moon shone on the scene below. She couldn't resist looking back, but all she could see was a line of soldiers standing on the edge of the river, rifles aimed, while their commander screamed at them to plunge in and follow the escapees. His words had no effect, the men were too terrified.

She ducked away from the river and scaled the hill, keeping her movements smooth and slow rather than risk catching the eye of an observant sniper. She looked right and left, but there was no sign of either Mrs Motswezi, Phumelo or Angelina.

She paused halfway up the bank. Should she stay for a few minutes to wait for the others, or make as rapid an escape as possible? A rustling in the bushes made her start, and something touched her hand, at first furtively and then it held on fast. Looking down she gazed into Angelina's eyes. Her first instinct was to grab the child, hug her, fuss over her and reassure her, but now was not the moment. She squeezed the small hand back, and made a gentle shushing noise and she thought she saw Angelina nod in the darkness.

A huge lump rose in Amie's throat. She could hardly believe they were together again. What were the chances of finding one small African child two years after a civil war where thousands had been killed? But miracles did happen and this was one of them. She sent up a brief prayer to whoever was in charge, and reminded herself they were not in the clear yet.

12 CROSSING THE RIVER

After their dip in the water, the cool air made both Amie and Angelina cold as they worked their way further up the ridge and ducked down over the top before turning east parallel to the far riverbank. Amie kept looking back to see if she could see Mrs Motswezi and her sister, but there was no sign of them.

Suddenly there was an enormous explosion from the direction of the camp and the reflections of the flames were mirrored in the water. Amie gasped and Angelina squealed when they saw what had happened. Shalima must have set off one of the explosives, or were the soldiers throwing missiles at them? Not a chance of hitting us here, thought Amie as she again hurried Angelina along, but as they moved farther away, she felt uneasy. Several times she thought she heard footsteps behind them, but whenever she glanced over her shoulder, she saw nothing.

Angelina was sobbing and beginning to lag and Amie knew she was struggling to keep up. She'd have to slow down; the child was gasping for breath and limping. Amie sank to the ground and pulled Angelina to her. Her little feet had several large gashes on the soles. While African children often ran around barefoot, Angelina must have stood on something sharp in the dark. The best she could do for her now was to tear strips off her shirt and wrap the material round like a bandage to protect them. It was easier said than done, as Amie hacked at the material with her knife. She was sweating as she worked as fast as she could, they were wasting valuable time and there was still no sign of Mrs Motswezi and Phumelo. Where were they?

Lifting Angelina to her feet Amie nodded and smiled, urging her on again. It broke her heart to be so cruel to the child, but Angelina appeared to understand the urgency and bravely squeezed Amie's hand in the dark as they continued their frantic dash, slipping and sliding on the loose earth, still damp from the torrential downpour only hours before.

Meanwhile Shalima was following the river on the other side, bumping over the rough ground causing Ben to moan in pain.

"Sorry," said Shalima cheerfully. "Best I can do. Not my bleedin' fault if they ain't finished the motorway yet."

"What?" Ben didn't have the faintest idea what she was talking about. He shifted his position on the back seat, to get as comfortable as possible.

"No, do not slow down," he said bravely. "They will be after us."

"Nah," Shalima giggled, high on an adrenaline rush. "Not bloody likely, not unless they wanna drive on flat tyres." Her laugh held a touch of hysteria.

"You ... you disabled the other truck?" Ben asked in amazement. This girl thought of everything.

"Sure did. Don't want those monkeys after us do we?"

Ben smiled in the darkness and leant his head back

against the seat. For now, he was content to let Shalima take charge; she seemed to have everything under control.

Stopping to bandage Angelina's feet had given Mrs Motswezi time to catch up. She nearly gave them both a heart attack when she appeared out of the gloom. One minute Amie and Angelina were alone and the next, she was right there beside them. Amie would never, ever get used to the Africans' ability to materialize from nowhere.

They hugged each other fiercely, Angelina squeaking in delight, but they had only taken a few more steps when Amie realized Mrs Motswezi was alone.

"But where ... where's ...?" she asked, but her old friend shook her head and hurried on ahead. Amie knew better than to talk at this time, she would not pry but allow the woman time to grieve in silence. They carried on, knowing they would soon need to cross back over the ridge and make once again for the river. Since none of them knew the area, and the British teenager had changed the plans at the last minute, they hadn't specified an exact meeting place. Amie prayed they'd be able find Ben and Shalima again.

The journey seemed to last for ages as they doggedly put one foot in front of another, not stopping to rest. Their breathing became ragged, gasps louder and legs and arms ached as they skirted trees, shrubs and termite mounds. So far they'd seen no animals, and Amie hadn't even given that danger a thought as they walked blindly further and further away from the camp. Still Amie couldn't shake off the feeling something was stalking them. It never came any closer but never felt further away. She thought about asking Mrs Motswezi if she sensed it too, but she didn't want to frighten Angelina, so she held on tightly to her little hand and kept going.

The night soon gave way to the pre-dawn light. Now they could see more easily, but it also increased the risk of being spotted. They had no way of knowing how determined the camp commander would be to follow them and make sure no one got out alive. At least, she reasoned, it would be easier to spot the Land Rover on the other side of the river.

Just before the sun crept over the horizon, they made their way up the slope and peeked over the top of the low-lying ridge that separated them from the river. They could see it shimmering in the early light, flowing steadily towards the sea. What they couldn't see was any form of vehicle.

"How far have we come?" Amie asked Mrs Motswezi, but the woman simply shrugged her shoulders. In the rural areas, distances were most often measured in days travelling by foot. Disappointed, they dropped back down from the ridge and continued trudging, but they'd soon have to cross it again to go down to the river to drink. Already the air was beginning to warm up and Amie could feel the sweat starting to trickle under her armpits and run down her back.

She suggested they stop and rest for a few moments, while she checked out Angelina's feet now there was enough light to see what the problem was. When she untied the bandages she was shocked to see the soles of both her feet were caked in blood. The child must have been in agony yet not once had she complained. The Africans were stoic but this was taking it to the extreme.

Mrs Motswezi ripped the hem of her dress and used it to pad the bottom of Angelina's feet and Amie reattached the bandages.

Angelia gave her a huge smile and wrapped her arms around her neck in a hug. Amie's eyes filled with tears as she held the child gently against her body.

"Let's try and make for that large tree over there," she said disentangling herself, "and then go down to the river. We need to bathe Angelina's feet and get all the dirt out. We don't want you to get sick do we?" Angelina shook her head.

Amie was suddenly overwhelmed with the responsibility of protecting this child. Now she'd found her again, there was no way she could abandon her, and she wasn't sure how she'd cope in the future. What did she have to offer her? How would she feed, clothe and educate her? Was the only answer to take her back to England? But they would never let her in would they?

The questions flew round her head, but Mrs Motswezi got to her feet and nodded. They must push on.

"Where the effing hell are they?" Shalima had climbed up on the roof of the Land Rover and peered in all directions. She'd chosen to stop by the river opposite a large tree on the other bank, hoping they might choose that as a landmark. Even from her lofty position, she couldn't see over the ridge, and if they had any sense, they'd stay out of sight as long as possible. She was sure the soldiers had seen them going downstream.

"You cannot see them?" asked Ben from the back seat.

He was in a great deal of pain, but refused to make a fuss.

Shalima clambered down and peered in through the back window. "So what's the matter with you?" she asked.

"Snake bite."

"You mean yer were bitten?"

"Yes. I did not see it, only a searing pain and my leg swelled up."

"And they didn't give you nuffing for it?"

"No. Why would they?"

"Yeah, well, I guess not." Shalima walked round to the back door of the vehicle and rummaged around through the various bags she had loaded at the camp earlier. "Might have sommat here which would help," she said. "Anyway, why'd they keep you alive? Have to feed you and all."

"For information? I do not know," replied Ben.

"And the other two, what's happened to them?"

"When the other vehicles came, bringing more soldiers, there was lots of shouting and arguments and before they left, they came in and dragged them out. Then the vehicles drove away. If they took them I don't know, they dragged them out of the tent and that's the last time I saw them."

"Ah hah!" Shalima triumphantly waved a small plastic box in the air. "First aid kit, magic, let's see what's inside."

The contents though were not too exciting. A few rolls of bandages, a small pair of scissors, some tubes of cream which had no labels on them and could be for anything, a couple of plasters, and a few packets of what looked like pain killers.

"Here try one of these, take yer pain away," Shalima pronounced optimistically as she handed one to Ben, while she dug out a water bottle from under the front seat.

"Filthy beggars," she said to no one in particular as she looked at the food wrappings, abandoned Coke cans and empty cigarette packets which littered the car. "Huh. Thought they taught you to be clean and tidy in the army."

"They are not exactly first-grade soldiers, more like raw recruits," Ben mumbled as he swallowed the tablet.

"Yeah, tell me about it. All they were really good at was terrorizing people and praying a lot. They even had trouble getting the flag up and down," she giggled. "Nasty buggers, cruel too. Not a glorious revolution at all."

"I do not understand why they are here," said Ben. "What do they want with rural people, they are not even African?"

"It's a holy crusade," Shalima told him.

"Pardon?"

"A crusade against the infidels," Shalima elaborated, but one look at Ben's puzzled face told her he really didn't understand.

"Hey, it's a long story, goes back years, to the war in Iraq, and even centuries before that."

"Iraq?" Ben had no idea what she was talking about.

"Yeah well, don't you worry, takes too long to tell."

"But do you know why they were hiding out in the bush, in the middle of nowhere? This is land put by for a nature reserve, so no one was allowed to live here. They are hiding?"

"Ah, explains why there ain't no people around, thought they must have got frightened away by the soldiers. The idea was to set up bases all over the place so you can get to lots of different places like embassies, airports, police stations, hey, even shopping malls. Lots of soft targets to choose from. Put the fear of God into the people. That's what it's all about. Bring everyone to the true religion or blow them to kingdom come."

Ben lay back and closed his eyes. Shalima's explanations made no sense to him whatsoever, but his pain had eased a little and for that he was thankful.

As the women struggled on, the going became harder and harder. They clutched their burqas and Amie still had the gun and the knife, but she had no water bottle. The heat began to take its toll. They were sweating less, but their mouths were dry and Amie's tongue felt several sizes too large for her mouth. The shimmering mirages across the valley to their left appeared to promise lakes of cool, clear water one minute, then waver, and in a burst of light, all she could see was the valley filled with clumps of bushes, trees and open patches of yellow, sandy soil. She was beginning to feel light-headed, and suggested it was time to cross back over the ridge and make for the river.

When they crested the ridge and scanned the landscape, Amie was pleased to see the vegetation was much thicker, providing more cover. One by one they slipped over the summit, keeping low in case they were seen. But as they descended the slope Amie still had that creepy feeling they weren't alone. She continually looked back, but could see nothing. She told herself she was imagining things, and tried to ignore the raised hair at the back of her neck.

They chose an area by the river where the vegetation

was less dense so they could keep a look out for any crocodiles that might be sunning themselves, and while one of them kept watch they took it in turns to drink and cool off. Amie gently washed Angelina's feet to get them as clean as possible. From the smile on the child's face, she guessed the water was having a soothing effect.

"The big tree is still a long way away," Mrs Motswezi pointed.

"Yes, I'd hoped to be there by now," Amie was disappointed, and when she turned her head she could have sworn something ducked down behind one of the bushes.

"Did you see something then?" she whispered to Mrs Motswezi, hoping that Angelina who was resting her feet in the water wouldn't hear her.

"See what? No I did not see anything. Where?"

"Oh never mind," Amie replied, "nerves getting the better of me I guess."

There was a rustling on the opposite bank and first one Thompson Gazelle, followed by three more came down to drink.

"Oh, they're so beautiful!" whispered Amie. Two zebra appeared and dipped their muzzles into the water, slurping and guzzling as they drank. She sat transfixed as a giraffe appeared and after waving its tall splendid neck in all directions, splayed its front legs and slowly lowered its head to the river.

"See," Amie whispered to Angelina who had joined her on the bank, "see how it stands to drink? That is the most dangerous time for a giraffe, time when a predator might attack."

No sooner were the words out of her mouth when there was a flurry in a nearby bush, a brief glimpse of a hidden, brown creature, and a young lion sprang out and leapt towards the giraffe. Quick as a flash it raised its head, butted the young animal and raced away. It turned to check its attacker.

The women sat stock still, even Mrs Motswezi, and Amie wondered if she'd ever seen much wildlife despite the fact she'd lived her whole life in Africa. Not for the first time, Amie found it amazing how predators could walk around a group of animals and most of them appeared to take very little notice of their enemies. Were they unaware they could well be on the menu very shortly, or did they reason their chances were good because the herd protected them? It wasn't until a big cat, hyena or jackal made a bid to take one down they would scatter and make a run for it.

The appearance of the young and very inexperienced lion had scattered the animals, and Amie feared they'd wasted too much time watching the unexpected free show. She was glad the giraffe had got away unharmed, but it was a reminder that there were other dangers that didn't have anything to do with the men who might be pursuing them.

They resumed their long walk, this time staying on the river side of the ridge, but keeping a sharp look out for danger which could come from any direction.

They walked for most of the morning and on into the afternoon, taking the opportunity every couple of hours to revisit the river to cool off and drink. They gathered leaves as they went, which not only helped to assuage their thirst but to a small extent, helped to fill their empty stomachs.

The long trek became a determined slog, one foot in front of the other over and over again. Every now and again Amie and Mrs Motswezi took it in turns to piggyback Angelina to give her damaged feet a rest.

All of a sudden, Mrs Motswezi grabbed Amie's arm tightly and pointed. There, on the opposite side of the river, she saw a glint. "Can you see it?" she asked Amie.

"No, what?" Amie stopped. What new danger was this? The sun disappeared, and whatever had reflected the light, vanished from view.

"A light, like that of a car," said Mrs Motswezi, and with that she picked up the pace. "Yes," she hissed with glee. "It is an army truck, it must be them."

"Whoa, not so fast," Amie pulled her back. "It may not be Shalima and Ben, we need to approach them while keeping out of sight. We could walk straight into trouble again. We've got this far, we must be careful."

Mrs Motswezi looked crestfallen, but reluctantly she ducked down behind the bush and they observed the vehicle. For some time nothing moved, and there was no sound of voices either.

"We will have to get closer," Mrs Motswezi insisted, and before Amie could stop her, she leapt up and walked towards the river calling out in Togodian. Amie held her breath, this was such a dangerous thing to do. It was a fifty-fifty chance it was the right truck. The air exploded out of her lungs as she saw Shalima's head pop up.

"Here," she called. "What took you so long?"

Amie and Angelina emerged from their hiding place and joined Mrs Motswezi. In a few moments they'd be back together again and with the added advantage of transport. They were nearly safe, they just had to cross the river again.

"We are coming to you!" Mrs Motswezi called out and she was about to step into the water when Angelina rushed forwards to stop her.

"No, no, Ma Nomsa," she cried, using the more familiar but respectful address for her old headmistress. "Look!" She pointed to several lumps sticking out of the water.

"More crocodiles," exclaimed Amie in despair.

"No, kiboko," replied Nomsa.

Amie didn't understand what she was saying and looked at the water. The humps had disappeared and she couldn't see anything.

"Kiboko killed the man in the water at the camp?" she asked.

"No, mamba killed the man." Mrs Motswezi opened and closed her arms in a scissor movement to imitate the jaws of a crocodile.

The humps came to the surface again and Amie could see that midway in the river, was a family of hippo. She slumped down on the ground in despair. How were they going to get past them? She knew hippo only ate at night, coming out of the water to graze on vegetation, but they were known to be aggressive if they were disturbed, fiercely defending their territory. She knew they'd overturned boats and people had drowned.

The head of one hippopotamus appeared above the water and stared right at her. It snorted and opened its mouth wide. She wriggled backwards; even a few feet further away felt safer.

"We cannot cross here," said Mrs Motswezi firmly. "We must go quickly."

The three women backed away from the river, keeping an eye on the animals, praying they wouldn't decide to come out just then. Dusk was approaching, the air was cooler and that made the situation even more dangerous. Soon it would be time for them to leave the water.

Amie tried to remember what Dirk had taught her about Africa's third largest mammal, but she could only remember two facts: one they sprayed their dung around and the other was they could run at thirty kilometres an hour. He'd never told her how far from the river they might wander in search of food, only that they followed age-old paths because grazing was a solitary occupation.

Shalima climbed onto the roof of the Land Rover and waved to them. "Go further downstream," she instructed them. "I'll follow you on this side. Get past them."

"That's the best advice we've had all day," Amie muttered. The fear of being attacked had given them an adrenaline surge and they made good progress for half a kilometre.

The river narrowed, lined on both sides by rocks that formed a roiling rapid as it squeezed through a narrow funnel.

"We might be able to cross here!" Amie exclaimed. "If we can find a branch, we can balance it on the rocks over the river and we won't have to get wet again."

Shalima's head popped up from behind the rocks on the other side. "Hey, wanna hand across?" she called out cheerfully.

"We're looking for some wood to use as a bridge," Amie called back, as Mrs Motswezi approached dragging behind her a long, thin branch that didn't look strong enough to Amie. She put her foot in the middle of it and grasped it at one end and pulled. It snapped in two and Mrs Motswezi looked disappointed.

Amie gave her a hug. "Sorry," she whispered.

"Here!" Angelina called out. She was pointing to a thick log, the trunk of a long dead tree.

"Ah that is better," said Mrs Motswezi, and using a short branch she poked all around it. While Angelina looked puzzled, Amie understood her older companion was checking to see what might be lurking around or inside the old log.

Satisfied there was nothing dangerous, the two women hefted one end and dragged it to the top of the rocks on their side of the river. The boiling chasm beneath them was not inviting and Amie went weak at the knees. If they fell, it would be unlikely any of them would survive, swept away in the turbulent waters and thrown against the stony banks on either side.

The two women heaved and tugged and pulled, and bit by bit they got the log closer and closer to the rocks but then it refused to move any further. No matter how hard they tried it simply would not budge another inch.

Angelina gave a squawk and pointed at something. When Amie followed her finger she could see where the log had jammed between two large stones. The two women managed to rotate it while listening to Shalima giving them a long list of instructions from the opposite bank.

"Tug it this way, no, further to the left, now right!" she urged them.

"We're doing our best," Amie replied through gritted teeth. "If you think it's so easy why don't you come over and do it?"

"Nah! Never was much good at long jump," Shalima replied with a rare show of humour, looking at the gap between the rocks on either side of the chasm. "Good Muslim girls like me weren't encouraged to do that sorta thing."

"Why am I not surprised?" said Amie under her breath as at last they managed to manoeuver the end of the tree trunk up to the narrowest point across the river.

Amie told Shalima to stand by to grab the log when they pushed it across. Out of the corner of her eye she was sure she saw movement in the bushes below. The moment she glanced in that direction the movement stopped, but once again, she had the feeling they were being stalked. She beckoned to Angelina. "Come up here Angelina and stand by me," she ordered in a voice that sounded firmer than she'd intended.

Angelina looked puzzled, but moved to obey. She'd only taken a few steps when a man dressed in black fatigues leapt out from a nearby bush and grabbed her.

Amie froze. No, no, not now, not after everything they'd been through. No please, she muttered, let us go, just let us go.

Mrs Motswezi was the first to react. Picking up a large stone, she flung it at the soldier, but her aim wasn't true and he ducked safely out of the way. Holding Angelina firmly with one arm, he used the other to gesticulate, first pointing at himself and then at the bridge.

Mrs Motswezi asked him a question in Togodian, but he shook his head. She tried what Amie thought might be a different African dialect, but again he didn't respond and only repeated his pointing and gesticulating.

"Do you speak English?" Amie called to him, but he put his head to one side. "I think he wants us to take him with us," she told the older woman.

"But he is our enemy!" she exclaimed, not taking her eyes off him.

"Do you recognize him from the camp?"

"No, but they all looked the same to me," was the answer.

"Oy! Take yer filthy mitts off that girl at once," screamed Shalima who was now standing on the highest rock on the far side of the river, lining the soldier up in the sights of a rifle.

Reluctantly the man let go and Angelina scampered up over the rocks and clung fast to Amie's legs.

Shalima kept her eyes on her target while Amie and Mrs Motswezi dragged and pushed the log into place. With one final heave, it reached the other side, but it slithered around on the top of the smooth surface of the rocks. They could anchor it in a cleft on their side of the river to keep it stable, but they could see no way of stabilizing it on the other.

A few moments later, Ben's head popped up. He was still suffering from the after effects of the snake bite and he dragged one leg behind him, but using one hand, Shalima hauled him to the top of the rock and passed over the gun. Ben kept it steadily trained on the soldier who hadn't moved a muscle since releasing the child.

Shalima was now free to help stabilize the log, but she could see no way of securing it to anything. "I'll have to sit on it and hope yer weight will keep it in place," she called over. "Who's coming first?"

"Send the child," Mrs Motswezi replied.

"No, you go first, show Angelina how it's done, then I'll send her over," Amie instructed while keeping an eye on both the log and the soldier who was now keenly watching the activity. She wasn't certain he wouldn't rush them at the last minute. If necessary, she was prepared to use her gun, and the knife. She knew Mrs Motswezi was unarmed.

"Do like a monkey," Shalima told her as she attempted to climb on the log. "Hang underneath and cross yer ankles over and pull along with yer hands."

Mrs Motswezi gave her a filthy look, before tying her burqa round her head, sitting astride the log and inching her way across.

"Where's yer sister?" asked Shalima conversationally as she was half way over, but Mrs Motswezi didn't reply. Her face was a study of concentration and then she looked down and couldn't go any further.

"No, do not look down," Ben said to her in their own language. "If you look down you will be fearful. Look at the other side. Look at Shalima and keep moving."

Still Mrs Motswezi seemed paralyzed and sat motionless for several seconds before she inched forwards again little by little.

"I can't help you off," apologized Shalima, "gotta keep hold of the log."

Next over was Angelina, who scampered quickly across, never looking down even once.

Amie admired the child's faith the log wouldn't break, or slip out of place, or that her feet wouldn't slide off. She wasn't so certain, as she commenced her own perilous journey above the teeming water. She half scrambled across, sitting astride the log, since there was no way she was going to attempt to cross commando style like Shalima had suggested.

She had almost reached the other side when in her peripheral vision she caught sight of the soldier moving towards her. For a second she panicked and slipped sideways, trying to get a grip on the rough wood to prevent her from plunging head first into the gorge.

13 THE STALKER

Ben immediately raised the gun slightly and yelled, "Stop right where you are!"

The soldier paused at the far end of the log, and held up his hands to show he wasn't armed. One by one he turned out his pockets then rotated full circle to prove he wasn't hiding anything. He joined his hands in an attitude of prayer and held them out like a beggar on the streets.

When Amie reached the other side of the gorge she sighed in relief. She looked back at the man on the other side. "I think he wants to come with us."

"Well, he can bloody well think again, I'm not having any of them filthy soldiers near me ever again," Shalima spat.

"Yes, yes I understand," said Amie, "but he could be useful. We might need him."

"Oh yeah sister, and what for? We've managed fine 'til now."

They gawped at the man as very slowly, keeping his hands in view he removed his uniform jacket and turned away from them. Even in the fading light they could quite clearly see the lash marks on his back, most of which had not healed and were still weeping. He turned to face them again. He was pleading.

"Poor bastard," Ben murmured. "Wonder what he did to deserve that?"

"Oh God," Amie exclaimed, "if they treated him like that we can't leave him here on his own, we have to let him cross."

"Oh yeah and what if it's a trap?" Shalima wasn't convinced. "They're all animals," she spat on the ground.

Ben answered calmly. "If the army was with him they would have been blasting away by now. I think he is on his own."

His words reminded them they were standing on a high point and possibly visible. Amie immediately ducked down.

"We'll let him across and then tie him up," she suggested. "He might be useful. And there's something else. He might know where they've taken Jonathon and Charles. We've not thought about anything but escaping. Has anyone an idea what we do now?"

They shook their heads. They had no action plan at all. They weren't happy to have the extra company, but they were scared to let him go in case he went back to fetch the other soldiers. Allowing him across was the lesser of two evils.

Amie and Mrs Motswezi nodded to the soldier. He replaced his jacket and began his slow journey along the log, while Shalima sprinted back to the Land Rover to find something to tie him up with. From his slow and deliberate movements it was apparent the soldier was in a lot of pain, and several flecks of blood oozed through his coat as he felt his way across.

When he reached the rocks, he showed no signs of

aggression, but Ben wasn't taking any chances and kept him firmly in his sights, never for a moment, losing his grip on the rifle.

Shalima bound his hands tightly behind his back, ignoring the blood on his jacket and frog-marched him to the truck. The rest followed behind, and squeezed in after him.

"So, which way?" asked Shalima, settling herself behind the driving wheel.

"Continue on down the river," suggested Ben who was now crammed in the back with both Amie and the soldier. "We could make for the coast."

"Could we find our way back to Dirk and Helen?" Amie asked as they bounced over the rough ground. Shalima's driving skills left a lot to be desired she thought, as the girl seemed to prefer to keep a straight line rather than steer round obstacles.

"I'm not sure," Ben replied. "If we go further east and then cut south we could maybe find them, but I'm not sure."

"Even if we took the road from Apatu to Umeru, I don't think I'd recognize the place where we turned off," Amie added.

"Let's put a bit more distance between them and us and decide later," Shalima was adamant. "I don't wanna be anywhere near those buggers."

"They could be anywhere out here looking for us."

"Not unless they want to hoof it," Shalima looked smug.

"She disabled the other truck before we left," Ben explained. "It will take them a while to get mobile again."

"Superwoman," muttered Amie uncharitably as her

head hit the roof yet again. If she's not careful, she'll stuff up this truck and then where will we be? The daylight faded quickly, and it was all too easy to hit something in the dark.

Up until now, Amie had not had a moment to think how desperately disappointed she was not to find Jonathon. She watched the landscape rush by as tears coursed down her cheeks. He was further away than before, and now he was in even greater danger. They could've taken him anywhere. Would she ever see him again? She could try to get information out of this unwelcome, injured soldier, but he didn't speak their languages. It was all such a mess.

She caught sight of Angelina sitting on Mrs Motswezi's lap in the front seat and that cheered her, if only she could work out what kind of future she could give this child.

Would it be kinder to leave her with her old headmistress? Could Amie stand to lose Jonathon and Angelina as well? She didn't know. All she was sure of was her heart ached and she wanted to cry herself into oblivion. But that was hardly an option sitting here in a truck bouncing through rural Africa at night. She'd have to 'pull herself together', as her father used to say.

It was now totally dark so they stopped for the night in what looked like a clearing and made camp as best they could. Everyone was hungry, tired and thirsty. Food and drink was a must and Ben rummaged in the bag to see what Shalima had liberated from the camp stores.

Ben burst out laughing. "I am not complaining Shalima," he chuckled, "but your uh, supermarket shopping is not very impressive." He held up several tins. "These are all the same. I cannot read the writing but I think it is some kind of meat." He continued to count them. "We have twenty cans of the same meat. I hope we all like it!"

Shalima shrugged and turned her back on him. "Next time, go and raid the bloody stores yerself," she snarled.

Oh dear, thought Amie, up until now we've all been pulling together. Let's not have any dissent. We need each other if we're going to get out of this alive.

"Before we settle down for the night," she suggested, "perhaps we should plan what we're going to do tomorrow."

There was silence. Now their mad dash to freedom was over, at least for the moment, it was time to make some decisions.

"We should start by asking each of us what we want to do," Amie continued when no one spoke. "Shalima?"

"Well, I ain't going back home, that's for sure," she replied. "Got some sort of relative in France, she went to live over there, think I might join her. She won't tell the parents either, she's cool. I've had enough of this war stuff, and it's about time I had a normal life."

"Right," said Amie. "Ben?"

Ben shuffled his feet in the sand for a few moments. "I will go to Apatu, see if I can get work again."

"You have family in Apatu?" Amie asked.

"Some, but then again I might go up north."

"But you are Kawa!" exclaimed Mrs Motswezi, "Your people are no longer the big people."

"Yes, but we want peace now, we did not start the war," said Ben. "We do not like war. We are peaceful."

"I have nowhere to go," Mrs Motswezi said sadly. "My village is all gone, all the people are dead. These people who attack us, they do not want peace. They want war! Where do I go now?"

"But your sister?" Amie asked gently, "you didn't say …"

"I do not know what happened, it was so dark and there were so many bullets as we crossed the river and then the crocodile took the soldier." She paused. "When I got to the other side, my sister was not with me, I could not see her anywhere. I think she went under the water or they put bullets in her."

No one knew what to say. Mrs Motswezi continued. "I must go to where the children need me. There are many AIDS orphans I can care for. They need me."

"Guess Amie you wanna find yer man right?" Shalima said.

"Yes, but I don't see how, I don't even know where they've taken him."

Everyone turned to look at the soldier who was propped against the back wheel of the Land Rover. His hands and feet were securely tied and since being thrown into the truck he hadn't uttered one word, not even when Shalima, none too gently, rubbed cream from one of the unmarked tubes she'd found in the first aid kit, all over his back. She had no idea what the cream was good for, but at least she made some sort of effort.

"Can't see we'll get any sense out of him," Shalima remarked. "None of us speak proper Arabic and he don't speak none of our languages."

"I have little Engleesh," said the soldier, taking them all by surprise.

Amie pounced. "So, where have they taken the two white prisoners? Tell me where they've gone. Who took them away? What are they going to do with them?" It took all of her self-control not to shake the information out of him.

The soldier looked alarmed and tried to ease himself away from her. The fear shone in his eyes as he tried to remember the few English words he knew. "Not know place, only big camp, many people, far away."

"Where, where is it? How far away?" Amie persisted.

The soldier shook his head. "I not know. Big place, many IS there. They make public display of power from secret place."

"That's no bloody help at all!" Shalima exclaimed. "He must know more than that."

"Why did you follow us?" Ben asked.

"They do many bad things to me and to women. They hurt me. They hurt me bad."

"Yes we have seen," Mrs Motswezi said. "You try to run away?"

"No, afraid to run. They hurt me they say I help women to go."

"So he got punished for what you did Amie," Shalima remarked acidly. "Ha! He's yer responsibility now."

"What's your name?" said Ben.

"Hussein."

"OK … Hussein … Not much help though is it. Still no idea where to go." Amie was dispirited. "Not even an idea which way we should start out tomorrow."

"Well, we won't get far," Shalima pointed to the Land

Rover. "The tank's only half full and the extra fuel tank on the back ain't full neither. No idea how far these things get on petrol, but we can't drive forever."

"So, we make for the coast?" Ben suggested. "We can follow the river."

"And then?" Shalima wanted to know.

"There are small towns by the sea I hear," Mrs Motswezi added. "We can get things there."

"Wiv what?" Shalima wanted to know. "I ain't got no money, have you?"

"No," Amie said, answering for all of them. "I don't even have my backpack any more, it's still in the hole across the river opposite the camp."

There was another long spell of silence until finally Shalima spoke up. "Well, if we don't know where we is going, let's decide where we ain't going," she said.

"Towards the camp."

"West."

"Back there."

At least everyone was in agreement about one thing.

"So we have the option of going north, east or south," Shalima observed wryly.

"Not north, sorry Ben," said Amie. "We have no idea if we'd be safe in Apatu and we'd stick out like sore thumbs. We must go where we can get help. It's all got too big for us to cope with on our own."

"To Mr Dirk's camp?" Ben asked.

"No, we need more help than that," Amie was positive. "The best idea is to make for Ruanga. We have to speak to people in power, people who can do something."

"Ruanga people not help here in Togodo," Mrs Motswezi said.

"I wasn't thinking of the Africans. No, the British."

"Why would they help us?" Ben wanted to know.

"Because Jonathon and Charles are British." Amie wasn't going to mention the part about the men working for the British government.

"Gee, thanks a bunch," Shalima snarled. "You think I wanna get involved with them! They'd pounce on me and lock me up. I can't get involved with British government people, no way!"

"We'd keep you in the background," Amie suggested. "Anyway, how do you think you're going to get to France? Hike across the Sahara? Look, none of us have passports, we're in a bigger mess than we realize."

"Yeah and how are we gonna explain him?" Shalima nodded at Hussein who was trying to follow the conversation.

Amie ran her fingers through her hair. "I don't know. I really don't know," she said. "But one way or another we have to get to civilization."

"So, we must drive to the nearest big town and find someone to help us," Ben said, feeling tempers were beginning to rise.

"Wait a minute," Shalima remembered something. "In that TV programme about you Amie, you stayed in Ruanga with a British couple. What about them?"

Ah The Robbins in Umeru, they would help. And then maybe we could then go further south to see the Mathesons! Amie realized that was an option, maybe their only ultimate option. If they had enough fuel to get as far as Atari, the capital of Ruanga, all the embassies were there. They could even hand Hussein over to one or other of them. She didn't look forward to the prospect of going to them for a second time after getting herself into yet another jam, but no other solution seemed likely.

"So, we all gonna stay together?" Shalima asked.

Everyone except Hussein nodded. He had no choice.

With the decision made, and after choosing who was to keep watch, they made themselves as comfortable as possible to grab a few hours sleep.

Angelina had been asleep for ages, curled up on the front passenger seat of the Land Rover, and while Amie watched her gently breathing, a small smile on her face, she couldn't help but wonder what the future would be for this little child of Africa.

No one slept very well. One by one they awoke and rubbed their aching joints. After grabbing a snack, drinking as much water as they wanted before refilling the bottles in the river, they set off in the early dawn light.

They continued east, following the ever-widening river, until they met the road that ran north-south along the coast. For a brief moment, Amie thought Shalima was going to turn left, but at the last minute she turned towards Ruanga.

The sheer bliss of travelling on a dirt road, even though it hadn't been graded in a long time, was so much easier than careering through the bush, and everyone seemed more cheerful. Everyone that is, except Hussein, who looked decidedly nervous. He had no idea where he was going, or what would happen to him when they got there.

At odd intervals they caught sight of the sea, sparkling and dancing as the sun rose and painted the waves a bright golden yellow.

Angelina was entranced, and Amie couldn't resist the urge to ask Shalima to stop for a moment so she could take the child down to the shoreline.

"You must be out yer tiny mind," grumbled Shalima as she slowed the truck to a stop.

"Only for ten minutes, promise," begged Amie, scrambling out as soon as the truck stopped. "Come on Angelina, come and put your toes in the sea. Here, it's called the Indian Ocean and the water is lovely and warm." This was not the first time Amie had paddled along this coast, and she knew the sea was seldom cold; people swam all year round. After the freezing seas that washed the shores of England Amie wanted to remind herself again, and show Angelina something new and exciting at the same time.

They tripped over the wide golden beach and Angelina was mesmerized. She hesitated by the water, afraid to go too close, even when Amie paddled confidently in the shallow waves.

Mrs Motswezi joined them and said she had never been in the ocean before, although she had often bought bottles of sea water that she used to cure all kinds of illnesses. Amie laughed when the teacher told her that in one old African folk tale she had heard as a child, the sea came to meet the land in the morning, but at night, it disappeared far away to feed. How else would you explain the movement of the tides? Amie reasoned. That would take a lot of complicated talking in a rural village a few decades ago.

With great caution Angelina approached the water, inches at a time, and when the first waves tickled her toes, she shrieked and ran away. She ventured a little closer and buried her feet in the wet sand on the edge. She giggled at the cool feeling on her ankles and watched in amazement as the waves came and went, and then suddenly she laughed. She bent over and scooped some water in her hands, and before Amie could warn her, she tried to drink it. Angelina pulled a face and spat it out. "Bad, bad water," she said and she laughed again.

"No. Good water," Amie said. "The water will help to make your feet better, but not for drinking." Then she laughed too, this was the first time Angelina had relaxed and enjoyed herself. How much Amie wanted to give the child many more years of happiness.

Shalima was already screaming at them from the truck to hurry up and reluctantly they walked back up the beach and climbed into the car.

It was a long, hot drive, even with the windows open, speeding past clumps of prickly pear, dusty bushes and the ever-present acacia trees. Occasionally they caught a cooling breeze blowing in from the sea, but as the sun rose, so did the temperature in the car. Shalima fiddled with the knobs to find the air conditioning, until Amie reminded her that turning it on would use up more fuel. It was unlikely, she added, that an old truck like this would even have air conditioning.

They sat and suffered, the sweat pouring down their faces and saturating their clothes. Amie was still dressed in the same outfit she had put on before leaving Dirk's camp and was longing for clean clothes and a good shower. But it was a lot better than walking and they only stopped for comfort breaks and to raid the food supplies to keep them going. They saw a few cars going in the opposite direction and overtook a couple more, but generally the road was quiet. Even Mrs Motswezi noticed there were only a couple of villages and not as many people on foot as was usual in Africa.

It was late afternoon when they saw a battered and faded sign announcing it was ten kilometres to the border.

"And now?" asked Shalima.

"We drive off the road and inland a little way until we can find a crossing," Amie replied.

"Oh shit," said the driver and veered suddenly off the road, throwing them all into a heap as the Land Rover's wheels fought for traction on the loose earth. They were back to bush bashing again, bouncing along dangerously fast, since Shalima showed no signs of slowing down.

"We stop here and wait for morning?" Ben asked.

"No, let's keep going," Amie thought it best to get to a friendly country as soon as possible, but she had no way of telling if the Ruangans would be friendly. It was possible that if the truck was stopped, they could all be smartly escorted back across the border. And then what would they do?

Although Amie had driven from Togodo to Ruanga illicitly several times, she didn't recognize any landmarks, except the rising hills between the two countries and she had no idea exactly where the boundary was marked. In most places there was no fencing, so they'd have to trust to luck.

They crossed the border sometime in the night, but were unaware of it. They'd stopped for a comfort break, put the last drops of fuel from the can into the tank and grabbed some food, while it was still dark. To Amie's enormous relief, the next day saw them driving into the suburbs of Umeru.

"I hope you can find this place quick," remarked Shalima, "we is driving on the smell of an oily rag."

While Amie giggled at hearing this old saying, all the others looked very puzzled. She reckoned they must have had long range fuel tanks to get possibly 800 kilometres or more.

At first all the streets looked the same; neat houses set out American style, with the roads at right angles to each other. Then she spotted a huge flame tree and knew they were in the right place.

"Here! It's here! Stop, it's this one!" she pointed to a high wall topped with barbed wire. She was out of the car and ringing the door bell before Shalima had manoeuvered the truck into a parking place between two other vehicles.

Amie waited impatiently by the gate, but there was no response. She rang the bell a second time. There must be someone in, there must be, she thought while she rang the doorbell again and again. Alice Robbins was in a wheelchair and didn't often go out. Even if she had, her maid Emily should be there.

Eventually she accepted defeat, but before getting back in the car, she thought the people next door might know. She pressed their bell and a moment later, a smiling black lady appeared at the gate. "Can I help you?" she asked, looking in horror at the young white woman wearing bush gear, who obviously hadn't had a bath in weeks nor put a comb through her hair.

"Good morning, I'm looking for the Robbins, but there was no answer when I rang their bell."

"Ah no, they are on their long leave in England I think," the lady told her.

"When will they be back? Soon?" Amie was so hoping it might be today or even tomorrow.

"No, not for many weeks, they go to see their family," the neighbour told her.

"All right, thanks." Depressed, she returned to the truck.

This was the worst possible news. She didn't think it would be a good idea to look for the mine where Tim Robbins worked, she didn't even know the name of it and she'd not thought to ask the neighbour either.

"And now?" asked Shalima looking out of the window.

Amie looked sad as she told them the news. "On leave in England."

"Oh great!" Shalima exploded. "What effing suggestion do you have now?"

They sat there for several moments until Shalima started the truck and announced she was going shopping. Still distraught, Amie didn't think to ask what she was going to use for money.

Shalima parked on the edge of a large car park in the town. She told everyone they had two hours to wander around and disappeared in the direction of a large supermarket.

One by one they climbed out of the Land Rover and looked at Hussein in dismay. His feet and hands were still tied together and they could hardly take him out in the streets like that. Mrs Motswezi solved the problem by retying one of his wrists to her own and the other to Amie's. "Now let him run," she beamed with satisfaction while Amie was convinced they must look like a freak show as the three of them walked abreast along the crowded pavement. Behind them, Angelina skipped along, keeping pace with Ben, who was still recovering from his snake bite, and unable to walk fast.

They passed the pavement sellers with their boxes containing pumpkins of all varieties, corn cobs, wilted cabbages, apples and trinkets from far eastern factories. Amie struggled to readjust to the hustle and bustle of the town, she found it almost overwhelming, as her senses were buffeted from all directions. There was a constant barrage of noise, smells, chattering, clutter all around her and she fought down the panic.

She noticed the others were taking the town in their stride and wondered what was wrong with her. They didn't seem the slightest bit bothered by the cacophony of human life, and Angelina in particular appeared fascinated by the sights and sounds. There was a buzz as people went about their daily lives: shopping, posting letters, greeting friends. As they walked past a coffee shop, Amie's mouth watered at the sight of the pastries and the smell of the coffee. She got a grip on herself remembering that for over twenty years she'd grown up on the outskirts of one of the largest cities in the world. She had no idea why she felt this way each time she came out of the bush.

As she turned sideways to avoid a man carrying a large sack of mealie meal on his shoulder, she bumped into a shop doorway and felt the gun in her pocket. She'd be in big trouble if she was caught with that. She suspected carrying guns was illegal in Ruanga. Apart from the clothes she stood up in, she had one gun and one knife to her name, so where did she go from here? And what was going to happen to all the others? What were any of them going to do?

She had no idea how long they wandered around the town; they were all a bit dazed, thought Amie. They made their way back towards the Land Rover.

It wasn't there.

14 SANCTUARY

"I'm sure this is where we left it," cried Amie.

"Yes it was," Ben nodded.

"So, Shalima's gone off and left us! I would never have believed she could be so cruel!" Amie was close to tears. They'd been through so much together and for one of them to take off and leave the rest of them stranded, it was too much. She wanted to scream. "Any bright ideas?" she asked no one in particular.

The others looked at her blankly, they had nothing to suggest.

As if by unspoken agreement, they turned and headed south, to where the road left for Atari. It was the only place where they might get help.

While the centre of town, with its chain stores, markets, pavement sellers and throngs of people was buzzing with life, the outer suburbs were tranquil and almost deserted. Amie, Mrs Motswezi and Hussein were still attached three abreast while Angelina had become very subdued. Amie knew the child had no idea what was going on and sensed the grown-ups were on edge. As the road widened, she came to walk next to Amie, gripped her hand, and smiled up at her. Looking down Amie squeezed the little hand and forced herself to smile back.

"Is it a long walk?" Angelina asked.

"Yes, I think we'll have to walk a very long way," Amie replied. "Some kind person might give us a lift though. We may be lucky." Secretly she thought that very unlikely. Who in their right senses would take on board a bedraggled white woman tied to an Arab and an elderly black woman plus a small child and a limping black man? We must look the strangest group on earth, she mused. We could easily have escaped from the nearest mental hospital.

On the outskirts the houses were set further apart, and the road stretched way ahead of them in a long, grey line into the far distance until it disappeared over the horizon. Amie remembered driving for at least two if not three hours the last time she'd made the journey. She doubted they'd have the strength to get that far and they were being stupid to even try it. Every few steps she glanced behind her in the hope they might be able to flag down an empty truck, but the few saloon cars that sped past didn't have room for the five of them even if they had been persuaded to stop.

Without a water bottle between them, dehydration was making them light-headed, so at first Amie didn't recognize the voice, which hailed them from a little way off the road.

"Betcha could do wiv some of this."

Grinning like a Cheshire cat, Shalima stood in the entrance to a farm track, sheltering under a tree. Behind her was the Land Rover and in her hand she was holding out a can of cold fizzy drink.

"What ... but ... how ... why?" Amie was lost for words, while everyone else's eyes were riveted on the cold drink can.

216

"No need to rush," chortled Shalima, "I got plenty, for everyone." One by one she handed each of them a can.

"OK, so where did you get all this?" Amie collapsed on the stubby grass beside the farm track.

"Piece o' cake," Shalima looked very pleased with herself.

"So ...?" Amie glared at her, but Shalima only smirked.

"Don't tell me," said Amie with a sigh, "you stole it, right?"

"Might have," Shalima replied, "think of it as a donation."

Amie peered into the back of the truck. It was crammed with all kinds of tins, packets and boxes. "All of this!" she exclaimed. "How, how did you do that? No one could walk out of a shop with all this stuff and not be noticed."

Shalima gave her a pitying look. "You don't walk out the *front* door, it's much easier out the *back* door innit? And don't look at me like that, yer eating the stuff ain't you?"

Amie looked guiltily at the half-eaten energy bar in her hand and hastily put the rest in her mouth. Yes, she was hungry, and no she wasn't going to insist they take any of it back. For now she would ignore her conscience completely.

Everyone rummaged among the goodies Shalima had 'liberated' and for a while they sat daydreaming in the sunshine, relaxed and content. Shalima had even managed to get some antiseptic cream for Hussein's back and Ben was applying it.

"They hurt you bad," he murmured, looking at the welts that crisscrossed the skin. Hussein winced but said nothing.

It was impossible not to feel sorry for him, Amie

thought. What was going to happen to him? Would he be arrested as soon as they contacted with the authorities? Which country had he come from? Did he have any family? So many questions she mused and no answers. He'd refused to reply to any of their questions about his past. But they weren't sure he understood what they asked him and he probably didn't have the vocabulary to respond.

Even under the shade of the wattle tree it was hot.

"Everyone ready to go?" Shalima asked, packing away the remains of their feast into the back of the Land Rover.

"Let me guess, we have petrol as well?" Amie enquired, doing her best not to sound too sarcastic.

"Yup, we sure do," Shalima chuckled. "Though I weren't able to fill the spare can as well."

"Why did you go and leave us?" Mrs Motswezi looked quite put out, though whether it was because Shalima had driven off, or because she had been blatantly stealing, wasn't obvious.

"It wouldn't have been too healthy for me to hang around after me shopping trip now would it?" Shalima replied sarcastically. "Knew you'd be making for Atari, so thought I'd hang out here and wait for you."

As everyone climbed into the truck Amie took Shalima to one side. "I don't want to know the details of how you managed to, uh … acquire all this," she waved her arm towards the vehicle, "but tell me this, would it be unwise for us to go back into Umeru?"

"Um. Possibly," Shalima replied. "And don't give me that prissy look Amie. Bet you grew up in a 'nice' suburb with friendly parents who didn't fight all the time. And you was at a nice school where you had everything you needed and I bet you even had ballet lessons didn't you?" She put her face so close to Amie's she was forced to back off.

She couldn't deny Shalima's supposition, but she wasn't going to mention the riding lessons and the annual overseas holidays as well.

"Well, we had to fight for what we wanted, and yes the more they tried to make me into a good, little Muslim girl the more I rebelled. Saturdays round the shops with no money what would you have done? You try living in the Sparkhill part o' Birmingham and see how you'd have been. So don't you go judging me, right?" Shalima spat out the words, flounced off and climbed into the driving seat. "You comin' or what? And while yer at it, no I ain't got no driving licence neither." She turned the key and the engine started. Amie climbed into the back seat without another word.

The road to Atari was tarred for most of the way and they made good time, though Amie secretly thought they were going much too fast. Her fears were realized when they heard police sirens from behind and, looking back, she saw a police car bearing down on them. Everyone held their breath as it got closer and closer and Amie wished Shalima would at least slow down a little, but she was afraid to suggest it. It might encourage the girl to put her foot down.

The screech of the sirens got louder and louder as the black and white car, lights flashing and liberally plastered with Polisi signs, shot past them. When it raced away everyone breathed a sigh of relief.

"Time for a pee break," Shalima shrieked and Amie could have cheerfully strangled her. It wasn't that she disliked the girl, and she had to admit that without her they would not have got this far, but she had the knack of getting right under your skin and irritating the hell out of you. She was hardly a role model for Angelina either, and Amie was slightly alarmed to see how the child seemed to enjoy the colourful language and how not to behave.

After the 'pee break', the rest of the trip went without incident, even though Shalima was not particularly adept at avoiding potholes, any more than she'd avoided obstacles in the bush. By the time they approached the suburbs of Atari her passengers were battered and bruised from all the bumping and thumping they'd suffered.

"Oh shit!" Shalima shrieked. "An effing roadblock!" Without waiting for a response, she careened off the road into the bush, catapulting Angelina onto the floor and banging Mrs Motswezi's head against the dashboard. Not that Shalima seemed to notice, and she wasn't about to apologize. Amie knew their driver was running on sheer adrenaline.

They jolted through the bush until they screeched to a stop in front of a fence, beyond which were fields of mealies and other vegetables.

"Oh! No, no, no! You are not going to drive over those!" Amie yelled and Shalima hesitated. "You do and we'll have every villager for miles gunning for us."

For a few awful moments Amie thought Shalima was going to ignore her, but then she backed the truck away from the fence and went round it until the narrow farm track brought them up behind an ancient smoke-belching tractor. The track was narrow and on either side lay the detritus of semi-rural Africa: old cans, broken bottles and general rubbish. It would be impossible to get past it. Shalima was forced to control her impatience. Even she realized it would be too easy to burst a tyre.

The tractor driver waved cheerily at them, turning round and grinning, while Shalima muttered expletives under her breath. Ben remained impervious, gazing out of the window, while Hussein, wedged in the middle of the back seat, was sweating and obviously in pain. In the front, Mrs Motswezi was rubbing Angelina's head where she'd bumped it and rubbing her own at the same time.

Amie concentrated on what she was going to say to the Mathesons when they arrived on their doorstep. They were a friendly couple and had been incredibly helpful to her in the past, but she'd not felt the same warm, fuzzy feeling she'd had with Alice Robbins. But they were the only people she knew in Atari, so there was no alternative.

At last the tractor turned and trundled off to the right and Shalima put her foot down. The track soon turned into a tarred road in the suburbs, with bungalows lining either side.

"So, which way? This Atari?" Shalima barked.

"Yes, yes it is. But I'm not sure which way to turn." Amie said. "So many of these roads look the same. I think they were in one called Poinsettia Drive."

"Great help," complained Shalima and Amie realized now they were back in civilization the teenager's aggressive attitude showed she was nervous.

"I remember it was off a wide road that ran past a shopping mall. So if we see the mall I'm pretty sure I can find it. And Shalima when we come to a four way stop, you stop, right? Then each driver takes it in turns to go. If you arrive last, you go last. We don't want to be picked up by the local police do we? Not with all those extra goodies in the back. They do have telephones here." Amie knew she was sounding prissy, but she had a sinking feeling Shalima was getting a little out of control.

"Yeah, yeah, don't nag," was the only reply she got.

They had a bit of luck when the car stopped at a crossroad and Mrs Motswezi leaned out the window and asked a passer-by where the local mall was. The fact she spoke in Togodian which did not seem to elicit any surprise, was reassuring and after a lot of arm waving and what sounded like high speed gibberish, Mrs Motswezi seemed satisfied she could direct them to the mall. She hardly had time, in the polite African tradition, to say thank you, before Shalima slammed her foot on the accelerator and the car shot forwards.

The mall was as Amie had remembered it and after driving round it a few times she pointed to one of the roads leading away from it. "Turn right here," she said "then take the first left. Yes, Poinsettia Drive, this is the one. Number 17, I think."

As they pulled up outside, she took a deep breath before climbing out of the car and approaching the house. At the exact moment she reached the gate it was flung open and she came face to face with Denise Matheson who stared at her in amazement.

"Amie," she shrieked, and air kissed her cheek. "What a surprise! We were expecting Jonathon soon, but not you! Come in, come in. I was on my way out, but that can wait. Tea, coffee?"

Amie resisted her efforts as she tried to propel her up the driveway.

"Mrs Matheson, wait, wait, I'm not alone," and she pointed back to the car.

"Bring them in, bring them all in," Denise said cheerfully, but when the ragged crew climbed out, her face fell.

"These are your friends?" she said faintly.

"Yes. I know we are a mess but it's a long story, and I can explain ..." For a horrible moment Amie thought Denise was going to send them all away.

Denise gawped at the bedraggled group and her eyes went wide at the sight of Hussein, in his blood-soaked shirt still tied to Ben. An Arab was not a common sight in Atari and she didn't know what to say.

"You'd better all come in. I'll get Mavis to see to uh ..." she pointed to Hussein. "No, introduce them when we're settled in the garden. Go round the back, there are tables and chairs on the veranda," and she disappeared into the house.

Feeling both unwanted and unwelcome, they trouped past the perfect lawn, around the sparkling pool and into the back garden, where another immaculate expanse of grass stretched to the far boundary wall.

Denise came out through the French windows and beckoned them up the steps to the patio. They looked at the clean, frilly covers on the chairs and hesitated, afraid to sit down, except for Shalima, who plonked herself down on the nearest one. Swiftly Denise whisked the cushions off the remaining chairs, took them inside, reappeared and urged them to relax.

"You must excuse me," she said, "it's such a surprise, I wasn't … wasn't …" she was lost for words.

Mavis came out of the house carrying a tray, but when she saw the assembled group she stared in amazement, particularly at Hussein. The tray wobbled dangerously in her hands and Denise Matheson quickly took it from her.

"That will be all Mavis, thank you. And no gossiping, do you hear me, no gossiping at all!"

While Denise poured fruit juice into glasses Amie introduced everyone.

"Mrs Matheson …"she began but was interrupted.

"No, Denise, please call me Denise," her hostess smiled.

"Denise. This must come as a bit of a shock, and I don't know what Jonathon told you when he was here last, but a lot has happened since."

Amie felt instinctively she should not tell the whole story, so she simply introduced each of the party by name with no explanation of who they were or how they'd ended up on her doorstep in Atari.

Denise regarded looked at each one of them in turn and nodded.

"I suspect your story is a long and complicated one," she rose. "I think it's best you all change out of those clothes and rest up. There'll be time to talk later."

Relief washed over Amie. She was exhausted, and a shower and sleep would give her time to get her thoughts in order.

"The company guest house is next door; we don't expect our British visitors to stay in the hotels around here and it's empty at the moment."

Amie smiled, remembering her experiences in the Grand Hotel in Apatu, where you paid for everything, even the towels.

Denise guided them through a gate in the wall into the next door garden and summoned Mavis to help get them settled. She insisted Amie stay in the main house, but when it came to Shalima she paused.

"Don't worry 'bout me, I'm happy to stay wiv this lot," Shalima waved her hands towards Mrs Motswezi, Ben, Angelina and Hussein.

"Ah, yes, quite," replied Denise. "Well, I'm sure you'll be comfortable here. Plenty of bedrooms." She bustled about collecting towels from cupboards, opening doors and smoothing down bedspreads.

Amie was about to protest and insist they all stay together, or at least keep Angelina with her, but she was too tired to argue and agreed to everything her hostess suggested. All she wanted to do was sleep. Waves of exhaustion engulfed her. Even while she peeled off her filthy clothes and stepped into the shower in Denise's guest suite, she battled to stay awake.

The next thing she remembered was Denise gently shaking her awake. She'd no idea how long she'd slept, but it was dark outside.

"You're needed in the lounge," Denise told her. "Come, you can wear this robe for now, Mavis has washed your clothes but they're not dry yet."

Amie sat up in bed and focused on her surroundings. For weeks she'd been on high alert, intent on survival and operating on adrenaline. Now she was back in a normal situation, she felt as if she was falling apart.

To her delight, Denise Matheson had left a tray of coffee next to the bed, and she poured herself a cup, thinking it was the best thing she'd tasted since Jonathon had brought some back to Dirk's camp. She was also ravenously hungry, and ate every biscuit on the plate her hostess had thoughtfully provided. But why was she wanted in the lounge?

There was only one way to find out.

As she walked into the main sitting room, Amie did not feel at all confident. To start with she was dressed only in a towelling robe, and Denise hadn't thought to provide her with any underwear. She tied the belt tightly around her body and crossed her arms over her chest.

Simon Matheson and a man she had never seen before were sitting on the sofa. Simon rose to give her a hug. "Hello Amie. It's great to see you again, but not, maybe, in this condition. You look like you've been to hell and back."

Amie managed a wry smile. "Yes, yes I have. And the others too. Denise told you …?"

"Yes, and I've met them all. They're welcome to stay as long as they like." While he was talking he guided her to a chair set at right angles to the sofa.

The other man also rose to greet her, but he didn't offer his hand or give her his name or tell her why he was there.

Simon sat on the other side of Amie, which made her feel as if she was the chairman of some company board, sandwiched between two directors as they both fixed their eyes on her and gave her their full attention.

"Can you tell us your story?" Simon asked her gently.

Amie nodded, it was pointless not giving both of them the whole truth, so she started from the beginning; from when Jonathon had returned to the camp. The only thing she kept back was the bit about Ben abducting her. She didn't want to get him into trouble. She had no idea why she didn't feel comfortable with this discussion, or was it an interrogation?

"So," she finished, "I know Jonathon was, is, a spy," she hastily corrected herself. "So it's no good pretending he was an ordinary engineer building a desalination plant in Apatu. I know that's why we were sent out to Africa in the first place, only no one thought to tell me."

"There are various levels of 'spies' as you call them Mrs Fish," said the man, who had still not introduced himself. "Many expatriates agree to report back snippets of conversation they might hear to their local embassy. It's as simple as that."

"Oh, I don't think so," Amie surprised herself at her boldness. "I think Jonathon was far more involved than you're suggesting. To start with, you lot had him somewhere up in Scotland for a year, and he wasn't practicing the art of eavesdropping was he?"

The stranger looked uncomfortable, but only for a moment. He asked, "You know where this camp is? Could you find it again?"

"Yes I think so," Amie replied without thinking, pleased she knew something this rather pompous man did not. Then she realized what this might imply. "Oh no, no, no. No. I'm not going back there, it's too dangerous."

"I wasn't suggesting you go alone," the man replied. "And I'm not suggesting you go on the ground either, but if you were in the air, that would be quite safe wouldn't it?"

"Oh, well, yes," Amie couldn't think of any way of refusing.

As if to push his point home her interrogator added. "In return, of course you'll need our help. For example, getting *another* passport?"

Amie did not like the way he put the accent on 'another'. They'd given her a hard time before when she'd nothing to prove who she was or where she'd come from. She'd left the embassy fuming at the way they'd treated her, as if she looked or spoke like an illegal alien trying to worm her way into England. While she might still be of some use, she decided to push the advantage.

"So, what are you going to do with the others?"

"As I understand it, only Shalima Jiskani is a British subject. We have no responsibility for any of the others because they're foreign nationals. They're not under our jurisdiction. If they need help they must apply to their own embassy or consulate."

"Even though they helped a British national to safety?"

The man was not interested. The others were obviously of no concern to him or his office.

"So what will happen to Shalima? She doesn't want to go back to her parents. I don't think she even wants to go back to England."

"I'm afraid I can't discuss another case, it would be quite improper. I shall be speaking to Miss Jiskani later."

"So you're not going to tell me what you're going to do

with Hussein either?" Amie wondered if Shalima's aggressive behaviour had rubbed off on her. She'd spoken rudely to this man she now disliked him more than ever. What had happened to her? Where was the shy, well-behaved English girl from the outskirts of London who had nice manners, respected authority and always tried to do the right thing? After everything she'd been through, it wasn't surprising she'd changed.

The questions started all over again, but this time in more detail. How large was the camp? How many men? What kinds of weapons did they have? What number of vehicles? Could she guess what country they were from? Any idea where the women had been abducted?

It went on for hours, or that's how it seemed to Amie, until at last Simon frowned at his visitor and suggested Amie still needed to rest. Denise had prepared a meal and the guest was very welcome to join them.

To Amie's relief he declined and rose to go, cautioning Amie on his way out, not to leave Atari and keep in close touch with the Mathesons. Just like they do in the detective series on the television, Amie thought as Simon showed the obnoxious man out.

When he walked back into the sitting room he sat next to Amie and took her hand. "You've been through so much," he said softly. "Don't let Edward upset you, he's only doing his job."

"So his name's Edward," she said. "He might have introduced himself. He was pretty rude," she added, preferring not to admit she hadn't been all that polite to him either. He started it, she excused herself.

"Come, let's have supper. I think Denise has found something more comfortable for you to wear."

By the time the meal was over, it was close to midnight, and far too late for Amie to go next door and see how everyone else was faring. She'd have to wait until the morning. A full night's sleep, in a comfortable bed under a cooling fan, would help unscramble her brain and relieve some of the aches and pains from the bruising she'd sustained on the drive.

The following day she was up bright and early, but not as early as the Mathesons. Lying on a chair next to her bed was a dress and, thankfully, a set of underwear and some flip flops. Another shower scrubbed off a little more of the ingrained dirt, and she felt almost human when she went to find Denise, or better still, the kitchen. She was starving.

She found Mavis buttering toast and the smell of the freshly brewed coffee was tantalizing. She noticed a pan of bacon and eggs sizzling on the stove and her mouth watered.

Mavis smiled at her. "I go to take food for other people too," she said. "You go in dining room, your breakfast there. I bring now."

"Thank you Mavis," Amie replied. She did as Mavis instructed and the moment she sat down at the large, polished table, Mavis appeared carrying a typical British breakfast; bacon, eggs, tomatoes and toast.

Amie stared at it deciding what to eat first. This was such a treat. As she ate, she looked around. The room was typical of many expatriate houses, not as modern as many homes, but comfortable, with large pieces of furniture, which at one time had probably been shipped out from

England and passed through a number of hands. The table, chairs, sideboard and occasional tables were all polished to a high sheen, and Amie suspected Denise Matheson made sure her house was spotless at all times.

She'd only just finished her meal, and was pouring herself a second cup of coffee when the lady of the house entered the room, closing the door firmly behind her.

Amie glanced up in surprise.

Denise sat next to her, helped herself to coffee and took Amie's hand. She looked almost furtive and a lot friendlier than she had been yesterday.

"I am going to tell you something I shouldn't," she said. "I thought long and hard about this last night, but I think us girls should stick together and I don't think it's fair you being kept in the dark."

15 TAKING TO THE AIR

At last, thought Amie, was she about to find out the real truth and have all her questions answered? Her heart pounded.

"About what?" she asked.

"What's really going on," Denise replied. "This whole situation is a lot more complicated than you think." She gave a short laugh. "I heard how Edward brushed you off last night and wasn't prepared to talk to you, and frankly that made me angry. I think you have a right to know, don't you?"

Amie nodded in agreement. "And you can tell me more?" she asked.

"You already know most of it, but often the men talk and they forget I have ears, even if I'm not in the same room."

Amie could imagine Denise listening at keyholes and she bit her lip to stop herself smiling at the pictures which sprang into her head. "So, what've you heard?"

"When Jonathon was here a few weeks ago he had a lot of meetings; some with men who are based at the British Embassy. There was a lot of talk about IS and the worry of how they could contain them."

"Jonathon told us he'd seen stuff on the news about

several incidents, people getting beheaded and villages being burnt."

"He didn't watch any television while he was here, all the information came from higher up in the embassy. It seems IS is a much bigger problem than anyone wants to admit publicly. They're afraid it will set off a wave of xenophobia in places like England where there are large mixed race populations. In fact they're trying very hard to keep the lid on it. As soon as anything is shown on YouTube or anywhere on the net, the western countries block it and take it down. Of course some information gets out and the investigative journalists have a field day, but most of the stuff they record is never shown on any media."

"If I've got it right," Amie said, "IS is a fundamental group of Muslims who want to convert others to their faith."

"It's more serious than that," Denise responded. "Not all the Muslims are united. They're divided into two main factions, the Sunni and Shia, and the split goes right back to when the Prophet Muhammad died. There was disagreement about who should take over, with some believing a new leader should be elected, those were the Sunni, but the Shia believed the new leader should come from the Prophet's own family, and to this day they don't recognize the authority of elected Muslim leaders."

"OK, but we've had a split in the Christian church as well," Amie said. "Surely we should be worried about the fanatics. Which side do they come from?"

"Sunni Muslims, who make up about 85% of all Muslims, but both factions have given rise to fanatics who are prepared to kill themselves to force their beliefs on others. It's all very complicated and the West is also to blame for interfering in other countries for one reason or another. Many people say that's what started this latest wave. But it's growing, and several western countries are very alarmed, including the British. That's why they sent Jonathon back to investigate the rumours of camps being set up in Togodo."

"So he knew about them, even before Ben came to Dirk's camp and told us!"

"That's the reason he remained in the bush and wasn't sent on to another contract somewhere else. He was more useful to them where he was."

"He often disappeared with Charles for several days on hunting trips. So that's what they were up to," Amie shook her head. She'd suspected Jonathon had a second career, or was it a first one? Now she knew for certain. She didn't know how she felt about that. It was all very well watching exciting spy movies on the cinema screen, but to be married to one in real life was a different prospect altogether. What were the chances they would ever settle in one place and create a stable home life with children, only to have him running all over the world poking his nose into dangerous situations? She was beginning to wonder if he had returned to Africa to look for her, or had he been sent back for quite a different reason? She put her head in her hands and shut her eyes tightly to hold back the tears.

Denise put her arm around Amie's shoulders. "It must be tough for you."

Amie was angry. She'd given up so much for Jonathon, she'd loved him, agreed to go with him to Africa, even though the idea scared her stupid, and what was she? A cover to make him look part of a normal family? If he wanted to play these dangerous games, he should have stayed single and only put himself at risk. Thank goodness I didn't know all this when I was in prison in Apatu, she thought. But did they guess? Is that the information they were after? Well she hadn't known then and she wished she didn't know now.

Yet she couldn't stop loving Jonathon, and suddenly she wanted to be with him again, more than anything.

"But now no one knows where Jonathon and Charles are," she murmured. "They could be dead already."

"Don't give up hope," Denise tried to reassure her. "Two white captives make good bargaining power and if they decide to make a public spectacle, they'll be sure to broadcast it loud and clear. In this case no news is good news."

"So what's our government going to do now?"

"Well, they obviously want you to show them where the fanatics are camping and then, who knows? Grab the leaders and force them to say where Jonathon and Charles have been taken."

Amie realized Denise must have heard every word of her conversation with Simon and Edward in the living room the night before. She knew exactly what was going on.

"I don't have a problem with them doing that," she said, "but I've had enough of this cloak and dagger stuff."

"Do you want to go back to England?" Denise asked her.

"No!" Amie said almost without thinking. "I ... I don't

think so. I wouldn't fit in. Too much has happened."

"Do you know what I think?"

"No. What?"

"I think they'll try and recruit you as well."

"That's the most ridiculous thing I've ever heard," Amie cried. "I'm an ordinary person, a housewife and I can make video programmes. That's hardly good material for a spy! What rubbish!"

Denise chuckled. "After what you've been through, the resourcefulness you've shown and the times you have escaped, I shouldn't think you would need much extra training."

Amie shook her head and rose. "Thank you for confirming my suspicions. What you've told me explains a lot, but I should really go and see the others. They'll be wondering what has happened to me." On impulse she leant over and gave Denise a kiss on the cheek. On her way to the door she paused. "Is there anything else I should know?" she asked.

"Only a few extra details, but go and see how your friends are getting on. I've got a couple of things to do. Edward's coming over about mid-day and he'll expect to find you here."

"So I'm under a sort of house arrest?"

"Not exactly, but they know you don't have any money, a passport, or legal transport, so where would you go?"

Amie nodded, and almost grinned. If her name was Shalima, those minor details wouldn't be much of a hurdle. Apparently growing up in Sparkhill, taught you how to solve problems like that.

Next door, she found Ben idly flicking through the three television channels one after the other. Angelina and Mrs Motswezi had gone for a walk, Shalima was mooching around, unable to settle, and there was no sign of Hussein.

"Where is he?" she asked.

"They came in the middle of the night and took him away," replied Ben.

"Noisy bastards, they woke everyone up, no bloody thought for others," Shalima moaned. "And how long are they gonna' to keep us here?" She kicked the leg of the sofa. Someone had provided Shalima with a long skirt and a loose t-shirt that looked all wrong for her 'tough girl' image.

"I'm sure you can leave whenever you want," Amie said. "You were talking about going to France right?"

"Well, you obviously ain't seen the guards out the front, and the back, and I ain't up to playing cat and mouse right now," Shalima pronounced and flung herself on the sofa. "And the bastards have made off with the truck and all our supplies. Bleedin' thieves."

"Poor Hussein, I wonder what will happen to him?" Amie was upset. She'd grown quite fond of the quiet, frightened man who'd never shown any aggression towards them, once they agreed to help him escape.

"They will want information from him," Ben said replacing the TV controller.

"And what about you Ben?" Amie asked

"They will send Mrs Motswezi, Angelina and I back to Togodo I think. Where else would we go?"

Amie's heart sank. She was to lose Angelina again? Her plans for adopting the child were looking very remote. She had no idea how these things worked, but she had no stable home to offer her, no employment and probably no husband either. She tried hard not to think of what Jonathon might be suffering right now. Were they torturing him? He would have information to give them. And Charles? What was his part in this? Denise hadn't mentioned him at all. What a mess!

"It felt better when we were all together," Amie said. "We did pretty well, didn't we?"

The others nodded in agreement and no one said anything for several moments, until unexpectedly, Shalima piped up. "I might go to the States instead." The other two gazed at her in astonishment.

"What?"

"Big place, easier to make yer way. I got big plans."

Sure you have, thought Amie. Now there's a fledgling spy begging to be recruited. She was all for running away to war a few weeks ago, I should suggest that to Edward, she's much better spy material than me. I'm sure spies don't need a conscience.

It was difficult to make conversation, the surroundings were all wrong. Ben told her briefly what it had been like in Apatu during the civil war. He had not been able to get work, and food and other basic necessities were short. There was a lot of suspicion between families and friends, with no one quite sure whose side they were on. All the defeated Kawa, who were the majority tribe, hated being subjugated by the M'untus, who put down any insurrection with immediate brutality. It was impossible to remain neutral, your tribe was a lottery at birth and the African tradition of 'if you are not with me you are against me' was paramount. Ben told her he thought Themba Rabasi, Amie's driver, now had a high position in the Togodo government.

Why oh why can't people live in peace and harmony? Amie mused.

"And the oil and minerals they found up north?" she asked. "Wasn't that what started all this?"

Ben looked uncomfortable. "I do not know," he replied and he didn't really appear to care either. It was unlikely his immediate future was too bright; he was from the tribe who were now the underdog. But the fact the Kawas were the largest tribe suggested that soon they would make a bid to take back power and another civil war would break out. It was a rare country that could exist peacefully under a minority government, especially in Africa.

Mrs Motswezi and Angelina returned, closely followed by two young men who Amie could only guess were some sort of bodyguards, jailors or minders, or whatever you called people who were there to restrict your freedom.

Angelina ran to Amie, gave her a big hug and whispered that she had seen a blue teddy in a shop window. She had lost hers at the camp, so would Amie get it for her?

Amie hugged her and promised to see what she could do. She didn't have any money, but it was possible Denise might help? She wasn't going to ask Shalima, who might go and steal it. An arrest for shoplifting in a developing country was not to be recommended.

"Shalima, did they offer to send you back home?" Amie asked.

"Said they'd talk to me later. But I ain't going and

that's that and they can't make me."

"How old are you?" Amie suspected she was younger than eighteen. If that was the case, she wouldn't have a choice.

It was as if Shalima could read her thoughts. "They have no proof who I am. Or where I come from, and they can't prove nuffin'."

"I wouldn't be too sure," Amie replied as she tickled Angelina, making her squeal. "One shot of your photograph on the BBC news and someone will recognize you."

Shalima's face fell. That was something she hadn't thought of. "Shit," she muttered. "Thanks for the heads up."

There was a knock on the door and Mavis poked her head around. "The madam says you go to her," she announced before disappearing again.

Amie sighed and got up. Edward must have arrived. Was it time for the plane ride, or simply more questions?

When Amie entered the lounge, Edward and another man were sitting on the sofa waiting for her. Edward didn't look any friendlier than he had the day before and Amie couldn't ignore her dislike of him. He was one of those rare people she'd met who had no warmth about them. She couldn't imagine him ever chatting about his family, taking his dog for a walk, or tucking his children up in bed at night. He appeared like a machine with no human emotion. She wished now she'd asked Denise about him. Did he have family? Did he go to the social events in the capital?

Amie gave herself a mental slap. What was she thinking? All that mattered was this man might be the one to help get Jonathon out of danger and save his life.

He rose politely as she walked in, but he didn't introduce his companion.

"I came to inform you we will be leaving in an hour," he stated. "I take it you don't suffer from travel sickness?"

"No," Amie replied.

Both men stood up again not taking their eyes off Amie, which made her feel like a specimen in a Petri dish in the laboratory. Gratefully, she turned to Denise who had bustled into the room.

"Can I get you some tea, coffee?" she asked.

"No, thank you, we were leaving. We'll be back in an hour to collect Mrs Fish," Edward replied. Staring at Amie he added, "I trust you'll be ready?"

"I suppose so."

Denise showed them out while Amie paced up and down. She was trying to get her thoughts in order. No one had asked her what she wanted to do, where she wanted to go, nor even offered their condolences on having her husband kidnapped and taken hostage by fundamentalists. It was as if Jonathon was simply some collateral damage and a nuisance at the same time. She was an even bigger problem. Apart from her helping them find the terrorist camp, she felt she was expendable.

Denise reappeared and briefly gave Amie a big hug, which surprised her because Denise wasn't the hugging sort. Her expression suggested she was fearful for Amie and that made her uneasy.

"Mavis has your clothes all ready, and I've told her to pack up a lunch for you," she smiled. "Men never think of these things do they? If it takes a few hours, I expect you'll get hungry. What would you like to drink? I'll get her to fill some bottles as well."

"Water will be fine, thanks."

Amie excused herself and went off to get dressed. As soon she was back in her own clothes she felt better. Silky floral shirt-waister dresses were not her scene, even her mother didn't wear those any more. She looked down at her clean bush trousers, t-shirt, and jacket and felt some of her confidence return. Mavis had even cleaned her boots for her.

While Amie dressed, she had a feeling there was something Denise wasn't telling her, but she couldn't put her finger on it. Her hostess was nervous, as if she was uncertain about what was going to happen. As soon as she was ready, Amie went to the kitchen where Denise was fussing around in the fridge, instructing Mavis what to put in the sandwiches. The huge pile of bread slices suggested there'd be enough to feed an army. She hovered in the doorway.

"Denise, how well do you know Edward? Who is he exactly?"

Denise turned to her, an uncertain expression on her face. "I don't know who he is, only that he's come to chat to Simon a few times. I can only suppose he's attached to the embassy in some way. Why do you ask?"

"Uh, no real reason," Amie hoped she sounded nonchalant. "Does he go to the social events at the club? I guess you have a club here?"

"Not at the moment. There's been a huge row over the premises we use. The landlord wants to take it back, and refuses to pay for all the improvements, the pool, the tennis courts and the bowling green. So right now, we have to put up with getting together at each other's houses. It's really curtailed our social life." As Denise prattled on, Amie could see she'd relaxed because she was on safer ground. She found herself tuning out as the older woman explained the difficulties they'd had in finding a suitable property anywhere in the capital that wasn't exorbitantly expensive.

Precisely sixty minutes after Edward had departed, a smart car drew up outside the Matheson's house and a driver stepped out and rang the bell. Amie said a grateful goodbye to Denise saying she would see her later, but she got the nagging feeling Denise wasn't expecting her back. She had to ignore her over-active imagination; she was committed. Why did her radar always go into overdrive? It was about time she learned to chill out without continually trying to predict the future. Goodness knows, her life had been a roller coaster ride for the past few years. By now, she should've learned to expect the unexpected.

The driver held the car door for her and she slid into the back seat. To her surprise, Ben and Shalima were already occupying most of it and they moved over to make room for her.

"I didn't know …" she was surprised.

"Neither did we." Ben grinned.

"Guess they wanna make sure we all agree where the hellhole is," Shalima said flatly. She was more subdued than Amie had ever seen her before. She was hunched up, stiff and very tense. She gave Amie the impression she was about to leap out of the car at any moment.

Edward was in the front seat. He glanced back at her

briefly, gave her a quick nod, then turned away.

They sped through the centre of Atari, which Amie thought looked very like Apatu. The three-storey high glass and chrome buildings housing the banking institutions were separated by low level adobe structures, housing a variety of shops and offices and the ever-present steel shutters that replaced the glass facades. In several places the local people had set out their wares on plastic sheets along the pavements, forcing the pedestrians to zig zag their way past, and step out into the road to avoid trampling on the fresh fruit, vegetables and meat on display.

The biggest difference Amie noticed was the larger numbers of donkey carts in town. Sturdy little animals pulling what appeared to be oversized loads behind their drivers, who were content to let the animals find their own way between the traffic and the walkers.

Soon they were driving though the suburbs on the far side of the city sprawl where the houses were spaced further apart until they were out into the open countryside. There was a small sign announcing Atari airport, and the driver took a sharp turn to the right. When they drew up next to what was simply a large wooden shack, Amie knew this wasn't the main airport. This was little more than a landing strip and the only plane she could see sitting on the hot tarmac was a twin-engine Cessna, which wouldn't hold more than half a dozen people. Still, if they were taking a brief flight they were unlikely to need a 737.

As soon as the car came to a stop, the driver climbed out and opened the back door for Amie. The others tried to get out of the other side of the car, but the child-proof locks were on, and they had to wait for the driver to open the door for them as well.

Shalima would have leapt out after Amie, but she was next to the door and Ben refused to move. She gave him a filthy look as she tumbled out of the car.

For a moment they just stared at the aircraft, then Edward motioned for them to follow him across the tarmac. He carried two laptop-sized bags, while the driver got a large suitcase out of the boot and wheeled it over to the bottom of the steps. Edward indicated they should climb aboard and he was right behind them as they went up the steps.

While they took their seats and buckled themselves in, Amie took stock. She'd never been in such a small plane before and it was the first time she'd been able to watch the pilot go through his pre-flight checks. He'd not even said hello when they boarded, but Amie didn't like to interrupt him. Edward sat next to the pilot, with Ben and Shalima one behind the other on the port side of the plane and Amie on the other.

No sooner had they got settled than the engines roared. Amie was reassured to see there were two of them. They taxied down the landing strip, bumping faster and faster over the rough grass runway until the plane lifted up, left the ground and they were in the air. As soon as they'd levelled off, although Amie personally thought they were flying a little low for comfort, Edward got up and sat in the empty seat in front of her. He had to raise his voice, as the noise from the engines was very loud.

"So this camp is next to a river?" he said.

"Yes, it's on this side of the river, on the south, in a valley between ridges. It's not the only river we crossed, when we drove down to Ruanga, but it is by far the biggest."

"Any other distinguishing landmarks you can remember?" he asked. There was no warmth in his voice.

"No," replied Amie and the other two shook their heads.

Edward nodded, got up and retraced his steps to the co-pilot's seat. He appeared to be giving the pilot instructions, but it was impossible to hear what he said.

It occurred to Amie they weren't really needed on this trip, so why had they been brought along? They could only give general directions to the camp, and if you flew around for long enough, surely you'd be likely to spot it. Yes, the tents were green but she didn't remember any camouflage material, and the IS flag had been blatantly raised every morning. How hard were these fanatics trying to hide? Word must have got out about the villages that had been destroyed and the bodies found. There must have been some sort of uproar in Apatu surely?

To Amie's discomfort the pilot didn't fly the plane at a steady height. One minute they were looking way, way down onto tree tops and rocks and the occasional herd of elephants, zebra and wildebeest which all took off running away from the shadow they cast on the ground below. The next minute they were barely skimming over the ground and she was convinced they were going to crash into a termite mound or one of the large boulders scattered about.

She glanced at Ben and Shalima. She'd dearly like to ask them what they were thinking, but she'd not been allowed a moment alone with them and she didn't want to speak in front of Edward. For some unknown reason she didn't trust him, even if he did work for Her Majesty's Government.

Ben looked as stoic as ever in the typically African way. It was impossible to guess what he was thinking.

Shalima on the other hand, looked sulky and disgruntled. She didn't keep still for a moment but wriggled in her seat without bothering to look out of the window. Amie could sense the animosity radiating across the narrow aisle between the seats and reckoned that even if she asked, Shalima was simply waiting to give someone a mouthful of invective. She turned back to admire the splendour of the savannah below as it stretched for miles and miles into the distance.

They'd been flying for almost an hour, when Edward turned in his seat and pointed to the river below.

Amie nodded. While most rivers looked the same, especially from the air, this one looked wide enough to be the one they'd crossed. She indicated inland and the plane banked, climbed several feet higher in the sky and followed the silver ribbon as it snaked west.

They were on the camp almost before they knew it. The rectangle of tents was still there and they could see only one truck parked to the side. They looked like small toys from a children's game. They could also see several figures running to and fro shading their eyes as they peered up at the plane.

They flew on past, and Edward leaned across to shout something to the pilot who shook his head. Edward was insistent and it developed into a huge argument. The pilot kept shaking his head and Edward kept shouting at him, until they banked again, and Amie realized they were going to fly back over the camp, this time, much lower. Her stomach lurched and she squeezed her eyes shut wishing she was anywhere but here.

In the meantime, Edward had pulled out a camera and was busy zooming in towards the camp.

Amie glanced at Shalima. She looked alarmed and even Ben was sitting up straighter. As they approached the tents for the second time, there was a whistling sound followed by a loud bang and the plane lurched violently in the air. More projectiles flew past them as they flew over and then away from the camp.

The passengers were terrified. Ben was shaking as he clung to the seat in front of him. Shalima looked scared out of her wits, and was bent over in the brace position, while Amie tightened her seatbelt, hoping it was the right thing to do. She was too scared to look out of the window and too scared not to. Briefly they glanced at one another and Shalima was praying rapidly under her breath.

The only passenger whose attitude hadn't changed, even a little, was Edward. He sat calmly in the co-pilot seat as if nothing had happened - as if getting hit by a bullet or a missile from an enemy camp while flying over it in a small plane, was quite normal. If Amie had stopped to think about it, she would now be convinced he had ice running through his veins and not blood like everyone else.

Even though Amie enjoyed flying, and liked aeroplanes, she didn't want to die in one. The thought of crashing, and falling from the sky like a stone, was one of those nightmares stored in the unconscious part of the brain but never truly considered.

The pilot was struggling to control the aircraft as it began to dive towards the ground. He banked to the left and cleared the river flying towards Apatu, and for several moments he got it back under control as they skimmed over the ridge on the opposite side of the water, crossed the valley and made for the second range of low hills where the women had taken shelter in the cave.

They were flying more slowly now, as the pilot pulled back on the throttle, and Amie could only hope and pray they didn't land too close to the camp.

The first engine died, and the plane tipped to one side as they came up to the next high ridge. A few seconds later, the second one suddenly ceased. After the screech and clatter of the dying engines, the quiet was deafening. They were gliding, and no one broke the silence as the ground came up to meet them. The pilot skimmed over the next high ridge, and the plane lost more height as he aimed for the long stretch of level ground, that formed the middle of the valley.

"Hold on! Brace yourselves!" yelled the pilot.

Amie had virtually stopped breathing. She was praying to the God she still didn't believe in, that they'd make it down in one piece. Their speed had dropped, and the pilot was controlling the descent, and although the ground still rushed up to meet them, it was at a slower and steadier rate.

There was a terrifying bang and the plane veered violently to one side, just as the wheels crashed onto the ground. The landing gear sheared, the undercarriage grated over the rock-strewn ground, and the nose of the plane ploughed into two massive boulders bringing it to a complete standstill.

Despite the seatbelt holding her in place, and her hands clutching the seat in front till her knuckles turned white, Amie was flung backwards and forwards like a rag doll. The webbing of her seatbelt dug painfully into her hips and she hung sideways out of her seat.

The plane was now resting at forty-five degrees, its nose crumpled like a piece of tissue paper. Tiny pieces of glittering glass from the front windscreen sprinkled the cabin, scattered around them like an ice storm.

16 AFTER THE CRASH

Amie hung suspended in the air, the weight of her body pulling her seatbelt so tight it was impossible for her to undo it.

Ben was the first to recover. He pushed Amie up towards what was left of the plane's ceiling, released the buckle and caught her when she fell onto the sloping floor. She was trembling all over and lay curled up for several minutes.

Shalima had managed to wriggle free, and was checking herself for any injuries. Her movements were jerky and uncoordinated. They were all in shock.

Amie struggled to stand, but the roof had caved in and she was only able to shuffle a little way to the front, to where the door had blown off. The nose and cockpit had crumpled like a large piece of bent tin foil and she could see that neither Edward nor the pilot had survived.

A shaft of metal protruded from the pilot's neck and Edward's body had been crushed between what was left of the front part of the plane and the unforgiving boulders.

"We'd betta get the bloody hell outta here," said Shalima in her left ear. "If them soldiers think they've shot us down, they'll be over here pronto. Go on, get a move on," and she pushed Amie towards the gaping hole where the door had been.

Shalima was right, they didn't have time to sit and recover and tend to the cuts and scratches. They needed to leave as fast as possible. They were in great danger.

Despite Shalima's urging, Amie gaped at the mangled bodies, she knew she would never erase those images, but another thump on her back from Shalima galvanized her into action. She staggered towards the exit, crouching down to avoid the sharp shards of metal and the broken glass until she reached the exit.

The plane had crashed head on and slewed to one side. It was only a short drop to the ground, and although Amie's knees were as wobbly as jelly, she jumped and hit the earth hard.

Ben dropped down beside her, but there was no sign of Shalima. Amie peered up at the open doorway and wondered what she was up to.

"Come on," she shouted. "What are you doing? It was you who told us we don't have much time. They'll be here any minute."

Shalima appeared in the hatchway, dragging the large case and the other two bags Edward had brought onto the plane.

"Thought these might come in useful," she replied, passing them down to Ben, who had evidently recovered faster than Amie.

She went back inside and called out to Amie. "Want yer packed lunch as well?"

Amie giggled, shock was setting in. They'd just survived a fatal plane crash and Shalima was thinking of lunch. Right now, her stomach was somewhere near her mouth, and food was the last thing she was interested in.

Shalima dropped down onto the ground behind her, carrying the packed lunch, which Amie now suspected had been packed for three people with enormous appetites, a knapsack full of water bottles and three blankets she had found behind the seats at the rear of the plane.

"We must go." Ben glanced nervously back the way they'd come. "We will take the two small cases and the water. Leave the rest, it will only slow us down. We must get over this ridge and down through the next valley as fast as we can."

Shalima ignored him and clung on tightly to the blankets.

They scrambled up the opposite slope. On the ridge Amie stopped and looked back. "Are we quite sure they're both dead?" she was ashamed she hadn't checked.

"As dodos," Shalima replied. "No one could've survived hitting them rocks head on." Briefly Amie wondered, for the second time that day, if Edward had had family somewhere. Who would mourn him?

"We must hurry," Ben glanced at the sky.

"Don't panic, they ain't sure we've gone down," Shalima was a lot more cheerful now, more her rumbustious self.

"No. Look." Ben pointed to the sky where a flock of vultures was circling lazily overhead. "The birds will tell them."

Shalima craned her neck. "Oh, yeah, right."

They scrambled down the ridge and set out across the floor of the second valley making for the other side as quickly as they could.

By the time they crested the top of the next range of low hills, they were exhausted. Going down the other side was a lot easier and they made better progress, until Ben stopped to wrench a branch off a tree.

"What the eff are you doing now?" Shalima snapped.

"Covering our tracks," Ben replied glaring back at her. As they walked, he swept the ground behind them.

"Wait," said Amie, "if I carry the case and the knapsack, you can work more quickly."

"Thanks." Ben handed them over.

"These guys ain't that good at tracking." Shalima sneered, shifting Edward's laptop bag from one shoulder to the other. "This'll slow us down big time!"

"How do we know that?" Amie snapped back. Already she was struggling under the weight of the food, the bag containing the water bottles and the second small case. "You're more likely to know, they trained you, remember? Did you have lectures in tracking?"

"No."

"And do you want them to catch us and do whatever they want with us?" Amie was angry.

"No," Shalima repeated, "but I wanna get away from here as fast as possible. Hell, gimme one of those bags," and she grabbed the smallest one from Amie.

"We all do," Ben said, but he still took his time bringing up the rear sweeping the branch leaves over the faint tracks they'd made in the dust.

By now the sun was high in the sky, and the landscape shimmered in the heat. In the second valley there was little cover, a few low bushes scattered around and the ever-present acacia trees. They laboured on in silence, sipping sparingly from the water bottles.

Amie's breath became ragged as the sweat poured down her face, stinging her eyes before dripping under her collar and trickling down her chest. Her clothes clung to her like a second skin and she took short, deep breaths as she put one foot in front of the other and plodded on.

There was little sign of wildlife in the valley, but Amie could imagine pairs of eyes peering down at them from the ridge behind. She wanted to ask Shalima how she had disabled the truck and how quickly the soldiers could make repairs. Hopefully, the fanatics had no transport and were still at least three valleys behind them. She tried to take her mind off her aching body by calculating how far they'd flown before they'd crashed, and how long it would take the soldiers to catch up with them in the truck or on foot. Every time she added it all together she came up with a different answer, until she just gave up and plodded on.

Peppered with rocks and boulders the next ridge was agonizingly high. Shalima was first over the top, and dropped her load, and slithered back to give Amie a hand as she slid on the loose scree. Ben brushed away the last signs of their footsteps.

To their relief the vegetation in the next valley was denser, with large areas of shade. Ben pointed to a grove about a third of the way across and suggested they make for that and rest up.

The trees may have looked close, from high up, but for each step they took, they appeared to get further away. At long last, as the sun lost its heat, they flopped down under the trees.

Their luck was holding, no lions or rhinos, no soldiers or elephants. They rummaged in the bags for food and drank deeply from their water bottles.

"Well, we got this far," Shalima said to no one in particular.

"True, but where do we go from here? Anyone any idea which way we were flying before the crash?" Amie's voice wobbled on the last word.

"I think it was north," Ben pointed to the far ridge, "Apatu is that way."

"I guess that's the most sensible place to make for then," Amie said, although she was nervous about what they might find there. "Would it be safe Ben?"

"Safer than being out here," he replied. "We don't have much food, or water."

They sat silently for several minutes then Shalima removed the lap top from its bag and turned it on.

"That's private!" Amie gasped.

"Says who? Man's dead ain't he?" Shalima smirked. "No harm in finding out what he was up to." She tapped away on the keys. "Ha! Silly bugger. Not even a password. How daft is that?" and she giggled.

While Amie couldn't resist continually glancing up at the ridge they'd just crossed, she was drawn to look at the screen too. There were hundreds of lists and folders. It would take weeks to inspect them all.

"Bloody hell," Shalima exploded. "Look here's all his emails, they'll tell us summat." She clicked on the first one. "Bugger, some sort of number code, can't read a thing. Drat!"

"It has nothing to do with us," Ben obviously didn't approve.

Shalima ignored him and continued scrolling through the files, but they all seemed to be in code, rows and rows of numbers, and she couldn't make head nor tail of them.

Amie ignored her reluctance to delve through something that didn't belong to her, and opened the small unlocked briefcase. Initially it didn't look as if there was much inside. She only found a couple of sandwiches, which she shared with the others, and a welcome bottle of energy drink. But there was a wallet containing a wad of British and Ruangan money along with some American dollars. Amie's curiosity mounted when she spied several driving licenses, all with Edward's picture on them but in different names. I guess we'll never know his real name she mused, sorting through the plastic credit cards. She found three British passports, only one in the name of Edward Simmons and two others in different names but with photographs of Edward. There was another bundle of blank passports all from various countries and filled with visas and entry and exit stamps. There was one dog-eared paperback and the last thing Amie found was a memory stick. She handed it to Shalima. See what's on this," she said.

Shalima inserted it into a USB port and opened the files. "Ain't nothing much here," she grumbled, "only a list of books. Didn't think Edward was the readin' kind."

"Um, nor I. So what does our secret service agent like to read in his spare time?"

Shalima went down the list. "Boring stuff. Lots of them desperate books we had to read in school, classic things."

She giggled, "'Cept for this one here. A Mills and Boon! I don't believe it. 'Love on the Ocean'. Ha ha. Listen to this! 'Lois falls in love with handsome Josh, but he's already in love with Leila. Can she get him to love her when his wedding is only four weeks away?' Stupid git, me mum reads stuff like this."

Amie looked thoughtful. "Wait a minute. We know that's a little out of character, but most people wouldn't, would they? And it's the same book here." She held it up and they glanced at the cover showing a curvaceous blonde in one corner gazing up soulfully at a couple in a romantic embrace.

"What do you mean?" Shalima glared hard at her.

"Those emails," Amie said remembering a film she'd once seen. "You said they were only rows of numbers. Well, what if this unlikely book is the code for that? Page numbers and the line number and the next number for the word."

"You mean, that poncey book is the key to what's in them emails?"

"Yes. Well, it's worth a try. We could check it out. Let's start with the latest email and see if we can get it to make sense."

Shalima insisted on passing the lap top over to Amie while she grabbed the book and found paper and pen from Edward's other case.

Ben shook his head. "You think you can read his emails from a book?" he asked. "They would be encrypted digitally or something?"

"Sometimes the old ways are the best, and least expected," Shalima said. "Bet you we can make out the messages this way."

Amie read out the first groups of numbers and Shalima tried to make sense of them by page, line and words in that order, but it was total rubbish. Next they tried line, page and word, but that combination only produced garbled nonsense too. It wasn't until they went for the word, followed by the line and lastly the page that the email made sense.

They were so engrossed in the transcription they barely noticed it was getting dark, but by then they had a good grasp of the contents of the two latest messages.

"Edward was planning to send me back to my parents, hand Ben over to the Togodian authorities and deport Motswezi and the kid!" Shalima was furious.

"But he didn't say what he was planning to do with me?" Amie asked. She was not sure she wanted an answer.

"No, he don't mention you. But at least we know now they think the guys have been taken to Libya."

Amie was totally despondent. "To Libya. We don't stand a chance of helping them there." She wanted to cry.

"Don't see why not," Shalima said as the battery died on the laptop making more work impossible.

"Don't be so stupid!" Amie exclaimed, not caring any more if she was rude or if she hurt Shalima's feelings. "You have some really crackpot ideas Shalima, beginning with your first one of leaving England to go and fight in some stupid Holy War!"

"Lot betta than hanging round the arse end of Birmingham," snapped Shalima. "You try growing up there and see what it's like. Any excitement is better than that!"

Ben suggested they get some rest. They seemed safe where they were because they were well hidden but they should take it in turns to keep guard. He offered to take the first watch.

Amie studied the trees in the grove and, grabbing one of the blankets, she chose the largest and started to climb it.

"Watcha doing?"

"I've got quite good at sleeping in trees" Amie snapped back. She was seething. She didn't like Shalima, she was not Amie's kind of person, and now she was suggesting they go haring off to a war-torn Arab country to look for Jonathon. Even if they got that far, then what? Bust him and Charles out of jail with a screwdriver and hijack a passing cruise liner off the coast and sail happily into the sunset? The girl was mad with her stupid ideas. There was nothing they could do, and she'd have to accept it. The best plan was to make for Apatu, and if they got there in one piece she'd ... she'd ... what would she do? Try to get back home to England? Did she have any other options? It was not what she wanted to do, but life didn't always give you what you wanted. On that thought, she fell fast asleep.

The night passed without incident, no sign of people or wildlife, and Amie was beginning to wonder how few animals there were in this National Park that Togodo had planned, or were they back in Ruanga now? It was impossible to tell.

After they'd finished most of the food, they tried to pack the contents of the two small cases into one, but that didn't work, so they kept both of them, along with the remainder of the food and water.

Watching the sunrise, Ben reckoned that if they struck out east, they should come to the road which linked Apatu with the Ruangan border. It wasn't going to be practical to walk the whole way, so their best bet was to thumb a lift to the capital.

By the time they finally stumbled onto the tar road their stomachs were empty and their throats were parched. They'd slogged non-stop for most of the morning and were all suffering badly from the heat. They stopped on the hot tarmac and peered hopefully in both directions, but there was nothing in sight.

Shalima slumped to the ground and put her head in her hands. "How d'you put up wiv this bloody heat all the time?" she asked.

Ben raised his eyebrows. Amie didn't bother to reply.

To the distressed travellers it seemed an age until the first shimmering in the distance indicated a car was approaching and heading north. By now, Amie would've accepted any lift, even if it was going south, back to Ruanga. She didn't think she could last much longer.

As it got closer they could make out it was an old pick-up truck with two goats in the back and two men in the front. Ben dashed into the road to flag them down.

The girls couldn't understand what was being said, but there was a lot of haggling and negotiating, which wasn't looking too hopeful until Ben pulled out a couple of American dollars courtesy of the late Edward Simmonds. All of a sudden their attitudes changed and the three of them scrambled up to join the goats in the back.

The goats weren't happy to be squashed in with the humans and were at great pains to show it. After only a couple of miles Amie reckoned they'd have been better off on foot, after receiving a couple of head butts in the ribs. Then one of the bad tempered goats gave her a hefty kick in the stomach.

Much to their relief, the driver stopped at one of the rare roadside fuel stops that also had a small spaza or tuck shop, and they were able to buy more bottled water and packets of crisps and biscuits, once again courtesy of Edward's stash.

Shalima eyed the sandwiches and hamburgers on sale, but Amie warned her it was much safer to buy pre-packed food. There was always the risk of cholera and they didn't need any more problems. Shalima glared at her, and unseen by either Amie or Ben, purchased a sandwich and gobbled it down secretly in the shade behind the building.

"Where do we go when we get to Apatu, Ben?" Amie asked him under her breath when they were back on the road.

For a few moments he didn't reply and she wondered if he'd heard her, the wind was whistling around them in the back of the truck.

"I still have friends in Apatu."

"Yes, of course." Amie hadn't been thinking. Ben was going home, but that wasn't true for her or Shalima. Was there a British representative in the city? And even if there was, she doubted Shalima would voluntarily walk inside the embassy, knowing they were planning to send her back to her parents. Amie could only guess what might happen to her. An arranged marriage, whisked back to her father's country to be united with some old man she didn't know. What future did Shalima have? Even though there was little love lost between them, Amie couldn't help feeling sorry for her. But there was nothing Amie could do to change things for either of them.

Soon familiar suburbs came into view, sprawling shanty towns with informal houses made of any materials their owners could find. Some were built of old packing cases, while others had stone walls, the rough shapes stuck together with mud. Most had corrugated metal roofs, held in place by old truck tyres and Amie could see women sweeping the areas around them with the handmade brooms that were on sale on every street corner. She remembered the brushes seldom lasted longer than a month before falling apart.

While the women kept the areas close to the houses spotless, the same could not be said of the outer areas where rubbish was piled high. She watched in dismay as young children played among the detritus, throwing handfuls of discarded waste at each other.

Closer to town, small bungalows lined the road on either side, and as they drove into the centre of town Amie recognized the main streets, that were looking a lot more dilapidated since her last visit. The presidential palace was about the only monument that looked smart and bullet holes were still visible in the walls of the Grand Hotel.

The building that had once housed the British Embassy was still in ruins, except it looked as if several squatters had moved in and lit fires on the balconies. The once-pretty gardens were now wildly overgrown.

Suddenly the truck veered to the left and pulled up sharply at the edge of the meat market.

"I've always loved animals, and I thought goats were

263

cute and cuddly, but I'm never travelling with one again," Amie hissed at the nearest goat. It gave her a filthy look back, bleated at her, and jumped around even more, hooves digging painfully into her legs as it fought against being offloaded by the driver.

Stiffly, the three passengers struggled to climb over the tailgate, which didn't appear to drop down and, nodding to the driver, they walked away.

"Ben, I can't see another white face around here," Amie said. "In fact I've not seen one white face since we drove into town. And the driver and his friend were giving us some very suspicious looks."

"Yes. We must cover you both," Ben answered. "Stay here behind this wall and I'll see what I can do."

Amie and Shalima hunkered down and tried to look as inconspicuous as possible. A few pedestrians gave them curious stares but no one bothered them as they hunched forwards pretending to be invisible.

It seemed an age until Ben returned, carrying two of the dreaded burqas. They groaned.

"I know," said Ben, "it must be hot wearing these, but it is the best way to hide you." He'd also thought to purchase a tin of brown shoe polish to rub over the backs of their hands and round their eyes. These burqas covered their faces and only left a small slit for their eyes, and even that space was covered with a dark, see-through veil of material.

"They should teach their bloody sons to keep their trousers zipped up," hissed Amie and giggled at the thought. When she was ready, she was sure no one would give her a second glance or believe she came from Caucasian stock.

"We need to find somewhere with a power source where we won't be disturbed," Amie said. "I think we need to find out more about the stuff on this laptop." Despite the long trip into town they had protected the laptop from harm. "And we must have a serious talk about what we're going to do."

Ben nodded. "A hotel room would be the best. Maybe the Grand is the only place with good wifi."

Amie groaned. Her memories of staying in the Grand Hotel when she had first arrived in Togodo, were not among her best, but she could understand Ben's suggestion.

"Yeah," agreed Shalima. "Let's go live it up on British government money and try out a bit of luxury for a change. We deserve it."

Amie sighed, not that Shalima would be aware of it from under the black clothing. She wasn't sure how much longer she could put up with the girl, she was just too much.

It wasn't very far to walk to the Grand Hotel, and the women hung back while Ben approached the reception desk and booked a room.

"How many rooms?" asked Amie as they all crowded into the one and only tiny lift, along with the blankets and the two small cases.

"One. For me and my harem," replied Ben with a rare burst of humour. "They expect me to share."

Amie could see the sense in that, but she wondered what was going to happen at bedtime. When they walked into the room, she was relieved to see one large double bed and a single. At least that solves one problem she thought.

Ben had also ordered food and drink to be sent to the

room, but the first thing Shalima did was to raid the bar fridge and pour herself a stiff drink.

"You'll need to keep sober if we're going to work Shalima," Amie told her sharply. "This isn't a holiday. We're in a mess and I haven't the faintest idea how we're going to get out of it."

Shalima flung herself on the bed and pulled a face. She ripped off the burqa. "Stop going on. It's all one big adventure. Chill out will you?"

It took several attempts to get the laptop connected to the Internet. It was very reluctant to accept the password handed over by the hotel, but finally they were online and almost immediately more emails dropped into Edward's inbox.

"Let's start with these," Amie said.

Once again, Shalima insisted Amie worked on the laptop while she sat ready with a pen and paper.

"Go back a few days, from when we arrived in Atari at the Mathesons," suggested Ben, "it will give us the story from the beginning."

"Good idea," agreed Amie. "How many days ago was it, and what's today's date?"

"Why don't you look on the laptop stupid, it's at the bottom ain't it?"

Amie sighed, why did the wretched girl always make her feel like an idiot? She scrolled down the list of emails, at least the dates weren't in code, and they began the laborious task of translating the messages. The teenager flipped backwards and forwards between the pages of the book, and laboriously wrote down the words in order.

The food and drinks arrived, and they continued to log down the transcription of each coded email word by word. By the time the sun set, they'd got the whole picture.

17 STIR CRAZY

Amie looked exhausted as she called out the last group of numbers from the screen and Shalima checked out the word.

"So, what've we got?"

Shalima squinted at the paper and replied. "Right. Edward was to hire a plane, check out the camp with the three of us and map the co-ordinates. Then fly on to Apatu and put me and yerself on a plane for London. Huh, fat chance," Shalima guffawed. "Then he was to return to Atari and complete the interrogation of Hussein, by whatever means possible. Torture I guess. He deserved it."

"I can't help feeling sorry for him," said Amie. "He was looking to us to protect him, as if he hadn't suffered enough already."

"No Amie," Ben warned. "We got to like him, but he is a fanatic and he helped to burn villages and steal women and children."

Amie nodded. She understood what Ben was saying, but when you grew fond of someone, it was hard not to worry about him falling into the wrong hands. They had no idea why Hussein was there, what his story was, how he'd come to be recruited and taken to Africa. He didn't behave like a fanatic who wanted to hurt others. He'd seemed a gentle sort of person. But there was nothing they could do to help him now.

"Do they mention Mrs Motswezi and Angelina?" Amie wanted to know.

"Only once and that was an order for them to be returned to Togodo, so they'll probably end up here like us," Shalima read from the transcript.

"Let's look at the paper files," said Ben, taking them out of the computer case. "They might tell us more."

"Give me a break," Shalima insisted, "I'm having a shower first and more food before we start again."

It was a sensible suggestion. They'd had a tough few days, a plane crash, an uncomfortable ride into town, head butts from goats and they'd been staring at the laptop screen non-stop since they'd arrived at the hotel.

Although they were anxious to find out what was in the files, they were too tired to do anything after they'd had a late supper and they crashed into bed. Whatever they might learn, could wait until tomorrow.

Ben was the first to wake the following day, and by the time Amie had opened her eyes he was already sitting at the table surrounded by papers.

"How did you sleep?" she asked rubbing her eyes.

"I thought I would sleep very well," Ben replied. "But I woke up many times. The bed was too soft."

"I went out like a light," Amie smiled, "though I think I kicked Shalima a few times. She was determined to take over the whole bed."

"No I weren't!" Shalima stretched and sat up.

"What have you got there?"

"The paper files that were tucked in the back pocket of the laptop case," replied Ben.

"Found out anything new?"

"There's information about their first 'talks', as they call them, with Hussein."

"So the same code works?" Amie was surprised.

"No, these reports are written by hand," Ben continued. "It says they were hoping to take the two captives, Jonathon and Charles, to Libya, which was also in that email yesterday, and either use them to exhort money or ..." Ben hesitated; Amie was not going to like this.

"Or what?"

"... or publicly execute them as a warning and a reprisal," he paused. "Is that the right word?"

Amie shoulders slumped. "Yes, it probably is reprisal. It means to get your own back." She rubbed the back of her neck. She'd been trying so hard not to worry about Jonathon.

Ben read on. "... in reprisal for past aggressions and a warning to the western powers not to interfere with IS activities."

"Fat chance, Britain and America will stand by and do nuffin'!" Shalima exploded. "Wha'd they think? That everyone will ignore them lopping off heads and sit and just watch them kids being kidnapped and used to keep those dirty old men happy?"

Amie was tempted to remind the feisty teenager that until very recently she'd been one of them - party to the executions and the kidnapping. She was still wasn't sure Shalima had had a complete change of heart. Could they trust her, even now? She imagined Shalima hadn't measured up in some way. Instead of being a glorious freedom fighter, lobbing grenades and shooting at infidels in Syria, she'd ended up as a prostitute in a desert camp way out in the wilds of Africa. They'd yet to hear the full story from Shalima.

"So, they're going to take Jonathon and Charles to Libya? Are you sure Hussein told them that?"

Ben looked down at the notes and nodded. "Yes, to a town called Benghazi. IS have a camp there."

"So, we go rescue them," stated Shalima as she made for the bathroom.

"Don't be so ridiculous," snapped Amie. "How are we supposed to do that? Walk in and ask them to release those nice white men? I told you yesterday what a stupid idea that was," her voice dripped with sarcasm.

"Just sayin'," Shalima spat back over her shoulder. "If it was my bloke, I'd go get him. But if yer a wimp, then okay." She slammed the bathroom door behind her.

Amie seethed. How dare she! How dare that brat tell her she didn't care for her husband! How dare she infer she was spineless!

Ben wisely went back to checking out the paper files. "They have a file for you and one for Shalima," he said.

Amie wrapped the blanket round her shoulders and scooted off the bed. "What does it say?" She looked over his shoulder at the notes.

"Not much. She does come from Birmingham and she does have a Pakistani father, an English mother and a few brothers and sisters. It says she was always in trouble at school and was suspended more than once." Ben raised his eyebrows.

"That means she wasn't allowed to go to school for a while because of her bad behaviour," said Amie, to his unspoken question. She knew it rarely happened in African schools, where education was highly valued and the children saw it as a way out of poverty and a path to a better future. They would walk miles, barefoot if necessary, to attend school, and those who might have been disruptive simply didn't go and no one would chase them up. Many children wouldn't even be allowed to attend school as they were often needed to look after younger siblings, or care for the animals and work on the land. She thought Ben looked a little shocked at Shalima's behaviour, but he would be too polite to mention it.

Amie flipped through Shalima's file and at the back there was a photocopy of a newspaper piece showing her parents making a plea on television for their daughter's safe return. She was so engrossed she didn't hear Shalima come out of the bathroom, walk over the carpet, and peer over her shoulder.

"They would've made a fuss," she said reading the headlines. "Can see it now, famous at last! Huh! See, I can be a national celebrity too, as well as yer been," and she dug Amie in the ribs.

"Shalima, it says your mother cries herself to sleep every night," Amie pointed to the lines of newsprint.

"I ain't fallin' for that. You don't know what it's like, so don't you tell me how to feel," Shalima was on the defensive. She picked up another file. "Is this the one about you? Does it say yer a little heroine 'cos you were brave and clever and managed to survive and had a programme on the effing telly about you? The great celebrity?" She flounced off and was about to leave the room, when Ben stopped her.

"No!" he cried. "Wait. You cannot go out like that!"

Shalima's shoulders drooped, and she returned to the bed.

Amie took a turn in the bathroom to allow Shalima time to cool off. She had such mixed emotions about her. On the one hand the Muslim girl had saved her life, and for that she was grateful. But it didn't necessarily follow she had to like her, or get on with her, Amie reasoned to herself as she turned on the shower. She'd never known anyone quite like Shalima before. She knew England was a class-ridden society, but it had never really affected her. All the pupils at her school came from similar backgrounds and even when she went to college, she mixed with other teenagers who had ambition and wanted to get on. They spoke normally, didn't use swear words in every other sentence and were as far away from the rougher areas of the major cities as it was possible to be. Sure there were programmes on the television that interviewed those on welfare handouts; free money from the government. She'd seen single mothers boasting about how much they raked in each week, while several young children hung round their legs, patting their Mummies bulbous tummies; more babies on the way. While she shampooed her hair, Amie acknowledged she'd had a very sheltered upbringing, which hadn't provided her with the survival skills she needed in Africa, and possibly not in some areas of England either.

By the time Amie rejoined the others Shalima was busy decoding more documents and Ben was heading out.

"Ben's gonna get some stuff for me," Shalima informed her. "If there's anyfink else what you need, yer better tell him now."

From the tone of her voice, Shalima was speaking about Ben as if he was the hired help and it took a lot of self-control not to retaliate. They needed each other, and it would only make things worse if they started a fight. She threw an apologetic look in Ben's direction hoping he'd understand how badly she felt.

"Ben, if I write a short list would you get a few toiletries for me please?" Amie asked him gently.

"Yes of course. You could come, but …"

"No, no. It'd be silly to take risks," Amie agreed. "There isn't a white face anywhere on the streets. I doubt the government is still after me but I really don't want us to take any more chances than we have to." She squeezed his hand.

"By the way, how much money did Edward have?" Somehow, it felt less criminal spending stolen money today, than it did yesterday.

"Several thousand dollars," Ben replied.

"What! What on earth would he need all that cash for?" Amie was amazed.

"So he wouldn't leave a trail stupid," Shalima answered before Ben had a chance to.

Ben took the list from Amie's hand and slipped out of the door before any more could be said.

"Do you want any help with the decoding?" Amie asked.

"No, I'm fine," Shalima replied abruptly.

Did Amie imagine it, or had Shalima's hand covered

the papers as if to protect them? Well, she couldn't blame her. It was something to do while they were holed up in this small hotel room with nothing else to occupy them.

Amie paced up and down. She was on edge, confined and wishing she'd gone with Ben after all, even swathed in that suffocating burqa. She was fretting about Jonathon. How must he be feeling? How scared was he? Where was he? What would life be like without him? Amie looked mentally into the future. She'd be alone. They'd never even had a baby together.

Her thoughts turned to Angelina. It was too cruel. No sooner had she found the child, against all odds, she'd lost her again. She'd had such plans for the poor little waif who had no mother, no father and no family she knew about. She'd had such a sad life. Amie had great plans for her. She wanted to give her the best education, help her through college; she could be a doctor, or go into business, or even politics. Amie wanted to give her the whole world. The only good thing was at least Nomsa Motswezi was caring for her. But what would Angelina think now? Amie had left that day, supposedly for a few hours and she hadn't returned. She had now done this twice. Angelina would have little reason to ever trust her again.

She paced to and fro and turned on the television, then turned it off because the picture was snowy and all she could find was a football game. She got an angry glare from her roommate, so she rummaged in the other small bag looking for something in Edward's luggage to interest her. But there was nothing. She would've had another look at the computer, but Shalima still had her nose stuck in it.

She thought briefly about insisting she help Shalima with the documents again, but decided against it. She flopped onto the bed and counted the cracks in the ceiling. She must have dozed off, because she was jolted awake by Shalima's excited shriek.

"Bingo! Effing marvelous!!!"

"What is?" Amie bolted upright.

"New emails in, sent from Atari to London."

"Wait a minute," said Amie sliding off the bed. "Is it likely they'd be sending him important messages if they haven't heard from him for several days? The embassy in Atari must have informed them the plane went down?"

For a moment Shalima looked nonplussed and squinted again at the screen.

"Yer right, it ain't for him, it's just a CC to him. My guess is that the person who copied it to him don't know yet as what he's snuffed it yet, or his laptop is missin'."

Amie cringed, "So, what is the marvelous news?"

"Little Hussein has been singing his heart out and they've intercepted messages from Syria to some of the camps in Ruanga and it gives their route. So we know exactly where they're going! Brilliant!!"

"What? Who are going? Where to?" Shalima wasn't making much sense. Amie leapt off the bed and went to stand beside Shalima.

"The lot what took yer hubby and the other one, Charles was it?" Amie nodded.

Shalima consulted her notes. "Well, they're making for Libya, but only by road to start with. They were to stop off at another camp for a few days and now they say they'll be travelling north through Togodo in four days' time. They'll be stopping off to get more supplies which they've asked to be airdropped for them and here, these are the co-ordinates for the drop. Brilliant eh!" Shalima dug Amie heavily in the ribs. "We know exactly where they're gonna be in a couple of days and we can intercept them and be waiting and you can get yer man back. Cool eh!"

It was all a bit much for Amie to take in. They were now actually ahead of the party that was transporting the guys? And now she knew precisely where they'd be? It was too good to be true, or maybe, just maybe, they'd had their first real stroke of luck.

Ben returned a couple of hours later, carrying bags with all the bits and pieces they'd asked for, to find the girls eager to share their news.

"Ben," Amie said hesitantly, "I don't expect you to come with us. This isn't your fight and there's no need for you to put yourself in danger."

"No, I want to help Amie," he replied. "We have got this far, I want to help you set Jonathon free. I feel bad you had so much …" he searched for the right word. "… so much pain from my people, so I want to do what is right now."

"Course he's gotta come," Shalima bellowed. "How we gonna walk around in these effing things," she pointed to the burqas on the chair, "wiv'out a male escort eh? Tell me that."

"I'm not going to use Ben simply to make life easier, especially when it'll put him in danger." Amie thought

Shalima was being particularly selfish.

"Well, don't come cryin' to me when you get yerself locked up again," Shalima said huffily. "Think you can do everything on yer own don't you?"

"Well, no, but ..."

"Accept the man's offer, he made it. Be gracious for once." Shalima packed away the papers and files, tucking them back into the carry cases. She powered down the laptop and put it back in its bag. "Time for a walk I think, don't you?" she suggested brightly. "Gonna go mad if I'm stuck in here much longer."

At that moment there was a loud banging on the door. Everyone stopped what they were doing and held their breath. Ben pointed at the bathroom door.

They didn't need to be told twice and grabbing the burqas, they collided in their frantic attempts to squeeze into the tiny en suite.

When Ben answered the door, all they could hear were murmured voices. It sounded as if Ben was thanking someone profusely. He tapped on the bathroom door looking serious.

"That was an old friend," he said, "he works here at the hotel. He came to tell me the police are doing a check on the rooms and asking the guests questions. We need to go. Fast!"

"But how? Which way?" gasped Amie struggling into the hated burqa.

"We cannot use the lift," Ben replied, "but I saw stairs at the end of the corridor."

"Let's go," Shalima was already packed and waiting.

"No time to hang around. Come on!"

Why does she always state the obvious? Thought Amie, collecting the other case and the shopping bags. She waited behind Ben as he opened the door to the corridor and peeped outside. There was no one in sight, so they followed him along the carpeted hallway and through a door marked 'stairs'.

Ben paused again to look over the railings to check the coast was clear, then beckoned for them to follow. They raced down the three flights as quickly and quietly as they could. When they reached the bottom, the door in front of them gave no indication where it would lead. Ben pushed it open a crack and peered through. There was another corridor on the other side, with several rooms going off in both directions, but for the moment there was no one in sight. One by one they slipped through and turned right.

They heard voices from one of the rooms, and were forced to duck through an open door into what appeared to be the laundry room. The voices got louder.

"Please don't come in here," Amie whispered. "Walk past."

The laundry room was large, with floor-to-ceiling shelves piled high with sheets, blankets, pillows and towels. They backed further in as two women, dressed in hotel uniforms, stopped in the doorway.

It sounded like they were never going to stop talking; they chattered on and on. The three of them crouched down and slid under the lowest shelf in the farthest corner. If the hotel employees turned round, they'd be sure to see them. The burqas would stand out like black squares on a chess board.

There was a shout from outside, and both women rushed away. Without saying a word, Ben, Amie and Shalima raced to the door. For now, the corridor was empty and the girls followed Ben, twisting and turning round corners and baggage trolleys as he tried to find his way out. They went past the kitchens and a supply room, and another room piled high with bottles, until at the end of the last corridor there was a door that led onto a back street.

It wasn't until they'd pushed it open and rushed through that Amie realized it was the kind of door that usually triggered an alarm, but like many things in African countries, it didn't work. They were out, free and clear.

They walked briskly down the narrow alley, avoiding the piles of rotting rubbish, and stepping over mud-filled drains. Everywhere she looked, it was filthy and Amie didn't want any of it getting on her clothes. She had no idea when she'd get an opportunity to wash them. She held her burqa off the ground with one hand while the other held the case and the shopping. When she looked down, she realized her white hands were showing and beside her, Shalima's hands were too light-skinned for an African. For once Amie was glad of her boots and her long trousers that were tucked into her thick socks which covered her legs and ankles. But after several showers, all the brown boot polish had washed off her hands and arms, and she didn't know if the replacement tin she'd asked Ben to buy for her, was in any of the bags they were carrying.

It was hot, itchy and suffocating under the full burqa and Amie wasn't sure how much further she could walk so quickly. Her breathing became short and tight, her chest felt as if a boa constrictor was playing hugging games, and her shoulders and legs ached. She didn't ask where they were going, or how far it was, but blindly followed Ben as he strode in front.

No one seemed to pay them any attention, but Amie felt everyone was looking at her, and imaginary eyes were piercing into her back as she doggedly followed her Togodian friend through the alleyways.

Eventually, they entered a park that had once been exquisite, full of shady trees, neat lawns and pretty flowerbeds. Now it was neglected and overgrown. No one had tended it since the civil war had broken out, and it was practically deserted. It was the perfect place to rest for a while and decide what to do next.

They slumped onto a stone bench, which was home to an ivy plant, and took several deep breaths.

"So, what now?" Shalima was the first to recover.

Ben looked at his watch. "It is too late to leave Apatu today, and if you have those co-ordinates, I will need to purchase a GPS, or we will never find the drop zone."

"Brilliant idea Ben," Amie said. "But how safe is it to sleep here in the park?"

"Not safe at all," Ben told her. "Come dusk all the prostitutes, pimps, drug sellers and addicts will arrive."

"So where can we go?"

"I have friends in a nearby township I can trust," Ben replied. "They will hide us for one night, two at the most, but I would not ask them to do it for longer. Someone would talk and we would all be in trouble. I cannot do that to my friends."

"No, I understand," murmured Amie.

"If you both wait here, I think there is a shop nearby where they might sell a GPS. I will be quick." Ben walked briskly out of the park.

Amie felt panicky again. Was she getting paranoid? She was frightened and scared Ben wouldn't come back. All kinds of scenarios tumbled through her mind. What if the police found them here now? What if they arrested her and put her back in jail? What if they couldn't find Jonathon and they wandered out into the bush and got lost and died from thirst and hunger? She slapped herself on the wrists. My over-active imagination again, she told herself sharply. At least this time you're not alone and you know so much more about living off the land. Pull yourself together Amie and focus on what's important. It might be easier to walk away and not try to rescue Jonathon, but could you ever live with yourself again if you didn't try? How could you not try and help him? Better to die trying than not to try at all.

She was amazed at how laid-back Shalima looked, as if she didn't have a care in the world. How did she do it? Amie wondered. Doesn't she imagine the dangers, or does she simply take one day at a time? More likely one hour at a time.

Rifling through the cases they discovered the tin of polish, but it was a very small tin and it didn't go very far. The results were less than convincing, it left streaks over their hands and wrists. No one will notice, Amie thought hopefully. Many people had skin with strange colourations and markings.

Ben was gone for a long time, and as the sun sank

behind the buildings, they began to worry.

"How long should we wait for him?" Shalima asked.

"I don't know, but when it begins to get dark, we should leave," Amie said. "And remember twilight doesn't last very long in Africa, one moment it's daylight and the next it's dark. I don't have a watch any more, but let's say when the sun starts to go behind the last tower over there, we move." To her surprise, for once, Shalima didn't argue.

Nervously they watched the sun sink lower and lower and still Ben didn't come. A few people wandered into the park, types that made Amie feel very nervous. She checked around her to see if there was anything she could use as a weapon, but nothing seemed obvious. She wished now she'd brought the gun Jonathon had given her, but it was still back at the Mathesons. She'd put it in a drawer in the bedroom before she'd changed her clothes, and afterwards there seemed little point in carrying it around, even when they went to overfly the camp. She could kick herself for not bringing it, though as she'd never even fired it, it was probably worse than useless, except as an empty threat.

At last Shalima got to her feet. "Well, I ain't waitin' around here any longer," she pronounced firmly. "I vote we leave now. We can get our own GPS and do wiv'out Ben."

Amie rose, discomforted by the people already staring at them. She'd noticed an empty syringe and some used condoms close to the bench and wondered who'd been persuaded to use the prophylactics. The ladies of the night might try to insist, but most African men weren't keen at all. It made the spread of AIDS more difficult to control.

She clutched the case and bag, and keeping her hands

out of sight as much as possible, followed Shalima to the park entrance. Even the once-imposing stone pillars were crumbling and the iron gates hung at crazy angles on either side, never to close again.

They paused, not sure where to go or what to do.

18 THE WITCH DOCTOR

They had just reached the pavement outside the park and were considering which way to turn, when Ben appeared out of the gloom.

Amie could have hugged him she was so pleased to see him.

"Come, I have everything. We can get a taxi near here, keep your hands hidden and say nothing."

Amie was familiar with the taxis, which buzzed like angry bees around Apatu and most African cities. Nearly all of them were in a poor state of repair, decorated with bumps, scratches, dents and peeling paint. Many were also decorated with names scrawled in bright colours, 'Road Monster', 'Speed Machine', 'Ace Tours', 'I'm the Best!' and other similar proclamations. A few were obviously the pride and joy of their owners, but most drivers were employed by one of the big bosses who owned a lot of these minibus taxis, and so were none too careful how they drove them. Amie thought not many would ever pass a roadworthiness test in England.

The girls followed closely behind Ben along the dark road. Very few of the street lights were working even this close to the middle of town. A vehicle came hurtling towards them, and Ben put out his arm and waved it up, down and round in circles and it drew to a screeching halt beside the kerb. Someone slid the door open and they squeezed in, wriggling to perch as best they could on seats already overflowing with men, women, a basket containing two chickens, plastic bags of groceries, babies sitting on laps, and even a rather mangy dog that stared up at them soulfully from among all the feet.

Ben handed money to the man in the front passenger seat, but not one word was exchanged. Amie wondered how the driver would know where they wanted to get off. The taxi stopped several times, suddenly and without warning. Each time the door opened and a few people got out, by Amie's reckoning, even more got in, until it was almost impossible to breathe. At one point she felt her burqa being pulled sharply to one side and she just grabbed it in time to stop it strangling her.

It was completely dark by now, and Ben nudged her to indicate they'd be getting off soon. Once again, they came to an abrupt halt. Ben scrambled out first and quickly took the bags so the girls could negotiate the steps without falling flat on their faces. As soon as they were on the pavement, the taxi roared off, even before the door had closed.

"Well, that was an effing awful ride," Shalima announced.

"Oh shut up!" Amie was fed up with being polite and from under all the black cloth Shalima wouldn't be aware of the dirty looks. "It was a hell of a lot better than walking. Thank you, Ben."

"It is not too far to go now," said Ben as they set off again.

"Tell me," Amie said, "How did you know that taxi was going in this direction?"

"From the way the driver's mate moved his arm out of the window." Ben held one arm up to demonstrate the particular waving patterns for the different destinations around Apatu.

"Clever," said Amie. "And you knew how much it would cost? And where the stops are?"

"Most trips are the same price around the city. It's only when you go out into the country the prices are higher. There are no official stopping points, only the taxi rank. They stop if they see people waiting and they stop where people want to get off."

Similar to taxis in London, Amie thought but also not quite the same. She couldn't help but grin at the thought of her family trying to cram into a beaten up old vehicle already jammed side to side with people and livestock.

"It would be wise not to say too much to my friends," Ben warned them. "I have told them I want to bring a couple of people to stay for one night, no more than two. They will be surprised to see you and may ask lots of questions and …"

"We'll say as little as possible."

"Yeah, well I hope they ain't gonna be too nosey," Shalima chimed in.

Amie sighed. If she'd been Ben she'd have simply refused to help her. Originally Shalima had been amazing during the escape from the camp, though come to think of it, Amie had set her free first hadn't she? Yet she wasn't the slightest bit grateful and did nothing but grumble. She'd be glad when this was all over. She hoped they'd pack the brat back to Birmingham and into the tender loving care of her parents. They could deal with her.

The area Ben had taken them to wasn't a suburb populated with neat rows of bungalows but something resembling an informal housing area or squatter camp. As they made their way down the narrow dirt road, there were shacks on either side built of wood, packing case materials, mud, stones and anything to hand that could be used to build a shelter. The usual tin roofs, held in place with either boulders or old tyres, were everywhere.

They met several pedestrians who nodded politely to Ben, but gaped at the burqa-clad women trailing in his wake. Amie thought this might be because the Muslim community didn't live in this area. Even in countries that never had apartheid, people would still live near others of a similar culture and background.

Despite being a mishmash of bits and pieces, each shack was surrounded by a patch of bare ground, many of them fenced with chicken wire to designate the garden. There were a few chickens, several half-starved dogs running loose and small children playing in the street.

After zigzagging through narrow gaps between the rows of dwellings, Ben stopped by one that looked marginally smarter than the others; it even had a gate to the garden. The front door flew open before he had time to knock and a smartly-dressed young man hurried them inside. His initial look of shock was replaced by a warm smile as he remembered his manners, and he ushered them into the living room and pointed to the sofa.

Ben introduced their host as Chibale, which he told them meant kinship.

"You related?" Shalima really couldn't keep her mouth shut.

"Most Africans are related." Chibale smiled. "Members of the same tribe are but in the tribe we have totem groups. Ben is also of the elephant totem like me. So that makes us brothers."

"Crystal clear," Shalima mumbled.

While the outside of the house looked uninhabitable, inside it was like a small palace. Amie gazed about her in wonder. She sank onto the black leather sofa, and rested against the fluorescent pink, fluffy heart-shaped cushions. There was a bright orange carpet on the concrete floor, two coffee tables next to the armchairs that matched the sofa, and on the other side of the room, a huge flat screen TV and video recorder sat beside what she thought were two laptops.

Meanwhile their host had rushed off to get them some tea, chattering in Togodian to Ben, and they heard the clink of china from the kitchen.

"Bloody hell," muttered Shalima taking in her surroundings. "It ain't nothing like the outside."

When they came back into the lounge with the tea, Ben politely talked to Chibale in English, so the girls could understand them, but every now and again they would add several phrases in Togodian that Amie sensed upset Shalima. She was further upset when she lifted her burqa slightly to drink her tea and nearly choked on it. Amie grinned. She hadn't warned the girl that tea meant sugar with a little tea added. It was an acquired taste and took some getting used to, but you never got to put your own sugar in, it was done for you, usually four to five heaped teaspoons per cup.

After the tea and biscuits, Chibale showed the girls into a bedroom off the lounge and indicated the large double bed. Once again Amie and Shalima were about to get up close and personal.

"Where's the bog?" Shalima hissed.

"The bathroom? I expect they have a long drop of sorts out in the yard or share one with a few other neighbours." Amie chuckled.

"So all this effing luxury and no indoor bathroom? Great!" Shalima snapped and went to find out. Sure enough when she returned, she pointed Amie in the right direction, and told her how filthy it was. It smelled beyond belief and she was sure she'd seen a rat in there.

After a quick trip outside it was wonderful to get rid of the burqa and collapse on the bed. Amie didn't care where she was, it had been another fraught day and nothing was going to keep her awake. She fell asleep in the middle of wondering what the penalty was for leaving your hotel room without paying the bill. Would the police be after them for that too? It felt as if everyone in the world was chasing her for one reason or another. For the moment though, she felt safe.

Amie had no idea how long she slept, but when she woke and got up, there was no one in the house except for Shalima who was still fast asleep. She dressed and went outside to use the long drop, not forgetting to keep herself well covered from prying eyes. When she returned, Shalima was still in bed, so she drifted into the kitchen and wondered if she could make herself a cup of tea or coffee. There was no note to say where anyone was, but she was reluctant to help herself.

A few moments later Shalima appeared and she had no such qualms. "Tea or coffee?" she asked, holding the kettle in one hand and looking around for a sink.

"I think the tap's out in the yard," Amie told her.

"Shucks, all this effing luxury in here and they put all the basics outside. Huh, think they'd get their bleedin' priorities right wouldn't you?" she sniffed. "Here," thrusting the kettle at Amie, "you go get the water while I use that stinking outhouse."

Amie sighed as she peeped out the front door. All seemed quiet as she rushed outside into the road to the communal tap. Someone had left it running full on, and she remembered the advertisements she'd seen on the television in England screaming for donations to provide fresh water for sick babies in Africa. They were a total waste of money. She wondered what the donors would say if they could see so much precious potable water being wasted. Not so likely to dig deeply into their pockets she suspected.

While the kettle was filling, she glanced around. There were few people about, a couple of half-naked babies playing further up the pathway and the odd chicken pecking in the dirt. A couple of houses away a very skinny goat was tied to a post with a bit of string, and two township dogs of indeterminate breed were sniffing each other. Amie couldn't decide if they were about to mate or fight.

The water spilled over her hand from the full kettle, but when she went to turn the tap off she saw someone had wired it full on and the water continued to pour out all over the ground. A wave of anger ran through her. Water was one of Africa's most precious resources and here they were deliberately wasting it.

Back in the house, Shalima was lounging on the sofa reading a magazine. "Took you long enough," she remarked waving as if she expected Amie to make her a cup of tea.

Amie bit her tongue. Once she'd found matches to light the single gas ring that stood on the kitchen cabinet, she checked out the cupboards, but there was no food in any of them. The gas fridge was almost empty; its sole contents were two bottles of beer and a piece of stale cheese. She did find tea bags and sugar in a couple of canisters on the side and shared one bag between two none-too-clean mugs hanging off hooks on the wall. She failed to find any milk.

By the time Amie and Shalima had finished their milk-less tea, Ben arrived with groceries and a big smile on his face. "I have brought food," he said, "and, I have arranged transport for us as well."

"So we don't have to tramp on foot to the drop zone?" Shalima smiled for the first time that day.

"We will travel in style. Well, not too much style, but it does have aircon of sorts," Ben replied.

The girls pounced on the bags. It felt like weeks since they'd had their last meal in the hotel, and they welcomed the fresh fruit and crackers with jam that Ben had brought.

"Are we safe here, Ben?" asked Amie.

"Not for too long. Chibale has already been questioned

about his visitors. People are always curious about newcomers, and want to know why there are Muslim women in the house."

Amie had forgotten how jealous and suspicious people could be. "Is this a Kawa area?"

"Most people are Kawa in this township," Ben waved his arm to indicate the surrounding houses. "For now, we are quiet, but the M'untu do not trust us. They do not want to lose their new power."

"Will the Kawa fight to get back into government and control Togodo again?"

Ben peered at her. "Of course. We are the majority tribe. The biggest, the bravest and the most intelligent. We will wait, and when the time is right, we will take back what is ours."

Amie sighed. This was the way in Africa, one tribe against another, one war after another, there was no way opposing tribes could live in peace. She daren't think of all the killing, shooting and destruction that was inevitable. No one could predict when it was going to happen. No wonder people lived only from day-to-day. How could you plan for the future when you didn't know when everything was going to erupt again?

Even Ben appeared eager for the war to restart. Despite the fact he was an educated young man with certificates from college, he still wanted to fight, rather than sit and discuss. There was no such thing as a graceful acceptance of defeat.

A loud banging on the front door startled them. Ben peeped though the lace curtains and gasped. "It is Ouma

Adede!" he exclaimed. "I must let her in."

"Who the eff is he or she? Tell them to go away." Shalima ordered, but Ben ignored her and opened the door.

Shalima had never seen a witch doctor or sangoma before. She gawped and her mouth dropped open. Amie thought she looked quite scared.

Ben bowed deferentially to the elderly, wizened lady who stood just inside the door. Her head was adorned with a variety of objects, bones, chicken bladders and dozens of beads in long strings that cascaded down her shoulders. She wore a long flowing, brightly-coloured skirt with a rather grubby white t-shirt advertising a local beer. Her bare arms and ankles were encircled with more beads and Coca Cola bottle tops strung together, that rattled and jingled when she moved. Around her neck she wore a scarf made of some animal skin and in her hand she carried a small bag made of uncured leather.

"We are honoured by your visit," Ben murmured softly, bowing yet again. "May I introduce you ...?" But she interrupted him.

"I know who they are, and why they are here. You do not need to tell me my brother." She patted Ben on the head as if he was a pet dog. "The spirits have sent me. I have words for you from them. I am their messenger."

Nobody moved. Ben indicated the sofa but the witch doctor ignored him and settled herself on the carpet. From somewhere among her clothing she pulled out a small raffia mat and placed it in front of her. She pointed to Amie and motioned for her to sit on the other side of the mat.

Amie got up from the sofa, knelt down and gazed at the

old lady. When their eyes met, Amie felt a bolt or small shockwave run right through her body. A minor electrical shock was the best way she could describe it. She had the uneasy feeling this woman could see right into her soul and read her every thought.

"You are not afraid, my dear?" Ouma Adede's voice was soft and low.

"N-no, not really, but I ..." Amie didn't know what answer to give. She wasn't afraid, but she was worried what the seer might tell her.

"But you respect, I can tell that. You were not born here, you come from a land far away across the water, but you are now a child of Africa. Africa flows through your blood. Africa has become part of you."

From behind, Amie heard Shalima snort. The girl had obviously regained her equilibrium and was treating this as a travelling circus show.

Ouma Adede ignored the interruption and continued. "The spirits called to me to see you this morning, to talk to you and tell you that you must take great care. You will suffer a great loss. You will cry many tears. But you must be strong and you must be true."

Not sure of the protocol during an exchange like this, Amie blurted, "Who will die? Who will I lose?"

"Wait!" commanded Ouma Adede as she opened her bag and took out four small bowls filled with wax. She lit each of these in turn. Next she took out a small leather pouch, shook it vigorously and opening the drawstring she poured out the contents. There were a number of small bones, tiny pieces of dried herbs, bits of twisted metal, sea shells, several pieces of what looked like desiccated animal parts and, much to Amie's amusement, two dice and more metal bottle tops.

The witch doctor studied these for several moments, humming tunelessly. She swayed backwards and forwards lost in her trance. The air filled with smoke and the scent of the burning wax cast a surreal aura over the proceedings.

"It is not for me to tell you of the loss, but the spirits have a warning for you. Do not take what is not yours to take. The child belongs here in the country of her birth and she should die here."

"Oh God!" Amie thought in horror. She must mean Angelina. She's telling me not to take her out of Togodo. But she also wanted to know about Jonathon: was he still alive? Could this wise old woman tell her? Did she know?

"You will lose many. You will weep many tears for them, but their time is almost up and they cannot escape their fate. The spirits have decreed this." Ouma Adede clapped her hands which startled them all, shattering the peace in the room. She waved Amie away.

Amie stood up and sat back down on the sofa. Could she believe anything she'd heard? It was a bit vague and there were many ways to interpret the words. She gave herself a good talking to. She was a child of the West, born and educated in England where life was predictable. Buses ran along the streets, the corner shop opened late at night and youngsters queued to get into the cinemas and nightclubs. Sitting in the gloom in this township shack next to a witch doctor was surrealistic. It wasn't just another country away, it was another planet away.

Ouma Adede beckoned to Shalima. "Come," she commanded but Shalima shook her head, refusing to budge. The old lady stared at her. "You do not believe the spirits, but you cannot escape what they say about you."

Shalima remained huddled on the sofa, but Ouma Adede gathered her trinkets, replaced them in the bag, shook it violently and flung them out on the mat once more.

"You come from many children," she said, "with parents from different parts. You ran, telling no one. They grieve for you. You made them very unhappy." She gave Shalima a hard look but only received a defiant stare back. She continued. "Life will not be as you expect. You are not as beloved as you think. The young man will not love you for long. You will not share a passion as you hope."

"I've heard quite enough," Shalima said rudely and disappeared into the bedroom.

Ouma Adede packed away the small bones, bottle tops and other objects into her little bag. She turned and smiled at Ben. "You? I have told you before what the future is for you. The spirits still see the shining light all around you. But beware, beware of betrayal."

Ben nodded. "Thank you Ouma Adede." He slipped some money into her hand before she rose and walked to the door. She turned once more to address Amie. "Go well my child and may the Ancestors protect you. You have endured much and will endure more but take courage." She added a few more sentences but they were in Togodian and Amie didn't have a clue what she said.

After she'd gone Amie looked quizzically at Ben. "Did you ask her to come? Was it to know what was going to happen in the next few days?"

"No, she just knows things, no one understands why, but she is a wise old woman. I feel easier we go with her blessing."

"What was that last part, in your language?"

"She asked the Ancestors to watch over us and save us from harm."

Amie wasn't sure what to think of it all. Her time in Africa had taught her life followed a different set of rules and it was unwise to sneer at things that, for the moment, she didn't understand. Could she compare Ouma Adede with the quacks on the pier in Brighton who offered to tell your fortune for a couple of pounds? Who really believed the horoscopes in the daily newspapers? Was it caused by the atmosphere, the smoke from the candles that might have induced a slightly hypnotic effect, or even the elderly lady herself? Despite the tinkling bottle tops, she exuded more nobility than anyone Amie had ever met in her life. She tucked the thoughts away to ponder later. Right now there was still a lot of planning to do.

The rest of the morning was spent plotting a route to the drop off point at the co-ordinates Shalima had read on the emails. They made a list of the supplies they might need, and even discussed the possibility of trying to get passports. Shalima had remembered there were several blanks in Edward's case, and Ben admitted he knew of someone who could insert photographs and fill in the details. As far as they could see, when they examined them closely, the passports themselves appeared quite genuine. A lot would depend on the time it would take, and if they could get them done before they left the next day. Ben was in favour of leaving late that evening.

After taking photographs of the girls with the cell phone he'd bought earlier that morning, he left them to it while he went out to source the rest of the supplies and collect the car.

It was a long, boring afternoon with nothing much to do. The girls both agreed, surprisingly for once, it was safer to remain indoors and Amie settled down to read the rest of the magazines that were scattered around the lounge. She'd have been quite content if Shalima had stopped prowling around, swearing and cursing under her breath.

First the teenager tried the television, but both stations showed football games with commentary in Togodian. She flipped through one of the magazines that was printed in English, and tried a couple of the puzzles but soon gave that up.

Amie felt as if she was holed up with a caged tiger as her house mate, one who couldn't sit still for a moment. There was a cuckoo clock on the wall which made a continuous tick tock noise and on the hour a bird appeared and went 'craw, craw,' like no cuckoo Amie had ever heard.

"Why don't that effin' bird shut the eff up!" Shalima snarled, but Amie ignored the outburst. She wasn't about to get into a fight with Shalima. The girl was street smart and Amie was quite sure she'd come off worst against an opponent from Sparkhill.

"Shalima?"

"What?"

"Look, I know we're very different ..."

"Sure we is. Knew that the moment I first saw you. Yer the kind what believes all that tommy rot the old woman was harking on about. You'd believe anything. Just 'cos you was a big star on telly, you think yer the cat's whiskers right?"

Amie sighed. She'd never even seen the television series, and she certainly had no idea if anyone had even noticed it or written about it in the papers.

As if reading her thoughts Shalima continued, "Don't tell me you don't know the fuss it caused?"

"Well, no, I don't." The thought of going home to face another barrage of press and TV cameras stuck in her face was a nightmare. It actually closed that escape route for her.

"Oh yeah, quite the little heroine you was, even that survival guy said he was impressed wiv' what yer done, all alone in the wild African bush! Yeah, right!" and Shalima sniggered.

Amie gave it one last try. "I know nothing about that, but if we're going out there tonight to try this rescue, and we want to live through it, why can't we just try and get along? Most probably we're not going to be stuck with each other much longer whatever happens, and we need to work as a team. So let's call a truce, right?"

Shalima considered Amie's suggestion seriously. "Yeah, well as long as you keeps out of me way and you don't tell me what to do." It was the best answer Amie could hope for. Shalima was a loose cannon and it was impossible to predict what she was likely to do.

19 THE DROP ZONE

It was almost dark when they heard a car engine stopping at the end of the narrow lane between the shacks, and a few moments later, Ben appeared carrying a mountain of bags. He gave them a shameful grin. "I thought we deserved some special treats. Some of the things I could not buy, as many shops do not have a lot to sell."

Shalima was already raiding the bags, grabbing a couple of energy bars and ripping the wrappers off them.

"Oh good, plenty of cool drink," remarked Amie peering into another bag.

"Yes. I got the small plastic bottles we can refill with water, they won't be so heavy to carry if we have to camp some distance away. And look, I got these." Ben waved a pair of binoculars and a GPS. And, I also got a map, though it might not be too correct."

"Can we work out how far it is?" asked Amie.

Ben unfolded the flimsy map and they searched for Apatu.

"There." Amie put her finger on the capital. "I'm not sure how we match the co-ordinates to the map."

"Give it here," Shalima snatched the map nearly tearing it in half. She studied it for several seconds and traced a line north, checking the numbers down the side of the map. She grabbed the pen she'd been using earlier and marked a large X in the middle of nowhere.

Ben pointed to the brown colouring. "I think this shows there are many hills around. That should help."

"Yes, and I think that's a river there, that's always useful," Amie added.

"If there is water in it, and no crocodiles or hippo" Ben reminded her.

"So when do we leave?" Shalima asked. She was itching to be on her way, desperate to get back in action.

"We should have a good meal first, and leave in a couple of hours."

Amie's suggestion met with general approval, so while Ben and Amie sorted and re-packed the purchases, Shalima disappeared into the kitchen and heated up the tins of stew Ben had bought, adding tinned potatoes and vegetables to the mix. The smells wafting into the lounge reminded Amie of days gone by when she would automatically expect to eat three times a day at roughly the same time.

"And the passports?" Shalima enquired through a mouth full of food.

"They were expensive but my friend promised to have them ready. We can pick them up on our way out of town," Ben replied.

"Cool." Shalima nodded as she fiddled with the new cell phones Ben had bought. They weren't the up-to-date smart phone variety, but the cheap, basic pre-paid kind. At least they could call and text one another if they needed to. Ben had warned them they were only to be used in an emergency. He had not been able to buy very much air time since many of the retailers were low on stock and would not sell him as much as he had asked for.

Shalima had pounced on hers as if it was a gold ingot. As soon as they'd exchanged numbers and keyed them into the memory, she shoved hers safely inside her bra.

All too soon it was time to leave, and the girls once again swathed themselves in the thick black burqas. Not only did they itch, but Amie's wasn't too clean either. After collecting the water that morning, standing in all the mud round the water tap, and a few visits to the long drop, it no longer smelt so fresh.

As soon as Ben had packed the gear away, and Shalima was taking her turn at the long drop, Ben pushed something into Amie's hands. It was a gun.

"Say nothing," Ben warned, passing over a handful of bullets. "I got one for me and one for you. She …" he pointed towards the outhouse, "… does not need to know."

Amie nodded. It was the last thing she'd tell Shalima. She'd probably hit the roof if she found out she was the only one unarmed. She knew better than to ask Ben where he'd acquired two handguns; they were readily available in most townships if you knew the right people. She was about to ask Ben how to load it when they heard Shalima returning. She lifted the burqa and stuck it in the waistband of her trousers, hoping she'd never have to use it, and wondering if she'd even know how, if the time ever came. It was a different model to the one Jonathon had given her.

At long last, packed and ready, they climbed into the truck, Ben and Shalima in the front, since she insisted she could read a map better than any of them, while Amie shared the back seat with a small mountain of supplies. Edward's money had been put to good use.

In a seedy street in the lower end of town Ben disappeared up an alley to collect the passports leaving the girls to wait in the elderly, battered Land Rover. Several thugs loitered nearby, staring at them, nudging each other and laughing.

"Effing idiots," Shalima snarled. "Think they're wide boys, oh yeah? They'd run a mile if they saw any real fightin'. Men? Pansies more like."

Amie wasn't so sure. If they were part of a gang, acceptance was often based on some brutal act, even a killing, before you became a full member.

Ben hurried back to the Land Rover, ignoring the cat calls from the youths, and climbed into the driver's seat. Finally, they were on their way.

It felt strange to Amie driving through the outer suburbs of Apatu as she had done so many times in the past, going shopping or to and from social events at the Expatriate Club. It gave her a feeling of déjà vu. Now the circumstances were so very different. This time she was smothered in a burqa and huddled in the back of an old Land Rover, with two people she'd not known all that long, and knew very little about.

Shalima was an enigma and she had never found out much about Ben's personal life. In fact all she knew about him was he was from the Kawa tribe, with the elephant as his totem. He'd studied hard at school and trained to work in film and television. She could also guess he knew quite a lot of what her mother would call 'shady' characters, those teetering on the wrong side of the law, or even a long way over the other side?

Yet the three of them had been thrown together, had experienced dangers together and, they'd survived. Once again they were driving into the unknown. She could understand why Shalima was there. She had nowhere else to go right now, and she'd put off returning to England for as long as possible. She'd travelled abroad for a cause and an adventure, and she was still there, playing the game.

But Ben? Amie couldn't figure that out. Why was Ben still here? What was there in it for him? He could as easily have stayed safely in his home city, so why was he prepared to take such risks? It didn't ring true with Amie. The more she racked her brains, the less sense it seemed to make, and the only possible answer she could come up with was he wanted to be near Shalima. Had he fallen in love with the girl? She tried to recall the exchanges between them but nothing she'd seen so far, suggested they were anything more than working friends, colleagues or whatever label you could put on any of their relationships? In the end Amie decided to give her brain a rest and, making herself as comfortable as she could, she fell asleep in the back of the car, as they left the suburbs behind and took the tarred road to the north.

She was woken by the sound of Ben and Shalima arguing over the map. The sun was visible over the eastern hills and they were parked a little way off the main road. The fierce discussion was over which direction they should go. Shalima was waving the map around, Ben was trying to get her to look at the GPS.

"Yeah, yeah. I know what yer trying to say, but that thing'll keep us on the road. We need to cut across here." Shalima was shouting. "Here on the map, see, if we go along by …"

"But the map is not very accurate. I programmed in the co-ordinates before we left Apatu and it will take us the shortest possible route."

"Guys we should trust modern technology," suggested Amie. "I'm sure Ben is right about the map. Let's trust the GPS right?"

"Oh yeah, take his side, wouldn't you know it," snapped Shalima crumpling up the map and sticking it in the glove compartment. "Go on then, get us lost. See if I care. Put us in more danger. Staying on a public road where anyone could stop us and wanna know where we is goin' and get us arrested!"

Amie sighed. Every time Shalima opened her mouth it was to complain or moan.

Ben replaced the navigation system in its holder on the windscreen and turned the ignition key. "I do not want to go driving off into the bush yet, we've only got one spare can of petrol. If we travel too far off road, we may damage something and have problems crossing river beds. It's only a few more kilometres on the road and then we will turn off."

Shalima didn't reply but hunched down in her seat and stared out of the side window.

There was very little traffic on the road, despite most Africans being early risers, out and about well before dawn. After half an hour, Ben slowed down and pulled over to the side of the road again.

"What now?" Shalima shot up in her seat.

"This is where we should turn off."

"So why don't you?"

"I'm waiting for that car to pass, so no one will see us."

But instead of racing past, the other car slowed down and stopped a little ahead of them. A man dressed in military uniform got out and walked towards them.

"Oh sheeeet," Shalima groaned. "You and yer 'we need to stay on the road longer'. Now we're in trouble."

Amie shrunk low in her seat trying to make herself invisible in the back. She was about to slide onto the floor when the newcomer stuck his head through the window. She felt the bile rise in her throat and thought she was going to throw up. No, not now, after so many near misses. Was this one Togodian soldier going to arrest them and force them to return to Apatu? It was impossible to see how Shalima was reacting, since she'd immediately pulled the burqa over her head.

The girls had no idea what was said, as the conversation went back and forth in Togodian. At last the man straightened up, knocked loudly on the car roof, walked back to his own car, got in and drove away.

Amie relaxed and gave sigh of relief. She'd hardly been aware she was holding her breath.

"And what was that all about?" Shalima asked.

"He thought the car was broken and he stopped to help."

"So what did you tell him?"

"I explained one of you ladies wanted to um …"

"Take a piss you mean?"

"Well, yes, and we were waiting until there was no traffic on the road."

"Nice one Ben." Amie smiled.

Looking both ways along the road, and seeing it was clear, Ben drove across the tar and onto the rough ground making for the low-lying western hills. Much to Shalima's disgust, he insisted on stopping again and walking back up to the edge of the road to sweep away the tyre tracks and his footprints, with a leafy branch he broke off a bush.

"It is wise," he said as he got back into the Land Rover, "that we leave no tracks close to the road."

"Paranoid," was Shalima's only reply.

Ben slowed the Land Rover and brought it to a full stop. He turned to look at Shalima. "I do not have to be here," he said. "I can drive back to Apatu and live my life. I want to help Amie, and if you want you can leave."

Shalima glared at him, shocked.

Amie was astonished. Nearly all the African people she'd met were very polite, and she was amazed to hear Ben speak so sharply. She could see he was very, very angry indeed. But this was between the two of them, so she closed her eyes pretending to be asleep. She wasn't going to get involved.

For several seconds a heavy silence hung in the car, then Shalima murmured a sort of apology. Ben put his foot on the accelerator and they moved forwards.

They drove for several hours, stopping only for comfort breaks and on one occasion they paused while a small herd of elephants passed by. The sight of the huge creatures even impressed Shalima and she gazed at them in wonder. She giggled at the antics of the two little calves that were struggling to keep up with the adults. They were still at the stage where they didn't have full control of their trunks and their clumsy attempts to feed like their elders were comical to watch as they tried to grasp small branches and pull off the leaves.

As dusk approached, Ben suggested they stop for the night. By his reckoning they were quite close to the drop zone, and there was a hill to one side covered with large boulders that would make excellent hiding places and give them shelter. This time Shalima didn't argue. She'd been very quiet for most of the day and Amie wondered if she'd had a change of heart.

After a cold meal, Ben made a small fire and Amie filled a pot with water and put it over the flames to boil. While she spooned in coffee, sugar and powdered milk she voiced the thoughts no one had as yet put into words.

"So, now we are close to the drop zone, do we know what we're going to do?"

"Thought the idea was to rescue yer hubby, right?" Shalima snorted.

"Yes, but how?" After a moment she continued. "The facts, as you discovered Shalima are that IS are going to drop supplies in this area, one of their convoys is going to arrive and pick up the goods. And we think it's the same group which is transporting Jonathon and Charles to Libya. Right?"

"How are they going to cross the Sahara?" Ben asked.

"I suppose they could cut further west, meet up with some of their allies in the Congo and Nigeria and go north from there. But didn't one of the emails say they would fly out?"

"Oh, yeah, yeah, of course." Shalima agreed quickly.

"It would be much easier. No one with any common sense tries to drive across the Sahara. That would be crazy." Amie said.

"They'll make for some airport and fly them out," Shalima agreed.

"But that could be anywhere," Amie said sadly. "They might even land the planes here and transfer them and we wouldn't be able to do a thing about it. All we could do is sit and watch it happen. How do we even know they'll stop and make a camp down there in the valley?"

"We do not know that," Ben joined in. "But if they still have Jonathon and Charles with them, we can follow if they drive further west or north. We may have a chance at some point."

"And if they do stop here for the night, and I'm sure that's what they'll do ..." Shalima sounded very certain, "... then we have the chance to rescue them right at the beginning."

"You make it all sound so easy," Amie moaned.

"You did pretty well before, and you was all on yer own when you did that," Shalima pointed out. "Do what you did before. Creep in and cut them free."

Amie wasn't convinced. She had a sinking feeling that this time the soldiers were going to be much more alert. They wouldn't be so easily fooled a second time. She knew Hussein had been punished because the women had escaped and that would be a sharp warning to anyone who was careless in the future. She remembered the suppurating sores on his back. They'd have to plan as they went along, but now they were here, she wondered how stupid they really were.

They'd decided it was safer to sleep in the Land Rover and take it in turns to keep watch. They would rotate sleeping in the back of the vehicle which was a lot more comfortable than a full night in the front seats.

Amie took the first watch and a few hours later, she was happy to change places with Shalima and climb into the back of the truck. She folded the burqa and snuggled down to sleep as best she could.

She wasn't sure what woke her up some time later as it was still dark. She lay quite still and listened. She could hear a soft moaning that sounded more human than animal. She sat up without making a sound and peered out of the window. Beside the Land Rover, Shalima and Ben were locked in a passionate embrace. Amie gasped. Yes, she'd wondered very briefly before if there was anything between them but not for a moment had she really believed it. Only a few hours ago they had been sniping at each other, so was Ben romantically drawn to Shalima? The idea was totally outrageous. She felt like a voyeur, and turned away, and hoped no predator would creep up on them while they were otherwise engaged.

She lay down again and decided it was nothing to do with her, but she couldn't help feeling a little betrayed by Ben. He was her friend and she wasn't happy about the, what could she call it, liaison, friendship, love affair, between one person she was very fond of and one she didn't like even a little bit. It was probably just a mad fulfilment of lust brought on by the dangers they were all about to face.

Dawn came and Amie was amused to see that as she sat up and stretched, the other two sprang apart as if they'd been scalded. She pretended not to notice, climbed out of the Land Rover and poured herself a cupful of water to wash her hands and her face. She did wonder who had been keeping watch if they had both been so occupied.

Looking down into the valley from their refuge among the rocks, Ben announced he was going to go and check the co-ordinates on the GPS. He wanted to be quite sure they were in the right place.

Shalima seemed reluctant for him to leave their makeshift camp, but he was adamant he needed to check their exact location. He argued that if they were in the wrong valley, the convoy could well pass them by and the whole exercise would be a total waste of time.

To Amie's surprise, Shalima didn't argue and then offered to go with him. She watched them clamber over the rocks and set off across the open plain. Her attention was diverted by the antics of a couple of rock hyrax peeping out from their hiding places among the large stones. They resembled large guinea pigs, with short grey coats, and pointed, twitching noses. They were constantly on the alert and the slightest movement sent them scurrying out of sight. From what Amie observed, they had little defence against predators, except their ability to run and hide. Pimbi was the local name for them, Dirk had told her, and she smiled at their cute little faces while they munched away on a lobelia plant, and scooped up any insects that came within reach.

There was a sudden high-pitched squeal from one of the sentries and, in an instant, they were all gone.

Amie looked up to see an eagle soaring overhead, and realized she'd not been on the alert for any danger to herself. Rocky areas were favourite haunts for leopards, and she prayed there were none around. She eased the gun Ben had given her out from under the seat, tucked it back in the waistband of her trousers and pulled her top down. It didn't feel particularly comfortable, but it gave her a measure of courage.

As she watched Ben and Shalima wandering back towards their temporary camp, she was astonished to see they were holding hands. Shalima was, in the vernacular, all over Ben like a rash. Amie was astounded. How was it she hadn't even suspected there was any real chemistry between them. Now, Shalima the tough, radical, fundamentalist fighter was gone, and she'd morphed into a simpering teenager hanging on to Ben's every last word.

Amie didn't stop to think about it any further. It was no business of hers and if Ben was happy about it who was she to complain? It was a surprising turn of events though. How Ben could be attracted to the teenager after the way she'd behaved was beyond Amie. But it was not for her to judge.

When they walked back up the rocks, they said that the coordinates matched exactly in the valley, and now all they had to do was wait. Amie would've been content to sit and wait patiently for the little hyrax to reappear, but Ben sensibly suggested they forage for branches and anything else they could find to cover the Land Rover. It would be very easy to see from the air, and they did not want to be attacked, or frighten anyone off if they thought the area was compromised.

Shalima was positively cheerful now, and she volunteered to throw her burqa over the roof of the Land Rover. Amie's was flung over it as well, while Ben placed large stones on top to keep them from blowing off. Amie remarked they'd come in useful after all. They'd used them as blankets, pillows, hiding places, as a disguise and now camouflage.

The sun beat down, the valley became a succession of mirages and the ground quivered in the heat. It was tempting to strip off as many clothes as possible, but there were too many insects about, and they were trying to save the insect repellent for use against the mosquitoes at night.

The day dragged on and still the brilliant blue sky was empty; and the valley floor below remained deserted. An occasional small group of wildlife wandered across, stopped to graze then moved on: zebra, wildebeest and an assortment of antelope. None paused for long, as there was very little to eat or drink, and very little shade.

It had occurred to Amie they wouldn't be able to hide behind the pitifully few trees and bushes when they made an assault on the camp. When they left the safety of the rocks they had a couple of hundred metres to go with virtually no cover. She'd had it easy in her first hideout by the river, but this time, she had a really bad feeling about their current position, but she couldn't quite put her finger on it. The only thing in their favour was the moon - it was in its first quarter and would give very little light.

They dozed on and off wriggling into the shade as the

sun moved across the sky. The hyrax grew bolder as they perceived no threat from the lazy humans who'd invaded their territory, until one sentry gave an excessively loud screech and they all vanished.

Ben jumped up. "What did they hear?"

"I don't know," Amie whispered back, it seemed safer to keep her voice low. Then they heard it, a faint drone from the sky, getting louder and louder.

"Yeah!" Shalima looked ecstatic. "Yeah. Right place. Right here. Brilliant." and she punched the air with her clenched fist.

As the planes approached, the watchers kept a low profile and the two small aircraft, Amie had no idea what kind they were, circled lower and lower. For a moment she thought they were about to land, but they came in very close to the ground, whipping up the dust on the valley floor. The doors in the belly of the plane were already open and several boxes attached to small parachutes floated down and came to rest on the sand. It only took a few moments and immediately after, the planes rose again into the sky, the doors closed and a couple of minutes later they had gone.

The packages lay there as the dust settled around them. There must have been a couple of dozen large, square and rectangular boxes covered in what looked like thick, black plastic.

Ben was the first to speak. "Shall we go and get one?"

"I'd love to know what's inside," Amie replied. "Guns? Food? Fuel?"

"Bound to be useful stuff," Shalima added.

"What if we're caught?" Amie said. "Just as we're out

there, right in the middle of an open valley and the convoy roars up. We'd be blown away in seconds."

"But the convoy might not arrive for hours, even a couple of days," Shalima pointed out.

"It is a risk," Ben agreed, "but we might be lucky."

They stared at the wrapped boxes. To go, or to stay?

"Well, if we're gonna get one or two we betta move fast," Shalima's suggestion made sense.

"Is that wise?" Amie was reluctant. "They might be too heavy to move anyway and we can hardly rip one open and leave the wrappings behind, that would give the game away.

"So, we go now," Ben decided. "We go and see if we can carry one back and if it is too big, we could fetch it in the Land Rover."

All Amie wanted to do was hide out and make one mad dash to see if they could rescue the men under cover of darkness once the convoy arrived. This was an extra risk to take, was it worth it? How many times was she being forced to be courageous? It simply wasn't in her nature, but the other two were keen, so she could hardly say no and stay right here. It would need the three of them at least to steal one box. The others were so enthusiastic there was no way she was going to argue with them, so she nodded her head.

They scrambled down the slope and set off towards the nearest box. Amie felt terribly exposed out here in the open. There was nowhere to hide and no shade. She imagined the zinging sound of bullets racing towards her back as she hurried across the open savannah. The grass was too short to hide them, even if they lay flat, and there wasn't a tree in sight. Even the termite mounds were miniature and the heat hit her like a sledgehammer. She found she was breathing in red hot air, gasping as the heat radiated off the ground.

When they reached the nearest package, it was a lot larger than they'd expected and they could only shift it slightly. It was impossible for the three of them to lift it and carry it back as they'd hoped. The outer wrapping was made of what looked like industrial strength black bin liners and these were kept in place by thick bands of woven straps linked together with metal strips.

Amie wondered if they'd be able to break it open even if they did get it back to camp. They had enough supplies for a few days, so why were they taking this added risk?

20 CAPTURED

Ben decided they needed the Land Rover and raced back up the hill to fetch it.

Amie had known this would be more trouble than it was worth. She shook her head while she watched Shalima try to make a hole in the corner of the box with a knife.

She glanced at Amie. "Don't you look so worried," she said. "If we get guns in this lot, it'll be a doddle gettin' the men out. No problem."

Inside Amie groaned. Why did this teenager always make her feel like a scared child? Wasn't she the one who was supposed to be older and wiser?

The roar of a truck startled her and she whirled round to see it speeding towards them.

"We must hurry," Ben pointed back up the hill. "I can see dust clouds fifteen, twenty miles off. We must get this into the back."

The fear of the approaching enemy jump-started their adrenaline and they strained to lift the box, but it was almost impossible to get it more than a foot off the ground.

"Now what?" Shalima asked. "It ain't that big but it's too heavy. How we gonna get it into the truck?"

Amie's mind flashed back to Dirk and his men using metal tracks to pull vehicles out of soft sandy soil. They'd placed a block of wood under the jack, and winched up the vehicle and placed the tracks under the tyres and they were out.

She peered in the back of the Land Rover, then dived inside, and reappeared with a smile on her face holding a pair of metal tracks. "We use these."

The heat made it agonizing work, and the black plastic burned their hands as they wriggled the box to the bottom of the tracks that now formed a ramp up to the tailgate. Bit by bit they pushed the box into the back of the Land Rover.

The moment it was secured, all three of them leapt into the front, and they started the slow drive back towards the hillside. The springs on the old Land Rover groaned alarmingly, and fearing something would break, the girls got out and scrambled up to the rocks.

After Ben reversed into the space between the boulders, they covered it again with the burqas and branches to stop the sunlight glinting on the metal.

If the convoy was close by, they could neither see it nor hear it. But Ben was right, there was a huge dust cloud to the south and they could only guess how long it would take before they arrived in the valley. It was unlikely the terrorists would miss one box from a couple of dozen, and the dust they'd kicked up with the Land Rover was already beginning to settle.

Amie grabbed Ben's arm. "Look! You can see our tracks from here. Tyre tracks and they lead right to our hiding place."

Ben's face registered horror. Did he have time to grab one of the branches and brush them away? They'd been so vigilant before, about leaving none behind, why had no one thought about it this time?

"What's the problem?" Shalima asked, coming round from the other side of one of the large rocks.

Amie pointed. "Our tracks, as clear as day, from there to here." She never knew what possessed her, but suddenly she was running headlong into the valley. She dragged a large branch behind her.

She refused to look in the direction of the approaching vehicles, and from the spot where the box had landed, she swept frantically back and forth. She ran backwards as she brushed over the tyre tracks.

Ben appeared beside her carrying another branch, sweeping away as fast as he could. They still had a long way to go. It seemed it would take forever as they moved inch by inch towards the hill.

Sweat was pouring down Amie's face stinging her eyes and making it hard to see. They could hear the rumble of engines as the convoy came closer and closer. The ground vibrated around her and it was difficult to keep her balance as she brushed away furiously. Then, she tripped over a rock and only just managed to fling herself to one side to avoid cracking her head open. She lay winded for several moments as the few clouds in the sky swirled like round-a-bout horses. Ben came to help her up, but she shook him off and scrambled to her feet.

"Keep brushing, I'll be fine."

They'd reached the bottom of the hill, and although an experienced tracker would have no difficulty in knowing exactly what had happened, it looked as if they'd covered the tracks pretty well.

Worn out, covered in dust and desperate for a drink, Ben and Amie reached the Land Rover, grateful to grab the bottles of water Shalima handed them. They flung themselves down in the tiny area of shadow and took deep, gasping breaths. Not that there was time to relax. The enemy was arriving and they would have to stay on the alert.

While Ben and Amie had been away, Shalima had managed to break open the box and found several assault rifles and ammunition, tins of food and powdered milk.

She looked very disappointed. "No bloody bombs or hand grenades. Those would have made the rescue a piece o' cake," she moaned to the other two, while they lay panting on the ground.

"We can't even begin to plan how to attack until we see if they're gonna to stop, and if they do, how they set up their tents and where the patrols go."

"They will stay," Ben said. "It is past the middle of the day and they must collect the boxes. No, they will stay for one night at least." He seemed quite convinced.

The afternoon passed all too quickly as, safely concealed among the rocks, Shalima showed them how to use the various bits of armaments she'd unpacked. She passed one of the guns to Amie. "AK47," she said.

Amie held it gingerly. It didn't seem too heavy for the size of it and she lifted it to peer down the sights and waved it around a little.

"It ain't no good like that," Shalima said, "you need this as well." She handed her a magazine and showed Amie how to slot it in underneath. Amie nearly dropped it.

"I can hardly lift it!"

"Don't be such a wimp," the teenager snapped. Her aggressive manner was back.

"These are the lighter kind, couple of bags of sugar, no more."

Amie wasn't convinced. She tried to heft the unwieldy rifle and keep it focused.

Next Shalima showed her how to change it from single to multiple shot and assured her she could kill someone a quarter of a mile away.

"So you don't have to get too close," she crowed, digging Amie in the ribs.

She demonstrated each of the magazines that contained thirty bullets and how she would insert a new one when they were used up.

Amie was aghast. She was quite convinced she would never be able to use it. How could she fire blindly at a group of people? She'd never even fired the pistol she still had in her waistband. If the time came, she'd probably fire one shot at someone, if she felt her life was in danger, and then drop the gun.

Meanwhile Ben was using the binoculars to watch what was happening below. The first two vehicles had arrived and several men in black fatigues jumped out. It looked as if they were unloading tents and other equipment.

In the second wave, there were three more vehicles that had parked near the packages. Despite the late afternoon heat, the valley was a bustling scene of well-organized activity. Taking the binoculars from Ben, Amie surveyed the scene below and her heart sank. These fanatics looked a lot more disciplined and organized than the previous group. They were as different as chalk and cheese. There was no way they were going to rescue anyone from this crowd. She sighed as she handed the glasses back.

The only similarity was the way they laid out the tents in a rectangle, but it wasn't until they were all set up that they opened the back doors of the last vehicle and removed a stretcher. It was difficult to tell but it looked as if the body on the stretcher was white, but Ben couldn't be sure it was Jonathon under the blanket. He watched to see which tent they entered and made a note of its position. There was no second stretcher and no sign of another prisoner either. So where was Charles? Or was Jonathon missing?

For as long as the light held, they watched the activity, noting down as much as they could. They took it in turns to monitor the scene below, until the sun finally set behind the western hills. Soon, all they could see were the flickering flames of the camp fires within the compound.

"So, when do we go?" Shalima was keen to get moving.

"We must wait until they are asleep," Ben said. "It is impossible to see how many guards they have, at least two I think and they keep walking around. We need to be careful."

Amie wished she was just about anywhere but where she was right then. How had she got herself into this mess? What was she doing? She was no fanatical believer, not driven by a cause, sure in her beliefs, riding on a crest of certainty that what she was doing was right. She certainly didn't agree with any one religion taking over the world and imposing their beliefs on anyone else. She thought it so wrong to kill people because they worshipped differently.

And it was barbaric to destroy priceless historical sites because they were a symbol of another people's past. All she knew was that she wanted to rescue her husband and take him to safety. Although, come to think of it, where would she go? Where would they all go supposing they got out of this alive? She realized they'd never even discussed an escape route, so were any of them expecting to survive? She only knew one thing for certain; she didn't want to die.

While they waited for the early hours of the morning, they took it in turns to doze to conserve their strength. At least it didn't look as if any of the camp occupants were scouting beyond the boundaries. They must feel quite safe.

All too soon it was time to move. The girls had talked about wearing the burqas. On one hand, they were excellent camouflage but on the other, they were hot, clumsy to move in and would slow them down.

They finally decided to wear them as they could always discard them if necessary. Amie pulled her burqa off the car bonnet and put it on. She tucked the bulky material into the waistband of her trousers, so she wouldn't trip over it as she slithered down the hillside. She slipped the gun Ben had given her into her pocket.

Once in the valley they'd have to move quickly and quietly, and hope they wouldn't be seen. The only possible cover was behind the boxes, several of which were still scattered over the ground, and although they weren't very high, it was better than nothing.

Amie shuffled in a crouch across the valley floor, as if making herself a little shorter was going to help. The moon gave them just enough light to silhouette the hills and their general direction, but it was difficult to make out the shapes of her friends as they moved closer and closer to the tents.

They'd agreed to approach the tent where they'd taken the stretcher, cut it open at the back as before, remove Jonathon and Charles, and retreat as silently as possible. They would hide up again in their camp and, if necessary, repel all comers. They hoped that Jonathon might not be missed until long after they made their escape.

To begin with, everything went smoothly. The sentries on duty could only be seen by the faint glow from their cigarettes on the far side of the camp. They weren't patrolling each side, but huddled in one spot. So far, so good.

Ben drew the knife while they hunkered down at the back of the tent and in no time he'd cut a wide slit and wriggled inside. The girls waited, ready to help if Jonathon couldn't walk.

For several moments nothing happened. Amie couldn't stand it any longer and she put her head through the gap. It was pitch dark inside and she couldn't see a thing. She wriggled in a little further. Suddenly a bright light hit her eyes and someone whooped in triumph. She couldn't understand a word he said, but as hard as she tried to break free, there were now several hands clutching her. There was no way she could escape. The AK47 was wrenched out of her hands and her wrists were fixed behind her back with plastic cable ties.

"Let go of me," she cried. "Let go!"

Someone lit a gas lamp and Amie was able to see for the first time. The tent was crowded with men wearing battle fatigues. A rough hand uncovered her face and one of the men compared it to a photograph he held in his hand.

"It's her all right," said a voice behind Amie and she twisted round to see Shalima smiling. "Told you I'd get her and now you should have the pair o' them. How's that?"

Amie was stunned. What was happening? What was the girl saying? Why was Shalima …? The girl was triumphant. She watched in horror as Shalima flung her arms in the air, gun in one hand a grenade of some sort in the other.

Then it dawned on Amie. It was a trap. They were expected. They'd been waiting for them. No wonder it'd been so easy. She felt sick. She felt the earth sway around her and the world went black.

When Amie came to, she was in one of the tents. A gas lamp illuminated the walls and the mattresses on the ground. Shalima was sitting opposite her drinking a mug of tea. She tried to move her arms but discovered they were tied behind her back. Her feet were also securely bound with cable ties. She looked at the teenager, who was grinning from ear to ear.

"You knew?" she gasped.

"Course I knew," Shalima said smugly. "And you fell for it," she giggled.

"But, I thought …" if she was honest Amie didn't know what to think, her brain couldn't put all the pieces together. What? Where had it all gone wrong?

"You thought what? That I would abandon the cause? Not a chance. Never!"

"But, but you said …"

"Said what? Did I ever once say I had?"

Amie couldn't remember. She'd assumed by running away from the camp Shalima had changed her allegiance. What a fool she'd been. She tried to replay everything that had happened since they fled across the river, but the events were all jumbled and confused.

"I don't understand Shalima! If you wanted to capture me why did you go back to the camp and help Ben and Phumelo escape, and drive the Land Rover and meet up and … none of it makes any sense!"

"Yeah, well, you don't know the half of it." Shalima was so smug that Amie wanted to hit her. As she leaned back she felt the pistol which was still in her trouser pocket, but she had no way of getting it out. With both her hands tied behind her, she wouldn't be able to use it even if it fell out.

"You really wanna' know what it's all about?" the teenager was simply dying to enlighten Amie and boast about how clever she'd been.

Amie was tempted to tell her she really didn't care, simply to take the girl's moment of glory away, but there were too many unanswered questions and yes, she really did want to know the truth. She couldn't believe she'd been so taken in by Shalima.

"Well, it's like this," the girl began. "It was all going fine until you had to come in and stick yer nose into what didn't concern you."

"But when I set all the women free you came with us!" Amie exclaimed.

"Yeah, wanted to find out who was helping you so I

could call the guys back to do you in. When I realized it were you, I went back o' course."

"Back to the camp?"

"Yeah, course I did. Told them you was coming back and they was gonna grab you."

"But, but no one did. You even helped us to escape!" Amie couldn't make sense of what Shalima was telling her. "They could so easily have captured me."

"Ah, but a change in plan. Fahid had left and I weren't gonna stay there without him."

"Fahid! Who is Fahid?"

"My boyfriend, stupid. Who else? They'd sent him away on the convoy wiv yer husband. So I had to get back wiv him. They told me to go find you and bring you back, like now they knew you was a famous celebrity an all. And that will go down well for the cause when they make a big thing about yer execution." Shalima sniggered.

It was still making no sense to Amie. "But we went miles away from the camp. You helped every step of the way, did you decide to give it all up and …?"

"Not an effing chance!" Shalima broke in. "Decided to see what info I could get while I was away. And I did too. That Edward, I could've fingered him for future capture. He was obviously important to the government, a good catch."

"So all the time we were in Atari with the Mathesons you were planning to …?"

"Course I was. I was waiting for the right time to spring the trap. I have friends everywhere."

"And your friends in Atari provided you with all those supplies?" Amie felt sick. Were there fundamentalists lying low in Ruanga as well?

"Yeah, well some of them," Shalima grinned. She was so pleased with herself. "And then the biggest stroke of luck, an aeroplane ride, in the right direction. What could be nicer?"

"But they shot at us!" Amie exclaimed, "We could all have been killed."

Shalima smirked. "Fortunes of war ain't it?"

"And if we'd not crashed then what? You'd have asked Edward and the pilot nicely to drop us off somewhere convenient?" Amie couldn't contain her sarcasm. She was so furious she was finding it almost impossible to sit still. She was prepared to fling herself bodily at the English girl if only to wipe that smile off her face, even though she knew it would be futile.

"Ah, but I was ready for a little cooperation," came the reply as the girl waved her gun around.

Amie realized Edward and the pilot were both doomed the moment they climbed into that plane. If they hadn't crashed, Shalima would have dispatched them anyway.

"I don't believe you!" Amie spat. "How would you know the convoy would be at this exact spot without reading all those emails? That wasn't another piece of amazing luck."

The response she got was a pitying laugh. "Don't be so stupid. I knew about this drop weeks ago, and I knew the convoy would come and that Fahid was wiv them. I made up all that nonsense about de-coding the emails. I pretended. 'Course they were protected and all that, not a code I could really break. And I read them out to you word for word and you believed me. Big joke that was. I had to get yer here to meet up wiv yer hubby and we'd have both of you and I'd be back with Fahid. Everything worked perfectly, see. And…" she added, "… as a bonus, I brought them Ben as well. You have no idea how important he is, do you? So now, we're all one big happy family."

Something Shalima had mentioned earlier permeated through Amie's brain. Execution? Her execution? And probably Jonathon's as well. She knew they filmed these events and posted them on YouTube as a warning to their enemies and to show off at the same time. It didn't sound as if they were going to be held as kidnap hostages, just blown away. There was worse to come.

"Of course," Shalima continued, with a crafty look on her face, "they might decide to stone you to death."

Amie gasped. She didn't know a lot about Sharia Law, but surely that was reserved for adultery? "But, but why?" she cried. "Why are you doing this to us, what have we ever done to harm you?"

"What a stupid question," Shalima was working herself up into a frenzy. "You don't get it do you? This is for the cause, this is a holy war and we're fightin' for glory, for what we believe. I only got to tell them you and Ben were at it, and they'll brand you a whore, with yer hair uncovered, showin' yer legs to any man, flauntin' it. Yer kind make me sick."

Amie decided it was best for her to say nothing. She was aghast. Her brain refused to take it all in. She couldn't believe what she was hearing and she wondered if she was dreaming, hallucinating, it was all just a terrible nightmare.

She bit her bottom lip and squeezed her eyes shut. She wasn't going to cry in front of Shalima. If she'd disliked her before, she hated her now. She pressed her back against the wall of the tent to stop herself shaking. She could feel waves of pure fear moving up through her body and even her teeth chattered. She prayed she wouldn't lose control of her bodily functions. That would be too humiliating.

Shalima got up to walk out, tired of taunting her. "Oh by the way," she said over her shoulder as a parting shot. "Yer precious husband is here, but Charles didn't make it. Good food for the animals right?" Her laughter was shrill as she lifted the tent flap and disappeared outside.

The hours dragged on. Outside, Amie could hear sounds of life as people carried on the day-to-day activities of cooking, practicing with guns and general chatter that went on uninterrupted. She wondered where they'd put Ben, and if he was with Jonathon, and how ill Jonathon was; she guessed he was the body on the stretcher. There seemed to be no way out at all.

She tried to bring her hands round her front by wriggling them over her bottom and threading her legs through, but it was impossible. Her boots were too large and strain as much as she could, she only succeeded in wrenching her wrists and shoulders. With a sigh of despair she gave up the struggle.

She tried to doze, but the images floating in front of her eyes were horrendous. Death by firing squad was scary enough, but being stoned to death would be so much worse. She imagined the rocks landing on her head and body. How many times were you hit before you died? Would it be dozens or even hundreds? She trembled with fear and hoped they might be merciful. She never thought she would pray to be taken in front of a firing squad.

Several hours later a young girl brought her some food. Amie suspected she was originally from the Middle East but she didn't speak English. She crept into the tent and held out a bowl containing some kind of stew. When Amie didn't take it from her, she put it on the floor along with a metal mug of water.

Amie tried to show her that her hands were tied behind her back and she'd be unable to feed herself. The girl nodded, but Amie didn't think she understood. To her dismay, the girl left the tent and the food was way out of reach. Was it better to starve to death or be stoned she considered in a moment of black humour.

A few minutes later, the girl reappeared and sat on the floor in front of Amie. She had a spoon in her hand and she ladled the stew into Amie's mouth. Even though she hadn't eaten for some time, the food was tasteless and Amie heaved several times trying to keep it down. She had no idea what sort of meat it was, obviously not pork, but its ancestry had been obliterated during the hours it had been boiled. It would have been more suitable for shoe leather. If Amie hadn't been so determined to keep her strength and spirits up, she would've spat it out after the first mouthful.

She refused the next offered spoonful and tried to talk to the young girl, but she shook her head. It was impossible to make out which country she was from as, besides wearing a full burqa, she kept her eyes down and didn't look at the captive at all. It was obvious she wasn't going to be any help and certainly not a source of information.

Amie was desperate to know how Jonathon was. What had killed Charles? Was it disease, an accident or did the men execute him and film it to send a warning to the world? She had so many unanswered questions. What was going to happen to her?

As soon as the bowl was almost empty, the young girl got to her feet and leaning over Amie, she offered her the mug of water. Even though she had no idea what toilet facilities were available and how, or even if, she'd be allowed to use them, Amie drank all of it, only pausing to take breath. As soon as it was empty the girl walked out of the tent leaving Amie on her own.

She thought she'd probably dozed off for when she opened her eyes again, Shalima was standing in front of her.

21 UNDER GUARD

"Big boss wants to see you," she said abruptly, hauling Amie to her feet. Once upright she swayed fighting to keep her balance.

"I'm sure there's nothing I can tell him he hasn't already heard from you," Amie said faintly. "What am I supposed to know?"

"See what he asks you," the young English fanatic replied while she cut the cable ties from around Amie's ankles. She held her firmly by one arm, covered Amie in her burqa and led her briskly out of the tent.

Amie squinted in the bright sunlight after being kept in semi-darkness for hours. She registered the lines of tents forming a rectangle and a few men dressed in fatigues strolling to and fro or lounging around cradling their guns. It was impossible to guess where Jonathon was, and even if she knew, she didn't have the courage to call out. Instinct told her the more submissive she appeared, the easier it might be, women with strong personalities and ideas of their own were not appreciated. She imagined how the freedom that women had fought for over the centuries, would be lost if these religious zealots succeeded in their aims. Didn't Shalima realize that? They'd never discussed it. She halted bringing the teenager to a stop as well.

"Shalima, have you ever thought about your future? If you take over countries and ban other religions and destroy ancient monuments, do you really think you'll have any personal freedom? You'll be forced inside the house not ever allowed out ..." She got no further.

"You still don't understand you pillock. I'll already be in heaven. I'll be rewarded for bringing everyone to the proper way to live. I'm prepared to blow meself up if that's what it takes." She thrust her face right up against Amie's. "Now d'you understand? It's for the glory and the reward in the afterlife. Not for some brief passing glory and material possessions in this one."

Nice one, Amie thought, not a chance there would be any help from that quarter. She could only wonder at the girl's absolute commitment to the cause she believed in. She'd been totally and utterly brainwashed.

Halfway across the compound between the tents, they met a young soldier who smiled at Shalima and Amie realized it was probably Fahid. While she couldn't see Shalima's face, she felt her whole body tense and quiver and had no doubt he was the boyfriend. He was certainly handsome and probably only a teenager himself.

Shalima stopped, abruptly pulling back on Amie's arm which caused the cable ties to dig deeper into her wrists. With her head bowed she whispered a hurried conversation with Fahid. Just as quickly she jerked Amie forward again and made for a tent at the far end of the compound.

They waited outside, eyes on the ground until one of the soldiers came out and nodded to Shalima who pushed Amie inside.

As Amie's eyes adjusted again to the dim light inside the tent, she observed three men sitting around a low table. They were all dressed in fatigues, drinking tea and smoking. The air was thick with blue haze. The one in the middle nodded to Shalima and she withdrew, leaving Amie on her own.

For several seconds the men stared at Amie making her feel like a piece of meat in a butcher's shop. She was still wearing her burqa but her face was exposed and she felt them staring at her blond hair. She stared right back at them, pretending she wasn't quaking inside, but if it was from fear or rage, she wasn't sure. What right did they have to take her prisoner? All she wanted was to take her husband and leave.

"You Amie Fish?" the man in charge barked at her.

It seemed pointless to deny it, so Amie simply answered that she was.

"Married to Jon Fish?"

"Yes, to Jonathon."

"So, Mrs Fish, you will be a good example to the people of your country when they see how we treat our enemies. I understand you have been famous once before, in a television series yes?" The man gave a short humourless laugh. "Now you are going to be famous again, and it will be on television have no doubt." He chuckled and the other men smirked.

Amie was tempted to protest she'd done nothing to harm them, and plead for her and Jonathon's lives, but she knew she'd be wasting her breath. These people were fanatics and no objection she could raise would have any effect on them. They were ruthless and vicious and would employ any means whatsoever to further their cause. She had escaped death before, but she wouldn't be so lucky this time. The only thing she could do, however hard it would be, was to maintain as much dignity as she could. It was unlikely she would gain their respect after all she was only a woman. She would do her utmost if only to represent Western women who lived as human beings, with their own agendas and their own freedoms. She continued to glare boldly at the men.

There was some discussion in a language Amie guessed was Arabic, and the man in charge indicated with a wave of his hand that she should leave. Amie turned to totter out of the tent. Her legs were aching and stiff and she wished she could've exited more gracefully, or with more dignity. She swayed slightly as a wave of nausea hit her, and she heard them snigger as she pushed her way through the front flaps.

Shalima was waiting for her outside, still whispering with Fahid and for a moment she wasn't even aware that Amie was beside her. She turned round suddenly and grabbed her arm. "They've laid on a bit of entertainment for you," she sneered. "Wanna see what they do to Ben?"

"Stop it Shalima. Stop it," Amie snapped. "Do you enjoy being cruel? Ben has never done anything to you either, in fact I thought …"

"Thought I liked him? You gotta be joking. Had to make sure he'd play along, didn't I? Especially at the end."

She dragged Amie across the open area and out a little way into the veldt. To Amie's horror she saw Ben blindfolded and tied to a stake. She whimpered and tears dribbled down her cheeks. No, this wasn't happening, they couldn't be that barbaric, they couldn't!

A group of five soldiers strolled towards him, taking their rifles off their shoulders laughing and chattering among themselves. They lined up opposite Ben and took aim.

Amie's legs gave way and if Shalima hadn't held her up, she would have collapsed. She couldn't watch. She wanted to shout words of encouragement to Ben, but her mouth refused to open and the words wouldn't come. She shook violently glad Ben couldn't see what was happening.

At the last minute the men raised their rifles and fired into the air. No bullets went anywhere near Ben. It was just a show of bravado. The air rushed out of Amie's lungs and she gasped, trying to get her breath but she could feel her heart racing. She was reduced to a quivering wreck, and only a few seconds ago she'd been telling herself to be brave and dignified.

When Shalima hauled her to her feet again, Amie thought she saw a spark of fear in the girl's eyes. Maybe she'd had a moment of regret, but it was gone in an instant.

Amie was dragged unceremoniously back to her tent, propped against the wall, her legs tied together, and once again she was left alone.

She drifted in and out of consciousness, but her dreams were full of dark, terrifying images. She could see Shalima's face, laughing hysterically at her. She pictured Angelina crying, Mrs Motswezi petrified, and she saw Jonathon's pale face lying lifeless on a stretcher.

Every time she came to, the tears would course silently down her cheeks, stinging her eyes and the minutes ticked by like hours. She tried not to think what might happen in the next few days, to her and the people she loved. At least the elderly headmistress and Angelina were safe and that was the only thing she could take comfort from.

It was dark the next time Amie woke. She thought she'd heard stealthy footsteps at the back of her tent and reckoned at first it was her imagination, but suddenly something exploded close by, lighting up the dark night. There was a second explosion and the sound of rapid gunfire. Men were shouting, feet running past the tent, followed by cries and screams and more explosions. The noise was deafening. The night was fractured by bangs, screams and rapid gunshots that lit up the darkness

Amie imagined they were being attacked and she slid down as close to the ground as she could. The cacophony went on and on, but with her hands tied behind her back she was unable to cover her ears. Her head felt like it was vibrating from the inside as guns spat bullets and the screaming continued, interspersed with shrieks of pain. It felt like hell, here on earth, right now. The noise permeated every fibre and cell of Amie's body while she lay curled in a ball. The last explosion was right next to the tent. It lifted her bodily off the ground and as she crashed down again, she blacked out.

By the time Amie came to, it was daylight and the early morning sun was beating down on her. A large hole in the canvas roof of the tent allowed a view of the bright blue sky above. The centre pole was leaning over at a precarious angle as if it was about to fall on her at any moment, possibly burying her under what was left of the canvas.

She struggled onto her bottom, her head spinning, then twisted until she got onto her knees and crawled forward. She didn't have the strength to stand, up her movements were uncoordinated and shaky. She could hear nothing but ringing in her ears, and the acrid smell of smoke permeating her senses.

When she peered out, she saw there were several small fires still burning but the camp was virtually destroyed. A few figures, clothed in a variety of garments, were rummaging among the wreckage while others beat out the last of the burning embers with blankets and sticks. She frowned, bewildered, not believing what she was seeing in front of her. Had they been attacked? If so, by whom? The British? The Americans? Another IS group? Nothing made any sense.

She tottered forward a little further and tried to stand up, but her legs wouldn't hold her. She fell sideways, her hands numb from the cable ties that anchored her hands in the small of her back. Without warning, someone grabbed her from behind and cut the ties. Her hands were free.

Amie tried to move her arms but the pain was excruciating and she rolled her shoulders several times to help the blood flow return. She twisted round to see Ben bending over her. He was grinning from ear to ear.

Amie gasped. "You're free! How?"

"Yes, and now you are too. Here, let me help you up." He cut the cable ties binding her feet.

"Jonathon? Is he here? Have you seen him? Is he still alive?" The questions spilled out as Amie attempted to stand.

"I don't know. We must go to look for him."

"They were going to kill us all," Amie spluttered.

"I know, but we arrived before they had the chance."

"We?"

"My people, from Apatu. There has been another uprising, we have been preparing to take our country back for a long time. Now it has begun."

Amie tried to focus on what he was telling her. Her head was still spinning and she wasn't sure she'd heard him correctly through the ringing in her ears.

Ben put his arms around her shoulders and gave her a very gentle shake. "Come, let us try and find Jonathon. Are you ready?"

Amie nodded. Shuffling like an old woman, and leaning on Ben, they went to look in the tents that were still partly standing. In many of them were the burnt remains of bodies, some were impossible to identify.

In the second tent, two bodies were recognizable. Shalima and Fahid. They were locked together in a gruesome embrace, their bodies melded into one by the heat. Amie could only stare, her emotions mixed between horror and morbid fascination.

Most of the structures had been totally destroyed and as they approached each one, Amie screwed up her eyes almost afraid to look. She desperately wanted to find her husband, but she dreaded seeing his dead body. Possibly one of the charred remains they'd already looked at might be Jonathon. She bit down hard on her bottom lip and tried not to cry. Her whole body felt as if it had been put through a wringer and she still didn't feel in control of her limbs.

There was a shout and one of the Africans beckoned them over. He called to Ben in Togodian who whooped with joy and gave Amie a squeeze. "They have found him," he exclaimed. "They have found him and he is still alive."

Waves of relief swept over her and adrenaline pumped through her veins. She immediately felt strong and alive. Her pace quickened and there he was, lying on the stretcher, awake but a little dazed as he blinked at Amie.

"I don't believe it," she cried as she fell on her knees beside him. "You're alive and we're safe and I'm never going to be parted from you again."

Ben excused himself and left them together but Jonathon still gaped at her.

Amie touched his shoulder "Jonathon! Jonathon, it's me, it's Amie!" Her voice broke. "Don't, don't you recognize me?"

Jonathon was still for several more seconds then hesitantly he replied, "Amie? Is it you? Is it Amie?"

"Yes, of course it is. We've been rescued. Ben rescued us, isn't that wonderful?"

Finally, it registered with Jonathon and he grasped Amie's hand and squeezed it hard. "But, we left you by the first camp," he spluttered. "You were to go back with Jefri to Dirk if anything happened. He promised me."

"Don't worry about that right now," Amie smiled. "It didn't happen, and just as well, or we wouldn't be here now and you would be on your way to Libya ... I think."

"Libya?"

Ben returned and told her he'd arranged transport to take them to the outskirts of Apatu. "There is a lot of fighting in the streets now, so it is not safe to go into the city. But I must get back and be with my men."

"Your men?" Amie asked.

"Ah, did I not mention it before, that President Mtumba was my uncle?"

"You? You are the nephew of the deposed President?" Amie was astounded. She'd known he was a Kawa and they considered themselves superior to everyone else. She could guess they would not accept being governed by any other tribe, especially a smaller clan they had no respect for. That's how it is in Africa. For a fleeting moment she wondered if it would all go back to the way it was. Jonathon working on the desalination plant, living in their old house, great parties at the club, helping out at the orphanage - except there was no orphanage now, it had been burnt to the ground.

"Is everyone dead?" Amie noticed there were a few still-smouldering tents but the only people walking round looked African. She could see no sign of prisoners.

"Should be by now," Ben sounded satisfied. "We do not want these people in our country, not because they believe differently, but for the killing and the damage they cause. They are fanatics and they have no place here. We don't think anyone escaped."

Amie turned back to Jonathon. "Where are you hurt?"

"It's only a broken leg," he said with a small grin. It's not been plastered but they took better care of me than I expected."

"All the better to kill you later on, when they were ready to film it and show it to the world," Amie said bitterly.

"What if we tried to pack round it with mud, that might help?"

"Sounds better than nothing."

The Kawa were systematically looting the camp of anything they could find that might be useful, and they collected up the rest of the boxes that had been air dropped.

During the morning, several more vehicles arrived and were loaded up. Someone came with food and drink, and Amie was aware that Ben was treated with great respect, bordering almost on reverence. As his close friends they were also getting royal treatment.

Two men arrived and tended to Jonathon's leg. To distract him from the painful procedure, Amie plied him with questions.

They'd kept Jonathon at the first camp for several days and he knew there'd been some kind of trouble, but he didn't know it was Amie who'd caused it when she rescued the women. While Amie was hiding out in the cave with Mrs Motswezi and Shalima, they'd put Charles and him in a truck and left Ben behind and another group of soldiers had driven him away. He had no idea what was going on.

At the next camp Charles had been brutally tortured, then forced to kneel down and was shot in the back of the head. The soldiers had unceremoniously thrown his body into a nearby river, and Amie could guess which creature had eaten well that day.

While she listened, Amie said nothing. There would come a time when she would tell Jonathon her story, but for now it could wait. After being surrounded for so long by people who didn't speak his language, he couldn't stop talking. She just held his hand and listened.

Before returning to Apatu, Amie and Ben walked back to where they'd left the Land Rover and collected it along with all their belongings. The drive back to the outskirts of Apatu passed in double time. The bungalow they were allocated by the government was a haven of civilization. True, the electricity supply was erratic and the water out of the taps was not potable, but to lie in a real bed, stand under a running shower and sit on a soft chair was heaven.

Amie was able to walk to the nearest tuck shop and use some of Edward's money to get basic essentials. There was plenty left over and she considered it Jonathon's salary after everything he'd been through. The funds came from his employers after all.

The local market was operating as usual, even though there was a civil war going on only a couple of kilometres away. They could hear firing in the distance, and for the first few days it was heavy, but the fighting lessened until it became sporadic and eventually stopped altogether.

They took a circuitous drive round to the hospital, which miraculously had escaped damage and was operating as normally as possible under the circumstances where they x-rayed and set Jonathon's leg.

Apart from visiting the hospital, for the first few days they did nothing but chill out talking, dozing or simply staring into space. They took time to get to know each other again, and they talked for long hours into the night. They talked about everything, except for Jonathon's second career, but as they lay together in bed at night, they rediscovered the love they had for each other and were at peace.

The fighting in the capital itself had only lasted about a week, and all the M'untu leaders were rounded up and Amie suspected they'd been shot. She chose not to ask. It was like turning the clock back, apart from more ruined buildings, lots of extra rubble in the streets and intermittent services for a while, life went back to normal. The shop keepers raced to pull their shutters up and the minibus taxis were soon flying along the streets, stopping wherever and whenever they wished. The banks, offices and shopping mall were once again open for business.

It took a little longer to restock supplies to their previous levels, but ships came into the docks and were offloaded with minimum delay. The airport was also busy, with planes flying in from all over the world. Since most governments hadn't acknowledged the rebel interim government it was back to business as usual. They even announced that elections would be held the following year, which would, most likely in true African tradition, return the ruling Kawa to power again.

Amie couldn't believe it was all happening so fast. Within a matter of weeks there were discussions about restarting work on the desalination plant and new expatriate families were arriving, mostly the husbands at first. There was still work to do organizing the schools and there was even talk of revamping the club. Were the Fishes going to stay and carry on as if nothing had happened over the past several months?

If she had any qualms about spending the money they'd rescued from Edward, Amie squashed them quite successfully. She felt she'd earned it, and if asked, they could afford to pay some of it back. To their amazement, they were told the money they'd left in the bank in Apatu, all those months ago, was still there. It'd been beyond the resources of the rebel government to break into the vaults, and the new government had won a lot of trust by offering to reimburse every citizen, worker and company in full. This was almost unheard of, but already large firms were swarming in with the prospects of mining the oil and minerals discovered some time earlier.

One morning there was a knock on the door and Amie opened it to find Ben standing on the doorstep. Mrs Motswezi and Angelina were standing right behind him and Amie cried for joy at the wonderful surprise.

"I don't believe it!" Amie swept Angelina up into her arms. "You're safe! Oh, how marvellous! Come in, come in."

Once again Angelina took a fistful of Amie's shirt and clung on as Amie carried her through to the lounge.

"Now all we need is Pretty to complete the party."

Ben shook his head sadly. "Pretty is late."

Amie sighed, another casualty in another senseless African war. She'd hung back from getting a new maid in the blind hope Pretty would materialize from somewhere. People in the local community knew they were back and the African grapevine was a lot faster than high speed Internet.

While Jonathon took Ben outside, presumably to talk business, Mrs Motswezi told Amie of her plans to start up a new orphanage. Would Amie help her? Nothing on earth would stop her and she knew together they could work wonders for the AIDS orphans. For the first time in months, Amie had a real, worthwhile project to work on, one that could only do good and she couldn't wait to get started. Not only would they take in AIDS orphans, but war orphans as well.

Gazing lovingly at the little girl who had now snuggled down on her lap, the idea came back to her that maybe they could find a way to adopt Angelina. She'd lost her twice, but Amie was determined not to be parted from her again. This time she hoped that Ben would help, for since the Kawas had reinstated themselves, he was now the Deputy President and could pull strings. After all the heartache and hardship, things were falling into place at last.

22 LAST DAYS

Three months later an excited child stood beside her foster mother and father in the departure lounge at Apatu airport. She was still not convinced they would be going up into the sky in one of the planes standing on the apron on the other side of the plate glass window. She fingered the new dress Amie had bought for her and looked at the bright red coat lying on the chair next to her. She was hot now wearing so many heavy clothes, but Amie had told her it was very cold in the country where they were going. It was called England and Amie was going to see her Mummy and Daddy, and her sister too, for a holiday. They would see all kinds of exciting things and go to lots of interesting places, but they would get on another plane and fly back to Apatu in time for Angelina to start school the next term.

Amie's family was expecting them and would meet them when they got off the plane.

There had been such a long silence from Amie they'd feared she'd been severely wounded or died. They'd received a call from the Mathesons to tell them Amie and Jonathon had come for a short stay; but then there was another long silence until the couple had returned to Apatu.

Amie and Jonathon both agreed not to talk about anything that had happened. If her parents believed they'd spent all their time in the camp with Dirk and Helen, so much the better. It was unlikely Angelina would say anything, she didn't talk much and when she did, it was to whisper in Amie's ear so quietly she had to concentrate to hear the child.

When the plane took off, Angelina clutched Amie's hand and shrank into her seat. Her foster mother spoke reassuringly, trying to calm her down, but it wasn't until the cabin crew brought the food that the little girl was distracted enough to relax.

The hustle and bustle at Heathrow airport was terrifying for all of them, especially Angelina. Even for her new parents, it was too easy to forget how many people were crammed into such a small space. The buildings seemed too close together as they were coming in to land, and Amie was unprepared for the shock of returning to the land of her birth.

If she was hoping to slip back unnoticed, she was in for a disappointment. True, there weren't the frantic number of reporters waiting for her this time, but there were at least two or three who'd got wind of her arrival and were waiting to ask her dozens of questions.

"Have you come back for good?"

"Are you planning to star in another television series?"

"Who is the child with you?"

"What are your plans for the future?"

"When did you last see your family?"

"What thoughts do you have on the state of affairs in Togodo with the new change of government?"

"Were you caught up in the second civil war?"

"Have you been in armed combat?"

Amie noticed Jonathon had slipped back into the crowd and no one seemed to realize she'd been travelling with her husband.

She pushed the reporters to one side murmuring, "No comment," over and over. She reached her parents and they made a rapid exit from the arrivals hall; but not before Amie noticed her mother's startled expression when she caught sight of Angelina. Amie had thought it better to explain her connection with the child face to face, so hadn't warned her parents there would be three of them.

Jonathon caught up with them and jumped into the car at the last minute managing to evade all the media.

They'd only just arrived at her parents' house, when her sister Samantha was on the doorstep with Dean and Jade in tow.

"You're back! That's brilliant!" Sam gave her a big hug. "And I hope you're not traipsing off again, we want you here at home, to stay. Understand?"

Amie nodded briefly. She didn't have the heart to tell Sam they were only home for a few days. She hadn't even told her mother it was just a short trip.

"And who do we have here?" Sam asked bending down to smile at Angelina. "Are you coming to live here too?"

Angelina looked wide-eyed at her and stuck her thumb in her mouth, holding on tightly to Amie's trousers. She hadn't said a word since they'd arrived. She looked scared to death.

"Come and meet Dean and Jade. Would you like to play with them?"

"Take them out into the garden for a few minutes Sam." Mary Reynolds made it quite clear she wanted to talk to her elder daughter in private.

"Uh, oh, yes of course." Samantha got the message, and gently prising Angelina's fingers off Amie's trouser leg she led the three children outside. Every step of the way Angelina looked back at Amie, unhappy to be parted with her for a second.

As soon as the back door closed, Mary turned to her daughter. "Amie, what are you thinking of? Are you going to adopt that child?"

"If I can," Amie was defensive. "It wouldn't have been possible before under the old government, but we now have connections very high up and it was quite easy to get a travel visa for her to come to England for a brief visit."

"Are you sure you know what you're doing?" Mary was worried.

"Yes Mum. I've had a special connection with Angelina since the first day I met her and I want her to have the best of everything. We think her parents died of AIDS and she was left at the gates of the orphanage. I want to give her a chance in life."

"But what if her family, there must be some, somewhere, what if they come and try and claim her back? How will that affect her? Being dragged from one environment to another in a totally different culture?"

"I think it's most unlikely Mum. You're not concerned because she's black are you?"

"No, no, not at all. Heaven knows England is a total melting pot of colours these days. I hope you've thought it through that's all and you're not relying on your emotions."

"No, I'm quite certain, and Jonathon feels the same way. We feel like a real family now."

"Well, the child is very sweet, I grant you that, but she looks quite shell shocked. It's going to take a lot of time, patience and understanding."

Amie nodded, reminding herself she wasn't going to mention how Angelina had escaped from the orphanage with Mrs Motswezi, taken refuge in a village that had been attacked killing most of the villagers and then taken to the IS camp where she'd been sexually abused. She didn't think that would help matters at all.

If Mary Reynolds wasn't convinced, she said no more but bustled around making the British remedy for all occasions, a cup of tea for everyone.

Sam came back inside. "She didn't want to stay out there," she explained, as Angelina rushed across the kitchen and clung to Amie again.

"No problem, it'll take a bit of getting used to, won't it Angelina?"

The child nodded and buried her head in Amie's lap.

"Uh, one thing I am curious about," Amie turned to her sister. "How did the press and media know we were coming? There were reporters at the airport. I wasn't expecting that."

Sam looked confused for a moment and not a little shamefaced. "You forget you're a celebrity now," she protested. "You can't expect people not to be interested in what you do. Have you any idea of the excitement the TV series caused? Everyone was talking about you."

Amie winced; glad she hadn't been around when it was shown live on air.

"You didn't tell the newspapers did you Sam?" her mother asked sternly.

"Of course not. I only told a couple of my closest friends," Sam protested.

"And what about all the social media?" Mary persisted.

"Ah, yes, well, um." Sam inspected her feet. "I did sort of mention it I guess. But only on Facebook and Twitter."

"There's your answer Amie, the whole world knows," said Mary.

"I'm sure they'll leave us alone now. I've got nothing more to tell them," she lied.

"They'll probably lose interest," Mary smiled. "At least the phones aren't ringing off the hook like last time you came home."

At that moment the phone rang in the hallway.

"I'm not here," mouthed Amie, but it was only one of Mary's friends asking if she was free for dinner the following week.

"So," Sam wanted to know, "how long are you here for? Are you staying?"

"No. We've come for a couple of weeks, just for a break, then Jonathon will be back on the desalination plant and it'll be business as usual."

The moment her mother walked back into the kitchen the phone rang again and she disappeared to answer it.

There was an awkward silence. Sam got out some biscuits for the children and Jonathon and Raymond Reynolds came in chatting about the possibility of a day out fishing. Dean and Jade began to fight over the only chocolate biscuit on the plate, but everyone stopped when Mary returned looking distraught.

"What's wrong love?" Raymond asked.

"Harriet. She died last night." Mary slumped onto a kitchen stool. "I can't take it in. She is, was, younger than me. They said it was a massive stroke and she died in her sleep."

Raymond put his arms round his wife while Sam, Amie and Jonathon looked askance at each other. The girls hadn't known their aunt too well, but they'd been up to stay with her in Birmingham a few times and remembered her as a bright, bouncy person who was always busy.

"When's the funeral?" Raymond asked.

"Probably next Tuesday. They'll let us know."

"We'll all go of course," said Sam and Amie nodded. She was not sure what she would do with Angelina, but the child had already seen death and would probably take it more in her stride than Amie's niece and nephew who were now rolling around on the kitchen floor both intent on taking possession of the chocolate biscuit. Sam reached down, removed it and calmly ate it herself. Jade burst into tears and the adults burst out laughing.

For the next few days, life went on much as it had done when Amie and Jonathon had lived in England. There were trips to the park to feed the ducks, a theme park, rides on the train and the underground, visits to the local shopping mall and drives in the country. They also spent time with Jonathon's parents and on one occasion they all visited a stately home.

Amie was a little worried about bombarding Angelina with too many new and different experiences. Most times she said nothing, her big brown eyes appearing to take everything in and Amie couldn't begin to imagine what she was thinking. Occasionally she'd smile shyly, but she was starting to worry about sensory overload for a little orphan who was used to the sprawling townships of a small African city, and the wide open expanses of the bush.

She could only guess that Angelina was suffering from post-traumatic stress, and nothing but patience, lots of love and a willingness to talk when the time was right, would help to heal the wounds.

Amie expected to feel more trauma herself after the ordeals of the previous weeks, but she'd remained quite calm. She decided it was the adrenaline rush to survive, together with her determination to care for and cherish Angelina, that had kept her from falling apart. She felt numb about everything she'd been through and had pushed it firmly into the background. Perhaps all the difficult situations she'd already survived had built her defenses.

Sometimes when they were out, Angelina would sit down and take her shoes off, wriggling her toes freely, but she always let Amie put them back on. You didn't walk around the outskirts of London in bare feet. Neither was the child keen on wearing so many clothes, she was always eager to rip off her coat as soon as they walked back into the house. She hated wearing gloves, even when her hands were freezing, and she was frequently cold even when she was indoors.

While Amie had occasional doubts as to whether she

was doing the right thing, she reminded herself they'd soon be back in Apatu, and Angelina would be going to school in the climate she was used to. After all, she reassured herself, if Angelina didn't want to be with her, she would've clung to Mrs Motswezi instead of showing her love for the white lady who'd previously taken her into her home.

The days flew, and the day of the funeral came around all too fast. Rather than drive to Harriet's place they decided to take the train to Birmingham and use a taxi at the other end. They wouldn't stay the night, but only go to the service and briefly to the wake afterwards.

To Amie's relief, Angelina didn't appear to be unduly perturbed by the proceedings, although Sam had to take her children outside, as they wouldn't sit still in the chapel. Since her aunt had asked to be cremated there was no visit to the cemetery so, after paying their respects, Sam and Amie decided to take the children to a local park and leave the others to go on to the wake and then meet them later back at the railway station.

While Dean and Jade shrieked with joy on the swings and slides, Angelina held back. When Amie tried to persuade her to try one of the rides, she shook her head.

They didn't stay long at the park, because the wind was bitterly cold. Amie suggested they visit the nearby mall, get milkshakes and look for a play area in the warm.

As they walked across the road, Amie asked Sam how everything was at home. On her last visit, her sister and brother-in-law had been going through a rocky period. Sam told her things were a little better, but she wasn't all that happy. Now the children were both in school she'd been looking for work, but it wasn't easy to find, especially a job with flexible hours to fit in with school times.

The mall was bright and cheerful, crammed with shops, restaurants, coffee bars and a cinema complex. In the main area there was an exhibition with several animals in cages. They walked over to look at them.

"Look Angelina, it's a monkey," Amie pointed out the vervet monkey who was screeching and leaping from one side of the small cage to the other.

"Monkey," repeated Angelina softly.

"Yes, a monkey, like they have at home," Amie said. "Do you think he's on holiday from Africa like us?"

Angelina would've stayed there forever, but by now Dean and Jade were clamouring for ice cream and milkshakes. They made for a table at the nearest café so they could still watch the animals.

Amie was amused by the smile on the little girl's face at seeing something familiar, and resolved to take her to the zoo once they were back in London; it would help to unite both worlds for her.

They ordered drinks and took their seats, but Angelina slid off Amie's lap and wandered over to watch the animals.

Amie's first reaction was to call her back and keep her close by but she soon relaxed. The child was still in sight, only a few yards away, and it was the first time she'd voluntarily left Amie's side. Was it a sign she was healing, feeling braver and on the road to recovery? Amie could only hope so. She smiled as she watched Angelina gaze intently at the monkey who'd calmed down and was in turn staring back at the little girl.

Amie nudged Sam. "Do you think they recognize a common bond, coming from the same continent?"

"That's not at all politically correct," Sam chuckled. "Okay, okay I know what you mean. Well, who knows? It's nice to see her take an interest in something."

Amie smiled. "Yes, it is," she replied. "We have lots of monkeys in the garden."

Cold shivers ran down Amie's spine when she thought of Africa. Suddenly, she had a blinding vision, so clear she was convinced she was back in the township in Apatu. As clear as day she saw Ouma Adede and her words rang out loud and clear.

"It is not for me to tell you of the loss, but the spirits have a warning for you. Do not take what is not yours to take. The child belongs here in the country of her birth, and she should die here."

The vision faded and Amie hastily cast around in a panic. Everything was normal, no one else had seen or heard anything. People were still shopping, eating and drinking in the cafes and riding the escalators.

At that moment a large trolley appeared at the end of the wide corridor moving swiftly towards them. Amie glanced at it and thought they were going to collect the animals, but she felt uneasy. Some instinct put her on alert, a feeling of danger she couldn't explain. She looked over to where Angelina was entertaining the monkey by making squeaky noises, but still her sense of danger grew. Sam was chattering away to the children and talking to her sister, but Amie was in a bubble, locked into the scene around her. Something was going to happen, something bad.

She took a fleeting look at the trolley that had almost reached them and leapt to her feet to grab Angelina. In a flash the world exploded. The last thing Amie remembered was the cry, "Allah Akbar!"

When Amie opened her eyes all she could see was a bright, white ceiling, but the effort to stay awake was too much and she slipped back into unconsciousness again.

In her dreams she heard voices and someone was shaking her shoulder gently but persistently. She didn't want to wake up, she wanted to go on dreaming, something was warning her it would be too painful to wake up. She knew she must be in hospital, but why?

It came rushing back. The shopping mall, the cart, the monkey and ... Angelina. Angelina! Her eyes flew open and she tried to sit up, but a nurse gently pushed her down.

"Angelina," Amie gasped. "Where is she? And Sam and the children? Are they all right? Please, please tell me."

The nurse smiled. "All in good time, when you're stronger."

"No, no. Tell me now!" Amie was shouting. She was aware of the door opening and her mother walking in. Amie held out her arms. "Tell me, tell me," she sobbed. "What happened? Was anyone hurt?"

Her mother took her hand and perched on the edge of the bed, ignoring the nurse's frown. "I'm sorry, Amie. I'm so, so sorry."

It was all over the evening news. It made the headlines in every national paper and gave birth to dozens of panel discussions and chat shows with numerous experts grilled for their views.

At 4pm on Tuesday afternoon a bomb went off in a Birmingham shopping centre, killing at least twelve people and injuring a further twenty-three. A group calling themselves Boko Haram UK have claimed responsibility and proudly announced four of their group had become martyrs for the cause. The explosive device was apparently wheeled into the crowded mall on a trolley, pushed by the suicide bombers. No prior warning was given and in a message posted immediately after the event, on Facebook and YouTube, the group stated this was in reprisal for the bombing of Syria by Western forces. They warned of further attacks to follow. The security forces are on high alert and reinforcements have been called in.

The names of the deceased are: ...

Mary Reynolds didn't know how to break the news to her bruised and battered daughter lying in the hospital bed. Jonathon rushed in and took Amie gently in his arms. He cradled her like a baby and whispered he loved her over and over again.

Without quite knowing why Amie burst into tears. "Tell me, tell me."

Jonathon pulled away and taking a deep breath he answered her unfinished question. Sam and the children had escaped with only minor injuries and only been kept in hospital overnight, but Angelina had not been so lucky. By the time the paramedics had reached her it was too late.

Amie's tears turned to gut-wrenching sobs. She had lost

her child twice and through a miracle had found her again. All the problems and difficulties she might've had adopting the child had been overcome, only for this to happen. Her child of Africa had died in a foreign land and had no future.

Amie blamed herself. If only she'd left Angelina safely with Mrs Motswezi, in her own country. If only she'd listened to Ouma Adede and heeded her warning. Her own selfishness had been the cause of the little girl's death. She wasn't sure she could ever forgive herself.

Amie was kept in hospital for three days while they ran a barrage of tests, and then she returned with Jonathon to her parents' home outside London. No one knew how to comfort her. Mary, Sam, her father and Jonathon's folks told her it wasn't her fault, but she sank into a deep depression. The other trials and problems she'd been able to handle, but this was the one she battled with, this was the one that had broken her.

"Amie, we must do something," Jonathon said to her one afternoon as they sat alone in the garden. "I have to know whether to find work here, or tell my bosses if I'm going back to Apatu. They won't wait forever."

"Yes, I know," Amie nodded. "I've been thinking too. I don't want to stay here with Mum and Dad. Jonathon I want to go back to Apatu."

"Are you sure? We don't have to if …"

Amie interrupted him. "No, I'm quite sure. It's where my soul can heal and I promised Mrs Motswezi I would help her build the new orphanage. Although I wasn't able to help Angelina …" her voice broke, "… I can help some of the other orphans. Will you take me back to Africa, Jonathon?"

"Yes," he said. "Yes, I will."

"And can we take Angelina's ashes back with us?"

"If you want to."

"I do. She was a child of Africa and that's where we should lay her to rest."

When Amie took her seat on the plane, she felt a very small part of her begin to relax. It was sad saying goodbye to her family again, but she knew they were doing the right thing. She had great hopes for the future. She would mend and one day, sitting out in the bush, surrounded by the vast African landscape, she would find peace.

The pilot welcomed them aboard and reminded them to switch off their mobile phones and electronic devices. Amie obediently pulled hers out of her bag and pressed the off button.

She wouldn't have been so relaxed had she stopped to read the message which had just dropped into her inbox.

We know who you are, and where you are going. We will never forgive you for the deaths you are responsible for. We will not rest until the martyr Shalima's death has been avenged.

ABOUT THE AUTHOR

Lucinda E Clarke has been a professional writer for over 30 years, scripting for both radio and television. She's had numerous articles published in several magazines, written mayoral speeches and advertisements. She currently writes a monthly column in a local publication in Spain. She once had her own newspaper column, until the newspaper closed down, but says this was not her fault!

Two of her books have been bestsellers in genre on Amazon on both sides of the Atlantic, she has won over 20 awards for scripting, directing, concept and producing, and had two educational text books published. Sadly these did not make her the fortune she dreamed of, to allow her to live in luxury.

Lucinda has also worked on radio - on one occasion with a bayonet at her throat - appeared on television and met and interviewed some of the world's top leaders.

She set up and ran her own video production company, producing a variety of programmes, from advertisements to corporate to drama documentaries on a vast range of subjects.

Altogether she has lived in eight different countries, run the 'worst riding school in the world', and cleaned toilets to bring the money in.

When she handled her own divorce, Lucinda made legal history in South Africa.

Now, pretending to be retired, she gives occasional talks and lectures to special interest groups and finds retirement the most exhausting time of her life so far; but says there is still so much to see and do, she is worried she won't have time to fit it all in.

© Lucinda E Clarke 2014

To my Readers

If you have enjoyed this book, or even if you didn't like it, please take a few minutes to write a review. Reviews are very important to authors and I would certainly value your feedback. Thank you.

Connect with Lucinda E Clarke on Facebook

https://www.facebook.com/lucindaeclarke.author

Webpage: lucindaeclarkeauthor.com

Or by email: lucindaeclarke@gmail.com

Blog: http://lucindaeclarke.wordpress.com

Twitter: @LucindaEClarke

If you would like to be notified when a new book is published, or there is a special promotion, please send me an email.

Also by Lucinda E Clarke

Walking over Eggshells

The first autobiography which relates Lucinda's horrendous relationship with her mother and her travels to various countries.

Truth, Lies and Propaganda

The first of two books explaining how Lucinda 'fell' into a career writing, her dream since childhood. First she had to get fired from her teaching job, and crash out in an audition at the South African Broadcasting Corporation. Then she found herself writing a series on how to care for domestic livestock, she knew absolutely nothing about cows, goats and chickens. And it all continued from there.

More Truth, Lies and Propaganda

Tales of filming in deep rural Africa, meeting a ram with an identity crisis, a house that disappears, the forlorn bushmen and a video starring a very dead rat. You will never believe anything you watch on television ever again.

Amie an African Adventure

A novel set in Africa, which takes Amie from the comfort of her home in England to a small African country. Civil war breaks out and soon she is fighting for her life.

Reviews

That Lucinda E Clarke can write and write well is not in question. This memoir left me breathless at times. She writes of her adventures, misadventures and family relationships in an honest but entertaining manner. I wholeheartedly recommend this book, (Walking over Eggshells) buy it, delve in and lose a few days, well worth it.

———————

This book was written with such consummate skill. I have enormous admiration for Lucinda E Clarke as an author.

She not only knows how to write an edge-of-the-seat, well-constructed story that would make a brilliant movie – she does it using beautiful, spare, intelligent, and amazingly descriptive language. By the time I got to the end of 'Amie' I felt as though I'd been to Africa – seen it, touched it, smelled it, heard it... loved it and hated it. Everything that is the truth of the country is there in this book. Can I give it six stars please? It deserves it. (Amie an African Adventure)

What a great book! I have so enjoyed this and love the tongue-in-cheek, self deprecating humour with which Lucinda Clarke relates her experiences. It's quite fascinating to read how she becomes involved in writing and broadcasting, and also really interesting to realise how much easier it was to get in touch with decision makers in the days before the digital onslaught. Either that or Lucinda is being overly modest and making it look simple! I loved the descriptions of her early experiences in Libya - both funny and frightening. And of course, there are lots of memories for me here as I moved to South Africa in the early eighties and always listened to Springbok radio. The style is easy and fluid, and I have enjoyed every page, riveted by the quantity of writing she managed to do without any previous knowledge of the subjects. Amazing. For me, this is the best one of Lucinda's yet in terms of keeping me pasted to my Kindle! I've read two of her other books before, and I'll definitely be reading the sequel to this one! (Truth, Lies and Propaganda)

I picked this one up purely on the basis of how much I enjoyed reading the first book and I was not to be disappointed. Lucinda E Clarke is one of those writers who can tell a story effortlessly in a way that just carries you along with her adventures. I have to say she is fast becoming one of my favourite authors. The book revolves around a period of her life as she returns to work in Africa and she uses her natural writing ability to not just recount events but to entertain along the way. Her skill is not in telling extraordinary tales but in making often ordinary real life stories come to life and it is in the smaller details of each story that I often found myself most enthralled. I cannot recommend this book and indeed the previous one highly enough. If your next book purchase is from the pen of Lucinda E Clarke you will have made a wise decision indeed. A thoroughly deserved 5 stars out of 5 from me. (More, truth Lies and Propaganda)

AMIE AN AFRICAN ADVENTURE
PROLOGUE

They came for her soon after the first rays of the sun began to pour over the far distant hills, spilling down the slopes onto the earth below. At first the gentle beams warmed the air, but as the sun rose higher in the sky, it produced a scorching heat, which beat down on the land with relentless energy.

She heard them approach, their footsteps echoing loudly on the bare concrete floors. As the marching feet drew closer, she curled up as small as she could, and tried to breathe slowly to stop her heart racing. No, please, not again, she whispered to herself. She couldn't take much more. What did they want? Would they beat her again? What did they expect her to say?

There was nothing she could tell them, she was keeping no secrets. She knew she couldn't take any more pain, every little bit of her body ached. How many films had she seen where people were kicked or beaten up? She'd never understood real pain, the real agony even a single punch could inflict on the body. Now all she wanted was to die, to escape the torture and slide away into oblivion.

The large fat one was the first to appear on the other side

of the door. She knew he was important, because the gold braid, medals, ribbons and badges on his uniform told everyone he was a powerful man, a man it would be very dangerous to cross. He was accompanied by three other warders, also in uniform, but with fewer decorations.

They unlocked the old, rusty cell door and the skinny one walked over and dragged her to her feet. He pushed her away from him, swung her round and bound her wrists together behind her back, with a long strip of dirty cotton material. She winced as he pulled roughly on the cloth and then propelled her towards the door. The others stood back as they shoved her into the corridor and up the steps to the ground floor.

She thought they were going to turn left towards the room where they made her sit for hours and hours on a small chair. They'd shouted and screamed at her and got angry when she couldn't answer their questions. This made them angry so they hit her again.

She'd lost track of the time she'd been here, was it a few days, or several weeks? As she drifted in and out of consciousness she lost all sense of reality. Her former life was a blur, and it was too late to mark the cell walls to record how long they'd kept her imprisoned.

This time, however, they didn't turn left, they turned right at the top of the steps and pulled her down a long corridor towards an opening at the far end. She could see the bright sunlight reflecting off the dirty white walls. For a brief moment she had a sudden feeling of euphoria, they were going to let her go!

She could hear muffled sounds and shouts from the street

outside. It was surreal there were people so close to the prison going about their everyday lives. On the other side of the wall, the early morning suppliers who brought produce in from the surrounding areas were haggling over prices with the market stallholders, shouting and arguing at the tops of their voices. Not one of them was aware of her, of her pain or despair. Even if they *had* known, they wouldn't give her a second thought, why should they care? She didn't belong here. Only a few years ago she'd never heard of them or their country. The sounds drifting over the wall that were once so foreign had become commonplace, then forgotten, and now remembered. She was aware of the everyday bustle and noise of the market, goats bleating, chickens squawking, children screaming and the babble of voices. But all these sounds could have been a million miles away, for they were way beyond her reach.

Hope flared briefly. Her captors had realized she was innocent. They'd never accused her of anything sensible, and she still didn't know why she'd been arrested. She knew she'd done nothing wrong. Her thoughts ran wild, and she tried to convince herself the nightmare was over at last.

All the doors on either side of the corridor were closed, as they half carried, half dragged her towards the opening in the archway at the end. The closer they got, against all reason, her hopes just grew, and grew they were going to set her free. She was going home.

As they shoved her through the open doorway, she screwed up her eyes against the bright light, and when she opened them, it was to see they were in a bare courtyard, surrounded on three sides by high walls. As she looked around, she could see there was no other exit leading to the outside world.

Then she saw the stake in the ground on the far side, and brutally they dragged her towards it. She thought of trying to resist, but she was too weak, and there was too much pain. It was difficult to walk, so she concentrated on putting one foot in front of the other, determined not to give the soldiers or police or whoever they were, any satisfaction. She would show as much dignity as she could.

The skinny one pushed her against the post and took another long piece of sheeting from his pocket and tied it around her chest fixing her firmly to the wood. She glanced down at the ground and was horrified to see large brown stains in the dust.

Not freedom, this was the end. She squeezed her eyes shut, determined not to let the tears run down her cheeks, but the sound of marching feet forced her to open them again. She saw four more men, all dressed in brown uniforms, with the all too familiar guns who lined up on the other side of the courtyard opposite her. They were a rough looking bunch, their uniforms were ill fitting and stained, and their boots were unpolished and covered in dust.

She was trembling all over. She didn't know whether to keep her eyes open to see what was going on, or close them and pretend this was all a terrible dream. She was torn. Part of her wanted it all to end now, but still a part of her wanted to scream 'let me live!! Please, please let me live!!'

The big fat man barked commands and she heard the sounds of guns being broken open as he walked to each of them handing out ammunition, then with the safety catches off, they shuffled into position.

To her horror, she felt a warm trickle of liquid running down the inside of her thighs. At this very last moment, she had lost both her control and her dignity. They had not even offered her a blindfold, so she closed her eyes again and tried to remember happier times, before the nightmare started. Briefly she glanced up at the few fluffy white clouds floating high in the sky as the order to fire was given.

The wedding day went without a hitch, and Amie, who was turning twenty seven in the summer, couldn't believe it had gone so well. It's not as if she really expected a 747 to make an emergency landing in the middle of the churchyard, or Uncle Oswald to get drunk out of his mind before the ceremony, but she had been worrying herself sick for weeks something awful would happen. Her mother was always teasing her about how much she worried about everything, but on the wedding day itself, the sun shone in a clear blue sky and there was hardly a breeze. No, not a single thing went wrong, but it was the calm before the storm. Life would soon take an abrupt turn and fate would redress the balance.

Both families approved of their new relations and on the day Amie and Jonathon exchanged their vows, friends and relatives from both sides had mingled well and enjoyed themselves. Even Amie's dad was secretly congratulating himself the bar bill was going to work out much lower than expected, thanks in part to the drink drive laws. Yes, all the planning and the time spent in preparing for Amie's great day had been worth it.

So far the biggest hiccups had been the usual dramas,

373

finding just the right venue, the perfect dresses for Amie and the bridesmaids and compiling the guest list. Amie and Jonathon had decided to pay for most of the wedding themselves, this way, they had control over the event with minimal interference from other family members. This took quite a bite out of their savings, but Amie felt it was worth it and Jonathon was quite happy to agree.

As everyone raised their glasses to toast the bride and groom, life had been just as Amie had imagined it. Now, all she had to do was balance her career with having a family and somehow she would manage that as well. Other women had coped and there was no reason why all her future plans shouldn't work out just as perfectly.

While Amie had always hoped she would get married and have a family one day, she didn't consider herself just a permanent housewife and mother. The idea of being tied to the stove, barefoot and pregnant in the kitchen didn't appeal to her at all. To begin with she enjoyed her job and had hopes of being promoted in the near future. She'd always dreamed of working in the television industry, but after studying for three years in Technical College, she found it was an industry that was very oversubscribed with hundreds of 'wannabe' Steven Speilbergs and Richard Attenboroughs!

Following advice from one of the younger lecturers, after three years, working at a variety of temporary jobs, she had eventually managed to get employment as a receptionist in a video production house which made short inserts for television, and product launches and training programmes for large companies.

'This was the way into the industry,' she had been told. 'Work your way up, learn how things are done from the inside and make yourself indispensable. The mark of a prospective and successful director is to know how to roll cables correctly, and how to make a good cup of coffee, especially when everyone else around you is faint from lack of sleep.'

So, from day one, Amie sat behind her desk in the reception area and not only answered the phone, took messages and greeted visitors, she also offered to order tapes, help source props, book locations and liaise with the agencies that provided actors and extras. It was often frustrating for her, since she knew how to operate a camera, and how to edit, but for the moment, she had to watch everyone else rush off on shoot, while she was tied to a desk in the front office.

In the three years since she'd been there, no promotion had as yet loomed on the horizon, but she was hopeful she would be offered the job of production secretary while the present girl was away on maternity leave.

On the social side, she had known Jonathon since they had been in school. When he went away to University to study engineering, she had had several dates, casual friendships, but no one ever meant as much to her as Jonathon. Each vacation, they spent every spare moment together, and soon after he graduated, Jonathon took a further year to complete his studies. Amie was disappointed he would be away for even longer, as the course was held at another college much further north and he didn't come home during the usual holidays. She worried he would meet someone else and fretted when she didn't hear from him sometimes for several weeks. She never admitted her fears to Jonathon, but then he came back and got a job in their home town with a company that designed and installed desalination plants and it was as if they had never been apart.

It wasn't long before they decided to move out of their parents' homes and get a flat together and for the last three years, life had been very good.

Had Amie noticed that so far life had gone exactly to plan? To be honest, it wasn't a very exciting plan was it? Of course she'd had dreams like so many young girls do. She once thought of being prima ballerina with the Royal Ballet Company, but then she changed her mind. She would take up horse riding and win the Olympics and feature on the front page of the nation's newspapers. Or maybe become an actress and win a standing ovation and rave reviews for her interpretation of Ophelia in Hamlet.

But like most of us, she came back down to earth, and realized she would lead an ordinary life in the town where she'd been born, and as long as she was happy, that was all she could hope for. Part of the plan was for Jonathon to propose, which he did, and the other part of the plan was for Amie to accept, which she did.

Both sets of parents had been born in Castle Bridge, had their children in Castle Bridge Hospital and expected to be buried in Castle Bridge Cemetery. While Amie's parents both lectured at the local technical college, Jonathon's family owned a small chain of hardware stores.

So in all fairness to Amie she more or less accepted the

same future. She did not yearn for distant horizons, she was happy as she was.

Amie's older sister Samantha was already married to Gerry who worked for the local council. They had two children, Dean and baby Jade and they also lived on the outskirts of town. Amie would often baby sit and she enjoyed spending time with her small niece and nephew, although she and Jonathon had decided to wait a few more years before starting a family of their own.

They had already started saving for a deposit on a house, perhaps over on the new estate they were planning south of the town, just large enough for the happy couple and the two children they were going to have.

But fate had quite a different future in mind for Amie, and the bombshell was dropped a few weeks after they returned from their idyllic honeymoon in Spain.

"What? Where?" shrieked Amie, as she almost jumped out of her chair.

"Shush," said Jonathon looking around the smart restaurant in dismay. "Don't shout, everyone is looking at you!"

"What do you mean don't shout, am I supposed to whisper? What exactly did you just say?" Amie couldn't quite believe it.

"That the company has offered me a promotion?" replied Jonathon.

"No, that bit I understood, it's 'where' the promotion is," Amie whispered very loudly.

"Oh, that bit, well yes, it's in Togodo."

"Well where the bloody hell is Togodo?" asked Amie.

"I'm not sure of the exact co-ordinates, but somewhere near the Equator, along the coast, on the east side, I think," said Jonathon miserably. He'd not expected Amie to react quite so badly. He'd imagined this moment and he had persuaded himself Amie would gaze into his eyes and say something like; "How exciting, I knew living with you was going to be thrilling and adventurous, do tell me we're leaving soon."

Well that was the dream. The reality was somewhat different.

"I thought you'd be pleased," he added.

"Pleased! You mean leave here, leave England! Go somewhere I've not even heard of? Wait. The west coast of where?"

"Africa," replied Jonathon. "And I think it's on the east coast."

"Africa!" Amie took a deep breath. "Go and live in Africa?" She enunciated each word slowly and carefully.

"I thought you'd be pleased," Jonathon repeated. "It'll be a whole new experience for both of us."

"A new experience? Yes." said Amie as the realization of what Jonathon had just said really began to sink in. "Let's start again, just repeat what you just said. I don't quite believe all this."

"The company has asked me, well us of course, to go and open a new branch office in Apatu, that's the capital of Togodo, and get a new plant up and running....er..." Jonathon fumbled for the right words. "It's the opportunity of a lifetime. I never expected to be a Project Manager so soon, even though they sponsored me through uni. It's a real chance for us. Oh Amie I thought you'd be as excited as I am!"

Amie looked at her new husband. She had automatically assumed he had the same plans for their future as she had. They'd talked about living in the town where they both grew up. They'd have a family, send the kids to their old school, socialize with the other people who'd also been friends since kindergarten, join the golf club, and look forward to the annual dinner dances. There was always the possibility of them moving a few miles away, perhaps as far as Scotland? But overseas, well that had never entered her mind.

"How long have you known about this?" asked Amie suddenly.

"Only since Tuesday and…"

"Two days! Two whole days, and you've not said a word?" Amie was astounded.

"I wanted the right setting, the right place to tell you," Jonathon tried to explain. "And you know how this place gets booked up and this is the first night they had a free table."

Amie wasn't stupid, she guessed Jonathon planned to tell her his news in a public place, it was a way of making sure she would keep her emotions in check. Not only that, but he'd chosen the most expensive restaurant in the area, everyone knew how exorbitant their prices were. Like a lamb to the slaughter, she'd followed him inside, wondering if it was an anniversary she'd missed, or a special occasion she'd forgotten, but no, it was to drop this bombshell.